ALL THE
NOISE
AT ONCE

ALL THE NOISE AT ONCE

DeAndra Davis

atheneum

New York   Amsterdam/Antwerp   London
Toronto   Sydney/Melbourne   New Delhi

atheneum

An imprint of Simon & Schuster Children's Publishing Division

1230 Avenue of the Americas, New York, New York 10020

Text © 2025 by DeAndra Miller

Jacket illustration © 2025 by Baraka Carberry

Jacket design by Debra Sfetsios-Conover

For information about special discounts for bulk purchases, please contact Simon & Schuster Special Sales at 1-866-506-1949 or business@simonandschuster.com.

Simon & Schuster strongly believes in freedom of expression and stands against censorship in all its forms. For more information, visit BooksBelong.com.

The Simon & Schuster Speakers Bureau can bring authors to your live event. For more information or to book an event, contact the Simon & Schuster Speakers Bureau at 1-866-248-3049 or visit our website at www.simonspeakers.com.

Interior design by Irene Metaxatos

The text for this book was set in ITC Slimbach Std.

Manufactured in the United States of America

First Edition

10 9 8 7 6 5 4 3 2 1

Library of Congress Cataloging-in-Publication Data

Names: Davis, DeAndra, author.

Title: All the noise at once / DeAndra Davis.

Description: First edition. | New York : Atheneum Books for Young Readers, 2025. | Audience term: Teenagers | Audience: Ages 14 up. | Audience: Grades 10–12. | Summary: "A Black, autistic teen tries to figure out what happened the night his older brother was unjustly arrested"—Provided by publisher.

Identifiers: LCCN 2024021908 (print) | LCCN 2024021909 (ebook) | ISBN 9781665952651 (hardcover) | ISBN 9781665952675 (ebook)

Subjects: CYAC: Autism spectrum disorders—Fiction. | Brothers—Fiction. | False imprisonment—Fiction. | African Americans—Fiction.

Classification: LCC PZ7.1.D3625 Al 2025 (print) | LCC PZ7.1.D3625 (ebook) | DDC [Fic]—dc23

LC record available at https://lccn.loc.gov/2024021908

LC ebook record available at https://lccn.loc.gov/

For Deon and for every autistic kid who has ever been told you can't do something. YOU CAN.

CHAPTER ONE

77 Days Until the Incident

Every summer, Brandon says it is hotter than the devil's ass crack, and I have never quite understood what he means by that.

> **NOTE:** *How hot is the devil's ass crack, exactly? And how many degrees hotter is it outside than said ass crack? The logistics. That is what I am concerned with.*

But here on this field, lined up in the sweltering Florida summer sun, my breath gathering in the enclosed space of plastic, foam, and metal that is this ill-fitting borrowed helmet, I think I feel the heat of that ass crack in my lungs.

I cough twice, clearing the swampish humidity from my throat, and focus on the field. It is summer tryouts for our high school football team. I stare at the tall, red-jersey-wearing boy in front of me. He shouts coded instructions to the offense with confidence. Then he claps and readies himself to receive the ball from the center. The quarterback. The star. My big brother, Brandon. The ball snaps and Brandon has it in hand before I can blink.

My time to move. Brandon drops back and pretends to line up for a throw. I rush forward, realizing his intentions easily. That twitch in his left calf, the subtle twist to the right, the imperceptible glance around. This pass is meant for me. I charge forward, grabbing the ball from his hands, and run toward the sweaty mass of bodies that awaits me. This is the hard part.

I practice these plays with Brandon often. Just me and him. A play action here, a draw there. The difference is, when it is just us, I do not have to crash my body into other people. I do not have to hear their breathing, feel their sharp exhales on my skin or their scrabbling fingers pulling at my clothes when the play is over. Those are the stressors. The things that push me over the edge. But so far, so good. The tryout has gone off without a hitch. I have dodged tackles and rolled away from contact like my life depends on it. Twenty more minutes of showing off and dodging touch and I will finally, officially, be on the football team with my brother. We can play together for his senior year—our last chance.

I have to focus.

I spot the opening in the defensive line, tuck the ball to my side, and push through. I know I have it. I always have it. I know where everyone is on the field. I can see it like a built-in map in my brain. I am going to cut through the hole in the defense and score a touchdown during this tryout and prove to these coaches that—like Brandon reminded me this morning—autism or not, I will be an asset to this team.

I lower my head and push past the defenders and the weak spot they leave open for me. But a harsh crash in my left rib knocks the breath from my lungs and I cough in response. A hand swipes up and tips the ball from my grip. I feel it slip out of my grasp as I careen toward the turf and bodies descend on top of me, desperate to recover the ball and prove themselves worthy of a spot on the team.

Most people have never been at the bottom of a football pileup. It would stress even the most mellow person out. Hands seek the ball, and when they do not find it, they poke instead at eyeballs, they tug at the corners of mouths, pull lips, hit, punch, and it only takes twelve seconds of this—three eye pokes, two lip tugs, and a thumb jammed past my face mask and halfway down my throat—before I am curled up, screaming and shaking.

I thrash, eyes closed, disconnected from my body to protect my mind, and push everyone away from me. I do not care about the ball. I do not care about the game. I do not care about the team. Right now, I care about my space. I care about my skin—on fire, burning all over, crawling with the sensation of searching hands. It is too much. I need space. I need peace.

The pile around me clears. My eyes stay closed, but I can feel the open space suffocating me. I struggle to catch a breath. The air shakes in my quivering airways and my throat constricts, stifling my screams. Then a shadow falls over me, blocking the light filtering through my still-shut lids. I brace for more rough contact, but the arms surround me and gently squeeze. I struggle against the pressure.

"Breathe, A." Vanilla and cinnamon and sweat mingle in my nose. "I gotchu. Breathe with me."

Brandon's voice is like my father's. Smooth. Marble but not cold. His voice is the feel of warm water sliding across skin. Brandon takes a deep breath and I mimic it. I struggle against the pressure, but he squeezes tighter.

"I gotchu, A. Just breathe. Just breathe. Don't worry about nothin' else. Breathe."

The sun burns red against my eyelids. My breath slows with every breath Brandon takes.

"It's all right," Brandon says now. "It's okay."

I look up at Brandon and tears sting at the corners of my eyes. I had it. I had it all mapped out. I knew where everyone was on the field. I knew how to reach the end zone. I had it.

Brandon takes off my helmet and holds me at arm's length.

Realization of my failure hits me and the tears finally fall.

"Is it the sun?" He covers my eyes with his hands, then stands and lifts me with him. I sniffle but let Brandon half carry me, staring at my cleats the whole way to the sideline. I try not to focus on the eyes I feel boring into me or the whispers building as we move. Brandon sits me on the bench.

"Dude, what the heck *was* that?"

Who is talking?

"Ay! Get back on the field," Brandon snaps at whoever

yelled. I focus on my brother's head instead of looking around. Looking around will only make it worse. I try to count the tiny hairs on his faded cut. "A, you all right? You think you good to get back on the field? You need a sec?"

"I think we've seen enough, Brandon." Coach Davis approaches, holding his clipboard up over his face to block out the sun. His long blond hair glints in the intense light. "Let him rest. We'll have team decisions up next week, Aiden. Why don't you head home?"

Brandon nods now. "Yeah, see, A? It's gon be all right. Just rest. Wait for me until the tryouts are over and we'll go home together, all right?"

I do not respond. Brandon gives me a crooked smile and tousles my locs.

"They understand, A," Brandon whispers now. "Don't worry about it. You did great today, all right? It's me and you this year. It's us. We gon be on this field, in matching jerseys, together." Brandon rubs the top of my head one more time, and I watch his retreating back as he leaves to join the rest of the players.

I feel the eyes on me as I sit on the sideline. I feel the glances from the assistant coaches. I feel the apprehension radiating from everyone around me. I close my eyes. I allow the grief of loss to wash over me, although my tears have dried in the heat. They will not understand. I know that already. I know how others react when I do not fit the norm. This is already over even though I was so close.

I had it.

8 8 8 8 8

I lie in the grass, grasping at random blades, rubbing my fingers along the faint prickle of each one, like mini cacti, before pulling them free from the ground. The front yard is quiet other than the breeze in the palm fronds. Everyone who would have been driving home this evening has already arrived, happy in their houses and welcomed by their families, smiling and celebrating some small win in their lives. I cannot stand to be inside my own home right now. I have no small win to celebrate.

I consider the tryout again, consider the overload I felt, consider the pileup and the resulting reaction. My skin crawls just thinking about it. I thought my mental preparation was enough. I knew what to expect. I knew what could happen. I was ready, but clearly not ready enough.

I find the Little Dipper—my favorite constellation—first before I pick out Orion's Belt in the sky, thinking about each star in that perfect line. Each knows its place. Each knows what it has been created to do. Burn and exist. Never moving. Never grasping for more than what it should. I should learn my place too. I should be content to quietly burn until my light is gone, never moving out of line, never trying to be more than what I am. I've thought this before. It is what kept me from trying out for the team for so long, but I had to try before Brandon graduated. This year was our last chance to play on a team together. I tried and here I am. Back in line.

Footsteps crunch to my left, but the cadence is familiar. I do not lift my head to look. It is my brother.

"Did you find the Little Dipper yet?" Brandon's voice is soothing. A balm on my nerves.

"First. Always," I say. I turn to look at Brandon standing over me, and he smiles. He lowers himself down and lies next to me on the lawn. We do not speak for three minutes and twenty seconds. I count.

"You thinking about how tiger pee smells like buttered popcorn?" Brandon asks.

I smile. "Nope. Thinking about how pandas do hand-stands when they pee."

"So, you ain't thinking about how only half of a dolphin's brain sleeps at a time?"

"Of course not. I am thinking about how crocodiles cannot stick their tongues out."

"Okay, you got me, I actually ain't know that one." Brandon laughs. He reaches for my hand and gives it a squeeze before letting go. "You all right?"

I do not answer. I do not want to lie.

"I mean, you can be. You *should* be. I think it's all gon work out, A," Brandon says now. "I think the coaches sounded good about it. I feel like they really saw your talent and they gon see that it's more important than anything else."

I listen. Brandon is all hope and light. A constant burning passion, like a star. He knows his place. The Big Dipper.

"I really feel like, regardless of anything, you gon get on the team this year. It's only your first time even trying out for the school team. And, I mean, if worse comes to worst and you don't make it this year—"

"Do not say that there is always next year," I interrupt. Next year, Brandon will be gone. He will be away at college and I will still be here. Even if I end up on a football field, which at this point feels highly unlikely, it will not be with him. It was supposed to be with him.

"Why not?"

"Because that was not the plan."

I can feel that Brandon is frowning without looking at him. I can feel it in the way his body shifts, how his shoulders grind into the ground below us. In the way his hand twitches back toward mine but stops short.

"Well, we can hold out hope that the plan is still in effect," he says.

I frown now. I know within my bones that it will not happen. I knew as soon as Coach Davis said that he had seen enough. I hear it in the tones of voices around me all the time—the moment when people write me off, when they decide that I am more trouble than I am worth. Brandon never hears it. All he sees in me are the bright spots. The shining. Polaris. The Little Dipper. I do not want to ruin his night, though. I do not want to ruin his hope, even though mine is already gone.

"We can hold out hope," I say now.

Brandon does not answer, but I feel his body relax. My agreement is enough to make him happy again. The promise of my hope—no matter how false—is enough for him, and I need him to be happy, even if it is short-lived.

I need him to be happy for the both of us.

CHAPTER TWO

7 Days Until the Incident

I can carry on conversations—I am just quiet. I am not quiet because I am autistic, which is what most people think. I am quiet because people are annoying. Well, most people. Like Dalton, tapping away at the text-to-speech program on his tablet, rattling off all the similarities between him and Stephen Hawking as his reason for why he will never need to do a job interview. Never mind that I have had science classes with Dalton since middle school, and the only lesson he passed with flying colors was when we made ice cream in Ziploc bags.

I chuckle.

Ms. Findley raises her caterpillar eyebrows at me. "Something funny, Aiden?"

Crap. Summer has not made my Life Skills teacher less strict.

I shake my head, lean back in my chair, and tap the edge of my desk. One, two, double tap. One, two, double tap. Three more times. I do not look up at Ms. Findley. Her expressions make me itch. Instead, I stare at the silly motivational posters all over the classroom. CHANGE with a picture of a tree. COURAGE with a picture of an army officer and a dog jumping out of a helicopter.

> **NOTE:** *Motivational posters are also annoying. Like most people.*

Ms. Findley lets out a long, drawn-out breath. I focus on the dot over the letter *i* in the word "disability" written on the board behind her. Ms. Findley is pissed. I do not like to piss anyone off. Not on purpose.

Ms. Findley's gaze bores into my skin. "So, as I was saying, *everyone.*"

Well, geez, make it more obvious that you are mad at me, please?

"Job interviews are on the horizon for all seven of you—yes, even you, Dalton. Most of you are finally sixteen and will be seeking out your first opportunities. I know that it might seem intimidating, but remember the tips we went over today."

Ms. Findley motions for Tucker to stand up. He glances at her, fiddles with his camera, and shakes his head like he wants his brain to fall out of his ears.

"Come on, Tucker," she says now. She's using her coercive

voice. That is just another version of her normal voice, which typically reminds me of raining needles. Light but just a little bit dangerous.

"It's Buck," he responds in a whisper. A few people laugh.

Ms. Findley clicks her tongue at us. She does that when she is upset. Like she is training dogs. "Oh, that's just a mean nickname. You shouldn't use it as a name."

He has been Bucktooth Tuck since third grade. Not gonna change it now.

Tucker huffs. His thumbs fumble over each other as he clicks at random buttons on his camera, which he hauls everywhere. It slips from his hands, and he scrambles to catch it before it hits the floor.

The new girl, Isabella, sits behind Tucker, stifling a laugh with the back of her hand. She catches me looking and her eyes water. I cough my way through a laugh. Isabella sits up and leans forward, letting her long black faux locs create a curtain over her face. I smile. She has a sense of humor like mine. It is nice to share a laugh like this with her for the first time.

"Tucker, come on." The pitch of Ms. Findley's voice increases. "All right, so remember, everybody. Don't force eye contact and make yourselves uncomfortable. Quick glances only." She demonstrates with Tucker. "People take handshakes seriously, so practice regulating your grip with your parents at home. You don't want to squeeze too hard by accident." Ms. Findley grasps Tucker's hand and shakes.

Tucker's hand is limp in hers. A fixed grimace on his face betrays that he would rather be anywhere but here. I don't know if it's the handshake itself or having to be on display for everyone, but it's definitely too much. He snatches his hand away and scurries back to his seat, burying his face in his camera.

I would not have to worry about job interviews if I did not screw up tryouts and had any future as a football player. One, two, double tap. I think about the film I watched with Brandon last night of the school's most recent football game. I mean, if our team could get a running back with a little more weight, he could have run that linebacker over in last week's game; I mean, if the current running back had more speed on him, he could have made it to the hole before the linebackers got there; I mean, had the running back had better awareness and seen the hole faster, he could have been there even with the trash 4.8 he runs now; I mean, if it was me—

"Mr. Wright," Ms. Findley snaps.

I glance up. Shit. Everyone is gone.

She clicks her tongue. "The bell rang."

Dog trainer noises. Twice today.

I lean down, grab my backpack, and sling it over my shoulder. I start toward the door.

"Aiden, you really need to pay attention in this class. Job readiness matters. What could possibly be more important on your mind than—"

I do not turn to face her voice. I could have been the bigger, faster running back in the film. I could have been part of the team. That is the more important thing on my mind.

"I am only sixteen."

"And sixteen is an important age. Did you even hear what I said about the group project?"

No. No, I did not.

"Yes," I lie.

Ms. Findley frowns. "Then who's your partner?"

"Bucktooth Tuck?" I guess.

Ms. Findley lets out a big breath. "Aiden, first off, do not call Tucker that. Next, you need to take this project seriously."

I stay quiet. I do not need the lecture, and I know that explaining myself will only lead to a much longer conversation that I do not feel like having. Ms. Findley frowns. She is unhappy. I take note, just like my occupational therapist used to tell me to do when I was younger. Take note of the people around you. Take note of their facial expressions and body language. Take note of what they say. It has always helped me understand people, helped me see what people do to put themselves into boxes, what they do to fit in, what it might take for me to fit into their boxes, even though I have no desire to do so.

"Aiden?" Ms. Findley asks.

"Sorry," I say now. "Can you explain the project again?"

Ms. Findley closes her eyes and bites her bottom lip.

NOTE: *Ms. Findley closes her eyes and bites her lip when she is irritated.*

"You are supposed to meet with your assigned partner and find a part-time job for the school year." Ms. Findley grabs a sheet of paper from her desk. "Here is the approved list of places that will be expecting students. You will go through the interview process and then work after school for class credit."

"But—" I start to say.

"Aht! No buts. You will do this. You can work out a schedule with whoever hires you. I've done this every year with my juniors, and it turns out amazing results." Ms. Findley walks back around her desk and sits.

I wait.

"You can go," she says now.

I frown and turn to leave.

In the hallway, Isabella is waiting right outside the door and stops me as I stalk out of Ms. Findley's class.

"Hey, Aiden, right?"

I look at her and nod. Her faux locs are wavy and hang down to her waist. Her hair was in a big curly Afro last week. And she wore it straight a few weeks before that. It hung almost to her waist.

"I'm Isabella. Your partner for the after-school project!" She reaches out her hand for me to shake, and I burst out laughing. Her eyebrows furrow.

I confused her. I stop laughing, grasp her hand firmly, and shake up and down, just like Ms. Findley demonstrated. When Isabella realizes what I am doing, she laughs too.

"The art of the handshake mastered so quickly, huh?" Isabella chuckles again and tucks a loose loc back behind her ear. She shifts from foot to foot. "So, Findley was really laying it on thick today, huh?" she asks. She alternates between looking down at her feet and up at me.

I watch her behavior. Yes, we are partners, but she is trying awfully hard to talk to me. I realize that she is waiting for an answer. I finally open my mouth. "Yeah, she was."

"Oh, it speaks!" Her huge smile brightens her face immediately. Her teeth are super white. I bet she goes to the dentist on time every year. "Glad I could get something out of you. I'm pretty sure I've only heard you talk once since the school year started."

I glance down at my watch. Four minutes to get to class. I start to walk. After six steps, I look back at Isabella. She stands, arms at her side, frowning. I gesture for her to follow. She grins and catches up.

"School only started two months ago." I shrug. "Not much to say."

"I don't know," Isabella says now. "Two months is a long time to say two words."

I bite at my curling lip. She is funny. "A word a month. Got a quota to meet," I say now.

Isabella laughs. It rings like shards of glass on a tile floor. Pretty. I glance down at her, but her eyes seem to want to catch everything as we walk. The bright blue lockers, some of them open with students standing in front, changing out textbooks between classes. The white tile floors, scuffed from years of kids not caring to pick up our feet. The ceilings, strung with banners and adornments every few feet advertising everything from Student Government Association to the basketball team. Or maybe only I notice all those things.

"A man of few words." Isabella nods. "I like it." She looks

down at her feet and I watch our strides. She takes two steps to my one each time. I laugh in my head at it.

"Why are you in Life Skills?" I ask now.

"What do you mean?" Isabella glances up, bites her lip, then looks back at the floor.

"You do not have a disability."

"That was not a question, and now I see you're a conversationalist at heart. You're breaking that two-word quota by a long shot." Isabella giggles and gently bumps her body against my side. Something about it makes me smile, though I am surprised that I am comfortable with the contact so soon. "How do you know I don't have a disability? Many disabilities are invisible, you know."

I nod. I do know. But I also pay attention. Ms. Findley does not approach Isabella the same way that she approaches the rest of us. I cannot explain how, but there is a difference I can feel but cannot put into the right words. I always try to find the right words.

> **NOTE:** *Life Skills is not just for kids with disabilities, but most years, it seems like we are the only students that the administration enrolls in the class.*

"But you're right, I do not have a disability. So clearly, I'm in Life Skills because I suck at life." Isabella smiles up at me.

I smile back. Don't we all, to some extent?

"I used to get in some trouble back at my old school in Nebraska, and I just transferred here this year. They signed me up for Life Skills because of my 'unfortunate history,' or whatever." Isabella glances at me out of the corner of her eye.

I return the look, then look down at the floor.

"That's not a problem for you, right?"

I shrug. Problem, by definition, means a matter or situation regarded as unwelcome or harmful. I am good.

"Ah, shy guy likes troublemakers. My interest is deepened." Isabella giggles, and it's like pennies clinking together. "Where's your phone?"

"Back pocket," I say.

Isabella reaches into my back pocket, grabs my phone, and starts typing.

I stop walking, but Isabella doesn't notice. She touched me without warning again. I wait for the itchiness to creep along my skin. It does not come. I wonder why.

"Well, you have my number now, so we can touch base about our project and stuff. We have a whole job to find together and we've got to hold each other accountable. I texted myself so that I have your number too. I'm gonna text you. We can work on our life skills together, or whatever," Isabella says, and I pause for a moment to really take her in. Her bronzed skin reminds me a bit of Brandon's. She has a beauty mark above the right side of her lip and one above her left eyebrow. Her heart-shaped face hides nothing. I can tell she is not the type who can mask how she feels.

I focus on her lips and not her eyes. I give her a quick second of eye contact and her smile gets bigger. She turns and struts down the hallway.

"Why are you being so nice to me?" I ask the back of her head.

Isabella turns on her heel to face me and shrugs. "I'm always nice to the coolest people I know."

I'm the coolest person she knows? I nod.

"Cool." Isabella nods back. "You better answer my text, or I'll bother you."

I stand in the hallway a full thirty seconds after she leaves, enjoying the feeling surging through me. I glance at my watch. I have to get to class, and then it's me, Brandon, and the football field.

I consider Isabella and her bubbly personality and smile. Compared to having to confront the football field for the first time since tryouts, being bothered by her does not sound too bad.

CHAPTER THREE

7 Days Until the Incident

My room, a football field, and hell are three places I would rather be than this packed hallway right after last bell. Everyone grabbing at each other and yelling like their lives have changed drastically since they last saw their friends in fifth period. They are acting like it's the first day of school instead of two months in.

A high-pitched squeal grates at my ears and vibrates across my skin. Sneakers squeak across the checkered linoleum tiles. Metal on metal clangs as people slam lockers shut. So much conflicting noise. My lungs seize up like someone is gripping them in their fists. I freeze in place, close my eyes, and drum my fingers against my thigh.

One. Two. Stop. One. Two. Stop.

My breath comes quicker and I squeeze my eyes until I see

neon. All this noise, all at once. It is overwhelming.

Arms wrap around me. Then quiet as headphones slide over my head. Cinnamon. Vanilla. Pine trees. Tabasco sauce. All those smells combined: Brandon.

I did not realize that I had left my noise-canceling headphones at home until first period, but of course my brother grabbed them for me. I welcome the soft padding and pressure on my ears.

Brandon nudges my side, and I follow his black-and-white sneakers. I do not bother to look up. I barely escaped one sensory-processing meltdown; I am not tempting fate. Instead, I embrace my muffled existence until we are through a pair of double doors, across mottled concrete, then onto grass. As soon as green is underfoot, Brandon yanks the headphones from my head. The breeze swooshes loud in my ears.

NOTE: *Air in my ear canals makes me feel dizzy. Do not like.*

"You know, Aiden, if I was autistic and hated a bunch of noise, I would never forget my headphones," Brandon says with a smile playing on his lips. "I'd be auspicious in my ability to remember them."

I count fourteen blades of grass taller than the rest. "Auspicious? Definition: Conducive to success? Favorable?"

The sun shines bright on the field. The orange glow gives Brandon's skin, only a shade lighter than mine now after a full summer of football practices, a golden-brown hue.

Brandon frowns, then nods. "Yeah. I'm sure I used that right."

Not at all.

"Well, auspicious or not, here we are, months into the school year, and just like yesterday, I had to remember ya headphones," Brandon says now. "You gon have to start paying me for top-notch noise-canceling provision services or something, 'cause I'm putting work in and I don't think I'm being accurately restituted, my brother."

I smirk. "Recompensed, maybe? Definition: to pay or reward for effort or work."

"Recomposed. Exactly," Brandon says with confidence, as though he had said the right thing from the start.

I chuckle. Here he goes. Out of the noisy hallway and into Brandon's endless chatter, not that it has ever bothered me.

"You know, if you wanted compensation for my headphones, you could have given them to me before first period," I say now.

"I forgot!" Brandon says. "I forgot I threw them in my bag and didn't notice them until after lunch. My bad!"

I roll my eyes. "No compensation for you."

"I'm gon ignore everything you just said and accept a thank-you and agreement for you to buy me some food the next time I ask," Brandon says now. "And you, my brother, are very welcome. What would you do without me? Oh! I just remembered! Did you watch the video I sent during lunch? The one with that crazy tackle by the safety from Florida

State? He hit that receiver so hard. Dude definitely got his bell rung!" Brandon's laughter echoes in the open air.

> **NOTE:** *Getting your bell rung, by football definition, means tackled. Not so hard that someone is injured, but hard enough that there is a satisfying clash of helmets.*

Brandon rubs the top of my head. I smile.

"You are gonna tangle my locs." There is no actual protest in my voice.

Brandon laughs. "How you tangle locs?"

The football field is empty. Not surprising, since practice does not start for another hour and a half.

"Whew, it's hotter than the devil's ass crack out here," Brandon says.

There he goes.

"I guess I will just radiate heat from my ears like a jackrabbit to cool down," I say now.

"Nah, you gotta vibrate your throat like a quail. That's where the real cooldown kicks in," Brandon replies.

"I will see your throat vibration and raise you a spinal regurgitation."

"Spinal regurgitation?" Brandon's face twists into a mix of a smile and horror. "Ostrich?"

I shake my head. "Pelicans."

"I always knew they were weird," Brandon says with a laugh.

"Why did you drag me out here?" I ask now. I have actively avoided the field since tryouts but could not ignore my brother's invitation.

"Way to change the subject!"

I stare at Brandon's forehead and wait for him to respond.

"Silence. We love that." Brandon gives my shoulder a push.

I shrug.

"First of all, you love being out here. Second of all, dragged. Definition: to drag. You walked out here on your own," Brandon says.

"Dragged. Definition: to—"

"Third of all," Brandon says louder now, "you used to always stay with me for practice. I been all alone this year, just suffering with no friends—"

"You have a lot of friends—"

"Just suffering," Brandon continues. "Because my brother don't love me no more. You got somewhere better to be, A?" He arches an eyebrow.

I shake my head.

"So, why you acting like you wanna leave, bro?" he asks now. His voice is gentle.

Still, anxiety creeps into the pit of my stomach and spreads out from my belly button, sending a skittering sensation like a million ants out across my body, up my back, and all along my scalp. I am itchy underneath my skin.

I close my eyes and tap at my thigh. One. Two. Stop. One. Two. Stop.

I have not wanted to be on this field since I saw that my name was not on the roster. Since I knew that they rejected me for my meltdown—for my autism. The same way I was rejected as a kid. The reason I barely made an effort at football tryouts ever again until this summer. The reason I kept my passion to myself all this time. The rejection for who I am. The rejection for being me.

Brandon reaches out and squeezes my arm and I open my eyes to look at him. "Hey, you're good." His voice thrums low like a hum. He does not ask. He tells.

"I just prefer not to come out here," I say now. Watching Brandon at practice is harder after this summer. It is Brandon's last year of school, and I will never play on a team with him. The thought is like a death, but I do not get to grieve.

Brandon frowns. "You used to always run a few drills with me before practice at least. I mean, dang, you already leaving me hanging with nobody filming practice, now I ain't even got a pre-practice warm-up buddy. It's just rough out here for a lonely quarterback." He pretends to swoon.

He sure knows how to guilt-trip. His face is contorted into some expression to make me feel bad.

I shrug.

"You been my drill partner all my life, A. That ain't 'bout to change now."

Here I am with my eyes closed, avoiding his facial expressions, ignoring his tonal inflections, dodging his guilt trips. I let out a breath, open my eyes, and focus on Brandon's nose. My expression must show some annoyance, because he rolls his eyes.

"This about the tryouts," Brandon says now. "You ever think, maybe, that the 'no' you got from the football team this summer ain't the end of the world and that you could easily get another chance?"

"Chances like the rejections from Pop Warner in elementary and the team in middle school?" Sadness gathers in a lump in my throat. I blink back the gathering tears.

Brandon chews on his lip. "Third time's the charm?"

NOTE: *"Third time is the charm" is not an exact science. In fact, it does not seem to be science at all.*

"Another try would be a fourth," I say now. "It is okay. They have you, B. Star quarterback. Black Tom Brady."

Brandon rests his hand on my shoulder. "Tom Brady needs Gronkowski."

My mouth twists. "Gronk is a tight end. I am a running back."

"It's an analogy, bro. Keep up!"

"Analogy? Definition—"

"Focus, A!"

"That is not what that is." I chuckle. "At all."

Brandon laughs. "Well, you know what I mean! I need you! And this year is your year!"

"Yeah?" I raise my eyebrows. "How is that?"

Brandon smiles. "Humor me." He jogs over to the sideline and fishes a mesh jersey out from his backpack.

Humor him how?

"I do not have anything to practice in," I say. "I left my stuff at home on purpose."

Brandon reaches back into his bag and out comes another mesh jersey. "You know, I always appreciate your honesty." He chuckles.

Now I am suspicious. The heck is he up to? I jog over to the sideline, pull my shirt off, and don the jersey.

"Happy?" I ask.

Brandon smiles. "Aren't you?" He pulls a football from his bag.

Even though I do not respond, I am a little happier. Most people are not calmed by a football's bumpy texture, but I am not most people. Not everyone is invigorated by the smell of fresh-cut grass on a hundred-yard field, but I am not everyone. Not all people perk up at the blast of a whistle, but I am not all people. Football is organized chaos. Rule-driven disorder. A route, perfectly run, is the most beautiful dance. A formation, altered on the fly, is the best improvisational theater. I have always loved it. I have always wanted to be a part of it.

"You know, A," Brandon says, "Coach was talking about trying to find a new running back for the team. Kevin—you know Kevin, right?"

I know of Kevin. I have watched him play—good trucking power, but misses obvious holes in the defense at times. He is a starting running back. That is it.

Brandon accepts my silence as a response. "Well, Kevin's dad apparently got a new job and his whole family gotta move like next week or something. And Henry, you know Henry?"

Henry. Other running back.

"Well, Henry broke his femur two days ago, out for the season. That's wild, ain't it?"

Clouds drift in front of the blazing sun, casting short shadows on the field. I can feel what Brandon is insinuating, but I do not want to make assumptions. Hope only sets up disappointment.

Brandon continues. "Bike accident, apparently—not motorcycle, just regular bike—but now we down two running backs."

Brandon is explaining a lot. Talking a lot. Even for him.

"What are you saying, B?" I ask now. "Are you trying to admit to breaking Henry's leg?" I know he is not, but the excited edge to his voice is enough to consider him a prime suspect.

Brandon cocks his head to the side and laughs. "I'm saying you should be on the team, A!"

My brows meet in the middle of my forehead. Of course that is what he is saying. I knew this was coming. I shake my head. "Not a good idea." Third rejection was the charm, or whatever he said.

Brandon sucks his teeth at me. "Come on, we gon be a great team! Like Shannon and Sterling Sharpe!"

"They did not play QB and RB."

"Bruh. Not the point! You keep ruining my analogies," Brandon says. "I'm saying we could be big, bro! Come on! Think about it. You can play with ya big brother for his senior year. Think about all the cool stuff they gon say about us. The Wright brothers: flying high or something like that."

"Flying high?" I raise a brow.

"You know, 'cause of the Wright brothers that invented

airplanes," Brandon says now. "I know that one's right. You can't even correct it."

A corner of my mouth lifts. He is right for once. I take in a breath and hold it, letting my lungs sear from the pressure in my chest. Brandon is serious about this.

My brother smiles with almost all his teeth. His eyes crinkle and twitch a little in the corners. The wheels are turning in his head already. He wants this. The look almost gets me.

"I already tried, B. You know what happened this summer."

Brandon bumps his shoulder against mine. "Summer was a fluke, bro. It was just one incident, and honestly, it was blown way out of proportion." He starts to walk to the other side of the field.

I count my steps as we make our way across the turf. Fluke. Definition: an unlikely occurrence. That was not a fluke. It was not blown out of proportion. I was overloaded. Full sensory meltdown. Just like with Pop Warner. I did not do bad in terms of performance or skill, but I did get overwhelmed. People do not always know how to handle overwhelmed. People stare. People avoid. People see it as a problem—a quirk. The coaches did not want to deal with my quirks. Now that is done. As people say—it is what it is.

"Regardless of all that, you're fast, you know plays, you analyze the field better and quicker than anybody else I know—besides me, obviously," Brandon says now.

Obviously. I chuckle.

"You can do this."

I shake my head and look down.

"Hey, Aiden?"

I look at my brother. I am not always the best with non-verbal communication, but even I can tell that Brandon's facial expression is earnest. Eyelids low, brows slightly furrowed, searching my face for a reflection of the comfort being given.

"I know you can do this." Brandon's voice is ice on a wound. Soothing. He is sure. "I know you can. Don't get hung up on all the *before*. You can do this *now*."

I nod. Maybe. It is hard to argue with Brandon when he is at peak motivational speaker mode, though. It could just be him in my head convincing me of something that is not real. "Okay, maybe I can talk to Coach? Let him know I am interested."

Brandon claps. "Yes! I knew you'd say that, so I already went ahead and told him you wanted to do it! This is ya practice jersey! You start today, bro!"

Of course he already said yes for me. I chuckle. I want to be mad that he told Coach I would join without asking me, but I can't. That's Brandon.

"I hate you," I say.

"Nah, you don't." Brandon rubs the top of my head.

"Locs!"

"They can't tangle!" Brandon guffaws.

"Are we running drills before people get here or are we talking?" I tug at the mesh jersey. The rough threads send tiny soothing shock waves up through my fingertips.

"Always about the business. A man of few words. That's why you my favorite brother, you know that?"

"I'm your only brother."

Brandon shrugs. "Still my favorite regardless. We ain't arguing semantics."

"You actually got that one right." I smile.

"You'd know, Encyclopedia Brown." Brandon reaches for my head and I duck away.

"Dictionary."

"Hate you." Brandon laughs and pushes my arm. "You know, maybe when Coach gets here, I can tell him you switching positions so that instead of a running back, you can be my *very* wide receiver. Get it?" Brandon doubles over, choking down laughter. He always laughs the hardest at his own jokes.

"Sorry, people that cannot tackle me do not get to laugh."

"Oh yeah? Maybe the real problem is that you can't hear me from way down there." Brandon uses his hands as a visor and stands on his toes to look down on me.

"Three inches," I say now. "You are three inches taller. At least I would not snap like a twig if I got hit."

Brandon drops the ball and tackles me right in the stomach. All the air leaves my body as he hits me, then I hit the turf. My head hits the ground and I blink away stars until Brandon's face comes into frame, upside down, grinning. His smile is bright against the backdrop of his dark skin.

"How's that for a snap, my boy?" Brandon asks.

I jump up and he takes off. His laughter ripples across my skin like rain. I let out loud whooping laughs as I push to pick up speed to catch him.

"Too slow, big boy." Brandon teases in huffs as he runs. "Got the power, not the speed."

I lean forward and my shoulder cracks him right in the

back. Brandon gasps as the air leaves his body, and we tumble around each other onto the plastic-feeling grass. I am certain I have lost at least my top layer of skin.

Brandon starts laughing again as soon as he can breathe. "Dang. Since when can you run a 4.2?" He sits up and swipes the grass from his brush cut.

> NOTE: *Completing a forty-yard dash at the NFL combine and running 4.2 seconds is rare and considered very impressive.*

> NOTE FOR NOTE: *I do not run a 4.2. Brandon is simply slow.*

I smile back at Brandon and shake my locs free of grass too.

"Hey! That's Big-Time Brandon!" a deep voice calls from the side of the field. We both turn to look. It is Greg. He jogs over.

I do not do eye contact. But I study faces. I study people. To study people is to understand people. To understand people is to decode people. Most people need decoding.

> NOTE: *Gregory Williams. Wide receiver. Senior—like Brandon. Half Black. Reminds everyone he is mixed at least twice a week. Licks his lips more than seems necessary. Thin, even for a receiver. Agile on the field. Least amount of dropped passes of all the receivers. Brandon's favorite and de facto best friend.*

Greg has a huge smile on his face for Brandon. Even with all that joy, I do not miss when he glances at me and his face falls ever so slightly. Brandon is his top choice. Me? I am just the side that comes with the meal.

"What you doing out here so early, my guy?" Greg offers Brandon an outstretched hand and they pull into their usual bro hug.

"Just running some plays with my brother. What you doing out here?" Brandon asks now.

Greg glances at me and shoots me a half smile.

NOTE: *Some smiles are fake. People who do not smile with their whole face—a half smile—are more likely to be faking the smile altogether. Half smiles can be because:*

1. *Someone does not like you.*
2. *You make someone uncomfortable.*
3. *They want to appear to be nice, kind, or polite.*
4. *They want to appease someone else around you.*
5. *Someone has a condition that does not allow them to smile properly.*
    a. EXAMPLE: *a stroke.*
        I. *To my knowledge, Greg has never had a stroke.*

CONCLUSION: *Greg might not like me. I do not care.*

"He knows the plays?" Greg whispers now.

His whisper sucks. It is loud as shit.

NOTE: *I have never known shit to be loud, but Brandon often says that things are "loud as shit."*

Brandon narrows his eyes at Greg and throws his arm around my shoulder.

"He knows 'em better than you do. Every route you ran this summer was trash." Brandon sings the word "trash."

Greg pushes at Brandon's shoulder. "Shut up. I'm just saying. I heard about summer—"

"Aiden's the best running back I know out here," Brandon interrupts.

Greg raises his eyebrows at me and chuckles. "Yeah, all right. Well, tell Coach to put him on the team, then." He slaps at Brandon's chest.

Brandon slaps his hand away. "Already did! He's gon be at practice today. While we adding people, though, maybe I'll tell him to put ya sister on the team too. We both know she can catch better than you on ya best day."

Greg drops his duffel bag and Brandon runs. I watch the chase. Maybe Greg is right. Maybe trying to be on the team is not a good idea.

I stroke the mesh and let the sensation tickle the nerves in my fingertips. My first practice will tell me if this was a mistake.

The rest of the team trickles out as we wait, and Brandon cracks jokes to kill the time. I note that a few players—especially the ones who clearly remember me from summer—nudge each other and whisper. I shift, suddenly more uncomfortable than before. I am instantly regretting this, but it is too late. I cannot walk away and disappoint Brandon after I have already said yes. When Coach Davis comes out, he does not regard me much, and for that I am thankful. Flanked by Assistant Coaches McDonald and Nielson, he quickly gets things started.

Coach claps twice. "Before we start, we have a new face today, though I'm sure many of you already know Aiden and remember him from summer tryouts."

Some of the boys snicker. I tap at my thigh and ignore them.

"Hey, it's all good. Ignore them. I'll handle that later," Brandon whispers to me.

I shake my head. I do not want him to do that. I do not want them to feel forced to accept me. Brandon already does this with his friends. They don't say it, but most of the people I hang around with are more Brandon's friends than mine because he always drags me along, and I do not think it is because they ask for me.

"Aiden has gratefully agreed to join us on a tentative basis to replace our losses, since we're down two running backs," Coach says. He pushes his blond hair to the side with one hand and smiles, freckles visible on the bridge of his nose.

Tentative, by definition, means not certain or fixed; provisional. Oh.

"He's mostly observing today, but I think things will go well and then he'll be able to stay on a more permanent basis, huh?" Coach Davis gives me a pointed look.

I look at the ground, studying each blade of grass on the turf.

"It'll be permanent, bro," Brandon whispers to me now.

I do not respond. He does not know—he hopes. I do too.

"Now we got pity joins," someone whispers.

I look up in the direction of the voice. Carter. Wide receiver. Sometimes Brandon's friend.

"Aye, nothing's out of pity. Cut that," Brandon snaps.

Carter clams up and nods. When Brandon looks away, he whispers to another player next to him.

I do not think that will be the end of that, but I cannot worry about it. I focus on the practice ahead. I feel the tension, but I know that on the field, I can be the best. I am ready for my turn. I can do this.

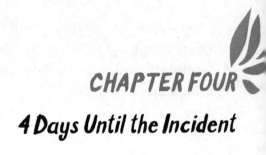

CHAPTER FOUR

4 Days Until the Incident

G ood hustle today, A." Brandon tousles my locs. "I gotta stay behind and talk to Coach real quick. You start home. I'll catch up!"

He takes my silence as a response and heads through the locker room doors to the coaches' offices.

My first practice is in the books. So much watching, talking, and explaining on an already exhausting Monday.

> **NOTE:** *Coaches ramble about plays, and positions, and routes, and field conditions, and players, and skill sets, but football is just Xs and Os and arrows and movements. I understand the Xs and Os and arrows and movements. The talking is unnecessary. It's simple to picture.*

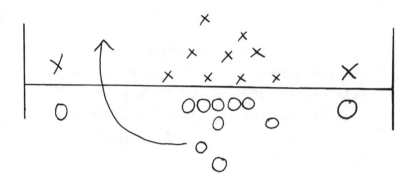

Overall, though, practice was good. I was good. I avoided excess contact. I kept my cool. My lungs ache from the work, and my limbs weigh me down, but my brain dances. I make my way out of the locker room.

"Later, Aiden!" someone says.

I turn to the unfamiliar voice.

NOTE: *Reginald Watkins. Junior—like me. Dark, curly Afro. Backup quarterback behind Brandon, all three years. Has played at least once in every game. Do not know his rushing and passing yards—need to check later. Tan skin—lots of red streaks from practice; he bruises easily. Often smiling.*

Reginald stops and frowns. He gives me a short wave.

I mirror the wave. "Bye, Reginald."

His smile returns. "Call me Reg. We're teammates now!"

Reg closes his locker and nudges Bernard Simmons, who sits on a bench nearby.

> NOTE: *Bernard Simmons. Defensive back. Junior. On the team since last year. Cropped black hair. Similar build as me—muscular and wide. Maybe a half inch taller. Will need to measure. Darker skin than mine. Scar on left arm, a few inches long—three? Long healed.*

Bernard smiles at Reg. They hold hands, fingers interlocked. "Bye, Aiden." Bernard waves with his free hand.

They are the first players to acknowledge me as a teammate apart from Brandon. I smile as I walk out of the locker room.

Panic surges in my throat once I am in front of the school. Two years of walking with Brandon has made me uncomfortable to start home alone. Still, I know the way, and that calms me a bit.

> NOTE: *It takes 2,392 steps to get home.*

I make my way to the sidewalk, thankful that the rain held off today—a miracle for September in South Florida. I have my umbrella, but I am wearing gym shorts, and something about damp legs sends my senses spiraling.

Walking has a beautiful rhythm to it. I stare at the ground and count my steps as I start home. One, two. Break. New sidewalk square. One, two. Break. New sidewalk square.

My headphones blanket my senses, filtering the sounds that typically make their way underneath my skin and instead letting them slip over me. I focus on my feet as I walk. Forty-seven more steps next to the row of coco plum bushes that line the entrance to the neighborhood right before mine. Sixty-three more steps of palm trees, all spaced exactly twelve steps away from each other. Almost to the front of the community— the home stretch. One foot in front of the other. Two steps for every sidewalk square. One. Two. Break. One. Two. Break.

A firm hand on my left shoulder interrupts my rhythm and the world spins, but the movement is not what makes me dizzy. Who is touching me? My left arm swings out and I dart to the right to create distance. I swallow the scream rising in my throat. Eyes up. Cop car. Green and white. County, not local. Lights on. Sirens? I push my headphones down around my neck. Only the bushes rustle behind me. No sirens. No other cars swish by.

The cop stands a few inches shorter than me. His dark sunglasses reflect my face back at me twofold. One hand rests on his hip, on top of his gun, the holster unclipped. I ignore the creeping feeling all over my skin, a reaction to the unwanted contact, and eye the weapon.

He smacks something—I assume it is gum—in his mouth, then spits. "You ain't hear me calling at you, boy?"

Of course, now would be the time when I instruct my body to move, but it does the opposite. Instead of shaking or nodding my head, or doing anything really, my arms hang at my sides and I stare at the officer's bushy brown mustache. The rest of his face is shaved and betrays a shadow on his pale skin, dotted with two razor cuts and at least three angry red bumps.

"You slow, boy?" the cop asks now.

Is there a correct answer to that question? The part of my brain that is functioning tells me to respond. It tells me to be polite and cooperative. It tells me to do everything my parents taught me to do when a cop stops me. The part of my brain that hates me—and that seems to be the dominant part right now—is drawing a blank.

The officer's mustache twitches when he talks. Four hairs hang past his lip. I wonder if they tickle.

"Boy, you don't hear me? You deaf or something?" The cop's tone is gruff. "What you doing out this way? You live round here?"

I dig my nails into my palm and finally nod.

The cop smirks. "Oh see, look, you can answer." He reaches out and claps a hand on my shoulder.

I shift under the weight and fight the roiling nausea tickling my esophagus. Do not pull away—it will look suspicious. Do not pull away—it will look suspicious.

"Where you live at, boy? I don't think I've seen you round here before." He is closer to my face now. He smells of motor oil and spicy cologne. My nose itches.

My mouth falls open, but words do not fall out with the motion. I stammer a few times.

"Sure you live this way, boy? Why don't you come on over here by me and we'll just do a quick check."

The cop steers me by my shoulder toward his car. Panic

flares in my intestines like a firework. Instinctively, I duck from underneath the weight of his hand. Then everything happens almost simultaneously.

The cop reaches out and grabs my shoulder, hard. My hands fly up in the air. Wings flap past me as two birds, startled by the sudden movements, flee the coco plum bushes behind me. And then, Brandon.

"Aiden?" Brandon calls out. "Aiden!"

Crap. Crap. Crap. I should have nodded, or shaken my head, or answered. I should have complied better. That is what Mom says to do. Comply. I panicked. I pulled away. Now I am probably gonna get arrested or die and he is probably gonna arrest or kill my brother and our parents are gonna be depressed because we are all they have and—

"Hands up! Hands—" The cop twists. He turns to Brandon and observes him from head to toe.

Brandon, clad in West Gate football apparel, strides up, hands slightly raised, with a sheepish grin.

"Brandon?" the cop asks now. "Brandon Wright?"

"In the flesh." Brandon shrugs and chuckles. His shoulders are still tense, his smile is still tight, his body still coiled—like a snake.

The cop's fingers no longer dig into my shoulder. A stinging ache resounds where the pressure releases.

"I thought that was you! Just coming up from practice, huh? You live out this way?" the cop asks now.

Everyone talks like I am not here, like everything was not tense just forty-seven seconds ago.

"Yeah, we live here and yeah, we just finished up. Coach held me back a bit. Gotta get my head right for the next game. Lot of cameras and scouts. My stock went up, you know? Number one recruit in the nation. The buzz is kind of crazy. Lot of people looking my way."

The cop nods. "Of course. Coach Davis all right, then? Good man. Done a lot for the community. Does a lot for the West Gate guys up at the local station."

"Yeah, he's good! He's planning another volunteer day for us for the station now." Brandon glances toward me and his eyes are a little wild. They don't match the smile he has plastered on his face.

"That's great! Y'all gotta come out to the county station one day." The cop shifts from his left to his right foot.

NOTE: *I believe the movement is discomfort?*

"So, you said you live out this way?"

He asked that earlier. Brandon already answered.

"Oh yeah," Brandon says. "Right up there in Acres."

"Acres?" the cop asks now. "Really?"

"Really," Brandon says with a smile. His cheeks are tense. His forehead smooth. His eyes flat. The smile is fake.

FAKE SMILE REASON NUMBER FOUR: *They want to appease someone else around you.*

   • *Brandon wants to appease this officer.*

Brandon gestures toward me with his head. "What's going on? My brother starting a little after-school riot?" He smiles and looks at me, his eyes a bit wider than normal.

NOTE: *I think the expression is fear?*

"Oh!" The cop claps down on my shoulder. The touch feels different now. Friendly. Casual.

Seriously?

"This your brother?" the cop asks now. "No riots for him. I was just checking on him, making sure he wasn't lost."

That feels like a lie. Well, no, it *is* a lie. I am almost absolutely sure he was not checking to make sure that I was lost when he was calling me "boy" and trying to get me to his car.

Brandon nods. "Yeah. He knows the way, but we appreciate that!"

The cop nods in return.

We stand in twelve seconds of silence before Brandon clears his throat. The cop lets me go. My shoulder feels cool, and the absence of pressure is comforting in a way I have never known it to be.

"Aiden here is actually on the team! New running back. Our own boys can't even stop him!"

"Oh, so you belong to West Gate, huh?" the cop asks, turning to me.

Belong to?

"One of Coach Davis's?" The cop scans me. Takes me in. Lingers on my shoulders, my arms, my chest. "That makes sense. I can see it. Built like a gorilla, this one. Good pick for sure. Can't wait to see him out on the field. Well, I won't hold y'all. Good luck in the next game. We need another championship! And let Coach Davis know the guys at the station are behind him," the cop says as he gets back in his car.

We do not start walking again for three minutes. I count. In that time, I realize that what the cop said about my build might not have been a compliment.

Tension ripples from Brandon like waves of heat, in stark contrast to his seemingly easy demeanor from before. I feel sweaty walking next to him, even though the air is not sticky like usual. Beads trickle down the middle of my back, a cool stream to calm me.

"Why did you tell him that I was on the football team?" I ask now. "You brought up football a lot."

I have other questions, but they bumble around in my brain, intertwining, interlocking, and, ultimately, getting too tangled for me to make enough sense of them to ask.

Brandon rubs the top of my head. "Sometimes with cops and stuff, you gotta make them know you're important."

My brows meet in the middle of my forehead. "What do you mean?"

"Coach Davis is a big deal around here, especially with the cops. I'm a top recruit and I brought in championships. You're a part of that legacy now. I'm also a starting player for our team. Everybody around here knows Coach Davis, you know? Some people know me. Some people see me as an extension of Coach Davis." Brandon rolls his shoulders. "Like, in some ways, I'm *his* to them. I don't like it, but it's true. You get me? Making who we are clear lets them know that if something happens, there might be coaches looking for us, you know? Coach Davis might be looking for us. That makes us important," Brandon says. "'Cause we important to someone who's important to them."

I frown down at the concrete. I am standing on a crack. I step onto the next slate. There are 526 more steps until we are home.

"Don't say nothing to Mom about the cop that stopped you on the way home. She just gon get all worked up," Brandon whispers to me as we walk up to our house. The long semicircular driveway and perfectly manicured lawn greet us. The driveway is the worst stretch, since it is a far hike from the street to the front door. We make our way to the front door, twice as tall as both Brandon and me, enter the security code, and push our way in.

I nod. Mom will get worked up. She will give us another version of *the talk*.

NOTE: *Short version of the talk:*
  • *Comply. Comply. Comply. Yes sir. No sir. Do not*
    reach for anything. Let them search. Get home
    alive.

We make our way through the foyer. Yellow and brown packages, most addressed to Nerissa Wright, litter the white marble floor. A few packages addressed to Ian Wright sit on the round table in the middle of the circular entryway. The packages stick out in odd contrast to all the white in the house. Mom thinks too much color is busy.

"Mom, what's all this stuff?" Brandon asks. He looks at each package to see if anything is for him.

"I hired a new attorney at my firm today, and I'm setting up their office. I got a few things so that it looks nice when they start next Monday. Also got a few new things for Aiden's therapy room. There's some stuff for you, too, sweetie," she calls from the kitchen. Mom's voice is chirpy as always. If I had to picture her as any animal, it would be a bird.

"I got 'em!" Brandon announces as he grabs two packages from the floor. He crosses the room and sits on one of the pale wooden barstools at the kitchen island.

Mom stands behind the large white island with a stainless-steel bowl and a pile of red salmon fillets in front of her. She meticulously separates the skin from each fillet. The whir of the food processor fills the air. Scallion, garlic, and Scotch bonnet pepper burn at my nostril hairs.

"Jerk salmon?" I ask.

Mom smiles, her long black hair framing her face. The lighting in the kitchen highlights her skin, the same color as Brandon's, slightly lighter than mine. "Your nose always knows. Hi to you, sweetheart. How was your day?"

I shrug and trudge across the great room that contains the kitchen and family room, then drop my backpack next to the sectional. I collapse face-first into the fabric and let the green velvet tickle my skin. Ugh, bad idea. Velvet irritates my joints. I can feel the smooth fabric in between my bones, creeping in, slimy like a snail. I need to get my skin brush and rub it over my arms a few times to relax, but I do not feel like moving just yet.

"You all right, Aiden?"

I turn my head and open my eyes. Dad lounges on the chaise watching television, his long locs hanging over the back. Brows furrowed, slight frown, hand reaching toward me. Concern.

I open my mouth to answer.

"He should be just fine." Mom's tone is cold water on my back. It is still chirpy, but deadly now.

Aw, crap. The cushion sinks in as Brandon settles next to me.

"What do you mean?" Dad asks now.

"I got a call that Aiden mouthed off to his Life Skills teacher, Ms. Findley," Mom says. There is an edge to her voice, and I just know she has at least one eyebrow raised and a frown on her face. I do not want to look.

Brandon taps me twice on the back, and I sit up bolt straight. That is his cue to me to get it together.

"Aiden, is that true?" Dad's calm, deep voice is like freshly sanded wood. There is a comfort in it that makes me feel more guilty than Mom's sharper tone. Even at her sweetest, she is about as soft as a dull needle.

"I'm sure Aiden ain't even really do nothing, Mom," Brandon says now. "Findley's probably being extra."

NOTE: *Walking out of Life Skills with an attitude after zoning out and not paying attention during class may not have been the best idea. I did do that. I do not always have the best ideas.*

"Thank you for the report from the class you weren't in, Brandon. Any other riveting revelations?" Mom raises an eyebrow at him. See, there's the eyebrow.

Brandon clams up. He knows better than to respond when she gets like this.

"*Ms.* Findley was not being extra, Brandon," Mom says now. "No. *Ms.* Findley is trying to teach your brother the skills he needs to be successful in life, Brandon. *Ms.* Findley is following your brother's IEP that we sat with her to set goals for, and doing her job, Brandon. *Ms.* Findley—"

"Was talking about handshakes. And eye contact. And letting HR know about our disabilities. And showing confidence through action. And understanding sarcasm," I say now.

Mom narrows her eyes at me.

"I was paying attention," I add.

"Apparently not enough to notice when the bell rang. She said you sat for two entire minutes staring into space."

I shrug. "I was thinking about football. And, to be fair, that was a few days ago. It did not happen today."

Brandon pushes me. "Dang, read the room. You could lie, bro." His laughter fills the room, and it is warm again.

Mom shakes her head, then chuckles. "I appreciate your

honesty, as always, but please try to take Life Skills seriously. It's really meant to help you with the day-to-day stuff we worry about."

I lie back into the soft cushions. "Mom, day-to-day stuff is easy."

"Mm-hmm, that's why I'm still doing your laundry and scheduling all your appointments, right?" Mom continues prepping the salmon. Dad has already refocused back to the television, flipping through channels for something to watch.

"*That* is Mom stuff," I say now. "I never realized I was supposed to be doing those things on my own. That is what moms are for, right?"

"Well, Mom stuff aside, is there anything else from Life Skills you want to tell us about?"

"Yeah, we have a project to find a part-time job," I say now, happy to be past her grilling.

Brandon snorts. "Why? We don't need one."

Dad raises an eyebrow. "And why not?"

Brandon raises his hand and gestures wildly in the air.

"I do not get it," I say.

"Yeah, neither do I," Mom adds.

"Well, why would we need to work? We get everything. We have everything. Look where we live."

"And so what?" Dad asks. Now Dad has the eyebrow. He almost never has the eyebrow. Brandon needs to about-face immediately. I try to tap him, but he ignores me.

"Dad, the only reason we walk to school is because it's so close that it doesn't make sense to buy a car." Brandon laughs. "Why are y'all acting like I'm talking weird? Am I wrong, A?"

I frown. I never really thought about everything we have. I never really thought about a part-time job, either, but I guess that is why. We do have a lot.

I shake my head.

"Well, a part-time job builds character!" Dad says. "I used to have one when I was your age."

"Really?" I ask.

Dad nods. "Supermarket."

I try to picture Dad working in a supermarket, but all I can imagine is him now, scanning groceries with a surly look cast over his face, a ratty apron hanging from his shoulders. I say as much to him.

"Why do you picture supermarket workers as unhappy?" Dad frowns and shoots Mom a glance.

What does that look mean? I shrug.

"Well, I think this is going to be great. A part-time job is amazing. Like Dad said, it builds character!" Mom says with a smile as she makes her way over to us.

"Y'all saying I ain't got character?" Brandon flexes and grins.

Mom pushes him on the shoulder. "Yeah, you see you? You have *too* much."

We all laugh. Mom rumples my hair, then heads back to the kitchen and continues skinning the salmon.

"Wait! Wait! Aren't y'all interested in why we're home so late?" Brandon asks.

Dad's eyes are trained on the television. "Aren't you both always back around this time?"

"Yes, we are," I say now. I am hesitant for my parents to find out about practice. They were not happy after the last rejection. Or maybe they were unhappy with my unhappiness. The way Mom raged for two days, threatening to sue the school for disability discrimination. The way Dad had to calm her and remind her that there was no proof that was the case. I doubt they will suddenly be happy for me to be on the team. Even now, I question my own placement.

"Thank you, Captain Obvious." Brandon pushes me and I pretend to fall over. "Aiden is on the football team! I didn't say anything before because I was still getting everything solidified, but he practiced with us today!"

Dad looks at me and I can see the joy plain on his face. "Wait, really? That's great, Aiden!" He reaches over and nudges me on the knee. "You excited? How was it? Were you good? No bad pileups or anything? Doesn't that mean your first game is Friday? Are you ready for that?"

I am surprised. I did not think Dad put much thought into me playing.

"Uh, yes really. Thank you. I think so. Fine. Yes. No. Yes. Maybe," I answer all his questions in order.

"Are you sure that's a good idea?" Mom asks. Her brow is furrowed.

"What do you mean, honey?" Dad's tone is not like it usually is. It is usually smooth, like river rocks. Right now, it is cut glass.

Brandon raises his eyebrows at me. He feels the change too. Mom looks up from what she is doing and looks at Dad with her eyes narrowed.

NOTE: *When Mom narrows her eyes, she is about to "light people up," as Brandon says. Being "lit up" is not good. Nobody glows. Anger ensues.*

"It didn't end well during all his tryouts, especially the last one." Mom sets down the knife she was using on the salmon. "I mean this in the best way, Aiden, honey, but I think being on the team is too much for you. This summer, you took ten minutes to calm down after being in that pileup. After twenty minutes, you were stimming so much in between plays that you couldn't even go out and finish," Mom says softly. She is concerned, I think. "And I am very convinced that all of that is why they rejected you. Is it worth it? I mean, do you want to be around people who rejected you for being who you are?"

"Well, it was his first time playing with so many people since the middle school tryouts. He had to figure it out and adjust," Dad says now. "Sometimes theory and practice are different. He's learned. He knows what to expect now. I don't think he'd do anything that he didn't feel like he was ready for. And we don't know if that is the reason they rejected him, Nerissa."

Yikes. A first name has been uttered. Reverse, reverse. Brandon scrunches his mouth together. He does that often when he is nervous. He does it before doctor appointments, on game days, and right before the first big drop on any roller coaster.

"Well, *Ian*," Mom says. Emphasis placed. "Aiden's disability hasn't changed since the summer, and neither has anyone's feelings about it, and he hasn't had additional experiences for us to know that he's past that kind of reaction, so I think your argument is unfounded." Mom is in lawyer mode now. Her arguments are ironclad, her tone as stony as her demeanor.

"Respectfully, I disagree, *Nerissa*," Dad says now. Emphasis returned. "Experience usually results in a lot of growth. Growth we've seen from Aiden in spades every single day. I don't see what the problem is here. If he wants to be on the team, and they'll have him, and he did good at practice today, then—"

"Do you want me to sue the school? Because if something happens, that's what I'll do. You all understand that, right? I will sue the school. I know the people to do it. I have the power to do it. I will exercise every power in my capacity." The words tumble from Mom's lips like rocks, each word piercing my skin, leaving a burning sensation where they land. She does not believe that I can do this.

It makes me believe that I cannot do this.

"This summer, the coach said that it might be best for you to focus on off-the-field activities, Aiden." Mom looks away from Dad and at me. "You could always consider being a volunteer coach for Pop Warner. They're always looking for—"

"So," Brandon interrupts, trying to defuse the tension. He winks at me. "Aiden got a girlfriend!"

My mouth hangs open like a blubbering fish. I told him about Isabella on the walk home a few days ago, and now he is trying to kill me with embarrassment.

"I do not," I say now.

"Do too. He told me on the walk home. Said a girl talked to him after class the other day and gave her his number, and then he bumped into her *again*, and sparks flew! They're already planning a wedding so that Aiden can escape us and go off to live his best life."

I jump on Brandon's back and he laughs as he shakes me off.

"Brandon!" I shout.

"Aht! Aht! You both know not to play in the family room. What is going on? Aiden, you met a girl? She likes you?" Mom asks, looking at me.

I cannot read her face. I scan my brain, thinking of my emotion cards to respond appropriately to what she may be feeling.

NOTE: *In speech therapy, you work with emotion cards to identify and pick up on nonverbal cues for emotions. Useful. 10/10, recommend.*

"I am unsure," I say now.

"Think she wants you to call?" Dad asks with obvious interest.

"It is unclear," I reply.

"Come on, A!" Brandon says. "Of course she does. Look

at my bro. Finally getting a little bit of game. Now you can put a peck on somebody besides Marcia that one time in first grade."

I laugh. "The only person who remembers that peck is you, and you are exaggerating it. She kissed me on the cheek."

"Marcia remembers!" Brandon says.

"Doubtful," I say now. "Can we talk about something else?"

Dad sits up. "Do we need to have the talk?"

I frown. Weird timing, but okay. "When a cop stops you, always comply. Put your hands up. Speak slowly and clearly—"

"No, not that talk, son," Dad says with a smile. "I mean *the* talk."

How many talks can there be? I glance at Brandon. He stifles fits of laughter in a pillow. What is so funny?

"Um—"

"Ian, don't harass him!" Mom scolds. "Is she nice, though? Can we get her name?"

"Isabella!" Brandon shouts. "She said she was going to text him so they could work on 'life skills' together." Brandon makes a kissy face at me.

"Okay, woman objectifier." I push Brandon's shoulder. "Assuming that any girl who is friendly wants to be my girl-friend? Shame. Mom, are you disappointed?"

Mom bites her bottom lip, then smiles. "I really am. Horrified, really. Shame, Brandon."

"Ah, okay, now I'm getting dragged. Fair, fair. Touché,

sir, touché," Brandon says. "I was indeed raised better." He pushes me and we all laugh.

"I have homework. Please feel free not to discuss me and my lack of social endeavors in my absence," I say now.

"And now that means we'll have to talk about nothing but you while you're gone," Brandon says through a smile.

I chuckle at their banter as I make my way up the spiral staircase.

CHAPTER FIVE

0 Days Until Incident

It is Friday, game day, which means that streamers line the already busy hallways. Red and black and silver. Metallic decorations everywhere. Painted banners with spirit slogans hanging from the ceilings. Add the bright blue lockers and doors. Add the cheerleaders and football players. Add the other students and the colors they're wearing. Add the yellow-and-white checkerboard tile floors. You get a hallway that is visually loud. Too loud. I am shaky. I hate game days, if only for this. I enjoy the sport, not the performance leading up to it.

Brandon walks beside me, and his football jersey is a beacon. It beckons cheerleaders. It beckons teachers. It beckons other players. It beckons people from other school teams— soccer, tennis, volleyball. People streaming by with *good luck*s, *break a leg*s, and *you look good*s, over and over. I expect this. What I do not expect is that now *my* jersey is a beacon too. Suddenly, I'm at the receiving end of these platitudes. By the time I'm ten steps into the school, I've garnered enough collective luck from my classmates to rival a four-leaf clover.

Halfway down the hall, we are stopped by our classmates, Georgia and Marcia, in their cheerleading uniforms. Georgia walks with her pom-poms up to her chest, at the ready, poised to shake them in people's faces at a moment's notice.

Brandon nudges me. "First-grade girlfriend," he whispers, and nods toward Marcia. "Keep piling them up, stud."

"Objectifier," I say now. He really has to let that kiss on the cheek go.

Georgia blinks a lot when she talks to Brandon. Her blond eyelashes are heavy with black mascara and flutter like moths against her almost translucent skin as she talks. She also constantly flips her hair. She moves too much. People who move too much bug me when they are not Brandon.

Marcia is Georgia's shadow. Always has been. She dyed her hair pitch black from its natural orange and covered up her freckled nose with makeup. She's quiet. An observer. It takes one to know one. I have always liked Marcia—her presence isn't overwhelming. I watch as her hazel eyes dart between Brandon and me.

Every time Georgia speaks or giggles at something Brandon says, she reaches for his arm. Always touching, touching, touching. That is irritating. I do not want anyone to touch me that much ever.

"Hey, Brandon! You excited about Superlative Night and

the game? I voted for you in a few categories!" Georgia swings her long blond hair behind her right shoulder. Four blinks. Is there something in her eye?

Brandon flashes his top-notch smile. "You know it. The cheerleaders had some categories too, right? I still have to vote."

I roll my eyes. He is not going to vote. He will forget between here and first period.

"Yeah?" Georgia blinks five more times. "I really want Most Likely to Cheer for an NFL Team! Don't forget to vote for me, 'kay?" She reaches out and strokes his bicep. "I'll be forever enthralled if you do."

"Using that word wrong," I say now.

Georgia turns to look at me. "What?"

I freeze, realizing I might have voiced my thoughts a bit too loudly, since Georgia is actually acknowledging me for the first time in this entire interaction. She seems mad. I look to Brandon to bail me out.

Brandon looks at the floor. His cheeks twitch. He is trying not to laugh. No help there.

I shrug.

"No, what'd you say?" Georgia asks. Her tone reminds me of when my mom calls our dad by his first name. She shifts her weight back on one leg and crosses her arms.

NOTE: *I believe this is irritation?*

"U-uh, um" I stammer. Damn. Should have kept my mouth shut. "Enthralled. Definition: to—"

"To be captivated or delighted by someone," Marcia says now. She speaks quickly, the words tumbling from her like blocks.

I close my mouth and nod. I give Marcia a small grin, which she returns.

Georgia looks at Marcia and frowns, then uncrosses her arms. "Well," Georgia says now, "that's what I meant. If Brandon voted for me, it would forever captivate me. I'd be delighted with him forever for it." Her head bobs up and down.

I glance over at Brandon, who has recovered from his mini laughing fit. He presses his lips together and nods. "Yeah, I, um, appreciate that, Georgia," he says. I know he will joke about this with me later. The fact that he doesn't joke about it in front of her means that he really likes her.

Georgia flutters her eyelashes at Brandon again. "Who wouldn't want someone enthralled with them, right?"

I roll my eyes. Riveting conversation. Brandon must be so intrigued. I am itchy. Everyone is touching. Marcia's sister, Beth, approaches with even more cheerleaders in tow. I want zero part in that—the air is tight enough. I am at my limit.

I check my phone. Ten past seven. Fifteen minutes until class starts. The air conditioner whirs and whines, a constant background track to the endless overlapping voices in the hallway. Random shrieks; the rustle of pom-poms shaking, plastic rubbing against plastic; a ringtone screeching like a fire alarm; the teachers' voices crackling over their walkie-talkies. I need quiet. I look through my bag for my headphones, but of course I forgot them again. I turn to Brandon to see if he grabbed them for me, but he's in the middle of a large crowd made up of cheerleaders and other teammates. I wave to get his attention, and he waves back. In his distraction, I think he thinks I'm saying bye.

I assess my situation. I'm starting to get overwhelmed, but the people in my math class come bumbling in after the bell rings, which means the classroom should be empty for a few more minutes. I head that way, watching my shoes. Pendulums swinging. Then I hit something solid. A hand tugs at my arm, pulling me down. No. No. I rip out of the grasp. My skin tingles. I roll my neck. Do not touch me right now. It is too much. Too many colors. Too much noise. Too many people. Too much touching.

"It's okay," says a voice at my ear. Arms squeeze me tight, pulling me down. The body is small. The voice is familiar.

"I've got you," Isabella says now.

My body shakes. My breath comes short. I need to slow it. Breathe in, one Mississippi. Breathe out, two Mississippi. Isabella rocks, back and forth, holding me tight. She smells of cranberries and lemons. Even her scent is bright and cool, like ice.

"What are they doing?" someone asks behind me.

We are in the middle of the hallway. People are probably staring. I take two more deep breaths and open my eyes. People *are* staring. Isabella keeps her head pressed to my chest. She hums under her breath. She rocks back and forth. Her eyes are closed.

"I am good," I say. Though I do not understand why I am good—Isabella is new. I am used to Brandon squeezing me. Used to his warm presence and scent. Used to his long body compressing me and calming me. I am not used to her, but I feel okay. I look at her and consider her face, smooth and peaceful. Her lashes long. Her face round and, even without a smile on it, happy. As though a ghost of joy stays with her no matter what.

Isabella holds me for two more seconds. I count. Then she lets go. She backs up, looks at me, and smiles. "Sorry! I shouldn't have stepped in front of you like that. I should have known you'd bulldoze me—you're clearly practicing for tonight."

I smile. Or at least I do in my head. I am not sure if it reaches my mouth.

She has pivoted from comforting me to joking, and it catches me off guard. I am so used to everyone making such a fuss. It is nice to just be able to move on.

Isabella rocks back on her heels. "Where you headed?"

Class. I think about her question, but again, my processing is not reaching my lips.

"Ah, I forgot. Man of few words. I shall assume from your direction, and the timing, and the fact that we are at school, that it's to class, but I don't know which, since we only have Life Skills together." Isabella laughs.

I smile despite myself, and this time my face reacts as it should, but then I notice two girls standing at a locker, watching us and whispering.

I squeeze my eyes tight until rainbows decorate my eyelids. I breathe and let go. It is fine. It is fine. People look at me strangely sometimes, which is not okay, but I cannot control what others do. I can control my reaction to it. I will not let them ruin my day, in the same way that this one moment will not define my day.

Isabella fiddles with a key chain on her bag. A sunflower. "I'm sorry, Aiden. I was just trying to help; I hope I didn't—"

"How did you know?" I ask now.

She stops. "Oh, I saw you walking this way from down the hallway, so I—"

"Why did you squeeze me?" I stare at her forehead. Not her eyes. "How did you know to squeeze me?" I ask. I feel a surge of appreciation in my chest.

"Oh!" Isabella grins. "I mean, I pay attention in class sometimes. I would hope I'd have learned something by now, right? Anyway, Ms. Findley talked about deep pressure like two weeks ago or something. I just hoped it would work and it did, so I guess they pay her for a reason?" She nudges me and smiles.

I nod. I start again toward my classroom. Isabella walks beside me. She is quiet. I do not mind the company.

At lunch, I sit with Brandon and his friends Greg, Louis, and Carter. They talk excitedly about the upcoming game, discussing which superlatives they might be assigned for Superlative Night. I was not on the team in time, so I will not get any.

"I bet I get Most Likely to Be Drafted in the First Round," Carter says now.

"Yeah, okay." Greg scoffs. "You acting like Brandon don't exist."

Carter shoves Greg on the shoulder, but Greg laughs despite the strength of the push. It did not seem friendly to me, but he still took it that way. Brandon's friends are always so rough with each other. Something about their behavior seems as though it is teetering somewhere between friendship and rivalry. Somewhere between friend and foe. Always on edge.

"Yeah, Brandon exists, but—"

"But everyone has a shot," Brandon says with a smile.

Ever humble, even though we all know that particular superlative will go to him.

"Exactly," Carter says now. "We all have a shot!"

Brandon takes a bite of his burger and nudges me. "Too bad you weren't on the team a little earlier. A few of those superlatives would have gone to you. I know it."

I do not know it, but I nod at Brandon anyway. Lunch is always a little weird. Even after years of being pulled into Brandon's friend group to exist on the periphery, it does not feel more comfortable today than it did the first day he introduced me to everyone.

I look around the lunchroom at people chattering away, enjoying their time. Probably more comfortable with their own friends than I am right now with mine. Though I am never quite sure if they truly are mine.

I spy Isabella—more on my radar now than usual—sitting

with a girl who I know is named Julia, giggling at some joke and holding her hand in front of her mouth. I smile before I realize I've done so.

"That her?" Brandon asks, breaking my reverie.

I look down at my lap.

"Aww, it's all right. I'm not gon be weird and go flag her down. I'm just asking." Brandon's grin seems sly, so I am unsure if I can trust what he is saying. Still, I know he wants an answer.

I shrug. "We're just project partners."

"Okaaaaay." Brandon singsongs the word.

That is sarcasm. I roll my eyes. Brandon always has to make things weird. Isabella and I are just partners in class, and Brandon is trying to make it something else. It keeps giving me ideas. Ideas I do not typically have. Ideas I do not think I need to have. I do not want to make things between Isabella and me weird when she is just being friendly to me.

"Excited for tonight?" I ask, redirecting the conversation.

Brandon beams his megawatt smile at me. "Of course! Superlative Night is my favorite night of the year other than Homecoming! It's finally my turn!"

I smile. Brandon deserves all the recognition he gets. Since his freshman year, he has dominated on the field. Beyond that, he's unfailingly humble, selfless, and kind. I kind of hit the jackpot with brothers.

"And soon, it's gon be your favorite night too. Just wait. This is just the start. I told you it was gon be us this year," Brandon says now. "I told you."

I chuckle. He did.

I listen to the guys argue about what superlatives they will get until the bell rings. Then, like always, I trail behind them out of the lunchroom. Always a part but never quite included. I wonder if after tonight, things will be different. After my first game.

I barely pay attention to what Ms. Findley says during class. There is more job talk today, but all I can do is envision possible plays for tonight's game and glance at Isabella when I think she is not looking. She is chewing gum. We are not supposed to. She stares off into space for most of the lesson. She answers two questions.

In front of Isabella, Tuck plays with his camera. Capping and uncapping the lens. Looking through pictures, and even turning around to take a picture of Isabella. She smiles and sticks her tongue out when he does. When the bell rings, Isabella comes straight to my desk.

"So, I didn't get to mention it earlier, but I didn't know you were on the football team until this morning in the hallway! But I can't be that spacey, because I know for sure that you have never worn a jersey on game day before, right?" she asks. "I know there's only been like two games, but still."

"Nope. Brand-new. First game today."

"That's amazing! See, I haven't gone to any games yet, but now I have an excuse to come and be into athletics. Football can be a bridge!"

"Football is a sport," I say now.

Isabella giggles. "Yes, you are correct. That it is. A sport, and now, a bridge. A bridge between you and me!"

I smile. A metaphor.

"What are you doing until the game starts?" Isabella asks now.

"I think I have to meet up with Brandon and do team stuff before the game. I am not really sure what that stuff is, though," I say.

"Duh, that makes absolute total sense. No clue why I asked," Isabella says. She still seems bright, but slightly disappointed.

"It was a good question," I say now. I consider her tone. Did she want to hang out? Am I imagining that because of Brandon's teasing?

Isabella smiles. "Okay, well, I am gonna hang in the robotics lab until the game starts and possibly google football terms to prep myself to understand my first game. Oh, and prepare to have your picture taken, because you're getting posted!"

I groan.

"Don't you use Snapchat?" Isabella asks.

"Only to keep an endless streak with Brandon. We are seven hundred and forty-six days in. He will not let it die. I ignore it otherwise," I say now.

"Well, I'm taking your pic, so prepare yourself!"

"Who'd wanna see a random player in a random football game in South Florida?" I ask now.

"Me!" Isabella beams.

I laugh as I head out of the room.

8 8 8 8 8

The warm air refuses to move as I stand along the sideline in full pads next to Reg, Bernard, and a tight end named Dustin. The crowd roars. I am ready for it, so the sound is not a bother. Football games have been a part of my life for a long time. This is noise I can handle.

The DJ starts. "All right, everybody! Welcome to Superlative Night for West Gate! The students voted, so let's hear what they have to say! We're starting with our star quarterback, who has already verbally committed to the University of Florida—even though University of Alabama wants him too." More crowd screams. "Our top dog here in Stallion Nation! Future Gator! Big-Time Brandon Wright!"

Noise erupts from the bleachers, so deafening it loses meaning. The roar is a wave—that deep rush I feel when water crashes over me at the beach. It is not piercing or over-whelming. It is a unified rush, sweeping over my body, pulling me under. With it, I feel a rush of pride for my brother, and after that a pang of sadness. He will be gone so soon, but that is why this night and the rest of the season matter. We have this final ride together.

"Brandon has been voted Most Likely to Get Drafted in the First Round, Most Likely to Win a Super Bowl, Most Likely to Win MVP, and Most Likely to Get a Jersey Number Retired. His team-mates say that without his leadership they wouldn't have won the state championships two years running, and now they are ready for the three-peat! One more cheer for Brandon, everyone!"

The wave sweeps over me again. Suddenly, I feel hopeful. This could be me during my senior year. I could be this too. Brandon waves out to the crowd, and he is in his element. The star of the show. Maybe next year, it will be my turn to shine.

It is the last quarter of the game, and I still have not played. I watch from the bench. I analyze. Brandon hesitates, then throws the ball to Carter. Carter slows up to match the new trajectory of the ball. He is only just in bounds. Carter catches, turns, then is immediately smacked with a tackle. I saw that coming. The ball flies from Carter's hands. Damn. Fumble. Coach will chew them out about that play. The guys pile on top of each other like piranhas on a cow head. The whistle blows and the referees step into the mess of jerseys and sweat, separating everyone. The crowd of players clears and Greg clutches the ball like his life depends on it.

The referees blow their whistles again.

"Stallions' ball!"

We got lucky with that recovery.

"We got lucky with that recovery, huh, Aiden?" Reg nudges me.

I nod. My thoughts exactly. Reg and I are bench buddies for this game. As long as Brandon is playing, Reg is not—the perils of being a backup quarterback to a star. They always give Reg a few plays once we are up by enough points, but we are not there yet in this game.

"Nah, Greg had it the whole time," Bernard says now.

No. He did not. Not everyone sees that, though. Football

moves fast for other people. Not me. Not since I watched Brandon play as a kid, and Dad tried to talk me through plays that I had already analyzed, broken down, and considered alternatives for by the time he started talking. I could always see everything happening on the field, all at once.

The teams set up on the line of scrimmage. The ball snaps. Brandon searches for an open man. None. Any throw will be intercepted. A pick. Maybe a pick six—taken back for a touchdown by the opposing team. Brandon tucks the ball and rushes forward.

Then, an eruption of cheers from the stand. The guys next to me on the bench jump and scream. Dustin shakes me by my shoulder pads and screams in my face. I keep my eyes on the field. Brandon thrusts the ball high, then spikes it into the grass.

The whole team rushes at Brandon. I let them carry me along. We all fall on him in the end zone.

"Touchdown," the DJ screams above the cheers.

It is my first game. I did not play at all. But we won. We won. It is different to feel that victory down on the turf instead of up in the stands. To feel the energy of the team surge and envelop me like a swarm of bees. It is frantic but warm, buzzing and vibrating together, turning up the heat. I jump up and down in a tangle of sweaty bodies, and we scream until our throats are raw. I did not watch a win. I was a part of one, even in my own small way. This win belongs to me, too.

After the game, Isabella finds me outside the field gate while I wait for Brandon to come out of the locker room.

"Hey! Picture! Picture! I need a pic with the star!" Isabella jumps next to me, holds up her phone, and snaps a selfie of us. "That was so fun! You did great," she says.

"I did not play," I say now. Still, the energy of the win surges through me.

"Still did great," she responds. "You didn't get tackled or snacked."

"Sacked?" I chuckle.

"All of those." Isabella's laugh jingles like bells. "You headed home?"

I shake my head. "Randy's."

"Oh, where's that?"

"Diner," I say now. "The team usually goes after Superlative Night every year."

"Oh, that sounds fun." Isabella bounces from foot to foot.

I nod. People file out toward their cars and walk down the sidewalk, headed home and to wherever else they go after games. Some are probably already headed to Randy's.

Isabella looks at me and raises her eyebrows.

NOTE: *My emotion cards have raised eyebrows as surprise, but I have also seen this expression as a look of expectation.*

"Do you want to come?"

"Oh, I—" Isabella's phone pings. She holds up a finger for me to wait as she checks the notification. All the humor on Isabella's face disappears. "I actually can't make it this time, but have tons of fun!" she says. "Take pics while you're there and send them to me. It'll make me feel like I'm right there with you."

I smile and look back behind me toward the sound of collective whooping. Brandon is finally coming with a bunch of guys in tow. "Who would wanna see what is going on at a random diner in a random town in South Florida?"

"Me!"

CHAPTER SIX

The Incident

Brandon, Greg, Carter, and Louis lead the pack, bumping into each other and joking around. Reg and Bernard walk next to me in silence as we make our way to Randy's. I count my steps—it takes 1,437 to get to the diner—and think about my impending order. Waffle, scrambled eggs, bacon. Same thing as always.

"Bruh, you lucky we won, or we would have all personally jumped you after that fumble on third down," Brandon says. He pushes Carter, and Greg and Louis laugh. "You was not about to make me lose on Superlative Night!"

"Mistakes happen." Carter rubs the back of his head, ruffling his short blond hair.

"Not with better receivers—" Louis starts, but Carter pushes him so hard that Louis ends up off the curb and on the street. A passing car honks loud as it barely misses him. The other boys laugh.

I do not find that funny. Louis does not seem amused either.

"A! You saw that fumble, man! I put the ball right where it needed to be, right? Carter could have held on to it, ain't it?" Brandon asks now. He smiles his big, flashy quarterback smile.

I consider the play. Truthfully, Brandon's late throw made Carter slow down to line up with the ball, which let the safety catch up to him, which meant that as soon as Carter caught the ball, he got hit, which caused the ball to get knocked from his hands right when he gained control, which meant—

"He doesn't know the game like that, dude," Louis says.

"Ignore him, Aiden," Reg says to me under his breath.

I narrow my eyes. "If Carter works on his control, he can maintain a better grip on the ball before hits so that drops like that are less likely. Maybe run a few drills," I say now. "Or maybe work on awareness so that he sees the safety coming next time. Stepping out of bounds to avoid the hit also works."

Brandon shoots me a huge smile. "See! That's what I'm talking about: real analysis. That's why you gotta hush when you don't know, Louis! Aiden knows what's up! Work on that control, Carter!"

"I got control for you," Carter yells as he hops on Brandon's back. Brandon laughs and fake falls to the ground.

"Hey, if you guys don't stop playing, everybody's going to leave before we get to Randy's!" Louis grabs Carter by his shoulder, but Brandon pulls him down to the ground. Greg jumps in and piles on.

I watch them, a tangle of arms and legs. Sweat and musk in the already muggy night. All the contact makes my skin itch. I focus on counting the bright red fruit clusters on the dahoon holly trees until the guys gather themselves. Reg and Bernard smirk at them and whisper among themselves.

When we get to Randy's, it is packed. Students stand around in the walkway leading to the restaurant, jumping on each other and taking selfies.

My heart pounds in my neck. My skin tingles. There were not this many people here last year. I stare at the ground, and an arm wraps around me. Brandon. He smiles. It calms me. My brother pulls me into him. The pressure puts my heart back where it belongs. I breathe deep.

"I got you. You know that," Brandon says now.

I smile and nod at him.

"Don't even worry about all this noise. We can eat outside on the patio if it's too crazy in there."

I shake my head. This is Brandon's night. It is his senior night and he won. This is not about me. I can do this for him.

"And don't forget, you can take this time to get to know the guys better too. Really get to be part of the team."

"Okay," I say now. "I'm good."

Brandon's smile gets bigger. I think he knows that I am trying for him.

Inside Randy's, every red leather stool at the bar has a butt on it. The server taking orders frowns and waves students off as they come up, interrupting her and asking for help at their booths. Packed red leather booths line the windowed sides of the restaurant. We head to an open one toward the back. I slide in and stare out at the trees. Greg, Louis, and Carter do not sit, opting instead to start making rounds at other tables, talking to everyone. Reg and Bernard also veer off to talk to a few people. Only Brandon sits next to me and fiddles with the plastic menu on the table.

"Gettin' the usual?" Brandon asks now. He talks to me, but his eyes drift from table to table. He waves back at whoever waves at him and waves off those that call him over. He wants to go talk to people.

I nudge him. "Go ahead. I am gonna eat," I say.

"Nah, I'm cool here with you." His voice means it, though his eyes are elsewhere. He is trying for me, too.

"B, go deal with your swooning fan base. I could never bat my eyelashes enough to make up for everything you are missing."

Brandon laughs and gets up. "Okay, okay. I'll be right back once I check in with a few people, all right? Wave me down if you need anything. Seriously."

I smile back and wave him off. When he walks away, I lay my head against the back of the booth and close my eyes. I need to not see all these people for a minute. So many eyes. I am so itchy. Forks scrape across plates, cups clink, people slurp and smack their food, a few argue loudly about the game's score. So many competing noises. I am irritated in my skin. I want to rip it off.

Breathe in. Out. Breathe in. Out. Breathe in. Out. Open eyes.

Brandon is talking to a group of girls sitting at a booth. He leans on one side of the stall with a weird smirk on his face. He looks so dumb sometimes when he tries to be cool. I chuckle. I open my phone and decide to send Isabella a video of the diner. She might want to see everything, since she has never been here. Her response is almost immediate.

Ooh 50s! A vibe! Having fun?

I am really not.

I am good, I respond. If I say it enough times, it might come true. Manifestation.

Greg, Louis, and Carter come back to the table and slide into the booth. They each take turns peeking at me in silence. Sitting here, on the other side of the table, I feel akin to an exhibit—a specimen to be observed and deliberated on by an audience instead of interacted with. The hope that swelled in my chest, that hope that I might be a part of something, that excitement after the win, it starts to show its cracks.

"I enjoy the lack of conversation," I say flatly. I also enjoy sarcasm.

Greg rubs the back of his head in a way that seems guilty. "You like your first game, Aiden?" he asks now.

I glance at him. He is Brandon's closest friend and the only one who actually tries to get to know me sometimes. I wish they knew that they did not need to try so hard.

"Yeah, good win," I say now. "Tight games are entertaining."

"I wish it wasn't so tight," Greg says. "Too many mistakes made in the first half."

He is right. Brandon threw an interception and there were a slew of incomplete passes by the receivers.

"Yeah, receiver awareness needs attention, and the other running back has to work on his handling," I say now.

Carter makes a face. Is he annoyed? Was I too blunt? Brandon always says that receivers are the divas on the team. I should have been more careful.

"Well, then, the people *on the field* will just have to work on that," Carter says. His face is taut and his tone harsh.

NOTE: *People swear that we on the spectrum do not understand sarcasm or changes in tone inflection. We do. Carter is annoyed. He is also annoying me.*

"I *was* on the field," I say now.

"Looked like you were on the sideline from where I was standing," Carter sneers.

A blast of air escapes my nose. The creeping feel of ants skittering up my neck and across my scalp sends shivers across my arms. This is too much. I close my eyes for a second. I should probably leave for a bit.

I slide out of the booth and do not bother to announce that I am leaving. I stand and look for Brandon, but he's lost somewhere in the quickly growing crowd.

A group of kids come through the entrance just when I am walking out and everyone is bumping up against me, rubbing past me, swarming around me. My chest feels tight. I burst through the throng and out of the diner doors. I can feel their eyes on me. So many people looking. I need to be away from everything for just a second.

Outside, underneath the covered patio, a few students linger, talking in small groups. A girl with black hair has her back to me as she swings her hair back and forth, taking selfies on the steps leading up to the patio. I walk past her, down the steps, and lean against one of the stone planters, gulping at the air, wishing it was a little cooler. I focus on the reddened tips on the leaves of the tall coco plum bush, concentrating on the transition from red to auburn, then yellow and green, trying to shake off the heat gathering in my neck. I should have gone straight home, but if I go now, Mom is never gonna let me hear the end of it for walking alone so late, as if I am incapable of taking care of myself. But I also cannot call and ask to leave on my own or she will definitely make Brandon leave early with me. That would ruin his night. And he wanted me to stay and get to know the team. And he wanted me to be comfortable. And—

I push all the breath from my chest. Okay, if I go home, Brandon goes home. That is a no-go. So, I stay. I am stuck. Stuck with people who feel like I am a tagalong, in a way-too-crowded, loud place. Stuck with people who feel like I am not a part of their team, no matter what number is on my jersey.

Whatever. I can be stuck. No big deal. I have always been the third, fourth, or fifth wheel. I can do this. Tonight is not about me. I can deal with this. I just have to go back inside and ignore Carter, the scraping and scratching of silverware on plates, the clinking of glasses, the competing pitches of voices, the constant grinding hum of the air conditioner—I wish I had gotten more sleep last night.

"Hey, Aiden, you all right?"

I glance around.

Reg. He walks toward me. Bernard trails behind, tapping on his phone.

I force a grin and nod.

"You don't look okay," Reg says now. "It's okay if you're not. You need anything?"

"I—" I stop. I do not know what to ask for. I am so used to Brandon being the person that helps me, and I never have to ask him to do anything—he just does. My insides are jittery to the point where I feel like I am almost vibrating. I feel like I need something but I have no idea what to ask for.

I shake my head.

Reg frowns a bit, then nudges Bernard.

"'Sup, babe?" Bernard says without looking up.

Reg nudges him again and he finally looks away from his phone and up at Reg. Reg gestures his head toward me.

"Oh," Bernard says. "Sorry. You good, Aiden?"

"He just asked that," I say now.

Bernard chuckles. "You're right. I wasn't paying attention. I kinda suck, huh?"

Reg laughs.

Something about their interaction makes a chuckle gather in my throat. The tingling on my skin dissipates.

"Should we head inside, or do you guys want to hang here for a bit, you think?" Bernard asks.

"Hang here, I think," Reg responds. "You think so, Aiden?"

I nod. I was not sure what I needed, but this is helping. I suddenly feel grateful for Reg and Bernard as they stand a few feet from me. Close enough to be close but far enough to give me space. They do not ask more questions. They stay close by and talk in low voices, loud enough for me to hear that they are not talking about me but low enough not to be loud. I take a few stabilizing breaths. I am almost ready to go back inside.

A few other people lingering outside head through the doors. Now it is just us and the erratic chirp of a cricket hiding in the nearby grass. Things feel easier. I tap my fingers on the rough brick of the planter, savoring the grainy texture deep in the spaces in my joints. One, two. Stop. One, two. Stop.

"Brandon's always bringing him, and look, he's acting weird, just like I said. Just like he did at tryouts this summer."

My body stiffens. I know exactly whose voice it is.

"Vanessa told me that new girl was like squeezing him in the hallway today because he was spazzing out," the voice continues. "Is that what they want us to do now? Hug him every time he freaks out on the football field or something? I'm not doing that. A few people already looked at us weird for walking in with him. They don't give a shit if he's wearing a jersey. That doesn't make him less weird."

Why the hell does everyone whisper so loudly? I open my eyes and turn around. It is not Greg this time with the sucky whisper. It is Carter. I see Carter standing with Louis on the steps to the patio, *whispering* and staring at me with a silly smirk on his face. A silly lopsided smirk, like he thinks he is clever, like he thinks he knows everything, like he thinks he is cool, like he thinks he is worth a second thought to anyone here on his own.

My mouth hangs open and words dance on the tip of my tongue. I could rattle off Carter's average field stats. He is mediocre as a receiver. No verbal commitments to any colleges or offers. He is an asshole. Everyone knows it. Even Brandon has complained to Greg about him. I could say mean things, but that is who Carter is, not me. I could say so much, but that would cause issues for Brandon, not me. Tonight is not about me. Tomorrow is not about me. Nothing is about me. It almost never is.

"Shit. Hey, guys, let's go inside," Reg mutters.

Bernard's eyes flash with anger. "Why? For them? Screw them. Ignore that, Aiden."

I roll my eyes. Bernard is right. I should ignore it. Carter has never liked me anyway. He does not know me well enough to dislike me, but he has never liked me just because I am autistic. At least, that is how I have always understood it. I remember being six at the community pool, crying because the water was too cold, everyone was splashing, there was too much screaming, the instructor kept touching my head, and everything was just wrong. I just needed comfort and understanding and quiet. Instead, all I heard over my own wails were Carter's while he complained that I took up too much space. Seven-year-old Carter, crying while I had a meltdown after he splashed water in my face on purpose, whining for his mom to stop helping my mom and pay attention to him. I hear him in my head now: *He takes up all the space, Mom. There's no space for the rest of us.*

But he is Brandon's teammate and sometimes friend. Carter never shows Brandon this side of him, though. I look Carter dead in the face. I am going to ignore him.

I tap my foot against the pavement. One, two. Stop. One, two. Stop.

Greg walks out from the diner and approaches Louis and Carter. "Aye, the food's ready. Y'all coming?"

"Yeah, in a second," Carter says now.

Greg hesitates and looks between the two groups of teammates. Maybe he feels the tension. He lowers his voice. "Wait, what's up?"

"Weirdo over there was talking shit about me."

What Carter says still does not classify as a whisper. At this point, I am convinced that he is loud on purpose.

"When?" Greg asks.

"At the table," Carter says. "What, you forgot already?"

Greg responds in his own too-loud whisper. "He wasn't really talking shit, man. He was just recapping the game, you know? He's a little blunt sometimes, but you know he don't mean nothing by it."

"Seriously, Carter?" Bernard asks now, joining the conversation. "You know Aiden wasn't talking shit about you. Your feelings are just hurt because you think it applies to you."

I was not talking shit about Carter. He dropped passes. He recovered a fumble. He did not do awful. He did not do good. It was not that deep. Not to me. Everyone can build better awareness. It was not talking shit. It was a fact. Why can people never handle facts?

"First off, Bernard, stay the hell out of it. You weren't even at the booth! You and Reg are always sneaking off, so how would you know?" Carter snaps.

"The hell is that supposed to mean?" Bernard asks. He almost spits the question at Carter. His anger is palpable.

Bernard charges forward, but Reg grabs his arms and pulls him back.

"Hey, hey. Leave him. Leave him. He's not worth it," Reg says now. His expression is flat, as though he is trying very hard to be detached from it all. Maybe if he feels too much, he will lose control too.

Bernard huffs large breaths out but does not respond.

"Ay, everybody freaking relax," Greg says. "Listen to all of us, Carter. Aiden didn't mean anything by it. Just chill."

"I don't know, man. It seems like he meant something to me," Carter says now. "He's always talking like he knows so much more than the rest of us. He said something about me on the walk here, then again at the table. He's acting like he can do better, when the last time he actually stepped foot on a field to play, his brother had to hug him for an hour because he can't handle playing with everybody else!"

"Ay, come on, dude. That's out of line. We all been cool since we been kids. You know what's up with him. Don't do that," Greg says now.

"No, we've been cool with *Brandon* since we were kids," Carter says. "We've just had to deal with Aiden because our moms and Brandon never want to leave him out."

I stiffen at his words. I have always felt that. Always suspected that. To hear it out loud is different.

"Don't say that, dude," Louis mutters.

"Why? It's true! And it's not like he cares. He barely has freaking emotions beyond screaming and losing his crap for no damn reason. Look at him. Look at his expressionless face," Carter says. He sneers at me with the utmost disgust, and I know in this moment that I hate him.

Greg frowns at me. Does he feel bad? Does it matter? He cannot change what Carter said. Nobody can. Carter stares at me, trying to force eye contact, even though he knows that it bothers me. Reg struggles to hold Bernard back from charging at Carter. I do not want anyone to fight for me. I also do not want to back down from Carter. My skin ripples and itches. Pressure builds in my temples. I will not back down. I do care. I have emotions. I should not have to prove it, but I will show him. I stare Carter down. One, two. Stop. One, two. Stop.

After six seconds, Carter breaks eye contact and whispers something I cannot hear, for once, to Louis. Reg and Bernard, who has finally calmed down, move closer to me but do not speak. I release a breath and look down. My body quivers. I need to get away from this.

Louis and Carter are about two yards ahead, blocking the stairs that lead back into Randy's. Two yards is not a lot.

NOTE: *My forty-yard dash is a 4.58. Two yards is nothing.*
  - *If the situation was a football play, it would be easy to execute:*

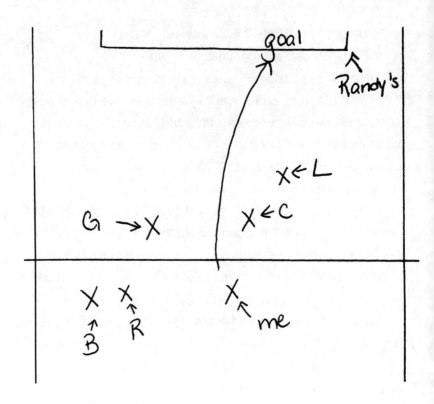

"Let's go," I say now.

"Okay," Reg agrees.

I stalk forward. I am going inside. I am eating my waffle. I am waiting for Brandon. I can do that. I can text Isabella. She can distract me. I can stay close to Reg and Bernard. They can keep me calm. I can do anything else. I just cannot stay here doing this.

I accidentally brush past Carter as I walk by. My shoulder barely bumps his, but he stumbles back as though I pushed him.

Carter straightens up and shoves me in the chest. I stumble back, bump into Bernard, then my head hits a concrete planter and everything rings. I squeeze my eyes tight and try to shake off the flashing lights in my vision. The spot where Carter touched my arm seems to burn even more than my head. I do not want to be touched. Especially not by Carter. I plant my hands into the ground and rub my palms into the rough concrete.

"Aiden!" Bernard shouts. "Are you okay?"

I want to retaliate, but I can still end this before it truly starts. I can still walk away from this. Carter deserves so much worse, but I can walk away right now. I focus on the rough feedback from the ground, running up my palms into the joints in my arm, traveling along my nerves.

Calm me. Please. Calm me.

Reg and Bernard hook their arms under my armpits, pulling me from the ground. The absence of the concrete underneath my fingertips sends a wave of emptiness through me. I have nothing to hold on to. Nothing to ground me.

"Hey, man, what the hell! Brandon's gonna kill you." Greg looks back toward the windows of the diner. Nobody inside seems to notice the commotion for the moment.

"Brandon's not here," Carter snaps back.

"Nah, man, why push him? Come on, dude. B's my best friend. I'm not about to let you mess with his brother."

"Neither am I," Bernard says. He wants to defend me just as much as he wants to defend himself. I doubt his anger from earlier has been dispelled.

"Didn't any of you just see him push me first?" Carter yells.

Greg plants a hand on Carter's shoulder. "That was not a push, man. If that's a push, then you need to get your weight up."

Carter pushes Greg's hand away. "So, what? Now you're on his side, right? That figures. Birds of a feather or whatever."

"The hell is that supposed to mean?" Greg asks.

"You both have more in common than *we* do, right?" Carter says now. "All of you do, I guess. That's why Reg and Bernard are helping him too, right?"

Greg raises an eyebrow at Carter. Carter finally stops speaking.

I need to take this moment to move while the anger is directed away from me. I will my legs to move. It does not even feel like they are attached to my body.

"I'm gonna need you to clarify and I'm gonna need you to do it now," Greg says.

"Clarify for me, too," Reg adds. He inches closer to Greg and Carter.

"More in common why, Carter? We not in the same grade. We don't have no classes together. The only thing we have in common is what y'all have in common, which is Brandon, and now this football team. Unless you mean something else," Greg says now.

"Dude, I'm just saying. You're *my* teammate, you were *my* teammate first, and you're taking *his* side. He hasn't been your teammate *or* your friend. You've made fun of him with me before. Now you're on his side? It doesn't take a genius to figure out why," Carter says.

I grasp at the light post next to the planter for support.

My head buzzes. My ears still ring from my head hitting the concrete.

"Well, call me the dumbest person in the room. Why?" Greg asks now. "Do you know why, Reg? Bernard?"

"Nope," Bernard says.

Reg crosses his arms and frowns.

"If you got something you tryna say, it needs to be said, because I know you not throwing out a race card. Right, Carter? I know you not saying I'm taking his side 'cause we both Black?" Greg says now. "I know you not saying that we're all taking his side because we're all Black, right?"

NOTE: *Reg, Bernard, Greg, and I are Black. That does not make us alike in any way.*

Greg and Carter are nose-to-nose. Neither of them blink. The tension makes the air feel thick, rigid. I feel stuck in place, watching it all unfold.

Carter shrugs. "Louis is on my side, that's all I'm saying," he says now. "Right, Louis?"

Louis rubs the back of his head and frowns. He does not say yes or no. He also does not leave Carter's side.

The ache in my head builds. I really need to get away from all this. I force myself to start back toward the diner.

"Wait, you don't get to just push me and walk away!" Carter yells. I turn as he sidesteps Greg and directs his attention to me. "You think you're untouchable, right? Because Brandon's always here to defend you and drag you along everywhere like a puppy?" Carter walks toward me. "Think you're accepted just because Brandon begged for you to be on this team?"

Greg stretches his arm in front of Carter. "Bruh, stop!" Greg cautions.

"Don't touch me!" Carter knocks Greg's hand away. "Where's your tough-guy energy, Aiden? You think Brandon's gonna stop me? I don't see him. Where's that energy from earlier now? Huh? You wanted to push past me. What about now, Aiden? What do you want to do?" Carter yells.

> **NOTE:** *I have never been in a fight. My mom always said not to start fights.*
> - *My mom also said that if someone else starts a fight, be the one to finish it.*

Carter is in my face and his breath is hot and wet and smells like grass and sardines. He screams and screams in my face until I cannot understand the words. It is all noise. He pushes me back, away from the stairs, farther away from where I need to go. I need to go inside. I cannot. I think a few people come outside and gather on the patio in front of Randy's. I think a few more spill out onto the grass to the side of the walkway. How many people are out here? Why is everyone just standing around? My chest tightens. My fingers dance at my sides. Sound is muffled because I am in a tunnel. Vision is blurry because I am underwater. Everything rushes around me like a wave at the beach. This is too much. I should have said screw the waffle. I should have said screw team bonding.

I should have gone home.

Carter pushes me again. His hands are hot. I feel them deep in my flesh. His touch is slimy. Searing. It is like my skin sloughing off after a burn. His touch is the absolute last straw.

I launch forward and tackle Carter. His body hits the concrete with a satisfying thud, and someone screams. The sound pierces through the waves. Thuds crash against my body. Carter punches me all over. I do not feel the pain, only pressure. Only pounding, like an unsteady drum. I raise my fist and punch. I punch and I hit jelly. I hit mush. I hit marshmallows. It is all soft underneath my fists even though I think my knuckles are bloody now and I think someone pulls at my shoulders now and I think I am flying backward away from Carter now and his annoying smirks and his insults and his dumbass loud-whispers.

I swing wildly.

"Aiden!"

I am in the tunnel.

"Aiden!"

Still underwater.

My back hits the ground and I see stars before I see Greg.

"Aiden!" Greg's face is contorted. Brow furrowed. Mouth open. He is scared. He pins me to the ground.

The pressure in my chest hurts. My heart slams against my sternum.

"Aiden! Shit, man. Shit. Are you good?" Greg shakes me. My body bounces against the rough ground. I turn my head to look around, but a stone planter blocks my view to the left and to the right are more planters, a light post, and the parking lot. Where is Carter?

Greg pulls me up. "Fuck, man. Brandon's gonna fucking kill me—"

Greg jumps back and I am falling forward, pushed from behind. The concrete scrapes my palms and my knees burn from the impact. The back of my head pounds. Grass and sardines assault my nose again.

"Get the hell off him, man!" Greg screams.

The pressure on top of me disappears. Bernard and Greg wrestle with Carter. Reg yells and holds back Louis, who is fighting to get to them. Carter flails, thrashing like a trout to escape them. On the patio and inside Randy's, a few people watch. I do not see their faces. I do not see anything. Everything is blurry. I only see red. Now I see blue. Everything flashes.

"All of you on the ground! Get down! Now!"

Two cops run forward. A blur of green uniforms. Guns between eyes and at the sides of heads.

"Get down now!" one cop screams.

The few people on the patio run inside. Nobody wants to get arrested. Nobody wants to get in trouble. We were just supposed to be getting breakfast for dinner, like everyone has always done on every Superlative Night.

I want to run too, but I hear Mom's voice in my head. *Comply.*

I drop to the ground. Hands on my head. I stare down the walkway, toward the parking lot. The world is sideways. Ever since we got here, the world has been sideways. My ankles itch, but I am afraid to scratch them. Most of my body lies exposed on the walkway. The grass lawn tickles my bare ankles. My shirt rolls up at the sides, my stomach rubbing the rough concrete, and my side brushes against the pitted planter. No cops have come to me yet, but I do not want to move. *Comply. Always comply.*

Feet scatter past me. Black shoes. Cop shoes. I try to look around without lifting my head. My cheek hurts as it rubs against the sidewalk. What is happening?

I see Greg struggling as a cop holds his arms behind his back. The cop hits Greg on his side and he crumples in on himself.

"Stand up!" the cop yells.

Carter fights to get away from another cop. Carter's eyes are directed at Greg. The cop blocks and redirects Carter a few times before wrapping him in a bear hug.

"Hey, calm down. Calm down!" the cop yells to Carter.

Louis sits in the middle of the walkway nursing a bloody lip from Reg. A cop stands vigil over him.

Two cops knee Reg and Bernard in the back, using their hands to pin their faces to the ground.

When did so many cops arrive? How many are here?

My body twitches from being so still. I want to move. My mom's voice. *Always listen to the cops. Do what they say. Don't react. Don't act in anger. Listen. Listen. Listen. Get home alive. I'll deal with it later.* That is what she says. *Get home alive. Your mom is a lawyer. I can handle it.* I have heard it since I was six. I cannot react. I have to lie here. I have to comply.

The cop dealing with Greg hits him again. The cop looks like all the others. They all look the same. He punches Greg in the back of his head. Greg screams.

The cop yells, "Stop resisting!"

Greg has not moved.

Are we under arrest? Did anyone say we were under arrest? Does being on the ground mean we are under arrest? Can we resist if we are not under arrest? Is not moving still resisting?

The cop wrestles with Greg on the ground. He lays his body on top of Greg's, punches him in the back of the head again, then pins his knee to Greg's neck. Greg cries out for air. A cop places his hand on Louis's back and guides him to the parking lot. Carter fights to get away from the officer holding him, but the cop just keeps trying to wrap him up in his arms.

More lights. More feet. Suddenly, a knee is on my back. Another knee is on my legs. No. Someone tries to force my hands behind my back. No. I have the right to remain silent. Anything I say can and will be used against me in a court of law. I have the right to an attorney. If I cannot afford one, one will be appointed to me. I am not under arrest. Nobody said I was under arrest. Stop touching me. Stop touching. I pull back against the hands.

"Stop resisting!" A punch fires at the back of my head and my forehead smacks the concrete. "Hands behind your head!"

Comply. I lift my hands up to my head. My arms are lead-filled. It takes everything to put them in place and keep them there.

"Stop resisting! Hands behind your back! Don't move!"

Stop resisting. I stop moving. I fight my instinct to turn inward, hold my torso, and rock myself into comfort.

"Hands behind your back!"

I move my hands lower. It takes everything not to reach out for the concrete, seeking some contact to calm me.

"Don't move!"

I stop moving. I try my hardest not to tremble. Not to shake. Not to fall apart.

Comply. Mom, what do I comply with? Who do I listen to?

They yank my arms. It is too much. I pull my arms to my side. I do not mean to, but I cannot take it. I need a minute. I need to give myself deep pressure. Someone keeps screaming. My throat burns and someone keeps screaming. My chest heaves and someone keeps screaming. I flail. Too much touching. Too many people on me. Hands grab all over me. The cops are saying something, but I cannot hear them because someone keeps screaming. Is it me?

"Aiden?"

Brandon?

"Aiden!"

Brandon, go back inside.

"Aye! That's my brother! That's my brother!" Brandon yells.

I feel pounding. It is everywhere. Brandon? I open my eyes and shoes surround me. So many shoes and legs and people. Everyone is on me. Hitting me. Pulling on me. Yanking on me.

"Aye! That's my brother! Hey! Hey! We're on the West Gate team! Call Coach Davis. Call my mom. Somebody!" Brandon shouts.

"Shut up! Get down now!" a cop screams.

"Aye, put the gun down! I'm the quarterback for West Gate! Aye! Wait!"

"Get down now!"

"Aye! Let me go! Let me—"

Brandon. My ears ring. I try to lift myself up. Another strike to the back of my head and my forehead hits the concrete.

Red and blue flashes all over. Someone is still screaming. My throat is raw. Someone is screaming. All I can hear is ringing and screaming.

Brandon?

Brandon.

CHAPTER SEVEN

5 Hours and 32 Minutes After the Incident

Ernesto Miranda was arrested and interrogated for two hours, during which he gave a confession to a murder, all while never knowing his rights to legal counsel.

It is cold in this room. A glass along the far side wall must be a two-way mirror. There must be cops on the other side of the two-way mirror. Waiting. That is what happens during investigations on crime shows, at least.

Goose bumps prickle on my forearms, and I rub them away. My arm smarts under my touch and I wince. I shift in my seat and my body screams at the motion. Everything hurts. My head pounds. I want to leave.

The door opens and an officer in a crisp white button-down shirt walks in, holding a folder and a mug. His bald head gleams in the bluish glow of the fluorescent lights, and gray stubble dots his face. I try to count the hairs, but he slaps a manila folder on the wooden table and I lose count at thirty-two.

"I'm Officer Brady. We got in contact with your mom, kid. She's on the way."

Officer Brady leans back in his chair and takes a large swig from the mug. He sets it down in front of me. I catch a whiff from the cup. Coffee.

"I figured we could take the time to talk before she gets here. What do you think?" Officer Brady asks.

I stare at his nose. Blackheads stand out. One, two, three, four.

He reclines in the seat and presses his fingers together in front of his face. "It's not an interrogation, kid, it's a conversation," Officer Brady says now.

Plot twist. I am prepared. My mom warned me about police officers and investigations. It is all an interrogation. Interrogation, by definition, means a formal and systematic questioning. This room? Formal. This questioning? Systematic.

"Am I under arrest?" I ask now.

"I mean, you resisted arrest, and—"

"Am I under arrest?" I ask again. I focus on the lights above me. Lights in police stations feel so dungeony. Dungeony. Not a word. No definition. Definitely should be. Dungeony. Definition: similar to or pertaining to a dungeon; an unpleasant, uncomfortable place; a place they put criminals. Like they think I am.

Officer Brady leans forward. "Yes, you're technically under arrest."

"I have the right to remain silent. Anything I say can and will be used against me in a court of law. I have the right to an attorney. If I cannot afford one, then one may be appointed to me." Ernesto Miranda. I think of Ernesto Miranda. Remember your rights.

Officer Brady frowns and knits his brows together.

NOTE: *Emotion card says confusion.*

I look down at my lap and count the threads woven together in my gym shorts. One, two, three, four, five.

"Is that why you won't talk?" Officer Brady asks now. "Would you like an attorney?"

I do not respond. I will stay quiet. I will not accidentally implicate myself in any way. People are usually uninformed with cops. He thinks I am uninformed. I am not.

"Look, kid, we already talked to some of the other kids that were there tonight. We have a pretty good grounding on what happened. We know you were involved in the altercation, so all we really want is your side of the story. Then you can go."

I tap against the armrest on my chair with my index finger. One, two. Stop. One, two. Stop. I drag my fingertips across the tweed-like fabric on the armrest. The scratchiness of the cloth winds its way into the spaces between my bones. I keep rubbing, back and forth.

"This process is much easier when you just talk to me, you know? All the other kids already went home. Like I said, they already gave me all the information I need to know, so—"

"Then you should not need to talk to me," I say now.

Officer Brady huffs at me. He takes another swig from his mug. "Well, we like to consider all possible leads."

Silence.

I tap. One, two. Stop. One, two. Stop.

He waits.

"My officers tonight responded to a call about a fight. How did that get started? Did you start it?"

I tap. One, two. Stop. One, two. Stop.

"The officers said you were being noncompliant during the arrest. I even have a report here that says there was an assault on an officer. We want answers on that. You want to explain that? What did you see?"

I tap.

"Hmmph," Officer Brady grunts. "Well, can you think of any reason why your brother attacked one of my officers?"

What? The shock breaks me out of my silence. "He never—" I start.

A knock at the door. A woman with bushy blond hair sticks her head through the gap.

"Sir, his mother is—"

My mom storms through the door past the blond woman.

"I'm not sure why anyone is interrogating my son without me—his mother—his *lawyer*, present. He's a minor." My mother seethes. Anger spills from every pore in her body. She is wound tight, coiled, and ready to strike.

"He's sixteen, and we're just having a brief discussion," Officer Brady says.

Mom narrows her eyes. "He's a minor. There are no discussions to be had without me or his father present." She rests her hand on my shoulder and squeezes. My skin tingles with relief at her touch.

"We just wanted to get his side of the events that happened tonight," Officer Brady says now.

"Have you said anything to them, Aiden?" Mom asks.

I shake my head.

"Good." She directs her attention toward Officer Brady. "I'm defense attorney Nerissa Wright. Partner at Henry, Lawler, and Wright. This is my son, though I'm not sure why it took so long for me to receive a call. I'm sure you have a marvelous explanation." Mom smiles, but her eyes are piercing and cold. "Is my son being detained?"

Officer Brady straightens up in his chair. "Ma'am, thank you for taking the time to come and provide counsel for your son, but truly, we meant no disrespect. We're just trying to get some information." His tone is different now. More courteous?

"Is my son being detained?"

Officer Brady chews his lip. "There's no clear consensus on who started the fight."

"I am not asking again without getting a clear answer as to whether my son is being detained, or you'll have larger issues on your hands." Mom leans forward and places a palm on the table. She looms over Officer Brady.

"No, ma'am, he is not being detained."

"Great." My mom tugs at my arm. "Then my son should have been released to me a long time ago. I'll be sure to let that be known to your supervisor. Where is my other son, Brandon?"

"Mrs. Wright, this is all still under investigation. Mrs. Phillips, Carter's mother, said she wasn't interested in pursuing charges against Aiden, but Brandon is a different story."

Mom stiffens. "Excuse me?"

The officer smirks. "Has no one explained the situation to you?"

Mom presses her lips into a fine line. "Enlighten me."

"Ma'am, your son is being held on potential assault charges."

Mom lets out a sharp breath and closes her eyes. "You just said that Carter's mother is not pressing charges—"

"Ma'am, your other son is being held for charges related to assault against one of our county officers."

Reality hits like a weight in my stomach. Officer Brady mentioned this earlier, but I thought he was trying to provoke me. There is no way anyone believes that really happened. I look to my mom to fix it. I need her to fix it the way she just fixed things for me.

Mom opens her eyes and purses her lips. She takes four full breaths before she speaks. "Has he already been processed?"

"He is undergoing processing now."

"When can he be released to me?" Mom asks. She sounds calm, but her voice is like a thread about to snap. She is too tight now. The strike after the coil has happened and now there is nothing left.

"When we complete processing and assess a bail amount."

"He is a minor!"

"Who potentially committed a felony. Ma'am, look, we know you're a defense attorney. Trust me, your son has reminded us constantly since getting here. He has asked us repeatedly to call both you and his coach. He has explained to us all, loudly and repeatedly, who he is, what team he plays for, and his stock in the national lineup for football recruits to colleges. We know exactly who Brandon Wright is. He is also seventeen and accused of a felony. He's being held and pro-cessed and will be here until the judge sees him and sets a bail amount on Monday," Officer Brady says.

If this news shakes my mom, she does not show it. She purses her lips and nods.

"I will speak to him before I leave," Mom says now.

Officer Brady grins. "Gladly."

Mom talks to Brandon without me, though I am anxious to see him myself. Anxiety courses through me like adrena-line, making my body vibrate as I sit in the bustling front room of the county police station. I watch as other students move past me, their parents keeping them close at hand. These are the people that Officer Brady said he interviewed. These are the classmates that Brandon was just mingling with, who apparently corroborated a story that he assaulted an officer. Something about it hasn't fully hit me yet, and laughter bubbles in my throat. It all sounds so ridiculous. Brandon attacking cops. Everyone telling on Brandon. It feels silly and unreal. The giggles grow into guffaws, and a few people glance in my direction warily, but I ignore them. I have to let out some of this energy, and this is how my body wants to do so at this moment, so I let it happen. Nothing is real anyway.

Thankfully, Mom finds me after my laughing fit ends and guides me out of the station to her car. The muggy night swarms me as soon as I step out the door. It is warm. I wish it would rain. Instead, humidity hangs in the air like a fog, a mist, water clinging to our bodies instead of falling from the sky. I hurry to the passenger seat of Mom's Audi and clamber in, sinking into the leather seat, still cool from the blasting air conditioner.

When Mom gets in on the driver's side, she rests her head back against the seat and lets out a long breath.

I wait. We do not move. Mom sits with her eyes closed. Her lips flutter, as if she is reciting something.

I lean back and stare out the windshield. The struggling lights of stars dot the inky sky. No moon tonight. The Big Dipper stands out among the sparkling lights. It was always the first constellation Brandon and I picked out as kids. I still do that. I hear my brother's voice in my head now. *I'm the big one, and you're the little one. Anytime you look up, they're always together. Like us.*

My mom sits up straighter in her seat. She taps at the steering wheel without a discernible rhythm. "Aiden, do you remember what happened tonight?" Her voice trembles a bit, but her tone changes. This is not Mom voice. This is lawyer voice. I am being interrogated. Any traces of laughter left in me are gone.

I nod. "Carter started an argument with me, and we

fought. I do not remember what happened during the fight, I was too overwhelmed." My fingers twitch. I trace the lines of a bruise forming on my knuckles. The raised edges of skin have not yet purpled with time. I feel along them, ignoring the sting of pain as I press gently down. "I know Greg tried to help and stop Carter. Maybe Reg and Bernard, too. Then cops were just there. I heard one say to get down, so I got down. I was listening like you said to do."

Mom nods. "Okay, the cops arrived, you get on the ground. And then?"

"I got on the ground and some cops were dealing with Greg, Louis, Carter, Reg, and Bernard. They were rough with Greg. I saw that. They were trying to stop Carter from still trying to fight—"

"Funny," Mom scoffs. "I saw Greg and his father walking out as I was coming in. Half of Greg's face is bruised, your lip is busted, forehead scraped up, and your eye is swollen, but Carter barely looks touched. What bruises he _did_ have apparently came from you, or at least that's what Greg's father said. I saw Carter and his mother inside the station before I got to you." Mom squeezes her eyes shut. "Okay, so you're down on the ground and all the other boys are being dealt with. You complied. Where is Brandon?" she mutters to herself under her breath.

I wait. I know that she is not asking me.

Mom shifts in her seat to face me. "Okay, you said you're down?"

I nod.

"The other boys are being dealt with?"

I nod.

"Okay, Aiden. So, where was Brandon?"

"I am not sure. He was inside when the fight started," I say now.

"Sweetie, I know it's stressful. I know, okay?" Mom faces the windshield. Her fingers flutter on the steering wheel.

The discordant pattern makes my insides turn over on themselves. I do not like this.

"I know that this is a lot, and you've been through a lot. I just—" Mom sighs. "I really need you to remember for me. Okay? I need you to remember what happened." Her voice cracks. "You are down on the ground, Aiden. You're on the ground. You surrender. You comply." She turns to me again. Tears shine on her cheeks in the starlight. "But, honey, Brandon is in a cell right now and I don't understand it."

This is too much. I tap my fingers against my leg and close my eyes. Her face is burned inside my eyelids. Maybe she does not know it, but I recognize the look. It looks like one of my emotion cards. It looks like blame.

"I am just not sure, Mom." My voice comes out barely louder than a whisper. "I heard his voice, but the cops were on top of me, and they were hitting me, and he was not outside, but then I heard him. I did not see. I do not know," I say now.

Mom slams her hand on the steering wheel. "You have to know!"

I flinch but do not look up.

"You have to know," she whispers. "I need you to know."

I stare at my hands. I run through the fight in my head. All the images run together, jumbled, bumping into each other. I got down, they hit me, I heard Brandon. Did I turn my head? Did I see? Do I have the memory somewhere locked away? Did I see?

"They hit me," I say now. "They hit me. Everyone was touching me. I heard Brandon say my name. I heard my name. I did not see. I—I did not see. I—" I wait for tears to fall, but they do not come. I search for sadness. We are supposed to name our emotions. Name them and you can understand them and control them. I search my soul and my heart for sadness. I find only panic. I cannot remember. "I'm sorry, Mommy, I did not see."

My breath comes short. I dig my nails into my palm and rock back and forth. I am back underwater. I cannot breathe. I rock and rock. I press my body back against the seat, but my breath does not slow. I wrap my arms around myself and squeeze tight. I am drowning. I wheeze for air and rock and squeeze myself.

It takes four minutes and two seconds for my breathing to slow.

My mom has her arms wrapped around her own body. Keeping her own head above water. She does not look at me.

"Mom—" I say now. I reach for her, and she flinches away. I pull my hand back and place it on my lap. The panic rises again, but I stifle it. I focus on my breathing. I tap.

One, two. Stop. One, two. Stop.

"I'm sorry," she says now. "Aiden . . ."

"I did not mean for this to happen. I never wanted this. I just wanted to play football," I say now. "I just—"

Mom pulls me to her and squeezes me. "I know, baby. I know," she says into my hair.

I take my first full breath since we got in the car. Her perfume is coconut and lilacs. I shut my eyes. Then the scent disappears. The hug ends too soon.

Mom straightens up, wipes her face, and puts the car in drive. "I'm sorry. It's going to be okay. I shouldn't act like this. It's going to be okay. This is all a big misunderstanding and they'll see that. It will be okay."

I lean back in my seat and find the Little Dipper. I follow its handle to the North Star.

CHAPTER EIGHT

1 Day After the Incident

The doorbell clangs repeatedly, like an off-key song rattling in my head. Someone is outside, hitting the button over and over. No breaks. Just noise. I shut my eyes and ignore the throbbing behind my forehead. I have not had a headache since I was six. That headache came after I ran headfirst into Brandon's stomach because he had taken one of my dinosaur action figures.

Brandon.

One, two. Stop. One, two. Stop. My fingers tap against my thigh.

I try to picture my brother, but all I can imagine is him in a cell, scared and crying and alone, and why is nobody answering the door?

I flip over on my bed, ignoring the screams of pain all

over my body, and push myself up. I step out into the hallway, which would be quiet if not for the current doorbell attack.

"Mom," I call out now.

Nothing.

"Dad!"

Nothing. Did everyone just leave and not tell me?

Now I have to get the door. Great.

I trudge downstairs and pause at the front door, my hand on the handle. I do not want to talk to anyone. I do not want anyone to ask me things, say things, do anything. What if whoever it is asks about Brandon? What if they are offering condolences?

Condolences, definition: expressions of sympathy.

I do not want sympathy. I want someone to understand. I need someone to understand what happened. Maybe then I can start to as well. How did everything go so wrong so fast? How am I home and my brother is in jail? Why did I have to explain the situation to my dad and watch his head fall in disappointment? Why did I have to hear my parents argue for an hour about what to do?

My hand shakes and my grip weakens. I realize that Brandon and I almost never sleep in different locations. That only happened once, for his safety patrol trip. The second time, Brandon tried sleepaway camp for twenty-four hours and came back home. Otherwise, for hospital stays, college visits, and everything in between, we went together. Now, for the third time—the time that is supposed to be the charm, according to Brandon—he is in trouble and I cannot figure out why.

The clanging is too much now and the vibrations of the doorbell tingle in my nail beds. I throw the door open, bracing for all the sympathy.

Reg and Bernard stand on the front porch, holding clear tins of lasagna. On the ground next to them in plastic containers are two tuna casseroles, a Tater Tot hot dish, and three homemade cakes—one smells like pineapple upside-down cake.

Reg and Bernard each shoot me a quick smile and hello, then breeze in past me.

NOTE: *Reg and Bernard have never been to my house.*

"Damn, I knew this place was big from the outside, but shit. You see how high these ceilings are, babe?" Reg asks.

Bernard nods, and Reg veers off to peer into my mom's office, just off the foyer.

"Not a living room," Reg says now.

"There's a big open walkway right here, but you look in the room with a door and say 'not a living room'? Just admit you're nosey and stop," Bernard says.

Reg chuckles. "Okay, I'm nosey. I've never been here. Sue me. Okay, living room."

They head for the great room while I still have the door-knob firmly in my grasp. I let go, stoop down, and cradle the tower of dishes in my arms, trying not to drop any as I maneuver my way through the house to the kitchen. I place everything on the counter and do not bother to put anything in the fridge. Since when do people send sympathy food for suspected criminal activity? I have not seen this much random food since Grandma died three years ago.

> **NOTE:** *When Grandma died, the neighborhood sent seven different lasagnas. Only four were good.*
> - *Brandon tossed one of the lasagnas out on the lawn for a raccoon when he found out it had eggplant in it instead of meat. It was the first time we laughed after Grandma's funeral.*

I walk around the island into the great room just as Bernard lies back on the chaise side of the sectional. Reg sits nearby, leaning forward, poring over his phone and scrolling. I want to ask what they are here for, but they seem so comfortable, and I wonder if the question will be rude. They have to know that Brandon is not here, right?

"Okay, let me find it. Let. Me. Find. It," Reg mutters.

"I thought you saved it," Bernard says, his eyes closed.

Reg shakes his head. "Thought I did too, but here we are. I'm gonna find it, though."

"What if they took it down?" Bernard asks now.

"Shit, I hope nobody did, that would be—oh, found it!" Reg jumps up. "Aiden, you need to see this," he says. He walks over to me, phone held at arm's length.

A post on Instagram. The page: @OnlyInWestGate. The headline: **TEEN STAR ARRESTED AFTER DINER PARTY!** The picture: Brandon in his uniform, smiling. Promo pictures for the team. The story:

Local star quarterback Brandon Wright was arrested last night during a postgame celebration at Randy's Diner. The local news reported that Brandon has charges pending and moderate injuries. Swipe to see submitted videos of the arrest.

Submitted videos? People have videos of Brandon getting arrested and beat up?

"You done reading?" Reg asks.

I nod. He swipes. I clench my teeth and my entire body. I do not think I am ready to see Brandon get hurt.

From the angle of the phone, it seems like the video was shot from the patio right in front of Randy's. The camera shakes a lot and police lights flash, but I cannot make anything out. People scream. Shaky footage of the floor inside Randy's. Brandon gets lifted by four cops. His eyebrow and mouth leak blood. He stumbles down the walkway, dazed. The phone drops. The video ends.

I grab Reg's phone and watch the video repeat, but it is not helpful. There is no footage to explain why Brandon got so hurt or what caused the arrest. I hand Reg back his phone.

"Everybody's been posting their BS videos trying to be the first people to get up footage of Brandon," Reg says now. "It's kind of wild. That's why we came—to tell you about it. What are you guys gonna do? What are your parents gonna do? Like, is Brandon gonna go to jail for real, for real? Is he okay? Is he gonna play the season? Is he here? I heard he's still in jail. Is that—"

I hold up a hand. Too many words.

"I do not know. I am not sure. I hope not. I do not know. I hope so. No. Yes," I answer.

Reg rubs the back of his head. "I actually think that was the answer for every question. You're good."

I stare at his chin. Three hairs poke out. Barely visible. Brandon once convinced me that shaving would make hair grow, so we used Dad's razor on our faces. We ended up full of scabs and told our parents that we had a vicious ant problem.

"Look, is Brandon okay?" Reg asks now. "When is he getting out? We really came to check up and see what's going on. We didn't want him to feel like nobody cared. I mean, he's going to jail. That's crazy."

"They didn't even press the charges yet," Bernard says. "You're getting ahead of yourself."

"Timeline is irrelevant." Reg rolls his eyes. "Charges are bad even if we don't know exactly what they are." He looks at me. "What are you guys gonna do?"

I blink four times. "I have no idea." It feels difficult to be at a loss this way, especially in the family I am in. With a lawyer for a mother and a research scientist for a father, all we get are answers. We were raised to have answers, find answers, give answers. We are expected to know what to do. Now I cannot even be sure that my parents are confident in their next actions, and neither am I.

Reg's eyes are bigger in his face than before. I stare down at the floor.

"Shit. Shit. Brandon can't stay arrested. That would be

really bad. What about UF? What about the rest of the year? What about . . ." Reg trails off.

"Babe, you're spiraling," Bernard says. His hand claps down on my right shoulder. It feels like there is a fist around my chest.

"Is Brandon okay, Aiden?" Bernard asks now. "Like physically? Mentally? Is he okay?"

I shake my head. "He is not home," I say now. "How can he be okay when he is not home? He has never been in . . ." I trail off. I cannot even bring myself to say it. Brandon has never been away from us like this. He could not even hack it at sleepaway camp. It does not make sense. Brandon might go to jail for a long time. He is hurt from getting beat up. We have not spoken since the fight. The police say that he assaulted an officer. People are rushing to post videos on the internet of my brother hurt, broken, bleeding. I do not understand it. I do not know how we got here.

Bernard rubs my back. Reg rests a hand on my other shoulder. We stand this way for forty-six seconds.

"Did you guys see Brandon attack anyone?" I ask now.

"I was tied up with the cop who was whaling on me. By the time I heard Brandon screaming . . ." Reg says.

Bernard shakes his head at the floor. "Same with me. Sorry, man."

My phone pings in my pocket, and I realize now that I have pending notifications. The first two are texts from Isabella.

Hey, are u ok?

Aiden, I heard about what happened. are u ok? Is ur brother ok? Just checking on u.

I start to respond, but just then my mom calls. "Give me a second," I say to Reg and Bernard. They nod and lean in close to each other, talking among themselves. I wander into the kitchen and answer the phone. "Hey, Mom, everything okay?"

"Hey, honey," Mom says. "Just checking on you. What are you doing?"

I squeeze my eyes shut until I see neon colors. "Nothing." I open my eyes, tilt my head back, and stare at the ceiling. I tap the side of my leg. One, two. Stop. One, two. Stop. "Sorry, I am lying. There are people posting about Brandon. There are posts saying he got arrested and stuff. That is a problem, right?"

Three rounds of breath pass before she answers. "We'll talk about that later."

"But—"

"Later, Aiden," Mom says now. "Please. I know, sweetie. Trust me, I know. Just—not right at this second. I just wanted to check on you. Do you need anything?"

"No," I say now. "Where are you?"

"Down at the office, trying to get with the lawyers and compile a few preliminary files just in case this gets bad."

Reg looks up with wide eyes. He can hear my conversation.

"Is it going to get bad?" I ask.

Papers shuffle in the background and something clicks, maybe a pen. "I doubt it, but it's better to be prepared and not need to be."

"Okay," I say now. "But the posts. Can you get them taken down? Nobody should see those. What if a recruiter sees—"

"Aiden, honey," Mom says. Her voice is snippy now. Conversation over.

"Later," I say. "Later."

"Thank you. I'll be home in a bit."

A surge of nervous energy rushes through me and my skin feels itchy all over. I want to see Brandon, but that is not an option. I want to talk about what is happening, but that is not an option. I want to make this all go away, but that is not an option. This is important. A cop hurt Brandon and he is getting blamed. I started the fight, but Brandon got hurt, Brandon got arrested, and now Brandon is getting blamed. He is the only one getting blamed.

Mom has to fix this. It is her job. She gave us all those talks. She always said the same things. Comply. Get home alive. She will fix it later. We complied. We are alive—even though only I made it home. She has to fix it now. She has to fix my mistake.

I want to throw my phone. Breathe. Identify the emotion. I close my eyes. The energy surges again. My neck and scalp prickle. My chest feels cold. Anxiety.

I understand the emotion. I understand why I am anxious. I need Mom to do something. That is why she is a lawyer, to do something. Brandon is getting blamed and the cop is getting away with it and I am the one who started the fight and I am not getting any blame and Carter was the one fighting with me and he is not getting any blame and people are trying to repost Brandon getting hurt and arrested and they are not getting any blame and she is not fixing anything and—

My phone pings. It is Dad.

Be home in 5. Went down to the station to try to get more info on Brandon.

My body shudders and I tap at my thigh to calm it. One, two. Stop. One, two. Stop.

"My dad is almost home," I say now, turning to Reg and Bernard.

They both nod. Reg frowns, but he does not look unhappy. Bernard gives me a small smile, though it has echoes of Reg's expression. If I had to place their emotion closest to one on a card, I would place it at sympathy.

I run upstairs. I need a minute.

"We'll let ourselves out," Bernard calls from the bottom of the stairs.

"You let yourselves in," I say now.

Reg laughs.

CHAPTER NINE

3 Days After the Incident

I should feel comfortable in courtrooms. In a way, I grew up in them. I played in empty ones while my mom packed her stuff up after late cases. I frequented them with my dad on days when Mom needed to see us after a heavy day. Courtrooms are not supposed to be intimidating; they are supposed to feel like a second home. So why am I walking up to this building, which I have entered so many times before, nervous, jittery, and uncomfortable?

My dad places a hand on my back when I stop at the steps in front of the courthouse.

"All right, Aiden?"

I do not respond.

"Hey, I know it's a lot, but there's nothing to be nervous about. It's a lot of formality and it's scary, but it'll be fine. They won't hold your brother, and we'll probably get things dismissed today if we're lucky. I'm sure it's all a misunderstanding. They know your mom. The community knows Brandon. It'll be okay, all right?"

I nod. I remember my mom's tears in the car. It will be okay.

The courtroom is filled with more people than I expected for a Monday morning. Some with minor infractions waiting for their turn to be seen by the judge, others waiting to have cases addressed. Courtrooms are typically like this when there is not a trial, which is funny, because that is not how it is depicted on television. People think that every case is packed with bystanders every step of the way, closed off to the public, some big show. Most times, the seats are filled with a bunch of people waiting to see the judge, and cases get knocked out or pushed forward, one by one, as quickly as possible. Much less dramatic than people think.

We wait for two speeding tickets and a domestic violence case to get preliminary hearings before Brandon is called. They bring him out, and I do not need a card to recognize his expression. Stress and fear. Brandon makes eye contact with me, and my heart drops into my stomach. Everything about him looks devastated. The bailiff walks him out to the defendant table one row in front of where we sit. Brandon, handcuffed and silent, stands next to a lawyer from my mom's firm.

Suddenly, I feel like I should have gone to school instead of sitting here, close enough to feel the stress radiating from my brother's body, but too far to do anything helpful. My mom, who arrived much earlier than me and Dad, pulls at her fingertips. I know she would rather be next to Brandon right now.

"All right, Brandon Wright. Charges are disturbing the peace, loitering, resisting arrest, and aggravated assault of a peace officer. Do you have legal counsel?" The judge sounds bored.

"Yes, Your Honor." Brandon's voice shakes.

"Okay, bail is set at twenty-five thousand dollars. If paid, you'll be immediately released so that you can continue to attend school until your next scheduled court date."

One gavel bang, one written check, a few hugs later, and Brandon is in the car and on his way back home. Though we do not speak on the ride home, I breathe a little easier with him in our midst.

Once we are home and through the door, Mom claps her hands twice.

"Family meeting. Now."

We all file into the great room. Brandon and Dad sit at the island. I collapse into the velvet couch, always forgetting how much I hate the texture until I am sitting on it.

Mom paces back and forth between the couch and the island, biting at her lip. Dad and Brandon exchange looks, and I stare at the ceiling, making patterns that are not there. Family meetings are like this—Mom ruminates, we wait, then she lectures. The last time we had a family meeting was when Mom got a new job. Before that, we had a meeting when Brandon broke his ankle. This meeting is more serious, so we give her time. After four rounds of pacing, she speaks.

"Okay, so, I anticipated the charges today. Honestly, I think that's the worst of it. We have the best people from my firm on the case. I hate that I can't be on the team myself, but our firm has rules. Either way, it'll be fine. I think that as long as we get everything together by the next date and present a good case, we can likely get this dropped. This could all be to scare you, and even if not, they'll maybe offer a plea deal, make you do volunteer work, who knows. I know that it all sounds very bad, but I think they're trying to use you as some kind of example."

"That's not fucking fair," Brandon mutters.

"Hey, language!" Dad snaps.

"It's not!" Brandon shouts.

"Hey!" Mom snaps her fingers. "We will not tear each other apart in here. It is going to be fine. I know it's stressful, Brandon—"

"What about when schools find out? Is my stock gonna drop? What if UF finds out? What if they pull my scholarship? What if they don't let me on the team? I may not need the money, but I need to be on a team. What if I can't play?"

"Honey, that's not going to happen!" Mom says now.

"You keep saying that, but what if it does?"

"It won't!" Mom yells. She stops pacing, closes her eyes, and takes a breath. "I just said that we will stay calm—"

"You said we will not tear each other apart. You never said—" I interrupt.

"Aiden!" Dad snaps.

My bad.

Mom narrows her eyes at me. "I am saying now that we need to stay calm. Those are worst-case scenarios, and we are not there yet. Okay? They're just making an example out of Brandon. We will work things out behind the scenes, maybe even before the next date, and it will all fall into place. The most important thing for you to do, Brandon, is to keep your head down and—"

"Aiden, you saw what happened, right?" Brandon asks.

"Brandon, this isn't helpful," Dad says now.

Brandon gets up from the barstool and comes over to me. I sit up straight.

"You saw, right? You know I ain't do nothing. You know!" Brandon says firmly.

"I—"

"Aiden knows, Mom! You keep talking about a plea deal or something like that. I ain't doing that. That's still gon be on my record. I don't want that. I want this to go away. I don't need this. It could mess up everything. If this gets bad, nobody's gonna want me. I'm the number one recruit in the nation. In the *nation*. Can't some charges stop you from getting accepted to college? This is my life. It's my whole life. Aiden knows. He can tell them. Right, A?" Brandon's eyes search mine.

"I—" I stop. "I am not sure what I know." I know this is crucial for Brandon, and I know what he needs to hear from me. It feels like hot oil all over my body to know that I cannot give him the answers that he is looking for.

Brandon's brows knit together. "What you mean?"

"I—I—" I stutter. "The cops were on me. I heard you, but—"

"A, you were there. You were right there. I could see you. I know they had you pinned or whatever. But I could see you. I could see you." Brandon grabs my shoulders. "You saw, A. I know you had to. 'Cause I could see you."

"There were planters," I say now. "And someone hit my head. My head hit the ground. I—"

Brandon shakes me. "A, you saw! You saw!"

I close my eyes. Tears gather behind my lids. I feel like I am failing my brother. He needs something from me that I cannot give him, and I do not know what to do.

"Brandon." Dad's voice is soft and low. "It's okay if your brother didn't see. We don't need to pressure him. He was in a bad situation too. You see he's still bruised and beat up. Give him some room."

I feel Brandon's breath on my face. Then the pressure from his hands disappears.

"You right. I'm—" Brandon stops. "I'm sorry, A. I ain't mean to come at you like that. It was a weird weekend. I ain't never even had detention before, you know? It's—I'm sorry, A."

I open my eyes. It is all hard. I know it is. It is not his fault. I know this. I cannot blame him for his reactions, the same way he has never blamed me for mine. I nod.

"Do not stress," Mom says now. "Either of you. I know it's difficult, but try not to. We have this. I just want you both to go to school, keep your heads down, let this kind of blow over while we work on it. Aiden, you'll go in for the rest of the day. Brandon, you'll go back tomorrow—you can take a day to reset. I know that's hard, it's a small town, but try your best to stay focused on being who you both have always been. In a few weeks, all of this will be settled and over and we'll be fine. Nobody's stock is dropping. Nobody's going to jail. Everything is fine. We have the best people on this. Just don't talk to anyone about it at school. Keep on as though nothing has happened. Got it?"

Brandon and I agree, and Mom and Dad both embrace us each in turn before we make our way up the stairs. Brandon stops me before we split off to go to our rooms.

"Hey, A. I'm sorry again, bro. I shouldn't have acted like that. It won't happen again, all right? You okay? I don't wanna stress you."

I nod. "Are you?"

Brandon shrugs. "I think so. It's weird, I can't lie. But it's gon work out like Mom says, right? It's all gon blow over. Can't be over here falling out and stuff over this."

I force a grin.

"Aye, don't look so stressed!" Brandon says. "We gon let the grown people take care of the scary stuff. You and me, though, we got practice tomorrow! Back to the field. Back to the grind." Brandon shoots me his megawatt smile.

I smile for real this time.

"Oh, I just remembered. I wanted to ask you if anybody said anything to you."

I look up. "Anyone?" I ask now.

"Greg?" Brandon asks. "Carter?"

I did not expect him to mention Carter. I shake my head. Brandon nods. I cannot make out his expression. I cannot match it to an emotion card.

"Yeah, me neither. I expected Carter. He wouldn't be that dumb, but I don't know where Greg's at. I mean, I guess he could be in trouble 'cause of the fight—his dad's real strict. That's probably it."

I am pretty sure that Brandon is talking more to himself than to me.

"But Louis ain't hit me up either. Reg and Bernard did, at least."

"Yeah, they stopped by to check on me and ask about you on Saturday," I say now.

"It's never the ones you expect." Brandon chuckles, but it does not seem to be in response to anything funny. The chuckle does not seem happy at all. "You know Georgia ain't called me? Got my phone back and not even a text. That's wild."

I rock back on my heels. "Is she your girlfriend?" I ask.

Brandon shrugs. "I don't even know. I thought so." He rubs the back of his head. "But like I said, we ain't stressing!" My brother plasters his smile back on. "Right?"

"Right," I say now.

"Wright brothers?" Brandon reaches out a fist.

I bump fists with him. "Flying high?"

Brandon's smile gets wider. "I knew you'd come around! It's good, right?"

"In a very cringy way, sure."

Brandon rubs the top of my head. "I'm never cringy, and you know it!"

"Locs!"

"Can't get tangled." Brandon chuckles, then walks to his room and closes the door.

I follow suit, but behind the closed door, I am not as relaxed as his easy laugh. My breath does not come as easily as his smile. A worry deep in the pit of my stomach will not go away. I cannot help wondering what will happen if everything is not fine. What is going to happen if everything ends up not fine, and it is all my fault?

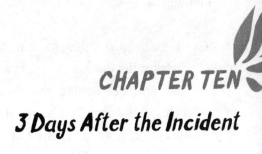
I still have to go to school after the court session, even though Brandon does not. Mom says we need to keep up appearances. If we act like everything is normal, then other people will follow suit. I am quiet in the car as Dad drives. He lets the radio play quietly—"Embrace of Silence" by Yiruma. One of my favorites. I know this is on purpose. I let the notes drift along my skin as I watch trees dart past my window. I observe people walking and wonder where they're going.

A man hobbles along with a cane in hand, wearing a jacket despite the sweltering heat. No bags. Nothing to indicate where he might be heading. I make up a life for him. A wife he is going home to, one he has been married to for twenty years. One who cooks his favorite roast beef sandwich for lunch in the middle of the day because she knows he comes home early on Mondays. Kids who are in school with me. Kids who have never talked to me. Kids who will stare at me today because of what happened. Kids who will stare at me because I ruined my brother's life.

Even my daydreams become nightmares. I try to shift my thinking to positive thoughts, but the doom and gloom haunt me until I look up and we are finally at school. I turn to Dad, and he clears his throat.

"You'll be all right?" Dad asks now.

I do not know. That is the honest answer. I do not tell him the honest answer.

NOTE: *My speech therapist once told me that sometimes you have to tell people what they want to hear. I asked her how you know what they want to hear. She told me that over time, you learn.*
   • I have learned.

I nod. "I will be all right, Dad."

Dad gives me a small smile and pats me on the shoulder.

That is my cue. I step out of the car, ready to brave whatever is coming. There are only a few periods before the end of the day, and I am coming in during the worst time: lunch.

Brandon gave me a pep talk before I left the house, and his words bounce around in my skull now. Nothing will be different. Nothing will be weird. Just walk in with my head held high and everything will be fine.

I make my way through the front office, sign in, and head

toward the lunchroom, suddenly brave and empowered by Brandon's words. He did nothing wrong. This will all blow over. Everything *will* be fine. I prep myself at the lunchroom doors. I close my eyes and take a few breaths, steeling myself against the negative expectations threatening to creep back into my brain. Then I throw the doors open, and the bravery escapes me, leaving my lungs devoid of air and my chest deflated when I realize that I do not know where to go.

I always sit with Brandon. I always sit with Brandon and his friends. I always sit with Brandon, Carter, Louis, and Greg. I scan the lunchroom. Carter is immediately a no. I do not even want to see him, and mercifully, he seems to be absent. Louis? He was more on Carter's side than mine that night. I see him sitting with his head down in a corner next to one of the guys from the football team that I have never spoken to. He glances up at me and looks back down, picking at his food.

I chew at my bottom lip. I look for Greg, but I do not see him, either. I did not plan for this. I do not think that Brandon did either. It hits me suddenly as panic rises in my chest in place of air, restricting my throat and tensing my muscles—I do not have a life outside of my brother. Everything that I have is because of him, through him, adjacent to him. I walked in with confidence because of him and lost it because he is not here. What do I have without him?

"Hey!" A familiar voice at my side. The scent of cranberries and lemons. Isabella.

I smile when I see her, but her face falls.

"Oh my gosh, Aiden. Your face!"

I forgot about the bruise on the side of my face from being forcefully smacked into the concrete. It is darker now, purpling as it attempts to heal.

"It looks worse than it feels," I say now. A lie. Tell people what they want to hear.

Isabella keeps frowning. I realize that I hate the look of a frown on her face.

"Come sit with me? Or do you have other people?" she asks.

I shake my head.

Isabella gestures to a table in the corner and I follow her. Eyes follow me. I feel them piercing through me, taking in everything. The rise of whispers settles like a unified hum across the lunchroom. I am the topic of conversation. Brandon is the topic of conversation. I know the question before it is asked: *Where is he?*

I sit next to Isabella, and though she seems worried, she plasters on a smile and chatters through the remainder of the lunch period. She ignores the stares. She ignores the whispers. And she does not ask why I do not eat.

I try to listen to her, but all I can think of is what I need to report back to Brandon. Everything is not the same. Everything is not okay. It is all different now.

After lunch, I zone out through Life Skills. I zone out to the point where, once again, I do not hear the bell ring. This time, Ms. Findley does not snap at me. She gently raps her knuckles on my desk, interrupting my wandering thoughts.

"You all caught up on the discussion, Aiden?" she asks. Her voice is gentle and soft.

"No," I say now. I am done telling people what they want to hear today. "I am sorry."

"It is fair, all things considered." Ms. Findley clears her throat. "I know you have a lot going on right now. I was reminding everyone of the job project. You should get started soon, which means I recommend going to a few of the approved stores today to see if you can get hired. I know that may be a lot to ask right now, but—"

I shake my head. "That is okay. I can do that." I need to take my mind off things, and avoiding home—avoiding telling Brandon what to expect when he comes back to school tomorrow—sounds perfect.

I look around for Isabella.

"I sent Miss Loft off to her last class, but I think she's ready whenever you are. Don't forget: you aren't in this alone. I paired you all up for a reason, so that you'll have someone to help you through shifts and during the interview. Having a partner should make this an easier undertaking."

I nod and stand, slinging my backpack over my shoulder. I start toward the door.

"And, Aiden," Ms. Findley says to my back.

I turn.

"If you need time . . ."

I look at her, my brows furrowed, tears burning just behind my eyes. I blink away the rising emotion. I do not need more time. I need to go back. I need to reverse time. I know that nobody can do that for me, but I also know, as my mom would say, that Ms. Findley means well.

I nod again and stalk out toward my last class of the day. I encounter more stares as I make my way down the hallway. I have always been solitary, but today is the first time I have felt lonely. It is the first time I feel truly alone.

I shoot Isabella a quick text about the interview after school and meet her by the front steps of the main building. She smiles when she sees me.

"No football practice today?" she asks.

I shake my head. "Ms. Findley got me out of it for the project."

"You know, I might have to do your makeup or something. They may not hire us if you look like a cage fighter." Isabella chuckles.

Her presence makes me feel a bit better. Soothed. I give her a small smile, though it hurts to do so, then look down at my feet. "If that is what you think would help."

Isabella reaches into her backpack, a pink affair with key chains hanging from every available clip. Puffy balls, plastic fruits, random symbols, and characters that I do not recognize. She pulls out a small compact and a sponge.

"Sit." Isabella gestures to the low wall by the stairs.

I plant myself on the concrete and grip it with both hands, grinding my fingers a little deeper into the rough material, letting the feeling calm my joints.

"You are really doing this?" I chuckle.

"Aht! Aht! You gave consent. No take-backsies!" Isabella says as she moves a hand to my face.

"Consent can be revoked at any time."

"Ugh, hate that you're right." Isabella freezes with the sponge.

"That is okay. You may proceed." I smile.

Isabella meets my joy, and suddenly I feel a pang of guilt. Brandon is at home, stressed, and I am just proceeding with life as though everything is fine. I glance at the other students milling around the front of the school. Everyone is proceeding as though everything is fine. Brandon's life is in limbo, but everything continues to move on without him. Even me. I close my eyes, hoping to block out the guilt from the inside.

"All right, so we're just doing some light work, 'kay?" Isabella says. "Just a little coverage so you don't look like you just stepped out of a ring with a prize belt slung over your shoulder."

I nod, keeping my eyes closed, and allow her to work. Her strokes with the sponge are gentle across my skin, though the sponge itself is slightly rough, almost the same as my skin brush. I focus on the feeling of the sponge rather than that of her light touch on my chin. The sponge drags back and forth across my cheek, under my eye, down and over my jawline, over my forehead, and along my hairline. It calms me, and I feel almost sleepy when Isabella announces that she is done.

She stands back to admire her handiwork. "Yep, I'm good. And so are you now! You ready?"

"I am," I say. Brandon still aches on my mind, but I know that I need to do this. I have to do more than feel guilty or else I will drown in it and never resurface to see the other side.

"Okay, so the first place on the list is the auto shop, but I figure that's really messy and just not the vibes. I know for a fact that a bunch of people are shooting for the fast-food places and diners because they want free food. And I heard like five people say they were going for the clothing stores at the shopping center, soooo, I'm thinking we can try the library! Thoughts?"

"Libraries are cool," I say.

"Cool!" Isabella echoes me. "Except, admittedly, I'm not sure where it is. Do you think we need a ride?"

I shake my head. "It is just around the corner from here," I say now. "I am not sure how many steps, but I know that it is close." I will have to count.

Isabella nods. "Lead the way, maestro."

I frown. "I am not a maestro."

Isabella giggles. "And that is correct. You just lead the way."

She touches my arm, and her fingertips feel warm on my skin. I suddenly feel hot all over. I shrug away from the touch and she lets her hand drop, her smile faltering slightly.

> **NOTE:** *I think I gave her the idea that I did not like the touch.*
>
> • *That was not my intention.*

"Follow me?" I ask.

Isabella nods but seems more subdued than she did before. I start toward the library, not knowing how to fix whatever it was I just broke in her. I do not want to be the cause of hurt for anyone else, especially her. Isabella has been a source of light in the darkness, so the thought of her dimming because of me breaks me a little bit too. I just hope this is a break that can be fixed.

We cross the street first, then pass the row of houses across from the school. The library is just around the corner from here. I count my steps as I go. One, two. Stop. One, two. Stop.

"Have you been to this library often?" Isabella asks now. She walks next to me but at a distance, and she is careful not to touch me again. I am unsure if I am grateful for that or sad about it. A part of me almost wishes to be touched by her specifically, which is confusing for me. I am appreciative that she always respects my boundaries but also upset that there are so many miscommunications along the way. I do know that I feel a way about her that I cannot quite place. I ponder that in the back of my mind.

"I used to go a lot when I was younger but not as much now. I read a lot more in middle school. Now it is mostly—"

"Football?" Isabella asks.

I nod. "Pretty much."

"What kind of books did you like? When you do read now, what do you like to read?"

I think about it. I have never paid too close attention to genres, but now that I am going through it in my head, I see more of a pattern. "Sci-fi, I think. Fantasy. A lot of dystopian stories."

"Love to see the world fall apart, huh?" Isabella asks. Humor returns to her voice, and it relaxes me.

"More that I like to see society for what it is," I say now.

Isabella whistles. "Whew, dark. You think the world is like dystopian novels? You're a cynic, I see."

My mouth falls open and I almost laugh. "I'm a cynic?"

Isabella smiles. "Completely."

"Cynic. Definition: someone who believes that people are motivated by self-interest. Alternatively—"

"Distrustful of human sincerity or integrity," Isabella finishes. "I knew what I meant, sir. Thinking the world is a dystopia definitely classifies you as a cynic, but it's okay as long as you don't think like that about me."

I rub the back of my head and chuckle. "Well, you are one of the special ones."

Isabella straightens up a bit and grins. "I am?"

"Of course," I say, surprised by my immediate answer. I know that I mean it, but it is interesting to see how easily the truth slips out when Isabella is around. "So, what kind of books do you like?"

"I mostly read romance. Romantic comedies," Isabella says now. "Stuff like that."

"That's cool," I say as we reach the library. "My mom loves romance novels too."

"Really?" Isabella asks. "Based on what you've said, she doesn't seem the type."

I consider that both my mom and Isabella like the same genre of books, and she is right. If the type is like Isabella, my mother does not fit the bill.

"I have never read a romance book," I confess. Isabella

seems to ponder what I said. Her nose scrunches in a way that is pretty cute, and she smiles.

"I'll talk you through one of my favorites one day," Isabella says. "Then maybe we can do a buddy read. Sound good?"

I nod. "It is a date." My face feels hot as I say it, and I look down at my feet. I peek up and Isabella mirrors my body. I wonder if she feels hot too. It did take 1,365 steps to get here.

Isabella takes a breath and raises her eyebrows at me. "Ready to go in?" she asks.

I look up from the ground and nod again. We turn toward the entrance. My stomach flutters and I am suddenly nervous to do this interview. I stare at the sliding glass doors.

"It's okay, Aiden. We can do this. It's on the preapproved list, so I don't think they'll give us a superhard time. It'll be easy."

Easy is relative.

I take a few deep breaths before stepping into the cool, air-conditioned building. The library is mostly white—the foyer has the welcome and checkout counters to the left, and to the right is a staff room. Straight ahead past the foyer, a double row of computers sits in the middle of the room, flanked by varying rooms on either side. To the left, there is a kids' room, then a middle grade and young adult section. To the right, there are endless rows of adult books.

Isabella and I make our way to the counter. A woman with curly black hair and large round glasses looks up as we approach.

"May I help you?" she asks. Her voice is welcoming and kind.

Despite her warmth, I open my mouth but nothing comes out. The nerves from this new situation have made me freeze up.

Isabella glances at me, then steps forward. "We're here from the West Gate High Life Skills class!"

The woman smiles. "Oh! You're the first ones who have swung by. We were worried that nobody would come."

"Here we are!" Isabella says cheerily. "What do you need us to do?"

The woman—whose name, we learn, is Hannah—explains the program, hands us applications, and lets us know that we will be interviewed as soon as we complete the paperwork. I take my time filling mine out. Once we hand the forms over, Hannah has us follow her down a hallway to a back room. Inside, a man named Adam sits at the end of a long table, and Hannah joins him.

Isabella and I sit. The interview is short, with Isabella doing most of the talking. Hannah and Adam explain what they expect of us: we will stock inventory, help customers find books, and help people access the computers. They are respectful of us both and treat us as though they have high expectations—expectations I have never experienced before.

As Hannah and Adam give us the full library tour and explain all the duties in detail, I observe the people gathered in the space. A man in a three-piece suit sits at a computer, bouncing his leg nervously. A woman with her toddler smiles as she shows him various board books, which he proceeds to chuck across the room. A young girl, settled in a beanbag, wipes away an errant tear as she pores over a thick book. I smile as I take it all in. My nerves calm a bit as I listen to Hannah and Adam, because I realize they are not speaking to or treating us like children. They are treating us as peers. There is an inherent belief that we will do the job to our best effort and that we can meet those demands. I realize suddenly the way I have been coddled for most of my life—how almost no one just places an obligation in front of me without some expectation of needing to assist me with it. Now I am being treated like someone who is capable and responsible. The person that I am and have always been. It feels good.

"Easy," says Hannah as she wraps up.

"Easy is relative," I say now. I am apprehensive—I have never had a job before. I listened a lot during the tour, mostly taking everything in and cataloguing my responsibilities. I can tell the job will keep me busy, but I worry that it will be too quiet. In the silence, I will have too much space to think about everything happening with Brandon.

She smiles. "We'll help make it easy."

"What are your availabilities?" Adam asks.

"After three thirty, I think," Isabella says now. She glances at me. "Because of football practice, right?"

I nod, grateful that she is thinking about me.

"I have robotics club, so I'll be around school until you're done," she says to me.

"After three thirty is fine," Hannah says. "And we'll work out the schedule week by week."

Once we finish the interview, they hand us welcome packets, and Isabella and I exit the library.

"So, how do you feel about it?" Isabella asks once we are outside.

I shrug. "Should be fine, I think." *Hope* is probably a more apt word. I worry about my performance, though Hannah and Adam made the job seem pretty low stakes. Brandon always says that I take everything too seriously, so I shake the bad feelings off. I am likely overthinking things before they even get started.

Isabella smiles. "We start tomorrow! And between you and me, I think we're going to make a pretty good team. A dynamic duo, if you will."

I smile back. "You think so?"

"Absolutely!" Isabella says. "Who could do better than us?"

I shake my head. "No one." Even though I am humoring her a bit, I am definitely starting to believe it.

"See, now you're catching on!" Isabella starts to reach for me, then stops, and her hand falls. She chews on her bottom lip and looks a bit nervous.

I raise my hand. "High five?" I ask. I have not high-fived anyone since I was nine.

Isabella brightens with a smile that shows all her perfect teeth and smacks my hand against hers. If she thinks it is corny, she does not say.

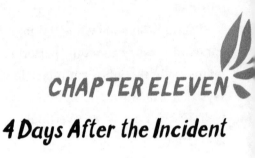

CHAPTER ELEVEN

4 Days After the Incident

Brandon is quiet before school on Tuesday. This would not be weird if I were not used to his endless chatter about one football game, or another football play, or some girl, or a friend. The dead air as we descend the stairs feels more irritating on my skin than noise. It worries me that Brandon is feeling differently toward me. Possibly starting to blame me the way that I am starting to blame myself.

Mom stands in her office, stuffing her briefcase with folders and prepping to go to work. She is always the last one out of the house in the mornings, since Dad leaves before the rest of us get up. I dash to the kitchen to grab a clementine and follow Brandon out the door, shooting Mom a quick wave before I leave. A very quiet morning.

I scratch my hand against my nylon gym shorts as we

walk outside, feeling the threads slip across my nails. It has not rained since the incident. The sky is, and has been, impossibly blue. I can count three large clouds and that is it. The sun is beaming down, probably frying the back of someone's neck right now. There is a family on a beach somewhere enjoying this weather. It is supposed to rain when bad stuff happens. Movies do it. Music videos do it. Books do it.

Rain would have been a good indicator of the day, but we are not that lucky.

Brandon stands frozen on the front steps, staring out toward the driveway and the gate of our property.

"What is up?" I ask now.

Brandon does not answer. He points.

At the gate to our driveway, a few men stand with cameras in hand. Some snap pictures of us at our front door.

I freeze now too, shocked at what I am seeing and suddenly feeling very exposed. Then my body reacts before my brain does. I back up, pull Brandon inside with me, and lock the door.

Note: There are four men. Three with hats. One with sunglasses.

Mom is standing in the entrance to her office, briefcase in hand, ready to go. She raises an eyebrow at us. "I thought you both already left."

I look to Brandon, waiting for him to explain, but he stares quietly at the front door. I might be imagining it, but he almost seems to have tears in his eyes.

"There are people with cameras outside," I say now. I never have to be Brandon's voice, but today is a day of firsts.

"People with—as in, newspeople?" Mom asks, sounding shocked and confused. She peeks out from behind the curtains to look for herself.

"Four. All men. One has sunglasses. The three others have hats. Maybe green?" I say.

"The only thing stopping them is our gate. I'm calling the police—" She stops herself. "I'll call community security to get them out of here. We pay our homeowner's fees for a reason. They shouldn't have even been able to get past the front gates." Mom pulls out her phone and starts to dial.

"Gates at the front of the community can't stop someone who's on foot." Brandon finally speaks. "We walk in and out every day, and now so can they."

Mom frowns as she explains the situation to security over the phone. As she talks, Brandon continues to stare at the door, lost in his own thoughts, and I wonder what is running through his brain. I bounce from foot to foot, anxiously waiting to see what will happen next.

I should comfort Brandon. Maybe a pat on the shoulder? Maybe a hug? He always knows how to comfort me. This should not be so difficult. I am just not used to him needing comforting. I am not really accustomed to being a comforter in general. Something about the responsibility feels heavy. Does Brandon always feel this weight?

"Should we stay home today?" I ask now.

Brandon looks at me and lets out a breath. His expression

seems almost pained but also somewhat more relaxed than before.

NOTE: *Is this relief?*

"Maybe we should—" Brandon starts.

"Mm-mm." Mom shakes her head. "We need to stay calm and act normal. Brandon, you missed school for the court date—any more extra days and it will look strange. You're both going to school."

Something flashes in Brandon's eyes that I have never seen before. He is always so confident, so composed, so happy. So why does the look in his eyes make me feel like the world is ending?

"Mom, walking does not seem like the best idea," I say. My tone, I hope, is urging her to see what is going on with Brandon without exposing him outright. I do not want to embarrass him, and I imagine that he does not want his intimate feelings out in the open.

Mom nods. "I know. I'm going to drive you both. I'm just waiting for security to come and clear these guys out." She peers through the curtains, and I follow suit. The men continue to mill about at the edge of the property. Two of them arch their necks and raise their cameras high over the gate and bushes. We are thankfully too far away for them to see us inside.

Fifty-eight seconds pass and finally the community security rolls up to our gate. The on-duty officer gets out of the car and does a lot of hand gesturing and pointing, and then the men with cameras walk away, though two of them look back to our house often.

"Okay, let's hurry and go before they try to double back," says Mom. She is remarkably calm, considering everything. She might be staying calm for us.

We hurry to the garage in silence. In the car, Brandon slinks down low, below the line of the window.

"What are you doing?" I ask now.

"I just don't wanna be seen, A." Brandon's voice shakes.

I do not push the issue further. He is not strapped in. That is a safety hazard. I purse my lips and keep my comments to myself. The drive to school is only four minutes anyway.

We pass the men with cameras on our way out of the community. They glance at our car but do not seem to know who is inside. Brandon's move to hide was smart.

At school, Brandon does not walk in with his usual vigor after a win. It is Tuesday. He missed the hype of the Monday after the game, he missed the excitement of celebrating in the hallways, he missed the camaraderie with other sports teams over the football team's win. I think missing that happiness took a lot from him. That must be why he walks with his head down, watching his feet swing the way I usually do.

I am going to ask Brandon today if he is okay. I am going to take care of him how he has always taken care of me. I just have to work up the nerve to do so without it feeling awkward or forced.

We turn the corner to the hallway where Brandon's locker

is, and I see Georgia lingering next to it. She rocks back and forth between her toes and heels, eyeing Brandon as we approach. I guess he can feel better now—she does care.

Brandon eyes Georgia and stops a few feet from his locker. "I gotta get to class. I'll catch you at practice, A," he says now. He does not look at me. He turns and walks in the opposite direction before I can get any words out. Class does not start for another twenty minutes. And I am pretty sure that his class is in the other direction.

"Brandon!" Georgia calls out.

Brandon does not turn around or stop. That does not seem like a good sign.

Georgia frowns at my brother's back, then looks my way expectantly before approaching me. First time for everything, I suppose.

"Um, Aiden," Georgia says. She almost never speaks to me, and she certainly never starts conversations. It is still a shock to me that Brandon even likes her. What does he see? Maybe she is different when you get to know her. I would not know.

"Is Brandon okay?" she asks. "Like, I meant to call, but . . . I think I screwed up."

Screwed up?

"How?" I ask now.

"I just . . . ," Georgia says. "I didn't call. I mean, do you know if he's okay?"

"He got arrested and spent the weekend in jail," I say flatly.

"Yeah . . ." Georgia looks at her feet. Her sneakers have rhinestones all over them. That is very on-brand for her. "I've been meaning to check on him. Like, I need you to know that. I'm not a bad person or a bad girlfriend. I've been meaning to check on him, but I just—I've been palled lately."

"You have lost strength or effectiveness, or you have lost interest or attraction?" I ask. "Because pall, by definition—"

"Uh, neither of those. I, umm . . ." Georgia scrunches her brows and frowns again. "I've just been, like, overwhelmed or something. Sorry. I heard that word in class the other day and thought it was right."

Georgia never uses the right word.

"Like, I know he's obviously mad at me, but can you tell him that I asked for him to call me? Or to, like, pick up when I call? I have a good reason for why it took me so long."

"What is it?" I ask now.

"What's what?"

"The reason."

Georgia runs her hands through her blond hair. "Aiden, I just need you to tell Brandon what I said. Are you capable of that? Like, can you do that for me?"

I nod and watch Georgia walk away, blond hair swinging like a pale curtain across her back. Her behavior was odd, and the fact that she could not tell me the reason was a little more than weird, but maybe it is not my business. She is right, though. Brandon is obviously mad at her, considering his aversion to her presence. I wonder if this is all just about her not calling, or if there is something else going on.

The hallways have not gotten crowded yet the way they do right before the ring of first bell. I watch my own feet swing as I head to class.

At the end of the day, Isabella's chair is disappointingly empty in Life Skills, which reminds me that I have not reached out to her since the library. Between Brandon and my parents stressing about Brandon, she completely slipped my mind. I cannot help but fight off a pang of guilt. I wonder where she is and if she will be at the library later. Considering how Brandon feels about Georgia not calling, I figure I should do something. I pull out my phone to text Isabella from underneath my desk, but I feel eyes on me.

I look up and Tucker is staring. Not blinking. Just staring.

I look away. The last thing I need him to do is tell Ms. Findley. I am supposed to keep my head down today. Act like everything is normal, even though it is not.

I lean my head back, close my eyes, and breathe. Last Tuesday was a lot easier. Last Tuesday still had perfect attendance. I had never missed any of school until Monday. Last Tuesday, my brother did not have to wait to figure out what his future might look like. And last Tuesday, none of these things were my fault.

"Mr. Wright?"

My head snaps up. The classroom is empty. I did it again.

"I'm sorry, Ms. Findley," I say now. I know I must be in trouble this time.

She holds up a hand. "It's okay. I told you yesterday that I understand."

I frown.

"I'm so sorry about what happened to you boys. I know you must be so stressed and tired. Cop interactions are stressful for me, and I'm an adult. You, you're young and . . . ," Ms. Findley says, trailing off.

Young and? I do not respond.

"Well, I just wanted to say that I have been thinking of you all. I see that you still have scrapes and bruises. Fight or no fight, children shouldn't have been handled that way. I just want you to know that my door is always open, and I'm glad that above all, you were able to just walk away from it and you can all move on without lingering consequences."

I nod. She does not know. It will not be my job to inform her.

After the final bell, I head to the field more nervous than I was before my first real practice. Nothing, really, has changed. At least, nothing has changed when it comes to the actual football—the routine. Brandon will still be here, I will be here, everyone will be here as usual. Everything is the same, but also, there is a truth aired out and lingering above and between everything now. Now I know that most of my teammates hate me, see me as a burden, see my placement on the team as nepotism. If they see me as a threat, it is not due to my talent. But that was never my goal. This was not what I wanted.

I make it all the way to the locker room before I realize that Brandon is not with me. Weird. I am very early, though. I always am. I backtrack to where I usually run into Brandon in the hallway by the football field and look for him. Nothing.

The field is also empty. I head back to the locker room. He could be inside, but he is never early for anything.

The stillness of the locker room feels like peace. There will probably be tension today. The first time seeing Carter since the fight. The first time back. I tap at my thigh as I make my way to my locker. One, two. Stop. One, two. Stop.

Closer to my locker, I hear low voices drifting from the coaches' offices.

"And I hear what you're saying, I really do. But these aren't our local guys, Brandon. This isn't West Gate police. These are county guys. You haven't given us assurance that this is going away."

Brandon?

"My mom said that by the next court date, everything's gon even out. That's Friday. I don't understand. Who else is getting punished?" Brandon asks now. There is an edge to his voice, an anger.

I meander through the locker room, following the voices to the source.

"Everyone involved, Brandon. Everyone involved is getting punished, but nobody else has any charges filed against them. You have to understand how it would look to still have you on the team with something like this hanging over you." That is Coach McDonald, I think.

"But y'all don't know if anything's even hanging over me, though. The game is Friday, the court date is Friday. Why can't we just wait until then to see what we gon do? I mean, be for real, I'm your best guy. If you take me out for practice this whole week and then everything clears up on Friday, how am I supposed to be ready for the game? How's anybody else supposed to be ready? I can't sit it out. One missed game and my stock might drop. My commitment to UF was only verbal. I ain't sign all the paperwork yet, Coach."

Silence.

"Coach D?" Brandon asks. His voice is full of desperation. I have never heard him like this.

I stand in the hallway to Coach Davis's office, peeking from around the corner so that no one notices me. Brandon sits across from Coach Davis and Coach McDonald. They all look tense, as if waiting for someone to make a move. Then Coach Davis glances at Coach McDonald, and there is an exchange of head shakes.

Coach Davis rubs his eyes with his fingertips. "I don't want to do this, Brandon. I need you to understand how much I don't want to do this."

"So don't," Brandon pleads.

Coach Davis sighs. "It's just not that simple, bud." His blond hair falls forward into his face. "Until we have clear insight that this issue is going to resolve itself, you have to be suspended from the team."

Brandon does not speak. Coach McDonald stares at the floor. Coach Davis's face sags.

Forty-nine seconds pass.

"Until when?" Brandon asks now.

Coach Davis shrugs. "Until all this mess gets worked out. Like you said, the court date on Friday is supposed to clear everything up. Once that happens, we'll reinstate you, and it might be last minute, but you know the plays, you're comfortable with the guys, you should be ready to start even with a few days off. Think of it more like a rest period. You still have some bruises—I can see them. This can be a time to rest and reflect. You'll be right back on Friday and everything will be fine. Like it never happened," Coach Davis says. I cannot tell if he means it. His voice sounds genuine, but his face seems doubtful.

"What about Carter?" Brandon asks.

"Carter has a lot of practice punishment to make up for what's happened. Louis, Greg, Reg, and Bernard too."

"And Aiden?" Brandon asks now. "It wasn't his fault. I don't think—"

Coach Davis holds up a hand. "I know that's your little brother, but Aiden is on this team now. That means he is getting punishment runs and extra striders and burpees with his teammates who also got into trouble. That's a nonnegotiable."

Brandon nods. "But no suspension?"

Even when Brandon has trouble of his own, he is still looking out for me.

Coach Davis shakes his head. "We don't have any plans to suspend your brother right now."

"Okay," Brandon says. "Okay." He stands.

I should move. I should leave the hallway and hide—make it less obvious that I have been eavesdropping—but of course, my feet do not move the way my brain instructs them to.

Brandon turns and immediately sees me. He seems surprised, but he gives me a small grin and gestures with his head for me to go. Coach Davis and Coach McDonald don't seem to notice.

I turn and walk back to my locker, collapsing on the bench and staring at the wooden door. Brandon plops his body down heavy next to me. We do not speak for a minute.

"Thinking about how squirrels see in slow motion?" Brandon finally asks.

I smile. "Nope. Just thinking about how tarantulas have pet frogs."

"So, you telling me the fact that caterpillars liquefy their bodies and turn themselves into soup in their chrysalis before turning into butterflies wasn't running through your brain?" Brandon asks now.

"I mean, that is interesting, but I was too busy picturing armadillos inflating their intestines to float across rivers."

Brandon reaches up and tousles my locs. "It's gon be okay, you know? It's just a few days, and you'll be all right without me. It's gon be okay."

I nod. Once again, Brandon is comforting me when I had planned all along to console him. Still, he seems okay, all things considered. I just wonder if it is real.

"Georgia wants you to call her," I say.

"I can't worry about that right now, but I'll think about it," Brandon says. "Anyway, I'll see you at home, A." He gets up.

I watch as my brother, who has played football since he was five, goes straight home after school for the first time.

Coach made sure to keep everyone involved in the fight separate during practice, so it went smoothly, even though I had to run and do burpees most of the time. Afterward, I hustled to the library for my first shift with Isabella, which mostly involved listening, watching, and learning. The ride home with Dad to avoid any lingering reporters was quick and quiet, and I welcome the strawberry-scented, air-conditioned breeze when we walk through the doors to our home. No guys with cameras outside, thankfully.

Mom stands in the kitchen chopping up greens, presumably for some sort of salad.

"Where is Brandon?" I ask now.

"Good evening to you too," Mom replies.

"Sorry. Good evening, Mom. Where is Brandon?"

"How was your day at work? Can't believe you're working."

"Yes. Me, working guy. It was good. Learned a lot. Where is Brandon?" I ask.

Mom rolls her eyes and chuckles. "Thanks for the details. He's in his room. You can actually go grab him, because we're about to eat dinner." She gives Dad a kiss on the cheek.

I bound up the stairs, two at a time, and knock on Brandon's door.

"Closed for service," I hear from inside his room.

"Requesting immediate reconsideration of closed status," I say now.

"Request denied."

Oh. I frown.

Brandon opens the door with a grin. "I knew you were gon take that way too seriously. What's up?"

"Mom says dinner is almost ready."

Brandon nods. His expression is flat, though, empty. I

think of the fact that he was alone at home all afternoon, and I wonder how he spent his time. What did he do when the thing he loves was taken from him?

I chew on my bottom lip. "Are you okay—"

Brandon holds up a hand. "We're fine, A. Remember? No stress, right?"

No stress. I listen, but the phrase does not reach me internally. My insides are knotted and twisted from stress. I cannot imagine how my brother is staying so cool about everything, but I am grateful for it anyway.

I follow him downstairs and see Dad setting out plates on the table.

"Brandon," Mom says. Her voice sounds tight, constricted.

"Hmm?" Brandon cocks his head.

"So, I wanted you to know that I got definite word about what's coming next."

Brandon lets out a big breath and smiles. "I thought it was something bad. You sounded scary for a sec."

"Well, I wasn't sure if it was stressful for you."

Brandon shrugs. "You said it would be fine, right?" He is nonchalant. His relaxed response to everything is shocking me. How can everyone be so wound up, while Brandon—who all this is happening to—is staying cooler than the rest of us? He really trusts that everything will work out. I can see that now.

Mom glances at Dad and grins. "Yeah, I did. I mean, honestly, we have the advantage because of my position and who I am. My place in the firm all but guaranteed you the best lawyers and resources you could need. Outside of that, I think the moves the prosecution is making prove that we have even less to worry about than I originally thought. I was worried that they were going to try to make you some kind of example, but I really think this will all be over very soon."

My shoulders fall in slight relaxation. Hearing that this will be over soon, truly, makes me feel lighter.

Brandon straightens up. "For real? Why? What happened?"

"Well, the prosecution pushed for an expedited trial since you're in school. They said they don't need anything to drag on. We approved and we're letting that go forward."

"And that's"—Brandon looks around at everyone, brows knitting together—"good?"

Mom chuckles and grabs his upper arms. "Yes! They wouldn't want to speed things up if they were trying to build some big case against you. You're clear! I wouldn't be surprised if we're able to resolve it at the next hearing, when they formally announce charges and how they plan to proceed."

"That's on Friday, right? I told Coach it would all be worked out by then! I didn't know for sure, but, like, I knew, you know?"

Dad laughs. "That's a lot of knowing."

Brandon laughs. And starts in on his salad.

"Can I come?" I ask.

Mom shakes her head. "No, you cannot skip school. Missing half a day was enough. It's not an important court date. We'll update you after."

I frown. Well, that sucks.

"I know it sucks," Mom says now.

Mind reader.

"But really, it's the best way to move forward with some sense of normalcy. This way, it doesn't generate a ton of attention, and Brandon goes back Monday in full swing of his senior year," Mom says with a huge smile.

She sounds so optimistic, which would not be weird except that my mother is a terminal pessimist. She is the person who plans for rain in a tundra. She will not put her odds on winning the lottery, but fully believes that she will get struck by lightning. For her to be this hopeful, well, it buoys us all.

"So, school?" Mom says to me.

I nod.

"And work?" Mom asks Dad.

Dad nods in his quiet way and digs into his salad.

"We don't need everyone there anyway. I'm confident that they're setting up to drop the case or give you community service at worst. Be happy, honey. It's almost over!" Mom reaches for Brandon.

He leans into her, almost falling off his chair. Brandon's body shakes a few times with sobs that he stifles in her shoulder. After eleven seconds, he comes up for air and sniffles.

"Whew!" My brother smiles despite the wetness in his eyes. "Almost over!"

"You good?" I ask. I am surprised by his sudden emotion because of how cool he has been playing it until now. I finally understand how much this has been dragging on him, regardless of the front he has put on. It makes me happy to see my brother this way after all he has dealt with.

Brandon nods. "Nothing but relief, bro." He holds up his hand for a high five.

I clap with him, and he holds my hand up, crossing it with his at the thumbs to form a makeshift plane. "Flying high," he says now.

I smile. With our hands together and the end in sight, I feel nothing but hope.

CHAPTER TWELVE

7 Days After the Incident

See, the major issue with autistic stereotypes is that they get everyone into trouble. Example: people assume that all autistic people are blunt and brutally honest. Result: people assume that autistic people are *always* honest. Further result: people assume that *I* am always honest. Final result: when I go to the front office on Friday morning and tell the receptionist that I have permission from my mom to leave early because of a "Brandon" emergency and that she does not need to bother my mom, who is in court all day, the receptionist wrinkles her forehead, gives me a sad nod with a pitying smile, and allows me to walk out the door, essentially skipping school with permission and no oversight.

See? Stereotypes are the problem. If they were not, I would be in math class right now instead of on my way to the courthouse that I am not supposed to be visiting, to watch Brandon when I am not supposed to, and to avoid my mom, who thinks I am in school. I will have to figure out that last part later. Fun.

I know I might get in trouble and I know my mom says that this hearing will fix everything, but I need to see and hear it for myself. I need to know, firsthand, that this is over. I need to feel the relief in real time. I need to know, right now, that I did not ruin my brother's life. That is all. I am sure my mom will understand.

It is six and a half miles, or roughly 13,642 steps, to get to the courthouse, which means it will take too long to walk, but I do not have a card to connect to a rideshare, so I have to take the bus. I have never ridden the bus, and for this, my first time, I am doing it completely alone.

I turn right on the sidewalk and head south toward the bus stop. Humidity clings to my skin, though it has not rained in a few days despite being rainy season. I focus on the concrete, counting my steps as I move. Two steps in each sidewalk square, skip the line. One, two. Break. Anything to shake the nervous energy gathering inside me over this bus ride. Why did my mom never take me on a bus? She always said that I would probably never need to step foot on one. Said I would probably have a car before I ever needed to go that far, so there was no need. Said I only needed to know how to ride one in theory, just in case, for emergencies. This is absolutely an emergency. Or at least it feels like one.

When I get to the bus stop, I settle on a metal bench and

look up and down the street. I check my phone and it is 9:47. The bus should come in two minutes. The ride should take about fifteen minutes, according to the transit schedule I find online. My breath is steady.

I go over the steps in my head, remembering the board game my parents made for me as a child to learn the neighborhood and how to do neighborhood activities. Visualize. Move forward one space. Roll dice. Pick up card.

You are riding the bus. Recite all the correct steps to move forward five spaces.

Wait at the bus stop. Bus arrives. Stand back. Doors open. Insert exact change or swipe bus pass. Wave to bus driver. Smile. Sit at the front so you do not miss your stop. Pull the cord along the side of the bus when your stop is coming up. Stand before you are ready to get off. Hold on to the bar overhead so you do not fall when the bus stops. Step—

A sharp hiss of air cuts through the quiet morning. My head snaps up at the sound of the bus's approach. I release a quick breath. I know what I am doing. I have reviewed the steps.

The bus stops and I board. Insert change. Wave. Smile. There are even empty seats right at the front. Relief floods my body when I finally sit. The bus lurches forward. Hard part over.

A man sitting across from me is wearing one shoe. The shoe is a dusty brown, though it looks like it was white once. A split between the sole and the rest of the shoe allows a peek at an exposed toe. Sneakers. Cannot distinguish a brand. A sock hides his shoeless foot. The sock is the same dusty brown. His faded black shirt hangs loose on his body, as do his worn jeans. He seems to be drowning in his clothes. He lies with his head back on the seat, eyes closed. Is he not worried that he will miss his stop? Nobody sits in the same row as him. Though the rows in the bus are strange.

Three seats line the walls by the front of the bus, facing each other—I am seated in one of them. Right behind these seats, there are two others facing forward, with a handicap sign over them. A ramp behind the handicap seats separates the front and back of the bus. Past the ramp there are doors that look wider than the ones at the front of the bus. Then, more seats. Every seat after that faces forward, everyone staring at the back of someone's head. The only seats that face a different way are these in the front. I wonder why.

The handicap seats are empty. A woman in black pants and a blue button-down shirt sits in the first seat on the right side of the back section of the bus. She wears sunglasses even though it is cloudy outside. She scrolls through her phone. She keeps a plastic bag on the seat next to her. She must not want anyone to sit there. Her black shoes do not have laces. They look like leather. They look comfortable. The type of shoe that you would be okay standing in all day. Her name badge says VANESSA. It is still relatively early in the morning. Is she going to work or going home? Does she have kids? A dog? A cat? A fish? A husband? A wife? A pet rock? I had a pet rock once.

Behind Vanessa sits another woman. She has no name tag. Brown plastic grocery bags almost overflow from a blue canvas-and-metal shopping cart in the aisle next to her. She holds it tight and stares out the window as the bus chugs along. All the way in the back, a man talks on the phone, his voice too low for me to hear, as a little girl—his daughter, maybe—swings her feet and swipes at a tablet. The man gestures a lot and rolls his eyes often. He wears jeans and a shirt that says TITO'S PLUMBING.

Nobody on the bus wears stiletto heels or Italian leather shoes like my mom or dad. No business suits, strong perfumes, lipstick, manicured nails, or purses with initials. Something about the lack of pressure in that is comforting. It smells like sunshine and air. Smog, every time the doors open to let people off and on. Weed, once, when a blond guy with bloodshot eyes walks by. Rain threatens, heavy in the dark overcast, as we roll toward our destinations. Clouds blanket the sky now, with not a single break for light.

A few stops, one cord pull, a long flight of stairs, a quick trip through security, and one elevator ride later, and I am in the hallway outside the courtroom, nervous, sweaty, and suddenly face-to-face with Dad.

"Aiden." Dad's voice is hard but warm. Mahogany. "What are you doing here?"

I freeze. He knows the answer, because I would not be at the courthouse for any other reason than to see Brandon's case, so his question is not literal. If I answer literally, I will be what Brandon calls a smart-ass.

NOTE: *Everyone knows that asses (on people) cannot be smart, but the term could relate to donkeys.*

   • *This works on the assumption that donkeys are*

not intelligent. Do donkeys lack intelligence?
Unsure. Will investigate.

Okay. No smart-ass answer. He knows why I am here. But wait—

"Why are you here?" I ask now.

Dad raises a brow at me. "What do you mean? I have leave hours. I can call off work. But there are no leave hours for school. Wait, I don't need to explain this to you. Aiden, why are *you* here? You're supposed to be at school."

I scrunch my lips. I have started this course of action and now I must follow through.

"Does Mom know you are here?" I ask.

Dad's eyes dart to the courtroom door.

That might be a no.

Dad rubs the back of his head. "I know she doesn't know you're here, Aiden. And you shouldn't be. Did you sneak out of school?"

"No," I say now. Not a lie.

Dad frowns. "Are you going to tell me why you're here, Aiden? Before I send you back on your way?" he asks.

"But the case—"

"Won't be seen by either of us if you aren't honest."

"I was worried," I say now. "About the outcome. Mom says not to be, and I hear her, but I have worried every minute since everything happened. Even now—" I stop and close my eyes. I am so anxious, I can hear my heart pounding in my ears. "I feel something heavy hanging in my stomach. Pressing down harder. Growing and taking up space. I felt better when I came here."

Dad holds out a hand to me. I grasp it.

"I understand," he says.

Dad leads me to the benches opposite the courtroom door. He moves slowly and deliberately. He looks tired. It might be the first time that I have really looked at him and realized how tired he looks. Just like my emotion cards, down to the saggy under-eyes and drawn face. He lowers himself onto the bench, head in hands.

"Dad, are you stressed?" I ask now.

Dad looks at me and frowns. "I think so, son."

I nod and sit next to him. I put my hand on his back. This is what Brandon does for me. This is comfort.

Dad rests his head back in his hands. I tap my foot and wait.

Stress. My parents say it often. Being stressed. Maybe it is the heavy feeling in my stomach? There is no emotion card for stress. Distress, yes—that looks like panic and sadness mixed. Not stress, though. When I asked my speech therapist as a kid what stress looked like, she said it was something that you felt on the inside. That it was hard to explain.

The door to Brandon's hearing looms in front of me. All the answers are behind it. Mom says not to worry. She says it will all be over soon. So, why is it so hard to relax? Why do I feel like ants are crawling across my skin? Why does my body feel heavy? Why are my eyes prickling? Why do I feel stress?

One, two. Stop. One, two. Stop. Dad still has his face

buried in his hands. The healing and comforting should start soon. Soon, he will feel the love from my fingertips. What else should I do? I rub my hand up and down the length of his back. He does that when Mom is upset sometimes. I just do not usually . . . Usually. Oh, I forgot.

I wrap my arms around Dad and squeeze as tight as I can. Deep pressure. It took me too long to think of this. It is not easy—he is thicker than me—but I make it work. Brandon's arms are longer than mine. I wish he was here.

Dad's body quivers. His breath comes fast. I think he is crying. I have never seen him cry.

"Dad, are you—"

He reaches for me. Now his arms are around me. Now he squeezes me. But why am I shaking? Was I shaking this whole time? Is it because my foot is tapping? Is it still tapping? My face is all wet. My breath is shallow. My chest heaves. He squeezes tighter.

"You don't have to comfort me, son. It's okay. You don't have to be strong for me, Aiden." His whisper spreads through my veins.

Sobs claw their way from my throat. Low and yearning. It is the first time that I have cried since everything. Since Randy's. And Greg. And Louis. And Carter. And Reg. And Bernard. And the cops. And the hitting. And the blood. And the handcuffs. And the arguing. And the interrogation. And the lawyers. And the judges. And I have not gotten to cry. Nobody squeezed me. My body was all pent up and I just kept going and I did not get to cry. Nobody squeezed me.

I lower my head into my dad's chest, and his heart beats against my face. I count the rhythm. He rocks me. I count the rhythm until I know it by heart. His tears fall onto my cheeks. Sometimes they mix with mine.

We rock for sixteen rounds of his heart rhythm. I am still. He is still. No more shaking.

Then Dad holds me at arm's length and looks at my face like he has never seen it before. I wonder what he is looking for. I wonder if something in my face is new.

"Are you okay?" His voice rolls out thick like fog.

I do not know if I am. I nod anyway.

Dad looks me over. "Are you ready?"

I do not know if I am. I still nod anyway.

Dad smiles. "Okay." He pulls me into a standing position, and I lean into him, letting his weight steady me. "I've got you," he says now.

Nobody looks up as we enter the room. Brandon sits at the table with his lawyers, and Mom is on the bench right behind them.

Dad and I slide into the last bench by the door.

"—and with all this being presented, we would like to move forward with the formal charges and designations." One of the lawyers on the prosecution walks around and hands a paper to the judge. The judge reads over the paper in silence for one minute and twenty-eight seconds, then nods.

"Brandon Wright, please rise," the judge says.

Brandon and his lawyers stand.

"Though the defense presented a decent argument on

your behalf, there was not enough evidence to dismiss the charges against you," the judge says now. "Mr. Wright, you have formally been charged with assault against a peace official, resisting arrest, and trespassing."

Brandon's shoulders twitch and he shifts onto his right leg. He glances at his lawyers, who give him a quick nod.

It seems like they expected this, so I do not panic. Everything is fine. Everything is fine.

"Brandon, I must also inform you that the state has decided to utilize their right to discretionary direct file and charge you as an adult for the third-degree felony of assault against a peace official—"

Wait. What?!

"What?!" Brandon shouts.

Exactly.

"Order," the judge snaps.

Brandon turns to my mom, eyes wide. I cannot imagine what he is feeling, but I know what I am: Shock. Dismay. Nothing makes sense.

"Again, the state has decided to charge you as an adult. They have also asked for an expedited process, so we will reconvene next week for plea bargaining and arraignment. Thank you." The judge bangs his gavel and leaves. That is it. No sympathy, no mercy, no further explanation. This was cold and to the point, as though he were not handing down life-altering news.

The prosecuting lawyers pack up, avoiding eye contact with my mom, who goes to comfort Brandon.

Dad looks at me, his eyes glassy. I meet his gaze and the weight returns to my body, worse than before. Guilt seeps into every part of me until I am saturated in it. Everything was supposed to be fixed today.

Brandon stands and turns, finally seeing us. Even from across the room, I see the tears in his eyes. Mom notices us too, and she looks too tired to be angry. They walk up to us but do not speak for a moment.

"Let's go," Mom mumbles. Her voice lacks its usual strength. We make our way to leave the room.

Brandon freezes at the door. His lip trembles.

"Not now," Mom says. "Not here. Let's go."

Brandon looks at her, blinks back tears, and takes a deep breath. He nods and pushes the door open.

Dad and I follow Brandon and Mom out, and on our way out the door, I think I see Marcia's long black hair from down the hallway. I do a double take and she is gone. Great, now my brain is trying to distract me by creating people from nothing. Maybe I still have Georgia on my mind from the other day, so now I am conjuring Marcia. Anything not to think about what just happened.

We walk in silence. We drive in silence. All the way home.

Even in the car, Brandon does not cry. Not even an eye twitch since the courtroom. I think he should. I felt better once I did. I wonder why he cannot.

We shuffle through the doors in silence when we get home.

"Okay, Brandon," Mom says now. "Come." She reaches out her arms to my brother.

"Not here," Brandon says. "Not now." He walks past her, through the great room and up the stairs.

Mom's composed expression does not falter as she lowers her arms. "He needs time to figure things out for himself. It's a hard time." Her voice is still weak. I understand why.

I look from Mom to Dad. Dad keeps his eyes trained on the stairs.

Brandon seemed close to breaking down at the courthouse. Now, for the first time, something about him feels cold. I look at my mom, already busying herself taking meat out of the freezer to cook for dinner later tonight. Her expression still has not changed. I wonder if she feels the chill. I wonder if she thinks this is her fault. I wonder if it is.

Showing up to the library right after Brandon's hearing is overwhelming. I considered calling out, but I did not want that to be Hannah's or Adam's impression of me as a worker. I also did not want to let Isabella down and make her do the shift alone. I arrive at the library just as she is walking up, and she waves at me, her grin as wide as can be. I smile back.

"Ready to keep kicking butt as the best library assistant interns known to mankind?" Isabella punches the air and takes a karate-like stance.

I laugh despite myself. A part of me was determined to be in a bad mood, and I still might be, but I cannot deny the way that Isabella seems to brighten it.

I chew at my bottom lip, and my thoughts shift to Brandon. He was locked in his room when I left, and I was not sure if I should have bothered him by knocking to say goodbye.

"You okay?" Isabella asks, brows knitted together.

I nod. The news has not broken yet, or if it has, it has not reached her. It seems as though the more time passes since the incident at Randy's, the worse things get, like ripples in a pond. A rough point of impact, and then, from there, everything only grows larger and more distorted.

"I think so," I reply. I try to be honest without saying too much. I do not think I am quite ready to talk about everything yet.

Isabella frowns but doesn't push the topic, instead lacing her arm into mine. Her touch is warm against my skin and tickles the hairs on my arm. In our time together, I have become accustomed to it. It is no longer a surprise, and now I welcome it. She gives my bicep a light squeeze and I smile at her.

"I am okay," I say now.

"Promise?" Isabella asks, raising her brows at me.

"I cannot promise," I say, honest again. "But I can promise that we will have a great shift."

Isabella seems to vacillate between wanting to ask me more and accepting things for what they are. I see the struggle in her eyes and played out on her scrunched-up lips.

"I'm going to get more words out of you, you know that?" Isabella continues toward the front entrance, pulling me along with her.

"I am already way past my two-word quota," I reply.

Our bodies bump against each other as we walk in a way that is not unpleasant.

"Oh, you remember what we talked about when we first spoke. That means it was an important moment for you," Isabella says cheerily. She swings her free arm animatedly as she speaks and looks up at me expectantly.

I raise my eyebrows, ready to humor her. "Life-changing."

Isabella's face twists into something that teeters between laughter and horror. "Are you mocking me, Aiden?"

"Me?" I smile. "Never."

Isabella rolls her eyes in a way I can tell is lighthearted and pushes at my chest. "You're terrible at sarcasm, honestly."

As we cross the threshold into the cool foyer, Hannah is there to greet us. "Ready to get going?" she asks.

Isabella and I glance at each other before nodding in confirmation. Today, Hannah gives us a quick rundown of the filing system, how to use the scanners, and the purpose of the many utility carts by the desk. Our job is to pull books for people when asked and reshelve books, keep the various areas clean, answer minor questions, promote upcoming events, and try to get people signed up for library cards.

I am initially overwhelmed by all the responsibilities since we only observed on our first shift until I break it down in my head and remember that I do not have to do everything at once, just when the need arises. With that, I start to relax.

Isabella and I take two utility carts and scanners and head to the young adult section of the library, ready to file books back where they belong. As we scan, Isabella holds up various books and attempts to mimic either the pose of the person on the cover or their expression. We stifle laughter as we sort books for thirty minutes until she falls over due to a particularly tricky pose. That is when a snort escapes Isabella's nose, and we fight to calm ourselves while checking to make sure Hannah did not see.

A small part of me feels wrong because I very much want to take things seriously, while another part of me feels relieved because Isabella's antics help me stop overthinking and just do the work. In an effort not to get into any trouble after Isabella's unfortunate tumble, we get back to business. It is quiet work that eventually falls into a rhythm. Find the spot where the book belongs, scan, place, move to the next.

Still warmed by our silliness, Isabella and I work in a comfortable and happy silence. Every so often our fingers brush against one another as we reach for titles, and the silence is only broken when we stop to answer questions—mostly about the computers—for a few kids who are hanging out in the area. By the end of our two-hour shift, all the books are reshelved, and I feel satisfied with myself. We head to the staff room, clock out, and leave with praise from Hannah, who missed out on the hilarities at the beginning of our shift.

Outside, Isabella dawdles, flipping a key chain between her fingers. "I think we did a good job today," she says now. "Mishaps aside, it wasn't bad. What did you think?"

I shrug. It wasn't bad. She is right. Work was methodical and I didn't have to talk to very many people, but I found that there was something about it that I liked. Being with Isabella made the work easier, and she distracted me enough that I did not think about Brandon. Even now, though, I feel reality beginning to crash around me. After this, I will return home to the aftermath of the day. I do not think I am prepared for it.

"A shrug from you is high praise, so I'll take it as enjoyment," Isabella says with a grin.

My mom's car pulls around just as Isabella finishes her sentence, and her face falls ever so slightly. She almost looks disappointed by something, but I am not sure what. I wonder if maybe I did not show enough enthusiasm about us working together.

I rub the back of my head, twisting my locs between my fingers. "I had a great time," I say now. "Cannot wait for the next shift."

Isabella visibly brightens. "I hope to provide just as much entertainment the next time."

I laugh. "You are going to get us fired." I start toward the car.

Isabella stays put, watching me go. "You only live once, Aiden," she says. "Get fired or whatever." She giggles.

"Fail a class or whatever," I respond with a chuckle.

I wave and climb into the car. I watch Isabella in the side-view mirror the entire time we drive away.

"Is that your friend that Brandon mentioned?" Mom watches her in the mirror as well.

"Yeah," I say. "Something like that."

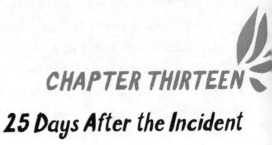

CHAPTER THIRTEEN

25 Days After the Incident

The news has been playing Brandon's face on repeat ever since he went back to court, pleaded not guilty, and officially started trial proceedings. Every news network is excited to report on the star quarterback in trouble, especially the sports networks. They run terrible headlines like "Fall from Grace" and "A Beast On and Off the Field." Meanwhile, nobody reports on what actually happened. Nobody reports on Brandon's bruised face, his still-blackened eye, and his bruised back and arms. They just sit and talk about scholarships and the upcoming trial. They just look serious for a few minutes, then smile and move on. I wish we could smile and move on too.

I grab an apple from a bowl on the counter and try to avert my eyes from the sports news network playing on mute on the television in the great room. I cannot hear what they are saying, but a clip of Brandon scoring a touchdown at the state championship his junior year plays while an analyst displays logos for schools. I do not need the sound to know that they are discussing his stock again. Discussing whether Brandon is still worth anything as a recruit. Discussing if schools will still want the problem kid.

Footsteps sound on the stairs and I turn the television off. It is Brandon.

He glances at the screen as soon as he enters the room, and air visibly leaves his chest. I cannot be sure, but I want to believe that this is relief.

NOTE: *It has been harder and harder to place Brandon's emotions on the standard cards lately.*

"Who's taking us to school today?" Brandon asks softly.

I shrug. The quiet downstairs is almost painful. Even Brandon speaks at almost a whisper.

Dad emerges from our parents' room, briefcase in hand, lab coat thrown over his arm. He's been leaving later to help Mom drop us off. "Ready, boys?" he asks.

"No," Brandon says now. Everything about him is flat. His tone, his face, everything.

"It'll be all right. You know how to handle it now, okay? Don't say anything. Ignore. Look ahead. When we drive by, don't look out the window. When you get to school, go straight inside. It'll be all right," Dad says.

Brandon nods. "Yeah, okay." His tone is the same. He does not sound convinced.

Outside, we drive past two reporters with cameras. Better than before, but I know we have yet to see what might be waiting at school.

"When are they going to back off?" Brandon asks. He seems almost angry.

"Well, things are only just getting started with trial proceedings. You just put in the plea. We still need to set a trial date. Right now, unfortunately, you're popular for some uncomfortable reasons. It will pass."

"The same way y'all said that this was all gonna work out?" Brandon says now. "That this was all gonna be over?"

Dad does not answer.

"It's gonna be worse at school," Brandon says.

He is cranky. He is cranky a lot now, which is not his typical mood. I would very much like to go back to when he was not this way all the time.

We are quiet the rest of the way and take our—now usual—evasive route to the teachers' parking lot to enter school without any reporters or cameras seeing. Brandon and I clamber out and run right into Georgia in front of the hallway.

"Brandon," Georgia says. She seems hopeful that he will stop and talk to her. Her eyebrows are raised, and she seems expectant.

I look at Brandon, searching for some cue about what to do. Should I stay? Should I leave?

Brandon looks at me and nods in the direction of the hall-way. I think that means go.

"I'll see you after school?" I ask.

Brandon nods.

I walk through the open doors that break up the hallway, but something makes me stop. I hide by the doors, out of sight. Georgia seemed strange the one time we spoke. Guilty somehow, maybe? I am unsure. I cannot place the emotion, but something was off. I want to know what is happening. It feels wrong to spy on Brandon, though. I hesitate, bouncing on my toes, ready to move at a moment's notice.

"What are you doing here?" Brandon asks now. This isn't the flat tone he has been using lately. This is harder, colder.

"I know you guys have been coming this way since things got kind of—" Georgia stops. "I've been wanting to talk to you."

"Not sure why you want to do that now," Brandon says.

"Because I care about you."

"And that care was where when everything first went down? You ain't even hit me up after I went to jail. Like, I actually went to jail, Georgia! Must not have given a shit once I wasn't the star no more."

"That's not it," Georgia says. Her voice is small, meek, apologetic.

"So what is it, then?"

"I was just dealing with something."

"Something more important than me going to jail?"

Georgia does not answer.

"Yeah, I thought so," Brandon says now. "Georgia, what's

really going on? I know you act superficial in front of every-body else, but I know you. I *thought* I knew you. You opened up to me. What's really going on with you? Because this ain't the person I said I wanted to be with."

"I know, Brandon. Look, I screwed up, okay? I just . . . ," Georgia says. "I should have reached out. I just got caught up with some stuff and I'm trying. I have been trying."

"What'd you get caught up with?" Brandon asks now.

A long pause.

"What'd you get caught up with, Georgia?"

"I can't tell you."

"You for real, Georgia?"

"I'm sorry, I can't," she says now.

"So why are you here? What did you stop me for?"

"I needed to talk to you. I wanted to tell you what's been happening. What people are saying."

"I don't give a shit what people got to say about me," Brandon says now.

"What about what they have to say about your brother?"

Silence.

"Everyone's saying you're going to jail for a long time. People are also saying that it's Aiden's fault. They're saying he sold you out to the cops or something."

Brandon snorts. "That's ridiculous as—"

"They're also saying that Aiden tried to kill Carter and that he should be arrested instead of you."

Brandon sighs. "Aiden would never try to kill anyone. And if anyone thinks that of my brother, then they're an idiot."

Georgia stays quiet.

"Did you think that?"

Georgia does not answer.

"You gon tell me what's been going on with you? Because this rumor mill convo ain't cutting it."

"No, Brandon. I can't."

"Well, I can't be with you," Brandon says now.

"Brandon, are you serious?" Georgia asks.

"So serious."

Footsteps sound in my direction, and I realize that I am in a corner with nowhere to go but forward. But if I go forward, Brandon will see me. But if I stay here, Brandon will also see me.

Shit.

Brandon comes down the hallway and almost walks past me, but four steps past the spot where I am standing, he turns on his heel.

Brandon narrows his eyes at me. "A, I told you to go," he says.

"I know."

He raises his eyebrows at me and gestures with his hands.

I frown. "Sorry, what?"

He sighs. "Why are you here, A? Why are you still here? I asked you to go and you're still here? That wasn't nothing that you needed to hear or know."

"I know. I am—"

Brandon holds up a hand. "Don't say sorry."

But I am. I stay quiet anyway.

"I just needed a minute to myself. A minute with my

girlfriend—ex-girlfriend. Just a minute! I needed a minute! You couldn't even give me that. You couldn't—"

I blink back tears. I do not know if I deserve this, but if it is coming from Brandon, I probably do. He only ever does right. He tries his hardest to be perfect. I am the problem. I got him into this.

I do not know what to say, so I do not speak.

Brandon closes his eyes. "I keep blowing up. I keep blowing up on people I care about. I keep going off and snapping at people."

Then he pulls me into a hug. I let him. I do not hug back. I am not ready.

"I'm not gon say sorry, A. I don't want you to feel like you gotta forgive me right now. I don't wanna put you on the spot. I do wanna say, I see how I'm acting. I'm taking my stress out in the wrong places and it's not right. It ain't cool that you eavesdropped, but I don't gotta talk to you like that either. You can forgive me on that when you ready. Okay?"

I nod. "Why did you break up with Georgia?" I ask.

Brandon frowns. "I'm gon be real with you, A. I think she's hiding something. I don't know what it is, and I don't know why, but something's giving me a bad vibe. I just don't feel like I can trust whatever she's saying to me, and I don't need that added stress right now. You know?"

"Yeah," I say now.

"Either way, I'm gon figure it out one way or another. Everything in the dark, or whatever."

"Everything in the dark what?" I ask.

Brandon smiles. "Everything done in the dark must come to the light, A. It means that if people plotting or doing dirt, it's always gon get exposed eventually. Just wait on it."

"What if it never comes to light? What if we have to go looking for it?" I ask now.

"Same destination, different journey, I guess." Brandon shrugs. "But I'm gon let the Georgia thing sit. I got other stuff to focus on. Anyway, I'm gon head to class. I'll see you later." He hugs me one more time, then disappears down the hallway without another word.

When I get to the locker room after school, Brandon is there, smiling.

"Good news or something?" I ask.

"Coach asked me to come by. I think he's finally gonna end my suspension, and honestly, I need that right now."

Greg walks up to us, and he and Brandon do their handshake. I am glad to see that they are still okay.

"My boy," Greg says now. "You gon be on the field today, Big-Time?"

"It's looking like it," Brandon replies. "Things starting to look up!"

"I can't catch the way I like to catch without my boy on the field throwing!" Greg says. He and Brandon bump fists.

Greg holds out a fist to me. "Aiden."

I bump fists. We are not close. We are not friends, but Greg has been polite even when Brandon was gone. Things with the team have still been tense, but I have Reg and Bernard at least. They have stayed close, they have walked with me to classes when they can, and they have even sat with me at lunch so I am not alone.

"And we trying out two new dudes today too, so you get to be here for that," Greg says.

"Oh, for real?" Brandon asks now.

"Yeah, one more backup QB spot and I think another receiver spot."

"Cool, cool," Brandon says. "I can't wait to show 'em the ropes. Arm been itching to get back out."

"I know that's right." Greg smiles. "I'mma go get dressed. I'll see you in there."

I smile too.

"Finally setting things right, huh?" Brandon says to me.

I nod.

"Let's go!" Brandon heads inside the locker room and I follow. He goes straight for Coach Davis's office, and I head for my locker.

I am mostly dressed when Brandon comes storming out of the coaches' offices. He punches a locker as he walks by.

"Aye, Brandon!" Greg calls out.

Brandon does not stop. He storms out of the locker room, and I follow. Greg tries to come too, but I hold a hand up and he stops.

Outside, Brandon paces back and forth, occasionally hitting the wall. Flecks of blood fly from his knuckles with each punch. I do not tell him to stop.

"Fuck!" Brandon screams into the clear afternoon air.

I do not speak.

"He kicked me off the team," Brandon yells. "He kicked *me* off the fucking team! Me! I did everything for this team. I finished a game with a sprained ankle. I played with a hairline clavicle fracture. I'm the number one quarterback in the—" He stops. He looks at me. Tears well up in his eyes. "I *was* the number one quarterback in the nation," he whispers.

My brother blinks and tears flow down his face. He swipes them away. "Not here," he says now.

"Why?" I ask.

Brandon stops and looks at me. "'Cause—I mean. Mom says—"

"Why not here?" I ask now.

Brandon's eyes fill with tears again.

"Why not now?"

Brandon's lip trembles.

I step closer to him.

"He kicked me off the team, A." Tears drip from his chin.

I wrap my arms around him.

Brandon stands and sobs freely at first, arms at his side, body heavy against mine. I hold him and squeeze. Then he hugs me back and the sobs come harder.

"I don't know what do, A," Brandon wails. "I don't know what to do. This is who I am. This is all I got. It's who I am. What do I do now? What do I do?"

I squeeze harder. I squeeze, and I rock, and I do not answer. No answer will be good enough.

CHAPTER FOURTEEN

25 Days After the Incident

I walk out of the locker room with my blue practice jersey thrown over my shoulder. Normally, Brandon would be next to me, singing "going up on a Tuesday," his favorite lyric for this day of the week. I want to keep my mind on him today. He deserves that much.

I pull my jersey over my head as I walk onto the field. I run my fingers along the mesh and savor the feeling. The tingle from the rough strands travels from my fingertips, up through the joints between each section of my fingers, until I can feel the texture all through my body, on my skin. I close my eyes and breathe.

After a few moments, I sit on my butt and stretch my legs straight out in front of me. The grass is wet underneath me, but I am not surprised. It rained all morning and the lingering clouds threaten more moisture, but practice will still happen even if the sky opens up and dumps its contents down on us. Games happen in rain; therefore, so does practice. I reach forward to touch my toes, letting my back extend, and try to focus on breathing and not feeling as angry as I am so often now. I want to think about practice and the fact that we are trying out two new players, but all that is on my mind is my brother and the fact that everyone else involved, even me, still gets to be on this field.

Instead of thinking about my anger, I go over drills and plays in my head. Cut drills, hand drills, maybe we will work with practice dummies, maybe we will do matchups against other players, maybe we will do single back formation, maybe we will do I-formation, maybe . . .

Another deep breath. Focus. After two more stretches, a few more guys come out onto the field in yellow practice jerseys. Peter, red hair shining in the light, leads the pack.

NOTE: *Peter played Jesus for a Christmas play once when I was six. He is a junior, like me.*

Two guys trail behind Peter. One is a lanky boy with dark skin and a brush cut whom I recognize as a senior, like Brandon, but I do not know his name. And Josiah, a head shorter than both Peter and the lanky guy. His long, straight, silt-colored hair lifts slightly as he walks. Must be new recruits. They walk straight toward me. I grab onto the goalpost, holding my right leg in my hand behind my back, stretching my quad.

"Hey," Peter says now. "Is it true Brandon got kicked off the team?"

"You have never spoken to me before," I reply.

Peter presses his lips together.

That was blunt. I know. I am not unaware. I just do not care.

"Sorry," Peter mumbles.

I drop my right leg and switch to my left to stretch my other quad. I do not answer. Not all apologies require a response. And not all apologies require forgiveness. The guy with the brush cut steps forward and drops onto the grass. He starts leaning forward and stretching his hamstrings. The guy with the long hair follows. We stretch in silence as more people file out of the locker room.

Once the field fills up, a mix of blue and yellow jerseys mill around on the grass. The offense members of the team gather in blue practice jerseys, and Reg, the now-starting quarter-back, wears a red practice jersey; his coily black 'fro bounces as he runs across the field. He waves at me. I wave back.

The defense, in yellow jerseys, lines up together, facing the boys on offense as we wait for the coaches. Greg, Carter, and Louis are all on my side of the field in blue jerseys. Greg finds his way over to me and keeps close by, quiet but present, stretching with his headphones in. Carter, as always since the fight, stays separate from us, and Louis—surprisingly—has been staying away from everyone altogether. Louis casts glances over at me and Greg every so often. I wonder if everyone is feeling guilty about Brandon. As I scan the crowd for the new players, Carter meets eyes with me briefly. My stomach bubbles and aches. My neck burns and it feels like my blood is rushing faster than normal. I feel angry, irritated, and nauseous all at once. My breath quickens and I close my eyes. I try to slow my breathing, but focusing on my breath is not helping. The threat of tears burns at my eyes. What is going on?

I tap my thigh in my familiar rhythm. My fingers shake as I tap, hands unsteady and rushing with too much blood. One, two. Stop. One, two. Stop. One, two. Stop. I focus on the rhythm. Breathe with each pause. A few more taps and my breath comes slower. I open my eyes. I look everywhere but at Carter. I do not know what that feeling was, but I do not want to feel like that again.

Coach Davis walks onto the field flanked by the two assistant coaches. Coach Nielson's pot belly pokes out ahead of him as he walks, and Coach McDonald trails behind them both.

Coach Davis stops in front of the two groups and claps twice. His muscles are obvious even through his shirt. He is the complete opposite of Coach Nielson, and yet they were both on this field once, just like Brandon and me. It makes me wonder what Coach Nielson was like in his prime. I know he used to be a running back. I consider how Brandon calls me his *very* wide receiver because I have always been stocky compared to his lankiness. Will I look like Coach Nielson one day, or more like Coach Davis, who was a quarterback? Are our trajectories set? Will we be like them? Will we play a little college ball and settle down as high school coaches, bringing up the next generation and having the privilege to recreate our glory days? Or will it end here for Brandon? Will he have any glory days to recreate?

"All right, y'all!" Coach Davis looks around. He smiles a large, toothy smile and rubs his hand through his long blond hair. "It's business as usual today, but I think we need to address the elephant in the room. Some of you may have already heard that our longtime star quarterback is no longer on the team." He takes a moment to look at everyone. "I know this isn't easy on anyone, even me. We've all been on a team with him for years, some of you longer, since Pop Warner. This is hard, but this decision was made in his best interest so that he could focus on the things shifting in his life, and we have to remember that Brandon would want us to keep pushing and keep winning, so that's what we're going to do!"

I look around, and the guys do not react.

Coach Davis clears his throat. "The offense is officially moving forward with our next up, Reg, who has been a great second-string for three years and has held us down during our past two games. I know we're in good hands. Let's clap it up for our new quarterback!"

I clap out of friendship for Reg, but only half the team follows suit. The field does not have the same energy it did last week. How can it, when Brandon is officially gone?

Coach Davis frowns. "Don't forget, after practice we are filling out ballots for new team captain, all right? We'll pick before the next game," he says now. "All right, so let's go ahead and get started. We missed yesterday, so we are going to do some conditioning before practice today! To the weight room, boys!" He claps twice, then turns, and we file in line behind him.

New team captain. The energy shift is almost immediate. I can tell that everyone simultaneously wants and does not want to fill Brandon's shoes. Without him, something feels empty, and I know I am not the only one feeling it. Everyone shuffles around, eyeing each other nervously, and it is quieter than normal. We quickly do some conditioning, then move back to the field to start practice formations.

"Offense to me!" Coach Nielsen calls, and we huddle around him. "All right, I want you guys in I formation. I want Watkins, Perez, Hilton, Franco, Wright, Daniels, Pierre, Dune, Williams, Ashley, and Mosley on the field. McDonald is likely to set up 4-3 or 5-3 defense, so be ready for that."

I jog onto the field just as rain starts to drizzle from above. I have to get this right. Brandon is not here to vouch for me anymore now that he is off the team, and I cannot prove Carter right. I cannot have everyone thinking that I am only here because of my brother. I need them to see that I have every right to be on this field. I know this formation. I have practiced it with Brandon forty-seven times.

Coach Kapoor, one of the position coaches, sets up the line of scrimmage on the twenty-yard line. The center, Francisco Perez, lines up on the ball. Perez has two offensive linemen to each side of him, his guards closest to him, and his tackles to the outside. Perez sets up to snap the ball to Reg. Reg lines up behind Perez, Bernard lines up behind Reg, and I line up behind Bernard. We form the *I* in the formation.

The defense sets up. I check the lineup and see that it is a 5-3 formation. They are ready for a run play, and I have to find a way through. I wait for the whistle. The coaches are not looking for us to knock each other's heads off—they are testing our awareness and skill in real-time situations. They are looking to see how fast I can find holes in the defense and push through to score.

My eyes are everywhere. Dustin lines up at tight end on my left, which means I need to find a hole in that direction. The receivers are lined up to the outside, just in case I cannot make the play. I pay attention to how everyone on defense is positioned, and I notice that Carter is lined up as safety on defense instead of as wide receiver like usual. That means I will have to play against him. I take a deep breath. Focus on the play, not him.

At the whistle, Reg gets the ball from the center and Bernard pushes forward to create a space for me. Reg steps back and twists, so I run forward and grab the ball. Bernard blocks a linebacker, and a hole opens in the defense. I push forward. The other two linebackers come at me. I rush through the hole with my arm extended, then push down one of the line-backers and spin around the other. The goal line is the focus. In my peripheral vision, Dustin misses a block and whoever got through is coming after me, so I push more, willing myself to speed up. Then, a clip at my heels, a tackle at the back of my legs. I come down hard. I tuck the ball, hanging on tight as the ground comes up to meet me, and curl around the ball.

I roll over to see who is keeping a death grip on my legs.

The same heat and nausea rise up from my stomach and I kick away from his grip when I realize it is Carter. He pops up from the ground and towers over me.

"The hell is your problem! What are you kicking for? You're always acting so weird! If you can't handle the game, then go!" he screams down at me.

I plant the ball on the damp grass and rise up from it. Now I am standing. Now I am looking down at Carter. The air in my nose is warm and wet. I let it fill my chest—expand it.

"You planning on doing something?" Carter's voice is low. He only wants me to hear. "Do it."

I bend down and clutch the football. I imagine the leather splitting under the pressure of my fingers, the air streaming out with a whistle and a pop, the ball deflating to nothing from just my touch. I feel it all at once, every bump, every notch, every ridge along the ball. I glare at Carter, but instead of seeing him, I visualize the ball. Spiking it, planting it, popping it. My jaw tightens—my teeth grind in my ears.

"First down," I say through clenched teeth. The ball pushes back underneath my grasp.

"Wright!" Coach Nielsen calls for me. I look in his direction. Almost everyone on the sideline is watching.

I turn from Carter, jog to the sideline, and toss the ball to Coach Nielsen. I do not speak.

"Next play!" Coach Davis nods in our direction and goes back to tapping away on his tablet.

We huddle together again.

"All right, same play, but this time, Dustin, I need to see

some real hustle. That block was an easy one. You left Aiden open from behind, and that's why he got clipped. Most teams are going to run a 5-2 or 5-3 defense. We have to be ready for them to try and stop the run play," Coach Nielsen says now.

The breath in the huddle is hot and moist. Mist settles on my skin as the drizzle picks up intensity. We break and start back toward the field.

"You're faster than Carter. You got more field IQ," Reg calls to me. "You got it this time for sure!"

I furrow my brow but nod. It is strange to get acknowledgment on my game from someone other than Brandon. I am grateful for it. It bolsters my confidence.

We set the formation again. I do not look at Carter this time. I focus on feet. I see where everyone is lined up. The whistle blows, and we are moving. Beads of water fly up from the grass as our cleats dig into the terrain. The rain falls harder now, creating a steady rush. A light pounding in my ears. A rhythm to follow. I rush forward, and Bernard sets up an opening. I possess the ball. I am through the hole. I focus on feet. A pair steps toward me, I juke around them, arm out. My gloved hand slips against a slick face mask, and I push hard. Keep rushing. Focus on feet. A pair to my left. I hold my arm out and keep going. The feet do not catch me. I am over the line. The whistle blares.

Feet rush up to meet me. Hands clamp down on my back and helmet. The thunderous rhythm of their approval makes me happy instead of anxious.

"I didn't know you were that fast, Aiden!"

"Good hustle, A!"

"Let's get this work!"

Someone throws their body against my side. I almost stumble, but I catch and steady myself. I look up. It is Bernard. He holds out his hand expectantly. I hesitate for a second, then reach my hand out. He reaches back and slaps my hand three times.

"That's what I'm talking about!" Bernard yells.

I smile.

Bernard claps me on the back and turns me around. All this encouragement is nice. It will never replace Brandon, but the feeling that I am included instead of apart is amazing. We jog back to the sideline together.

The next play is easy. I focus on feet. I get passed the ball. I run forward, then a hit to my right side knocks me off-balance. My ribs burn from the impact of shoulder pads to bone. The world twists around me as I roll through the grass, tumbling after the hit. It is a clean hit. It is okay. I pop up. Look at the grass. Focus on feet.

Then, a voice near me. Quiet enough for only me to hear. "You needed that wake-up call. You don't belong on this field, fucking spaz. Only a matter of time before you show everybody who you are."

I close my eyes. This is Carter. The same Carter who whined until he was allowed to blow out everyone else's birthday candles when we were little. The same Carter who squealed and had his mom lock the car doors—with Brandon and me inside—at a gas station on the way back from the park, because a man two shades darker than my brother, but lighter than me, walked by. The same Carter who is on this team while my brother is not. I would know his voice anywhere.

I bite my lip until I taste metal and salt. Ignore it. Ignore it. Take a step. I picture my foot rising, knee bending, heel lifting from the ground, body propelling forward to the sideline. I picture myself at the ready, hands open, eyes scanning the field, prepared for the next play. I picture my lips pressed together, tongue still, throat clenched. Silent.

I wish I could always do what I visualize.

"Fuck you, Carter," I say now.

Carter laughs derisively. "Yeah, it's 'fuck me,' but at least I didn't get my own brother arrested and kicked off the team because I can't handle being a normal person. Now we won't get to States because of you."

My eyes open. Carter's helmet is in the grass, probably knocked off during the play. My heart pounds in my ears as I look up, straight into his cold blue eyes.

"The only spaz that got my brother arrested and kicked off the team was you," I say through clenched teeth. My stomach churns, and vomit gathers in my throat. The back of my tongue pushes down the sour liquid.

Carter's nostrils flare and he pushes me hard in the chest. "Take that shit back!" he yells.

He shifts, and I know a punch is coming, but I beat him to it. I swing out with my right hand, fist connecting with his jaw. The pain splinters in my knuckles, but I ignore it as I cock my other hand back. The wind almost whistles around my left fist as it comes down again on Carter's face, and every punch that connects makes me feel a little less nauseous, a little less jittery, a little less breathless. Now Carter's fists are coming at me. Punches land on my side. I duck as he throws a punch at my head. Should have let him hit my helmet.

Then someone yanks me back and my helmet flies off. Voices boom around us, but I fight to get back to Carter. I am numb all over. My skin is stone. I feel nothing. I just want to keep punching. I want to keep punching until all the bad feelings are gone.

Someone taps at my face, but all I can see is Carter. I windmill my arms even though he is not in my reach. I scrabble to get out of the grips of all the hands around me, frustrated at the restriction. Anger surges under my skin, but I feel disconnected from my body. I am lost within my emotions, drowning in them, letting them consume me. Everything burns and my nerve endings are fried. Hands are on me, and I can't feel them. There is only the anger.

"Wright!" A yell directly in my left ear catches my attention.

I turn. It is Coach Davis. He grabs my face in his hands, and I stop swinging. Water drips from my chin. My throat is ragged. Tears mingle with sweat and rain in one big, salty mess.

"Aye, aye, look at me," Coach Davis says now. He looks me directly in the eye. I stare him down.

My blood is hot. It is running too fast in my veins. My breath is coming too fast. I just want to keep swinging, but I do not. My energy is spent, though the anger bubbles just under the surface.

"You're going to waste all the time your brother spent convincing me to let you on this team, huh?"

I try to turn my head to look for Carter, but Coach Davis turns my head back to face him. My eyes keep searching.

"You hearing me?" he yells in my face.

Air whistles from my nose and my chest heaves. I try to count my breath to calm down. I reach thirty-two, when my heart no longer pounds in my ears, before I finally look back at Coach Davis and nod.

"Good! Now! Are you going to waste your brother's time and my time? Yes or no?" He looks at me expectantly.

I do not bother to blink away the tears. My body begins to vibrate with emotion as the anger fades and something else sets in. I cannot quite place what I am feeling, what the anger is morphing into. I shake my head.

Coach Davis lowers his voice so only I can hear him. "I know it's hard right now, but you have to be better than this. What you're doing right now, it's what everybody expects from you. You want to be what everybody expects?"

I want to shake my head. I want to say no and go with it. I want to do what is going to get me on the team, but just past Coach Davis's head, Coach Nielsen walks Carter back toward the locker room with an arm around his shoulder.

NOTE: *An arm around the shoulder typically signifies comfort.*

> • *Carter is being comforted. I am getting yelled at.*

No.

"What about what everybody expects from him?" I murmur.

"What?" Coach Davis asks. He seems genuinely confused.

"What about what everybody expects from *him*?" I yell, and point at Carter. I shake out of Coach Davis's grip, and he reaches for me again but I pull away.

Coach Nielson and Carter stop walking and turn to watch.

"Nobody touch me!" I shout as hands approach me. "I am not gonna go after him. But what about him? Why is nobody worried about him? Why is it all on me? Big, scary autistic kid with big, scary tantrums! But what about him?" I point at Carter.

Coach Nielson looks at me and Carter looks at the ground.

"*He* is a damn problem! He is a problem, and nobody notices it because there is no diagnosis for it. Or is it just because he is the right color to get ignored? Which is it? You all talk about what you expect from me, but *he* got my brother arrested. He did that! You would still have your quarterback if *he* was not a problem. What about that shit, huh?"

Rain drenches me and I shiver—cold to my core—but I know it is not the weather. The initial anger has cooled, but a new kind of rage builds, a controlled wrath, a pointed fury. My frustration finds form, and in it, I feel satisfaction. Water droplets drip from my eyelashes and trickle down my lips. In this moment, I think of Brandon. I think of us in the car, watching raindrops race on the window, oblivious to the world flying by beyond. We can never go back to that—ignorant of what the world around us will bring. I can never go back, not after this. Not after all we have both been through. I will never be innocent and oblivious again. I will also never again be silent.

Coach Davis stays quiet and refuses to meet my eyes. I look around and everyone turns their face away. Now only Carter looks at me. His lip is bleeding. I feel better just seeing that.

"If you are only letting me stay on this team as a favor to my brother, then keep it," I say to Coach Davis. "I want to earn it. I want to deserve it. I do not care what anyone expects. I do not like to be touched all the time. I do not like to talk. I do not do crowds and eye contact. I can hear bugs chittering in the trees and sometimes it is louder than the voices right in front of me. Sandpaper calms me and velvet makes my bones shiver. I do not love everything, but I love football. I love seeing the field from a bird's-eye view even while I am standing on it. I love watching a linebacker shift on the turf and knowing where he will be in two seconds. I love knowing exactly where the holes will open on the defense just by looking at everyone's feet. If I gotta pretend to be somebody else, if I gotta pretend to be good with everybody and everything, and dealing with this bullshit to play the game, though, it is not worth it."

I turn and head toward the locker room. If anyone speaks, I do not hear them. I storm past Carter, daring him to say something. He does not. Inside, I walk straight to the back corner locker where I stashed my clothes, pull my jersey off, and toss the wet mesh cloth on the floor. I need to get changed.

A creak and slam of wood-on-wood alerts me that someone

else is entering the locker room. The footsteps move away from me. Good, whoever it is, he is not in here to bother me. Then the steps get louder—now they are headed this way. I close my eyes and let out a sharp breath through my nose. It had better not be Carter.

"Wright." Coach Davis stops directly to my left, at the end of the aisle, between the back wall of the room and the last row of lockers. He walks toward me and sits on the nearest bench.

I stay standing, hanging on to my exposed shoulder pads and staring at the speckled linoleum tile underfoot.

"I can't say that I'm happy with how you acted on the field just now, Wright." Coach stares at the lockers in front of him instead of at me. "I will say, though, that I understood where you were coming from." He crosses his arms and lets out a heavy breath. "It's not easy on us here, without Brandon. I can't pretend that we feel what you and your family are feeling, but I can tell you that if what we're feeling is a fraction of it, then I know you're hurting bad."

I tap at my shoulder pads and listen. One, two. Stop. One, two. Stop.

"Even so, fighting isn't the way to deal with this. If you remember, that's what got all this mess started in the first place," Coach Davis says now. He frowns a bit, but he does not seem unhappy. He seems . . . apprehensive? I cannot tell.

I close my eyes. Blood rushes in my ears and all sound is muffled. I shake my head to clear it.

"I know it's not what you want to hear, but that's what

it is. That goes for you and Carter both. If fighting started it, how is fighting gonna fix it?"

"Did you ask Carter that?" I ask now. I look at him as I speak. I have never spoken to him this way. I have never spoken to any adult this way—it is just not how I was raised—but my rage fuels me in a way I have not felt before. It gives me a bravery that is new to me.

Coach purses his lips. "Not yet, no."

"You are dealing with me only?"

"I plan to talk to him next," Coach Davis says. He shifts and glances at his feet for a second as he speaks.

"The night we fought, the night Brandon got arrested, the cops did not tackle Carter. He never got handcuffed. He did not get beat up. Neither did Louis," I say.

"He had a bloody lip," he responds.

"That was from our fight—he had the bloody lip before the cops got there."

"Well, Louis was not fighting."

"Neither was Greg, but half his face got bruised up anyway," I say now. "Reg and Bernard got tackled too. I still have bruises on my sides."

Coach Davis unfolds his arms and leans sideways against the locker. "What point are you trying to make, Aiden?"

"None. I am just asking questions. Carter and Louis got treated with kid gloves by the same cops that beat up me and Greg and accused Brandon. Why?" I strain my throat, forcing my voice to stay below a certain volume. My neck hurts from the effort.

"Well, I would guess—" He starts.

"Don't blame autism." I stare Coach down. The bravery is still pushing me forward.

He looks at me for a second, then runs his hand through his blond hair.

"Why did Coach Nielson walk Carter back with a comforting arm around his shoulder while I got yelled at in front of everyone?" I ask.

Coach Davis does not answer.

"It is because you are all white, right?"

"Now, hold on, Aiden," Coach Davis says, frowning deeply. He rubs the back of his head and his eyes shift, as though looking for a way out.

"My mom used to try to explain racism to me when I was younger," I say. "It was confusing then, and it still is now, but she used to call something obvious the elephant in the room. You said it earlier too. The elephant in the room. I never understood that. I used to picture an elephant standing in the middle of our house, too big to turn left or right, too cramped to raise its trunk, until all it could do was stampede forward, blowing a hole through the walls and destroying everything. I get it now. That is how this feels. Everybody is talking about everything else, but nobody is talking about what this is. My mom has been talking about this since before I could understand, but everyone calls me oblivious. Right now, I am either the only one that sees it or the only one that is saying it. The cops that night were white. Carter is white. You are white. Coach Nielson is white. The parents of half the players on this team who comment under news stories and videos of Brandon getting arrested and blame him for what happened—they are white."

"And what are you trying to say, Aiden? That we're all racist? We all just sit around and conspire against you kids? Come on now, son. This is a good town. A tight-knit town. We're all family out here, you know that. You have all been family. We've gone to pumpkin patches in the fall together, and I was one of the first people to call your brother after—" Coach Davis stops short. He stands and rocks back on his heels. "Aiden, what you're saying isn't fair, and I think you know that."

"It does not need to be fair to be true," I say now.

Coach does not acknowledge this. "I didn't come back here to argue with you about this."

"Then why did you come back here?"

"Look, a team is a family. Families don't always get along, but the boys on the field are brothers. Brothers fight. Does that mean they should? No, but they will. As coaches, we know that. We expect that. Football is a rough game, and this is a tougher time than usual for this team. Still, we're family. That means even during conflict we stick it out together."

I stare at the University of Florida pin on Coach Davis's lanyard as he speaks. Will Brandon ever get to go?

He waits for me to respond. I do not. I am out of things to say, but it seems as though Coach is not done with his appeal. I consider what he has said so far, and I think of what I know about families, but the only thing I have to compare it to is my own. My family has never been like this. We have been better. Can this team be better?

"What I'm saying, Aiden, is that I'm considering you a part of this family. That's why I'm back here."

"I cannot be a part of a family that does not treat everyone equally," I say.

Coach Davis nods. "That's true, and that's fair. Aiden, I can't claim that we're perfect. I can't claim that it all boils down to race, either. There's a lot happening right now. The other coaches already know Carter—that could be a factor."

I had not thought of that.

"There might even be some people who expect negativity from you after that other fight at the diner—"

"Carter started that," I interject.

Coach holds his hand up. "I hear you, but we weren't there, and of course we only got Carter's side, so that might be a factor."

"And whose fault is that? Why has no one asked about my side?" I ask.

"That's a fair question and something we need to examine," Coach Davis says. "Carter came to us about it right away and we took his word as law, but we shouldn't have done so. I can see your side. We didn't ask enough questions. That could be a factor."

I nod, happy that this is being acknowledged.

"And we're both being honest here, so I can openly say your disability might also be a factor. The meltdown you had this summer during tryouts—you lashed out at a few people.

Coach Nielsen was one of them. That could be a factor."

I knew that.

"So, I can't say it all comes down to race, but I also can't say that it's not a factor among many other factors. I also can't say that it doesn't matter. And I can't expect you to trust a team as your family if we don't address those problems to make you feel like family."

I glance up at Coach Davis. His eyelids hang low. Is he sad?

"If I have in any way made you feel less than, Aiden, I'm sorry. If any of the other coaches have made you feel the same way, I apologize for them, and I know they'll be willing to apologize themselves. There's tension right now, but a lot of what you've said has made me consider what we've done to address it. The truth is, we haven't done enough. Now, I'm willing to fix that if you are, because you have the talent, Aiden. You do. And I still have hesitation—I can't pretend that I don't—not just about you, but about Carter, too. I'm willing to look past my own misconceptions to see you as more than that, and go further to accept your differences and take you as you are, not as what we think you should be."

Coach reaches up and rubs the back of his head. "Honestly, if fights didn't happen at damn near every practice, I'd probably write you both off right now, but I'm giving you a chance to choose to really be a part of this family. Being a part of it means that you can be pissed, and you can have it out with your brothers, but you don't leave the field. You guys start shit together on the field, you get punished together on the field, you ride out your punishment together on the field, and you move on." He straightens up and crosses his arms. "Before, we wouldn't let you on the team, but now you've got a choice. You can put on your jersey, come back out, and do striders for the rest of practice as punishment for fighting with the rest of your team, or you can leave. I won't stop you either way." Coach shrugs at me.

"Talentwise, though, you were one of the best out there today. You read movements faster than anyone else on the field, you adjusted to changes quick, and your observation skills helped you make great decisions on the fly," Coach Davis says. "You may have reservations, but this is the same team your brother called his. I can't fix every problem you presented to me, but I sure can think about things and start to try. Can you give me that chance if I'm giving you this one?"

I do not speak. I look up at the back wall. Three state championship banners adorn the walls—a reminder of what kind of team this is. I waited for so long to be a part of it, and now the choice is mine. In some ways, I am in a more powerful position than I have ever been in. It is not what I expected, but most things never are. My dream came with flaws. Now it is up to me to decide whether I am willing to accept those flaws with the hope that we can get to a better place. I have to decide if I can trust my coach and my teammates to be more. I have to decide if I still want this, even though it does not look the way I thought it would. And if I still want it without Brandon.

"I'm in the business of building a great team, Aiden. We've

lost your brother, and he was the cornerstone of our offense."

I consider the fact that Brandon is gone because of him and the other coaches. I want to ask how much he truly wanted to make that call, but I do not. I am unsure if I will get an honest answer. Or maybe I am afraid of the answer I might get.

"Starting over with a backup quarterback is going to be tough, but if I can secure the run game with the best I can find—and right now I think that's you—then we may be able to defend our district title, maybe even our state title," Coach Davis says now, his tone shifting to something more hopeful. "That's my focus as athletic director and head coach, all the other drama aside. So, are you going to get out on that field and be a part of this team?"

I hesitate. The speech is a good one, but I do not know if Coach Davis will really think more on anything I have said. I do not know if anything will be fixed. Carter is still a problem too. The truth is, it does not feel like enough, *but* this is what Brandon wanted for me. He fought for me to be on this team. This is also what I wanted, even if it does not look as perfect as I have always pictured it. I do not know whether leaving or staying is a betrayal to Brandon. I do not know what the right thing is anymore. Now it comes down to me deciding for myself.

"You said you wanted this to be about your talent, Aiden. Well, it is. What do you think?"

That is what I said. I wanted to earn my place on this team, and I did.

I chew at my bottom lip. I do not know if what I am deciding will make Brandon happy. I do not know what comes next or if it will make me happy. But I do know that for once I am being seen for my abilities and nothing else. For once, my talent is at the forefront.

I nod.

"Even if that means working with Carter?" Coach asks now.

I stare back up at the banners, then back at Coach Davis, and nod again. I want to be a part of this legacy too. I want to be able to say that I got here and I did great things. I want to be able to look back and say that I tried.

He smiles at me and nods in return. "That's all I can ask."

I grab my jersey from the floor and pull it over my head and pads. Coach Davis claps me on the shoulder, shaking my pads underneath my jersey, and we jog out the double doors and onto the field together.

I ignore the pang of guilt broiling in the pit of my stomach as I run back out to the team without my brother, but I know that this is something that I cannot change. I cannot change Carter. I cannot change Brandon being on the team. I cannot change anything that has happened before now. I may not be able to change what happens to Brandon in the future, but right now, the rain is not falling, and the sky is clearing as I jog out into the brassy glow of the evening as the sun lingers above the horizon. It feels like something is shifting.

CHAPTER FIFTEEN

25 Days After the Incident

I linger after practice, puttering around, not wanting to go home and settle into Brandon's grief about the team. Also, not wanting to deal with the stress of the trial after all the tension on the field today. I already stim more than usual at home these days. I need time to myself, but I do not even have work as a valid excuse to avoid home today. I stow my practice gear, shower, and walk out of the locker room with no purpose or destination in mind.

I walk through the school, watching my feet swing until someone calls my name.

"Aiden!"

I turn, and Isabella runs up to me, smiling. I am surprised she is still here so late.

"Hey!" she says now. "What are you still doing here?"

I tap at my thigh. How do I explain that I do not want to go home? "Just finished football practice."

"Shouldn't that have been done a little bit ago?" Isabella asks.

"Yeah," I reply. I hope the answer is enough for now.

She nods slowly. "Well, I just finished with robotics club. Wanna hang for a little bit since you're around? I barely see you outside of Life Skills or work anymore."

"Sure," I say. Anything to not go home. And besides, Isabella is always nice to be around.

She and I walk around the back of the school, toward the portables. The sky is a purplish orange, and the post-downpour clouds are still splitting, casting streams of light as the sun buries itself beneath the skyline. I glance over to Isabella and the light catches her eyes, giving them a pretty caramel glow.

"So, what's up? I know things have been really weird since the plea—I heard about the trial. We haven't gotten a chance to talk about it and stuff. You've been busy," Isabella says.

Busy. That is a word for it. "Yeah," I say now. "All of this probably would not have been made into such a big deal if Brandon was not who he is. It is funny—sometimes, cameras came to big events because he was the top recruit in the nation, but it was never like this. This feels like everyone is just waiting for something bad to happen."

"That might be the most I've ever heard you say at once." Isabella's face is grim.

I give her a small smile. "It has been on my mind, I

suppose. Brandon being tried as an adult changes everything. The consequences are worse, and the outcome of this trial is going to drastically alter his life. If he is guilty, I do not know what his sentence will be, but I know it will be bad. I do not know what to do."

"And it's fair to be a little lost right now, to be honest. I don't know, though. I guess it sucks that we only ever see how things turn out and not every outcome, right? Almost makes you wish you could see the future to know how all our choices would turn out," Isabella says now.

I shake my head. "I would hate to know all my choices. I think I would still choose wrong."

"What's right and wrong is subjective," Isabella says. "You can't ever really choose wrong if you feel it's what's best for you at the time."

I stop walking. We stand between two portables, watching the final vestiges of light flicker away. Isabella rocks back and forth on her heels and chews on her bottom lip.

"But what about the consequences? Does it matter whether I feel like the choice is right if the consequences are bad?" I ask.

"I guess that's a different conversation, right? What if you get a good consequence from a bad choice? Does that make the choice good? I don't know," Isabella says now. "But what I do know is that we can only do what we can, because we're humans who can't see the future, even if *some* of us wish we could."

I smile. "Thank you," I say now. Talking to Isabella does not fix the lingering heaviness that weighs on me, but it does make me feel a bit better. She sees things through such rose-colored glasses that it is difficult not to do the same, even when everything is falling apart.

Isabella laughs. "Not sure what I did, but you're absolutely always welcome!"

I smile and we walk a little farther, our sides bumping lightly as we move.

"—can't believe you did that!" Someone's voice cuts through the air.

"Who is that?" Isabella whispers. "Crap, can we be back here at this time?"

I shrug. I genuinely am not sure. I have never stayed at school this late before. I peek around the portable and Isabella follows suit.

Georgia and Marcia stand facing Tucker, who is backed up against an adjacent portable. Weird, I did not realize that they all knew each other. Tucker never struck me as the type to follow after the cheerleaders.

"Tell me you deleted it!" Georgia snaps, and pushes Tucker in the chest. "You better have deleted it!"

Tucker does not answer. He seems disinterested, especially considering the vitriol in Georgia's voice. I cannot see the girls' faces from here, but Georgia's tone is enough. Tucker almost looks bored, as though this is not his first time dealing with Georgia acting this way.

"Ugh! I swear you're impossible sometimes!" Georgia throws her hands up in the air.

"Hey, relax. This isn't necessary," Marcia says. She turns,

and I can see her face now. She looks concerned, maybe for Tucker. She glances over her shoulder as though she is afraid of being caught, but she does not see me.

"Seriously? You think this isn't necessary? Marcia, this is life-ruining. Like, I am not even trying to be funny with how life-ruining it is. Brandon already broke up with me because of this, and he doesn't even know about it!"

Brandon? I turn to Isabella and her brows furrow. She nods at me in what I know is an unspoken agreement for us to stay and listen. I heard my brother's name. There is no way I am leaving now.

"If he doesn't know about it, how could he break up with you for it?" Tucker asks now. His tone is matter-of-fact, as though he is pointing out something very obvious.

"Oh, *now* you answer!" Georgia rolls her eyes.

"Relax, GiGi," Marcia says.

Georgia sighs. "Tucker, I just want to know if you deleted it, okay? Because I will personally go into your room and smash every camera you own until you give me an answer."

"That wouldn't help," Tucker says now.

"You're determined to ruin my life. That's what this is. You, like, hate me as a sister, and you want to ruin me. Is that it?" Georgia asks.

Georgia is Tucker's sister? Why did I not know that?

"No," Tucker replies. "I never said that."

"Like, I know you had your camera out," Georgia says accusingly.

"That doesn't mean that he was recording," Marcia says,

trying to keep the peace. "And even if he was, it doesn't matter. It doesn't mean anything is going to happen with the video, GiGi. You have to calm down."

"What do you mean?" Georgia asks.

"Because the only people who know are us. And Tucker knows that the video is important for several reasons if he *does* have it. Right?" Marcia looks at Tucker.

He does not answer. What video are they talking about, and what does it have to do with Brandon?

"Look, it matters to me, too, but we're going to be fine. Right, Tucker?" Marcia asks again.

Once again, Tucker does not answer.

"I'm going to take that as a yes," Marcia says now. "GiGi, just talk to Brandon. He's mad because you didn't reach out. That's fixable."

No. Brandon is mad because he felt Georgia was hiding something, and apparently he was not wrong.

Georgia sighs again. "You're right. You're right. I can fix this. I will not stress this. Like, it's going to give me early wrinkles, swear to god!"

Marcia smiles, but something about it seems forced. I cannot place the expression. I look to Isabella, and she frowns.

When I turn back around, Marcia is looking right at me. She nudges Georgia and gestures to me and Isabella.

We duck behind the portable. Shit.

"Should we run?" Isabella whispers.

I shake my head. "Looks guilty."

"We *are* guilty!" Isabella says now.

"That is true."

"Oh my gosh! Okay, okay, they're probably coming—just let me do the talking, okay?"

I nod. I am a bad liar.

Twenty-four seconds later, Georgia and Marcia pop up in front of us. Georgia's face is livid. I do not need a card to clarify. Marcia looks wary, as though she is trying to decide what to make of the situation.

"Are you guys, like, spying on us?" Georgia asks now. Her tone is not as angry as her face—it is forcefully lighthearted, as though she is restraining herself. I note that Tucker is not with them. Where did he go?

I shake my head. Not intentionally.

"We were walking," Isabella says. "We just happened to come this way." She sounds surprisingly confident. I definitely believe her.

"Who are you?" Georgia puts a hand on her hip. "I don't know you, and I know everyone."

"I'm new, actually. Isabella! Nice to meet you." She holds a hand out.

Georgia looks at Isabella's outstretched hand, then looks at Marcia. Marcia's hand twitches as though she wants to reach out, but she glances at Georgia and seems to think better of it.

"Why are you two out here?" Georgia asks us. She does not return Isabella's greeting.

"Because it is an open campus and a free country," I say now.

Georgia narrows her eyes at me. "You know what I mean. I swear you and my brother are the same."

"What does that mean?" Isabella asks. She raises a brow, and there's an edge to her voice.

Georgia holds up a hand. "Definitely not whatever you think it does. I mean, they always have a smart answer to a question when people ask. What exactly did you think I meant?" She cocks her head to the side and smiles.

Isabella does not answer.

"What did you hear?" Marcia asks us.

"Nothing," Isabella replies. "Like I said, we were just walking and ended up this way, just like you did."

"Was there something to hear?" I ask.

Georgia narrows her eyes at me. "No, but eavesdropping is rude, so we had to check, didn't we?"

"Well, we didn't hear anything," Isabella says now. "So, we're gonna go." She nudges me, and we both turn to leave.

"Hey, Aiden," Georgia calls out.

I turn back toward her.

"Tell your brother to call me."

Marcia nudges Georgia.

Georgia rolls her eyes. "Please."

I shrug. "Tried that once. Did not work."

Georgia's mouth falls open, but she quickly recovers. "Well, try again," she seethes between closed teeth.

I shrug again. Isabella pulls at my arm, and we speed-walk away.

Back in front of the school, Isabella stops and bursts into

laughter. Her whole body vibrates with humor, and the sound rings through the quiet evening. I watch with curiosity until she regains her breath.

"Sorry, I laugh when I'm nervous. I do not handle things like this well. I laugh at funerals, too. Did you know that? Don't judge me."

I raise my eyebrows at Isabella and smile. "No judgment." I can relate.

"Whew," she says in relief. "Okay, but what the heck was that about? They were talking about a video and Brandon and their lives being ruined?"

I shrug. "Not sure, but I do plan to find out."

But first, I have to tell Brandon.

I walk through the front door, ready to tell Brandon about what I overheard, but I can feel the tension rippling across my skin as soon as I walk in the house. I start to tap at my leg. One, two. Stop. One, two. Stop. See, this is why I stayed late at school.

"Aiden, can you come in here, please?" Mom calls from the great room. Her voice is tight, as it often seems to be now.

I sigh. Here we go.

Mom, Dad, and Brandon all sit around the dining table. The television plays on mute. Brandon's face is, once again, on the screen as the sports networks discuss his future. The logos of schools pop up next to his name. I know they are debating who might still want to take him and if any of it is going to matter. Already, Brandon's scholarship to University

of Florida hangs in the balance. They have not pulled it yet—
they may be waiting to see what happens with the trial—but
we may not have that much time.

I sit and stare at the table, waiting for whatever they need
to share.

"Hi, honey. I'm glad you're home. How was your day?"
Mom starts.

"I got in a fight with Carter at practice," I say now.

"What?" Mom shouts.

"What?" Dad snaps.

"You kick his ass?" Brandon asks now.

"Brandon!" Mom says.

"He deserves to have his ass kicked." Brandon shrugs.
When Mom turns to me, he winks at me. I smile.

"Aiden, you truly cannot afford to get in trouble. What if
someone took pictures or a video? We need you to be on your
best behavior. You may not be on trial, but your image matters
right now too. It matters for all of us," Mom says.

I nod.

Mom sighs. "Well, did you?"

I am confused. "Did I what?"

Mom's face is pleading with me to know what she means,
but I am at a loss. "Did you get in trouble? What did your
coaches do about the fight?"

"Oh," I say now. "They made me run."

Mom's mouth falls open in confusion, and she looks at
Dad, who shrugs. "That's it?" she asks.

"That's football," Brandon says wistfully.

Mom purses her lips in a regretful sort of way before taking a breath. "Okay, so actually, while we are talking about your images, let's touch base about the trial. We were waiting for you to get home, Aiden." Mom shuffles a few papers in front of her. "The media has gotten worse since Brandon's not-guilty plea and the charges went fully public."

"I wish they'd make the cop's name public too so his face can be national news," Brandon grumbles.

"You know that can't happen right now. They're invoking a law that protects the cop as a victim of a crime. His name won't be released."

"I'm the victim," Brandon protests.

"I know, but right now, I need you to focus. The trial date is set, and it's closer than you think. Everyone knows Brandon is going to be charged as an adult, and people have opinions. There are some blurry videos going around online, none of which show or prove anything, but people—even those we know—are commenting, and public opinion is less than sympathetic."

"Why? Brandon is the one who got hurt," I say now.

"Yes, son, but Brandon wasn't seriously injured, not enough to garner some level of sympathy, and it's his word against an officer's. Those aren't good odds," Dad says. His face is sagging and exhausted.

"Exactly," Mom says now. "So, we need to discuss a few changes and some strategies moving forward."

Brandon and I exchange grimaces, preparing for Mom to go full lawyer mode on us.

"The first thing is that you both need to continue"—Mom eyes me—"to be on your best behavior at school and in public. Limit going out if you can so that there can't be any stories printed about you. Don't talk to anyone that you don't trust."

Brandon and I both nod. My brother twiddles his fingers in front of him and does not look up. I wonder if he is thinking about Georgia. I wonder if anyone else in his friend group has betrayed his trust.

"Next, we are recording a statement tonight that will maintain Brandon's innocence and also paint him in a more positive light, to hopefully hold on to any offers and scholarships he has and may receive. We will release this tomorrow."

"A statement?" Brandon asks now. "Saying what?"

"We're still pulling that together, but don't worry." Mom reaches out and pats the back of Brandon's hand. Brandon grabs her hand and gives it a squeeze.

Even with the unexpected, Mom is ready with a plan, like always. Always ready to pivot. Lawyer mode is not fun, but it works, and she is putting it in double overtime for us.

"Lastly, Aiden." Mom turns to me. "We've just been informed that you will not be called to testify during Brandon's trial."

"What? Why? He was there!" Brandon shouts.

I am surprised too. Witnesses are usually a good thing.

"Brandon, relax," Dad says soothingly. Sanded wood. Calm. As always.

"Well, they say that his testimony may not be reliable because by our accounts, he never saw what happened," Mom says.

"Okay, but he heard what happened," Brandon points out.

"And that means everything he says will be pure conjecture. Nothing he can say is based on what he has seen, and he will automatically assume you did nothing wrong because you're his brother. It's not strong enough."

"Haven't people who only overheard crimes been called on to testify before, though?" Dad asks.

"Of course," Mom replies. "But the defense is trying to combat an institution that automatically has support and believability because they're law enforcement. If it's Brandon's word against a cop's word, then the police are going to win. They want to avoid too many answers of 'I don't know' on the stand."

"Well, who *is* getting called?" Brandon asks now. He sounds exasperated, and I feel the same way. I will not get to help my brother out of the mess I got him in.

Mom shuffles through the papers. "So far, Carter, Louis, and Greg."

"What about Reg and Bernard?" Brandon asks.

"Same issue as Aiden," Mom says. "They're even dicey about calling Greg, but we'll see."

"So that leaves the two people who were messing with Aiden the most to testify that I didn't do something when they clearly hate us," Brandon scoffs.

I consider this too. Brandon's defense is in their hands, and that does not feel very hopeful to me. Would they be spiteful enough to let Brandon go to jail?

"Brandon, Carter and Louis have been your friends since

you were kids." Mom puts her hand on Brandon's shoulder. "I'm sure they wouldn't paint you in a bad light."

"Did they even see what happened?" Brandon glances at me. I shrug.

Mom sighs. "Based on reports, no, but the prosecution has decided to call them."

"Which means they believe that Carter and Louis will be helpful to them, right? Isn't that what that means?" Brandon asks.

"They may be called as character witnesses to speak against you and suggest that your character fits the crime. We will argue against that, don't worry."

"And why can't we use Aiden for that on our side?" Brandon asks.

"Honey, it's not my case. I am not representing you. If I was, I would call Aiden. I've already made that point, but my colleagues don't agree. I can't speak to their decision-making, and I don't want to argue it now. Now, I just wanted to let you both know the latest information so that we can all be aware and move forward."

I do not speak. I do not know if I wanted to speak on the stand at all. I do not know what I would even say if I was there. I have seen trials. I have watched them as a kid following my mom around on days when I could not be anywhere else after school. Trials are nerve-racking. The lawyers pressure the witnesses with questions, cut them off, stop them when they object. I would get overwhelmed, and I know it. Maybe it is better this way. Maybe I would not be much help.

"I am too scared to testify anyway, B," I say now. "Do not worry. Things will work out."

Brandon frowns. His expression does not comfort me. He seems disappointed, and I do not want him to be disappointed in me.

"The deposition is scheduled for three days from now, on Friday, and we are prepping to begin the jury selection shortly after. We are officially going to trial," Mom says. Her tone is flat.

I frown now too. "They never offered Brandon a plea deal?" I ask.

Mom nods. "They did, but it just wasn't something that we could agree to. Beyond that, it would have put a guilty plea to a felony on your brother's record—that would affect college applications. We don't need that."

I glance at Brandon, and he seems miles away. He wears a vacant expression and stares off into space. I wonder what he is thinking.

Mom claps. "Okay, all the big stuff is announced and out of the way, so let's quickly draft this statement." Her ability to keep pushing from problem to problem is both amazing and scary, somehow both warm and cold simultaneously. Still, there is not a single person I would want on our side more than her.

"What will I say?" Brandon asks.

"It's short," Mom says now. "It says: 'Many of you know me as Big-Time Brandon Wright. I am here to say that I am still that person. Though I respect the work of the county officers doing their jobs and trying to uphold duty and order—'"

"Pssh, arresting me ain't duty and order," Brandon interjects.

Mom side-eyes him. "'Though I respect the work of the county officers doing their jobs and trying to uphold duty and order, I maintain my innocence in this matter. In the past, I have volunteered alongside local officers and done amazing things for the community, both with my team and on my own. My focus is college and my future, both of which are being derailed by this unnecessary charge against an innocent person. I implore the public not to take sides. I ask the public not to deem me guilty in the court of public opinion, and wait instead for my innocence to be proven. Please continue to follow my lead as your number one. Thank you.'"

Brandon smirks. "That's a little cheesy, ain't it?"

"Yes, well, cheesy pulls at heartstrings. We got a few good people together to write this, so you're going to read it, we are going to flank you, and everything is going to be fine. Okay?"

"You already said that," Brandon says now.

"Huh?" Mom asks.

"You keep saying that everything is going to be fine, and then things keep getting worse. I'm just saying, maybe we should stop saying that it's going to be fine."

"Well, what would you prefer we say, son? That everything is going to be awful?" Dad asks.

"I don't know," Brandon says. "Say that everything is gonna . . ."

"Be what it is," I suggest.

"Yeah," Brandon says, looking at me with a gentle smile. "Everything is just gon be what it is."

Mom frowns. "Fine, everything will be what it will be."

"You had to class it up." Brandon laughs.

And finally, for the first time in a while, we all laugh with him.

After we film the very cheesy statement, Brandon and I head upstairs. In the hallway, he stops me before I turn to go in my room.

"Hey, A, about Carter—" he says now.

"I am sorry about the fight," I interrupt.

"No, no." Brandon holds his hands up. "I mean, I'm not saying to fight. Fights can cause issues as, I mean—" He gestures wildly in the air with his hands. "Look at where we're at, right? But I do want you to learn how to stand up for yourself without me. In a way that's not fighting. I need you to learn how to assert yourself, have confidence, and show people that you're more than what they think you are."

I frown but nod. Then I remember. "Oh, I saw Georgia today."

"Uh-uh, nope. I don't wanna hear about her," Brandon says.

"No, but, B, I heard her—"

"A, please, please. I know. She probably keeps asking for me and she probably has all kinds of crap going on. I don't wanna know. I don't wanna hear about her. I need to focus on the trial. I can't focus on her, you know?" Brandon says now.

I nod. "Okay." I will bring it up to him later. He needs to know.

Brandon smiles. "Thanks, bro." He reaches up and rubs my head.

"Locs!" I say now.

Brandon chuckles and goes into his room.

I frown. My brother does not want to hear about Georgia, but I think she knows something. I could go to her myself, but she does not seem to want much to do with me. I could ask Tucker, but he has never been that forthcoming with information. He never even mentioned that he and Georgia were siblings. That leaves one option.

I head into my room and pad onto the white carpet, letting the fibers tickle between my toes. The navy-blue walls have always soothed me, and I instantly feel my body relax. I make my way to my bed, flopping onto it as the white sheets fly up around me, swallowing me whole. I bring out my phone. Isabella answers on the second ring.

"Hello, hello, hellooooo," she practically sings into the receiver. I am immediately happier at the sound of her voice.

"I do not think we can go to Tucker about what we heard—"

"He barely talks in class," Isabella jumps in. We are already on the same page, which makes me happy. She gets it. She gets me.

"Exactly!" I say. "But what if we go to Marcia?"

"Do you know her?"

"A little," I say. All I can think of now is Brandon teasing me about that kiss on the playground. I decide not to mention it to Isabella.

"Think she'll spill?" Isabella asks.

"I have no idea."

"Well . . ." Isabella pauses. "Everything's worth a shot!"

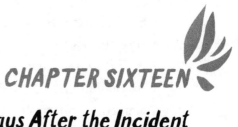

CHAPTER SIXTEEN

26 Days After the Incident

I tap my fingers against my thigh, waiting for Isabella. One, two. Stop. One, two. Stop. I ignore the anxious feeling like bugs crawling underneath my skin. I ignore the urge to itch. My life went from simple and peaceful to full of confrontation and secret missions in less than a month. How did that happen?

"Hey, you skipping practice for this?" Isabella's voice calls from behind me. I turn toward her as she bounces down the front steps of the school with a huge smile on her face.

"Have to," I say. "I've never skipped anything before."

"First time for everything, bad boy. You ready to go?"

I nod. "Marcia lives pretty close to my house. Near the front of my community, so we should be able to walk."

"Hopefully we won't get bombarded by any reporters on

the way." Isabella tightens the straps on her backpack. "I've never been to your house. We should go there after, yeah?"

"I have seen fewer cameramen lately, but it might get worse once the statement is released this evening." I frown. "Is going to my house something you would want to do?"

"Why wouldn't I?" Isabella asks. "Also, what statement?"

"Statement of innocence from Brandon," I say now. "Also, I just never thought that my house was very interesting. Why do you want to go?"

I have never really had friends over. Then again, I have really only counted Brandon as a friend before. Not by choice or from lack of desire, but maybe by design. Too many people with no patience to learn me.

Isabella looks at me with a raised brow. "Would you want me to come over?"

I had not thought about it. "Sure, it does not matter."

I start walking forward. I am seven steps ahead when I realize that Isabella is not beside me, so I turn back. I gesture for her to follow, like when we first talked in the hallway.

Isabella frowns and looks down at her feet. She tugs again at her backpack straps and starts forward. Once she is caught up, I fall as in step with her as I can, which is hard, since I need fewer steps. I watch my feet as we walk. I step in each individual cement section of sidewalk twice, once with each foot, and step over each crack between sections, counting all the way.

On step 207, Isabella turns to me and stops walking. "Don't you want to know why I'm quiet?"

I stop, blink at her five times, and suddenly, in my nervousness, feel the urge to look at everything except her. I look at the mottled sections of sidewalk, the yellowing fronds on a palm tree, the bright red hibiscus flowers decorating a bush behind her. The colors muddle with the orange of the sun under the cover of clouds.

"Well?" Isabella asks.

"I was not thinking about it," I say now.

She huffs. "So, you don't care?" She turns and starts walking again.

I frown and catch up to her. Care, by definition, means to feel concern or interest, or to attach importance to something. Not caring and not thinking are not the same thing.

"I did not say that," I say to Isabella. I slow down next to her and keep counting my steps. Walks were easy with Brandon. I did not have to talk or wonder why he was talking or why he was not talking. This is harder, for some reason. I cannot figure out what Isabella wants me to say, but I know that I do not want to say the wrong thing. I want to say the right thing. I want her to be happy.

"You just don't seem very excited at the prospect of me coming to your house," Isabella says now. Her voice is low. It is normally so musical, like wind chimes, like bubbles bursting in cold air. Now it is the deepest chord of a cello. Deep, vibrating, almost sad.

"Oh," I say now. I tap at my thigh. "You are right."

Isabella's brows knit together on her forehead. She seems like she is waiting for an explanation.

"Well, I have not really had friends over before, so I had not thought about it. But it sounds nice. And, I mean, we are friends. Friends going to each other's houses is supposed to be normal, right? I did not think to be excited," I say now. "Sorry."

Isabella scrunches her face and looks down. Her faux locs cover her face now. I walk for fourteen steps before she looks back up. "Yeah, you're right. We're friends. Sorry." Isabella still sounds like the open C string on a cello. Low.

I am not sure what I said wrong this time. I rack my brain trying to figure it out as I keep walking.

We pass the fire station and the undeveloped land that separates it from the community. Most of West Gate is made up of a bunch of communities. Ours is an older neighborhood, but I remember Mom mentioning that it is one of the biggest. She said the new ones all have small lots and more people. Mom says where you live and how much land you live on is a status symbol in our town. I do not get the difference.

"Isn't this where you said you live?" Isabella asks as we approach the front entrance. She was quiet for most of the walk. It was not our usual quiet—not like the comfortable silence of the library. I try to consider how I might change that.

I nod. "Marcia lives in Sky Isles, inside West Gate Estates. My community is Skyline Acres. It is close to the front," I say now.

Massive stone columns frame the large white iron gates at the front of West Gate Estates. The fountains on either side of the entrance and the perfectly manicured grass and hedges fill me with a feeling of comfort. I am almost home. The clinical smell of chlorine and the rushing sound of the fountain calm me. Through the gates, the streets and sidewalks expand in every direction.

"Okay, this is a little confusing," Isabella says as we approach a crossroad between several of the neighborhoods.

I am so used to it that I did not realize she might be disoriented. "Um, okay," I say now. "The main road and this main sidewalk go all the way back. Every road that turns off from this one is a community."

We walk along the sidewalk and come to a crosswalk, where the first two communities branch off on either side. To the left, the street turns into my neighborhood, Skyline Acres. To the is right Skybridge Acres. They are the two oldest communities in the development.

"My neighborhood is there." I point to show Isabella. Water-wall features and bushes manicured into perfect balls and cubes frame the entrance.

Isabella nods. Her eyes are wide, and she seems to be taking everything in.

"We live 462 steps in, closer to the golf course," I add.

We cross the street and continue down the main sidewalk, farther into the development. As we do, the entrances become a bit less opulent but still beautiful.

"It's weird—a community with, like, mini communities. There's a gate to get in, but then there's still gates to each of these communities too," Isabella says now. Her voice isn't as low as before. It seems like she is starting to feel a bit better.

"Is your community the same way?" I ask.

Isabella shakes her head. "I don't live in a community.

Just, like, a neighborhood? No gates or anything."

"Oh." I nod. That is different. I am not sure why I assumed that her home would be like this, but then, I have not been to too many other neighborhoods. Now I wonder what her neighborhood must be like.

When we reach Marcia's community, we walk in past the gatehouse. Gates do not do much if you are not in a car—the journalists and cameramen figured that much out. Isabella's wide eyes dart everywhere, and she cranes her neck to look at the houses as we walk past. I follow her gaze. None of them look much different than my own home. If anything, they are smaller. I suddenly feel like I should be self-conscious about inviting Isabella to my house.

Squared-off hedges frame the stone walkway to Marcia's front door. Her large, manicured lawn spreads out around us, leading up to a glass door about triple the width of a normal door. The house's exterior is white and angular, like a modern art museum.

I ring the doorbell and sway back and forth as we wait. Isabella angles her head, peering through the glass to observe the interior of the house. Only the living room—decorated with plush white carpet, white couches, white marble stone on the fireplace, stairs to the upper level, and a hallway to what is presumably a kitchen—is visible from the glass panels in the front door.

Marcia descends the floating wooden stairs into view. Her expression is flat. Her eyes dart back and forth between the two of us as she pushes open the huge door.

"Hi, Aiden." Marcia's mouth forms a half smile as she nods to greet me. She leans against the doorframe, crosses her arms, and eyes Isabella up and down. Her smile to Isabella seems pinched, pointy, forced.

I look to Isabella, expecting her to say something the way she did with Georgia. But Isabella just raises her chin toward Marcia. I turn and see that Marcia's eyebrows are raised at me. I get the feeling that I am missing something important.

Looks like I'm going to have to say something. "Hi, Marcia. Sorry to bother you," I say now.

"It's fine," Marcia replies. "Just doing homework. I see you brought your new friend." She eyes Isabella from head to toe again.

"Isabella," she says now.

"Marcia."

It suddenly feels very icy.

"Um, I will not take up much of your time, but I just wanted to ask if you saw anything the night that Brandon got arrested. I did not mean to eavesdrop, but I think Isabella and I overheard you and Georgia talking to Tuck about it?"

Marcia's body stiffens and she narrows her eyes at me. "You heard wrong. I had some stuff going on that night, and Georgia has her own stuff with Brandon. Nothing we were discussing was about the fight."

"Yeah," I say now. "But it really sounded like—"

"I actually need to go. That homework." Marcia pushes off the doorframe and motions to close the front door.

I speak up before she can complete the gesture. "You

guys mentioned Brandon. And Georgia sounded like she was hiding something about him. His trial starts in a few weeks. You seemed like you know something. And even if that is not the case, you both were coming down hard on Tuck like *he* knows something. Does he? Can I ask him? This is for my brother, Marcia." My voice comes out a little louder than I anticipate.

"Tuck doesn't know anything, Aiden. Neither do I. You're making a lot of big claims. If Brandon needs help, you were there. You help your brother," Marcia says now. Her face looks conflicted, though her tone is firm. She seems to be at war with herself over something.

"I didn't see," I say.

Marcia rolls her eyes. "Well, neither did I."

"I think I saw a video online of you there," I say now.

Marcia narrows her eyes. "What video?"

Isabella looks at me and cocks her head.

I have seen many videos with many students. None where I can definitively recognize Marcia, but this tiny lie is worth the risk.

"A video of a girl with black hair," I clarify.

"And you know that's me because?"

"You have black hair—"

"So do Ginger, Caley, and Becca." Marcia looks at me with her brows raised.

I knew that would never work, but I am certain that Marcia knows something. She knows something, and she is lying to me. Why?

"Marcia, I am just trying to help my brother," I say now. I do not understand what is causing her to be so secretive. We have known each other for a long time. We may not be close, but still.

"Help him how, Aiden? I don't have any information to give you. I didn't see anything. I don't know anything. If you didn't see it either, then I'm sorry. I can't be of any help." Marcia starts to close her front door, but Isabella reaches out and stops it.

"Dude, come on, we both heard you and Georgia. What's the deal? Don't you care? If you can help and you don't, are you prepared to live with that on your conscience?" Isabella asks. Her voice is strong and insistent.

Marcia stops pushing the door and looks to the side, away from Isabella. "Yeah, I do want to help. I'd love to help. I just—look, everything's not as easy as you think it is, okay?"

"Well, what is it, then?" I ask.

Isabella backs away from the door but stays nearby, just in case Marcia tries to close it again.

"Look, I can't help you, okay?"

"Withholding evidence is illegal," I say now.

Marcia purses her lips and tilts her head to the side. "Your mom's the lawyer, Aiden. Not you."

She is not wrong. I barely know anything about the legal system. I only know what my mother has told me to say over the years and what I have heard her say. Even then, I have not always had context.

"You can't just throw things at me and think it's enough

to make me admit to something. My dad's a cop, you know? I know stuff too." Marcia looks between Isabella and me.

"Then what makes this not easy?" I ask now.

Marcia looks down at the floor. "It's not easy because I can't help you. I don't have whatever it is that you're looking for. That's it."

My fingers lose the rhythm against my leg. Marcia is not making sense. I heard her and Georgia talking. Now Marcia is pretending like it is nothing, but that cannot be right.

"Are you positive you can't tell us anything helpful?" Isabella asks.

Marcia lets out a quick, sharp breath. "No, I can't think of anything."

"I do not understand—" I start to say.

"Aiden, forget her, she's not going to help," Isabella says. She's angry, I can tell. "Let's go."

Isabella turns to walk away. I stay put. When she notices that I did not move, Isabella turns back around and waits. Marcia does not move either. I focus on a button on her white oxford shirt. Her sleeves are rolled up. Her pitch-black hair contrasts where it falls on the fabric.

I stand and focus. I do not move. If there is information to gather, then I need it. I do not want to just give up. Brandon said that I need to assert myself. This seems like a good time.

"You know, a lot of people got questioned that night, Aiden," Marcia finally says. "Or at least that's what I heard . . . A lot of people got questioned, and I think everyone already did what they could. And now with all those videos of Brandon's arrest going around on socials, I don't know." She looks at me. She shakes her head, and she seems tired.

Footsteps echo on the tile behind Marcia.

"What's going on here?"

Marcia's mom, Mrs. Lewins, only a few inches taller than Marcia, stops just behind her. She wears a knee-length, tan business skirt, a tucked-in ivory silk shirt, and tan high heels with pointed toes. Her blond hair hangs halfway down her back, and her powdered face looks smooth. Bright red lips curl into a pained smile as she surveys the scene.

"Are you going to invite your friends in, Marcia?" she asks.

Her words make me shift back and forth on my feet. The question seems innocent enough, so why do I feel uneasy? Something about it is forced, as though she is just trying to be polite.

Marcia shakes her head. "No, they're just leaving, Mom."

Marcia's mom narrows her eyes at me but keeps the smile plastered on her face. "Your brother's doing well, Aiden?"

I nod. I focus my gaze on a painting on the wall behind her. So much of the interior of their house is white, but this painting has blue splattered across the canvas. Not navy, not cerulean, not cyan, but electric blue, speckled and spotted across a white background.

"Hmm," Marcia's mom says as she looks me up and down. "That's good." She turns on the balls of her feet and disappears down the hallway. "Go ahead and let your friends leave, Marcia. We'll be having supper soon." Her voice trails from another room.

"Okay, Mom," Marcia calls back. She looks back at me and frowns. "She saw a video that everyone is saying shows Brandon attacking the cop," she says in a low voice.

"You *know* Brandon," I say now. "We've all known each other a long time. You've been friends with him. You know his character, Marcia. Did you forget that?"

Marcia hesitates, then closes the door and disappears down the same hallway as her mother.

I let out a breath I did not realize I was holding.

Isabella starts back down the walkway. "Well, that was kind of useless." She sounds annoyed, and I feel the same.

I shake my head. "This doesn't make sense." I follow Isabella out of Marcia's yard.

"I mean, it's like you said—she's lying. We don't know why, but we can't force her to tell us, right?"

I nod. "I know."

With Marcia a no-go and Georgia completely out of the question, I am not sure what to do next. It seems that they are central to this issue, but Marcia's insistence that Tucker does not know anything might actually be true. Or is it? I cannot tell what is a lie anymore. But I do know that something is happening, and I need to unravel it.

Isabella's phone rings, pulling me from my thoughts. Her eyes widen as she looks at the screen.

"Oh no, it's my dad," she says. "And it's a video call."

"What's wrong?" I ask.

"I'm technically supposed to be at robotics, but I'm here instead and that's bad, because remember how I said I used to get into trouble before I moved? Yeah, well, I am definitely not supposed to lie to my dad about where I am—he's going to freaking kill me." Isabella's words tumble from her lips. "I lied to him. And we have an agreement. He calls. I answer." She tugs at her hair before she swipes to answer.

"Hey, Dad! I was just going to—" Isabella starts.

"Stop," her dad says now. He is stern and dismissive. "Don't bother. The adviser for robotics club already called me to ask where you were. He said they had a meeting today, but you weren't there."

Isabella stares at the screen without speaking. I look at my feet.

"Isabella, I thought we were done with this. I had enough trouble getting you into this school after the stunts you pulled with your mom. Cutting class, vandalizing bathrooms, skipping school . . ."

I look over and see Isabella's eyebrows shoot up.

"Dad!" she shouts. She glances up at me, turns her back, and starts to walk away. "Please . . ."

"I asked you, Bells, and you still lied to me. Now, where are you? Better yet, who are you with? That might give me a better idea," her dad says now. He is harder to hear as she drifts farther away.

I feel a sudden urge to run. I do not want to talk to this angry man.

"I'm with Aiden." Isabella's voice is barely above a whisper.

"Is that the one whose brother just got arrested?"

"Yes, but—"

"May I speak with him?"

No. No. No.

NOTE: *I barely like dealing with my own parents when I am in trouble. I do not want to deal with someone else's.*

"No, Dad. Please don't. He's not making me do anything," Isabella pleads.

My ears almost twitch from how closely they are paying attention.

"And yet here you are, lying to me, not at robotics club, out god knows where," her dad says now. "Why can't I speak with him?"

"It would just make him too uncomfortable," Isabella says.

"And what about my comfort, Bells? Why can't I speak to him?"

"Because, Dad, he's different," she answers.

Her dad sighs. "What does that even mean, Isabella?"

"He's on the autism spectrum," she says now. She glances my way. She seems embarrassed.

"And what does that have to do with him getting my daughter to lie to me?"

"That's not his fault," Isabella says.

"Well, he's sure a part of the blame," her dad says now. "Being on the spectrum doesn't absolve him of guilt. And you using it as an excuse is a disservice to him."

I stare at my shoes. The scuffs in the toe. The creases. I focus on anything except the words rattling in my head.

My phone pings. It is Reg.

Hey, a few of us heading out in a bit to do something important. Meeting at school. Wanna come?

I look up and see that Isabella is hanging up with her dad.

"What is it?" she asks me. She blinks away tears in her eyes.

"Reg," I say. "He needs me back at the school. You okay?"

Isabella shakes her head.

"Want me to walk you home?"

She shakes her head. "I live just past the school; we can split off there."

I wonder if I should put my arm around her or hug her. I know how to comfort my own family, but figuring out what is right with someone else is difficult. I also have no clue how to ask.

"I am going to pat you on the shoulder," I say now.

Isabella gives me a small grin. "Okay."

I pat her twice.

"Thank you, Aiden," she says. She leans into me, and I let her weight fall on me for a bit. I rub at her shoulder and she sniffles before looking up at me with a grateful expression. I guess I did something right.

Now, on to Reg and this big "important" meeting.

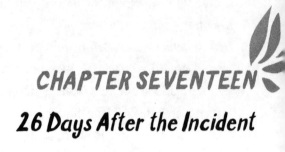

CHAPTER SEVENTEEN

26 Days After the Incident

Isabella and I part ways at the front of the school. Following the directions from the text, I walk until I find Reg standing with Bernard and Dustin in the student parking lot. When he sees me approach, Reg heads over to me with outstretched arms. I dodge a hug.

"Consent," I say now.

"Fair," Reg replies. His arms fall to his sides. "But! Official introductions: Aiden, Dustin. Dustin, Aiden. You both have backs. You both run. Dustin's in our crew now. Aiden, we need to talk to you."

I'm worried. Marcia and Georgia are enough of an issue—I can't handle much else.

Bernard pulls his phone from his pocket. "Somebody sent me this anonymously." He angles the screen so I can see. I read the message:

Hey! I saw that you're on the west gate team and wanted to msg. I was at randys the other nite and saw the cop who arrested and accused brandon. I know where he lives. Wanted to pass along because a lot of us are mad abt what happened to brandon and want justice. Heres the address:
78567 Pine Lane
West Gate, FL 33171

I hand the phone back to Bernard. My neck throbs with anxiety. Someone knows who did this? To just be given an answer feels too easy. It makes me nervous.

"Okay," I say now.

"What do you mean, okay?" Reg asks. He looks at me as though I am missing something obvious.

"I am confused," I reply. My mind is still racing from this new information, but I am also wondering what Reg wants from me. I feel jittery and my skin blazes, though the sun is beginning to set.

"It's the cop's address, Aiden! We have to go. We have to do something."

"Like what?" I ask. "Are you even sure that it is real?'

Bernard nods. "We searched it. Came up as someone named George Jensen. Another search confirms that he's a county officer. It checks out."

The pain in my neck grows. "Still, I am not sure if—"

"Look we don't have to do nothing bad, but we can, like, pop up. Ask questions or something. I mean, it's our chance to do something for Brandon! Nobody else is doing shit!" Reg says, almost yelling.

"What are we doing for Brandon?" Greg pops up behind me, startling us.

"Lower your voice," Bernard says to Greg.

"Reg is yelling, bruh. Y'all should have tried being quiet earlier. What are we doing for Brandon?" Greg asks again.

Reg sighs. "You're late," he says to Greg. "Someone sent us the address of the cop who arrested Brandon. He lives in town! We about to go over there."

"Wait, no, we are—" I say now.

"Y'all sure it's the guy?" Greg asks. He is immediately interested—I can see it all over his face.

Reg and Bernard nod.

I try to speak. "No, they are—"

"All right, I got my old man's car today. We can ride over there and see what's up," Greg says now.

Bernard claps Greg on the shoulder. "Good deal, man."

A huge lump in my throat refuses to clear no matter how much I swallow. I cannot shake the bad feeling gathering in my stomach. "You guys, I am not sure if we should—"

"Can we stop by my house on the way?" Dustin asks. "I need to grab something."

Everyone else is talking and no one is hearing me. Then, before I can try to speak again, the group is moving and Bernard and Reg take hold of my arms and suddenly we are out of the school, in Greg's dad's car, and driving.

Dustin is only inside his house for a few minutes before

he comes sprinting back to the car, stuffing things in his backpack. I am a bit overwhelmed by the speed at which all of this is happening. I have not had a minute to catch my breath and process. I squeeze my eyes shut until the darkness turns to Technicolor and take a few steadying breaths.

"Navigation says Jensen's house is like seven minutes away," Reg says now.

I am wedged between Bernard and Dustin in the back of the car. Reg navigates from the passenger seat and Greg drives. I wiggle away from the skin-to-skin contact.

"Sorry you had to sit bitch," Bernard says to me.

NOTE: *As I learned today, "sitting bitch" means having to sit in the middle seat in the back of the car.*

I shrug. "It is fine."

I want to call off this trip. The negative emotions broiling in my stomach are only getting worse, and vomit is threatening with every passing second. This feels like a very bad idea. I do not understand what we can accomplish on our own and do not see how pulling up to a cop's house ends well for any of us. Worse, I have never done anything like this before and know that if I get caught, I will be in a ton of trouble, especially since Mom told us to keep our heads down.

"Okay, so when we get there, we're just gonna see if anybody's home, you know? And if the cop is there, we take out our phones and record, you get me, and we ask him why he's lying on Brandon and make him show us the injuries he got from Brandon on camera. I think if we catch him on camera and he's not injured, nobody'll believe him, and we clear Brandon's name. Then no jail!" Reg says now. He bounces up and down in his seat.

Reg makes the whole affair sound simple, but what if it is not? What if it gets complicated? Once again, my mom's warning about keeping a low profile rings in my ears.

Greg turns a corner into a neighborhood, and I count palm trees and house numbers.

One palm tree. 78561. Two palm trees. 78563. Three palm trees. 78565.

The house is blue. White shutters. One-car garage. There is a swinging bench on the front porch. The lawn looks like it has not been cut in a few weeks. There are no cars out front. It seems that nobody is home.

This is it. This is where the person who ruined my brother's life lives. A part of me feels sick. Someone inside this house has been living in peace while my brother has dealt with nothing but turmoil. As the thought crosses my mind, I want to move. I want to jump out of the car and make something, anything, happen to get justice for my brother and all he has been through.

"It don't look like nobody's here," Greg says now. He parks along the street.

"I'mma go see," Reg decides. He clambers out of the passenger seat.

"Wait, babe," Bernard calls. He follows Reg out.

Then Dustin climbs out from the other side of the car.

Greg sighs. "Guess we all getting out." He turns the car off and joins them.

I sit for twenty-two seconds, focusing on my breathing, considering what to do. Do I go against everything my mom has been asking of me for a moment of satisfaction? There is no guarantee that anything is going to happen, so maybe it is fine to get out. But what if something does happen? Then what? I rub my tongue against my teeth as I think, until a calm comes over me. We are already here. Everyone is already out of the car. No other choice now. I get out and slam the door behind me.

The five of us stand on the sidewalk, observing the house from a distance as though a force field keeps us from proceeding. We all glance at each other, silently daring someone to move, when Reg finally shrugs, walks up to the porch, and peers in the windows. I glance around, hoping the cover of darkness will protect us from being noticed by anyone nearby.

"You're gonna get arrested, dumbass," Greg says now. "You can't just be on people's property."

"It's not illegal to be on a front porch," Reg replies. "Or else delivery drivers would be screwed!" He looks in a few more windows before coming down off the porch. "Damn, I don't think anybody's here for real."

"Okay, nobody's here." I cannot ignore the relief flooding my body. "Let's go," I say.

"Wait," Dustin says now. He pulls two cartons of eggs from his backpack. A mischievous smile spreads across his face.

"What?" I ask. I glance at Greg, Bernard, and Reg.

They are all returning Dustin's smile.

Greg nods. "Bet."

"Bet what?" I ask now. I feel like I am missing something important. "What are the eggs for?"

"Throwing," Reg says. He lobs an egg at the blue wall, and it bursts open, splattering yolk all along the siding.

My mouth falls open. This is turning from a quick drive-by into chaos. I am worried about anyone seeing or hearing us. I am shocked at everyone's willingness to do this. But I am also somewhat thrilled to see it happen. Still, I think we should stop. "Wait, I do not think we should—"

Dustin pitches an egg and it hits close to where Reg's landed, spraying more yolk. Dustin lets out a whoop.

Greg laughs and grabs two eggs, throwing them at the front of the house. Then Dustin pulls rolls of toilet paper from his bag. They each grab a roll and start to toss the toilet paper across the palm trees in the front yard, over the porch railing, on the swinging bench, in the bushes, and on the roof. Bernard cheers them on, grabbing a roll to paper the house with himself.

It unfolds so fast that all I can do is watch. Then Greg is next to me.

He places an egg in my hand and folds my fingers around it. My hand closes around the cool, smooth surface. I can feel every little bump and notch on the shell as I rub my thumb across the length of the egg. I relish the texture under my fingertips, my skin catching at times against the exterior. I glance up at Greg.

"You'll feel better," he says to me.

I look down at the egg, then back at him. Greg nods. This is the person who arrested my brother. He ruined Brandon's life. *My* life. He is lying about my brother and hiding behind a law to protect him, his name, this house. The sick feeling subsides. The nerves dissipate. The anxiety is quelled. Now I feel calm and sure. I look at the egg again, then pull my arm back and throw it as hard as I can.

The egg smacks against a window, and I hear a resounding crack.

"Shit!" Dustin yells. "I think you broke it!"

My mouth falls open. "Oh no, oh no, oh no—"

Then a laugh erupts from Reg's mouth. He doubles over, holding his sides, laughing until tears stream down his face. Bernard watches him for a split second before he starts to laugh too, then Dustin, then Greg. Before I know it, they are all laughing, and it takes me a second to realize that I am laughing right along with them.

I broke a window. I got in two fights. I egged a house. I did all the things I was not supposed to do. And all we can do is laugh.

"What are you guys doing?!" A voice behind us cuts into the laughter.

I turn and see that five boys—all of varying heights, hair colors, and builds, but all white—stand in the street by the car. Their faces are angry and their stances aggressive.

"Uh, redecorating?" Reg says. He still has a trace of laughter in his voice.

"You can't just do that to this house. This used to be our neighbor's house." The boy who is speaking is tall and lanky. His dark brown hair is gelled down to one side. "You guys really thought this was a good idea?"

No. I did not. But I got outvoted.

"Used to be? So no one lives here now?" Bernard asks.

"Shit," Greg mutters.

"Told you guys," I say now.

Dustin pushes me on the arm.

"Maybe we didn't give a shit if it was a good idea," Reg says. He puts a hand on his hip and raises his chin.

"Maybe you should have," lanky boy responds.

"What do you want?" Bernard asks.

"You guys have to pay for that window," lanky boy says now. He punches into his own hand.

"Why?" I ask. "It is abandoned, right?"

"My dad's a cop. I'll call him," a stocky boy threatens.

"Do it, then," Greg taunts. He sounds surprisingly confident, all things considered.

I would rather that did not happen. I open my mouth to protest, but Bernard puts a hand up to stop me.

"What did you say?" lanky boy asks. He takes a few steps toward us and his lackeys follow.

"He said, 'Do it,'" I say matter-of-factly.

"You're going to jail, you monkey," a short boy says.

"The hell did you call him?!" Dustin says now.

"Why are you even with them?" short boy asks. "You don't feel like an odd man out? Just you and all these nig—"

Dustin sprints forward and tackles the lanky boy in the stomach, and the other boys jump on Dustin. Greg, Reg, and Bernard do not hesitate. They each rush forward, swinging wildly and grabbing at Dustin to get him off the ground. Five full seconds pass before I move, launching myself in the middle of the chaos, hitting whatever comes across my fists. Everything is a blur for exactly sixteen seconds as curse words, screams, and insults fill my ears and punches land on my skin.

"We got Dustin. Let's go!" I hear in my ear.

I break out of the mosh pit, run toward the car, and dive into the back seat. Reg and Bernard clamber in after me and Dustin jumps into the front passenger seat. Greg starts the car and pulls off with the driver's-side door still open. The group of boys run after us for a few seconds before finally giving up. Greg finally slams the door shut and his eyes dart between the rearview mirror and the front windshield. I stare out the back window until Greg turns a corner and the boys are out of sight. Once they are no longer a threat, I collapse in my seat.

"Well, shit!" Dustin says now.

Silence. Then we all burst into laughter.

"Yo, I almost got my ass beat!" Dustin yells.

"Nah, we all did. The hell were we thinking?" Reg chokes out between laughs.

"Not gonna lie, that was dumb as shit," Bernard says now. "I guess that 'tip' we got was crap."

I do not speak. I just laugh and laugh until all I can do is cry.

Greg looks back at me as he speeds through a neighborhood. "You good, Aiden?" he asks.

I do not know. I have not felt this way before. I feel joy, almost. Laughter that will not stop, but also sadness. Brandon is not here. He is not here to see this thing that happened. These fights. These moments. And relief. We are safe. And surprise. And guilt. And I did not even think of Brandon once this whole time, not until now. And—

"It's okay if you're not, you know?" Bernard says now. "It's okay if you not okay."

I nod. Greg watches in the rearview mirror, then swerves onto the lawn closest to us. We all slide around in the car, jolted by the sudden turn.

"Greg, what the hell!" Reg shouts. "You want us to die?"

The streets in the quiet neighborhood are empty save for a few cars parked in driveways. The evening air is still, and it is only us and the streetlights.

"We almost already did that," Greg says now. He lets out a whooping laugh and swerves onto another lawn.

I look behind us as Greg leaves tire tracks on lawns and dirt trails in the street.

"Fuck it!" Greg says now. He lowers his window and yells out, "Fuck it!"

Bernard and Reg laugh and wind their own windows down to yell with him. Dustin leans forward, fiddling with the radio, changing stations until it settles on one playing loud rock music, then he collapses back in his seat.

"Fuck it," he says with a shrug, then chuckles.

I look around at them all, tears in their eyes, smiles on their faces, screaming out the windows. I have never felt more lost. I have also never felt so found.

I stick my head out the window just as Greg swerves onto another lawn.

"Fuck it!" I scream to the sky.

I keep screaming until my voice gets lost in the warm evening air.

Greg drops me off in front of my house before leaving to take everyone else home. I am energized, my entire body vibrating with leftover exhilaration. I am excited to tell Brandon about what happened. I need to share this with him, the way we share everything else.

Brandon is asleep in his room, earlier than usual, when I get there, and I hesitate to wake him. I watch him for a while, looking like himself for once without all the stress and expectation weighing down his face. After forty-two seconds, he opens his eyes.

"Hey, A," Brandon says now. "What you doing in here? Everything good? When'd you get here?"

"Two minutes and fifty-three seconds ago."

Brandon chuckles sleepily. "I can always count on you to be specific. You coming from practice? How was it?"

I shake my head. "We went to a cop's house because we thought it was the cop who arrested and accused you and then we egged it and then we put toilet paper everywhere and then some boys came and told us the house was abandoned and then they got mad and then one of them said his dad was a cop and that we were going to get arrested and then one of them called me a monkey and then Dustin tried to fight and then we all fought and then we got in the car and drove around and messed up people's lawns." The words tumble all over each other as they fall from my mouth.

Brandon opens and closes his mouth a few times. "Who is 'we'?"

"Greg, Dustin, Reg, Bernard, and me," I say now.

"Okay, so y'all went—A, wait. Why the hell? I—what!" Brandon shouts.

> NOTE: *Brandon's eyebrows are raised. Mouth open.*
> *Cannot speak. Emotion cards say he is shocked.*

Brandon's face is the tipping point, and the confused joy from the car bubbles over in me again. Laughter spills from my lips and I gurgle on for thirty-three seconds before I realize that Brandon is not laughing with me.

"What is wrong?" I ask.

Brandon frowns. "That's not what you supposed to be doing, A."

"What do you mean?"

Brandon sighs. "You supposed to be focusing on football, on the team. You supposed to be earning your spot. Getting noticed. Getting your talent out. Helping Mom and Dad and stuff—helping me. But you out fighting and shit. A, that's not what we do, man—"

"You mean it is not what you do," I interrupt.

Brandon stops and raises an eyebrow at me. "What's that mean?"

I shake my head. I did not come here to fight. I wanted to share this weird joy with my brother. This strange happiness I found lurking in the sadness and anxiety. I wanted to share it.

"Nothing," I say now. I lie.

"You don't lie, A. You bad at it. You bad at it right now. What's up with you? We had a goal. A plan. I can't play football right now, A. I could go to jail. Like for real, for real, go to jail. They trying to charge me as an adult, Aiden. I'm dealing with all this and what you out here doing?" Brandon asks. His face is filled with an anger I have not seen from him before.

"Having fun," I reply. "I think. I am having fun. I am just doing stuff. I am hanging out with people and doing things that I never did before—"

"Because those things are pointless. What the hell—"

"And laughing, because I can never laugh anymore without feeling bad because I think about you, and how you are here, and you are not laughing, and it is my fault!" The words tumble out before I can stop them.

Brandon purses his lips. I stare at his forehead for one minute and thirteen seconds. Anger slips from his face and he just looks drawn.

"A, I'm not saying you can't have fun. I'm saying that's not what we do—"

"Why?" I ask now. The expectation of constant faultlessness overwhelms me, and I am suddenly sick of it. "Because we have to be perfect? Because *you* have to be perfect?" I yell.

"When have *you* had to be perfect?" Brandon snaps.

I clam up. Brandon never yells at me. Tears sting in the corners of my eyes.

"When have you had to be perfect, Aiden? You get to mess up! You get to mess up and keep messing up and Mom and Dad will accept it, they'll even expect it. I'm the one who has to be perfect. I have to be the perfect son, the easy one. I have to be the perfect brother to be—" Brandon presses his lips together.

I stand up and back away from the bed. "You blame me," I say now. I have thought it. I have thought it so many times. I have even blamed myself, but I never knew for sure if Brandon did. Knowing makes everything in me fall apart at once.

Brandon rolls his eyes. "I ain't say nothing about blaming you for nothing, A. Look, I—" He sighs. His tone softens. "I'm sorry. I ain't mean it how I said it. I'm just saying that you ain't have all the expectation, and now when it's getting handed to you, you just messing it up. You just messing it up 'cause you used to having all these chances."

I shake my head. "What chances?" I ask now. I am used to getting none. I am used to people making assumptions about me the second they find out that I am autistic. People who believe I am either a problem to be had or fixed. People who believe I am either incapable or somehow super capable due to autism being some "secret superpower." I am used to watching that shift from a normal interaction to a stereotypical one the second the word "autism" is uttered. No one gives me chances to show who I am, the extent of my abilities, the depth of my thoughts, or the limits of my mind. What chances have I been getting?

Brandon rests his head back and closes his eyes. "A, I don't wanna fight with you. This ain't the time to be fighting."

"Maybe it is," I say now. "Maybe it is if you blame me the way everyone else does."

"Stop, I ain't ever treated you like everybody else—"

"You are now."

Brandon opens his eyes. "I just want you to appreciate all the good that's coming to you, Aiden. You can't see that? All I been tryna do is get you to a good place where you happy and thriving—"

"That is not your job," I say now.

"But it has been," my brother says. "And that's okay. I ain't mad about it. I just feel like you throwing it away right now."

"I do not want all this pressure on me," I respond. Brandon and I speak, but never like this. Never about the reality of our positions in life. There is some torch being passed to me that I do not want to carry and that I do not believe Brandon should carry either.

"Neither did I," Brandon says now.

Our eyes finally meet. Out of all people, Brandon is the person I truly look at the most, but for some reason it is like I am seeing someone new. Not less than, not more than, but different. Changed.

"I am sorry," I say. I do not know if I know what I am apologizing for, but I feel like I should apologize. I know that this is where an apology goes.

"Why?" Brandon asks.

I shrug.

Brandon nods. "You don't gotta be sorry, A. You ain't do nothing to me. I'm sorry. I love you, bro. I need you to know that. I really, really love you."

He reaches a hand out. I lower my head and he tousles my locs. Somehow, though, it feels different. Something is missing. I am unsure if we will be able to find it again. Every day, it feels like things morph and shift into a new place, and I have to relearn the people around me who I have had mapped all my life. I knew Brandon, but now it seems I must get to know him all over again. Or maybe I am the one who is changing? Maybe I need to relearn me to get us back to where we were.

I leave the room and realize that I never told Brandon about how I felt. I never even told him about the joy. I never told him how I learned to laugh even when I am crying.

When I walk through our front door after practice the smell of soy sauce and ginger hangs in the air. Chinese food. I do not announce that I am home. I walk through the dark foyer, not bothering to turn on the lights. Mom sits at the kitchen island, scrolling through a page on her laptop. An open takeout box of beef and broccoli with pork fried rice sits untouched in front of her. Dad lounges on the couch, his long locs draped over the back of it, flipping through TV channels with the remote.

"Hey," I finally say when I walk in the room.

"Hey, son," Dad says without looking my way. "How was school?"

"Good," I answer. "What did you guys get me?"

"Fried rice, no onions, no peas, and no carrots. Four egg

rolls and pork pot stickers," Mom answers, but does not look up from her computer. "The usual, honey."

The order might be the usual, but the behavior? The distracted separation instead of everyone gathered around the table, focusing on each other while we eat? That is unusual.

"Thanks," I say now. I grab the paper boxes and settle at the island, leaving two seats empty between Mom and me. I eat my fried rice and egg rolls in silence. When I open the box of pot stickers, I toss the plastic cup of sauce to the side. Brandon usually steals a few pot stickers and uses the sauce, but he is not here. Weird.

"Where's Brandon?" I ask now.

"Went for a walk, I think," Mom says.

"Is that a good idea?" And since when does he go for walks?

"Well, things calmed down—which is why we held off on releasing the statement. No need to rile things up. I think he'll be okay."

I hope so. Still, I wonder how he feels if he is just walking around. That has never been his thing, mostly because he is too tired after practice to do much else. Without football, though, I suppose I should not be surprised that he is finding other ways to clear his head.

"How was your day, Mom?" I ask before I bite into a fried dumpling. The still-hot pot sticker fills my mouth with steam, burning my tongue. Still, the flavor of the pork is good—salty and a little bit sweet.

Mom tilts her head to the side. "Uneventful."

I nod. Somehow, with everything going on, I am relieved

to hear that. No news is good news. "You, Dad?"

Dad turns and looks at me. I think he is a bit surprised. Brandon usually does the after-school check-ins, but I figure I am here, so I might as well. "It was all right, Aiden. Training some new research assistants in the lab today. Nothing groundbreaking, but we need the help before we start this new clinical trial." He turns back to face the TV and keeps flipping through channels.

I nod. I consider the conversation I had with Coach Davis and what Isabella's dad said. I want to tell my parents about the football team, about the driving around, about Marcia, but instead I think about what I really want to ask them after talking to Brandon.

"Did Brandon get arrested because of me?" I ask now.

The TV stops on a cartoon. A talking dog dances on-screen, but the volume is too low for me to hear what he is dancing to. Mom looks up from her laptop and Dad turns in his seat again to look at me. They both look a bit stunned by the question.

"What makes you ask that?" Mom asks. "Did someone say something to you?"

I shake my head. I would rather not rehash the conversation with Brandon.

Mom breathes hard and rubs at her eyes. Then she turns to look at my dad. I cannot understand the face he is making at her. It is a yes-or-no question. They seem to be struggling, so maybe I need to rephrase my question.

"Do you both feel like he got arrested because of me?" I ask again.

"Of course not," Dad says now.

Mom presses her lips together.

"Does Brandon?" I ask.

"I don't think so," Dad replies. His voice wavers. He sounds unsure.

"But do you know?" I ask now. I need to press him on this. I know what Brandon has said, but everyone seems to be walking on eggshells around me, and I want to know why.

"I don't think—" Dad repeats.

"You do not know," I interrupt. "Not for sure." I stare at the countertop, seeking striations in the stone. He is not confirming anything, but at the same time, he is. Confirming what I believe, what Brandon will not admit. I sigh.

"Aiden, sweetie. Did something happen?" Mom asks. Her voice is softer than I am used to.

"Brandon has not talked to me much. I think he is avoiding me."

"He had a hard day today," Mom says now.

"Why?"

"We started choosing the jury and it's been difficult, especially with the trial in a couple weeks," Dad says.

"Why?"

"It's been hard to get a jury of his peers," Mom answers.

"What does that mean?" I ask now.

"It's been hard to get people on the jury that are representative of a diverse population."

Now Mom is talking like a textbook. She does that when she is still processing. "Everything about this case is so difficult. Everything keeps changing and getting worse. Is that normal?" I ask.

Mom looks at me. Her eyes seem puffy and sad. "Do you remember the talk we had when you were seven and started walking home with your brother? When we finally stopped driving you both to and from school?"

I nod. "You told Brandon and me what to do if we ever got stopped by cops."

"Do you remember what we said?" Mom asks now.

"You said to comply, no matter what. You said it was better to come home beaten than not to come home at all. You said do not argue, let them search us if they asked, and . . ." My voice trails off.

Mom looks at me, eyebrows raised.

"I do not remember the rest," I finish.

"We said to remind them that your mom's a lawyer, your dad's a research scientist, and you are important," Mom says.

That is what Brandon said the night the cop stopped us when we were walking home, before everything happened.

"What does that conversation have to do with what I am asking?" I ask, a bit frustrated by the tangent.

"Do you remember why we told you that?" Mom asks now.

I shake my head. I remember a lot of what she told us to do, but I do not remember what sparked the conversation or why.

"Since the day you got your diagnosis, we worried, Aiden. Not just because you had autism, but because of what that meant in the world we live in. We're Black, Aiden," Mom says now. She emphasizes the word as though it is something I am not aware of.

"I know. You say that Black people are disproportionately—"

Mom holds her hand up. "I know you can repeat my speech back to me word for word, baby. Do you really understand what it means, though? Do you know what it means when I say we're Black?"

I take a breath and play with the zipper on my pocket, thinking. Before everything happened with Brandon? No.

"It's all obvious now; when you were younger, it wasn't. You didn't think about those things. Autism didn't think about those things. You're Black, and you'd have big emotions, big reactions—all warranted, of course—but your dad and I were very aware that we live in a society where those emotions in a Black body aren't as acceptable."

I twist my mouth to the side. I am not sure what to say.

"I work in the legal system. I see too many cases of police brutality disproportionately impacting Black people. Even in Miami, a Black healthcare worker got shot trying to protect an autistic patient who left a care facility some years back. Black bodies are over-policed, and it's always the same story: non-compliance, they seemed older, excuses," Mom says now. Tears dance on the edges of her eyes. "We moved to West Gate because it was small. We figured if it's a town where everyone knows everyone, then nobody would ever see you or your brother as a threat. We thought you both would be safer if the town knew you, and that maybe it would give people pause. Maybe, if anything ever happened, they'd think you both are different."

"Different than who?" I ask.

Mom shrugs. "Other Black people."

"What do you mean?" I ask.

"We had to move you both to a place where you would be the exception, not the rule," Dad says. "We can't change what people think of everyone, but we can alter what people think of *us*. Unfortunately, we've found that when people get to know you, they tend to see you as a good person *despite* being Black, rather than accepting that maybe Black people aren't what they thought in the first place. Us presenting ourselves one way doesn't end racism or prejudice, but it helps our family."

"Is that not kind of messed up?" I ask. "Does that not position us against other Black people?"

"Probably," Mom admits. "But we were willing to do that to protect you both. It isn't the best strategy. It isn't clean or pretty, but survival never is."

Survival. I never saw our existence as something we were surviving. The talk my mother has given us takes a different shape in my mind now.

"So, you are saying that Brandon got arrested just because he is Black?"

"We're saying it's more complicated than that, Aiden," Dad says now. "A lot of factors are at play."

He sounds like Coach Davis. "Are you saying other Black people deserve that?" I ask now.

"No! No! That's not what I meant," Mom replies. "Ian?" She looks at Dad.

"Your mom means we both hoped that our plan would help people who don't look like us think you were different from their underlying prejudices or biases. Enough to not do harm," Dad adds.

"People who don't look like us?" I ask now. "White people?"

Mom nods. "Not exclusively, but yes."

I am confused. West Gate is predominantly white. There are Black families, but most live on the east side of town, so it is not like we solely live around them. Even so, we are easily outnumbered in the larger community. I have always been aware of this in a passive way. I just did not focus on that sort of thing. I did not focus on people much in general.

"Is that why we're having issues finding a jury that is 'representative of a diverse population'?" I ask now.

"Thank you for the direct quote." Mom gives me a small smile. "And yes, that is why."

"So, why not move us to live around more Black people?" I ask now.

"We figured that was more dangerous," Dad says.

"Why?"

"Black and low-income neighborhoods are more heavily policed than white and high-income neighborhoods. We figured this would help lessen your number of interactions with officers throughout your life," Mom says now. "And so far, it's worked."

"Because we are Black?" I ask now.

"Well, yes and no," Mom replies.

"That makes no sense," I say.

Mom furrows her brows. "What do you mean?"

"Moving us away from Black people did not fix anything. Brandon got arrested anyway, and now he cannot even find a good jury. Moving us to live around white people did not fix anything. Brandon still got in trouble. We should not have to worry about where we live and who we live around to be safe. That feels unfair."

I am antsy and itchy in my clothes. In my skin. Under my skin. In my veins. I shift in my seat and drum my fingers on my leg. I feel like I have been hearing all this for many years, but now is the first time that I am comprehending it.

"It might seem unfair, but we had to do those things. For one, because we're Black, but also because you're autistic," Dad says now.

It always comes back to that.

"So, Brandon *did* get arrested because of me?" I ask.

Dad holds up his hand to stop me. "You weren't verbal until you were three, and you weren't fully verbal until you were about six. Even then, you didn't want to talk to other people. You were much more reactive then, when you were touched or grabbed, and we worried that increased police exposure would put you at risk, specifically."

"How?"

"Do you remember how it was for you? When the cops were on you at Randy's?" Mom asks.

The truth is I do not—not clearly, at least. Not for lack of trying. Every night, I go to sleep and I dream of lights—all red and blue. Brandon yells my name over and over. In my dreams, everything is blurry. Muddled faces, coarse surfaces, the smell of cigarettes, coffee, grass, and wet stone. I do not remember anything clearly, but my body remembers the fear. My neck throbs, blood stretching my veins, as the blurry images flood my mind. My body has not forgotten the fear.

I stare at the TV screen, listening to my parents as the talking dog drinks coffee straight from the pot. I am trying to reconcile all I am hearing with all that I already know. I am vacillating between regret for asking the question and appreciation for being trusted with the answer.

"We know it's hard for you to understand, Aiden. It's hard even for us to understand sometimes, but we had to do things this way. We've always protected ourselves this way, for generations—even more so with Dad and I being immigrants. You have two uncles that can't even come stateside anymore since they got deported," Mom says now. "You know how wary we have to be of law enforcement, and the only way to really be safe is to keep doing what we're doing."

"What we are doing does not work. It just makes us quiet," I say now. "People still get arrested. Do you know that Brandon feels like he needs to be perfect? What if he had gotten shot? If he had died, he would have died trying to be that: perfect and quiet."

Dad gets up and walks over to me and Mom follows suit. He places a hand on my shoulder. I accept the weight of it, the pressure exactly what I need after such a heavy conversation.

"We might die perfect and quiet, but the hope is that we

die old. Sometimes that means silence. We can't put you at risk. That's why we chose the way we did," Dad says.

"Anything that put you at risk also put your brother at risk. That's why we moved here," Mom says now. "You have to trust that sometimes silence is the best way."

"I do not agree," I say now. And I will not. I cannot. Not when my parents' decision is making it worse for Brandon now, even though he did everything right. And then, are there other Brandons? Other Black boys suffering under the same decision-making? Or worse? I squeeze my eyes shut until every color spirals around like a light show. "But that still does not answer my question. Did Brandon get arrested because of me?"

Mom and Dad look at each other.

"Pointing fingers doesn't solve anything," Dad says.

"But if you had to point a finger?"

"I'd point it at the person who attacked your brother and put the cuffs on," Mom says now.

How can that be true? We moved here because being Black can be dangerous and my autism can be dangerous and those two things can be a danger to me or to Brandon and it is and was, and Brandon might go to jail now.

"Whoever put the cuffs on would not have been there if it was not for me," I say now. My voice trembles as the reality of my words shocks me.

"Whoever responded didn't have to put the cuffs on, baby." Mom reaches out and holds my face in her hands. She does not make me look at her. She looks at my forehead and plants a kiss. "You're shouldering a lot of blame for this. You're holding on to so much and you have to let it go. This isn't on you, honey. It's not on you."

My eyes sting with tears. I do not blink. I let them gather, teetering first on the edge of my lashes, and then I let them fall.

"They are going to send Brandon to jail for a long time," I say now. It is not a question.

Mom lets my face go and steps back, sitting on the edge of the back of the sectional.

"They're going to try," Dad says.

"Because he is Black," I say now.

"I'm not saying that if he was white, they wouldn't have done this, or that the fallout wouldn't have been this bad," Dad says now. "But I am saying that if he was white, there may have been pause."

I consider what Dad said. We were all fighting that night— all struggling, none of us as compliant as we could have been, even though I tried to be.

"Greg got punched and hit as much as I did," I say now. "Reg and Bernard, too."

Dad nods. "And your brother got the worst of it. We talked to their parents, and they feel like we do. Greg said that you and he were treated similarly—Reg and Bernard too. When we said something at the station about it, the police denied it and said that you five were the most combative, the most difficult, and the most threatening at the scene."

Were we?

"At the end of the day, honey, we think a lot of factors

contributed. It wasn't just one thing," Mom says now. "We can say for sure, though, that this isn't your fault. And *none* of us feel like it is."

Even Brandon? I do not ask. They are going to say no, even if they are not sure.

Dad squeezes my shoulder. "Just remember the things we've tried to teach you, okay?"

I nod. My mind races. I was upset with Coach Davis because I felt that Carter was treated differently, not just by the coaches but by everyone, and I called it out. But to have it confirmed is different. Now, what do I do with this information? It has been scratching away at the back of my mind. It feels weighty, dangerous, and unwieldy now that it is out in the open, here and ready for me to confront it. It feels too big for me to deal with. With all the factors at play, is there any way for Brandon to win this? Is there any way for me to help him?

The TV cuts to a commercial and I let out a breath.

Then Brandon walks through the front door, slams it behind him, and stomps up the stairs.

"Brandon!" Mom yells after him.

He does not answer.

Mom starts up the stairs, but Dad stops her. "Give him space," he says now. She hesitates but takes a step back and nods, then settles onto the couch next to him, pretending to watch TV but casting furtive glances at the stairs every few seconds.

I wait a minute, then pop off the chair and head up the stairs anyway.

"Aiden," Dad calls to me.

I ignore him.

When I open Brandon's door, he turns to face me. He sits on the bed, under the sheets. His Adam's apple bobs in his throat. We look at each other for three minutes and two seconds, saying nothing, saying everything.

"I heard about the jury," I say now.

Brandon nods, blinking back tears.

"Are you afraid?"

Brandon nods again.

"You have been avoiding me."

"I know." His voice sounds like sandpaper.

"Why?" My voice cracks. I blink away the burning blurriness building in my eyes.

Brandon opens his mouth, his bottom lip curling in over his teeth. He runs his tongue along his bottom row of teeth on the right side of his mouth and rolls his eyes to the ceiling. Tears fall heavily, skipping past his face and dotting the white sheet on his lap.

"I, uh . . ." Brandon clears his throat. "I'm happy for you, you know?"

I do not bother wiping my face. I let the tears cool my warm skin.

"I just, uh . . ." He lets out a cough. "I just, um . . . I ain't know it was all gon turn out like this." His lip trembles and his voice cracks. "I ain't know you was gon have everything and be doing everything while everything in my life is falling apart. I ain't know you was gon end up doing all this without me."

Brandon bites hard on his bottom lip, and ragged sobs fight to escape his closed mouth. His cheeks puff with each hard breath. His mouth finally opens, and he lets out a low wail like a lost wolf searching for his pack. It vibrates deep in the pit of my stomach and I feel sick. I rush forward and grab my brother. He leans into me, and I squeeze him as tight as I can, his arms caught to his sides, his head cradled in the nook between my neck and shoulder. His tears dampen my shirt as I cry into his hair.

"What am I gonna do now?" Brandon wails. "I was supposed to be out there with you. We practiced together! We did that!"

My tears fall faster. I do not know what to tell him. I worried so much that we were falling away from what we were and that things were changed between us, and now here I am. My brother needs me, and I do not know what to say to save him.

"What am I supposed to do now? I don't wanna do nothing else, A." Brandon crows like a vulture. "I don't wanna do nothing else, man. I don't know what to do now. I don't know what to do."

We stay like this, crying, until Brandon's exhausted frame sags into his bed. When I am sure that he is asleep, I let my big brother go, still sniffling in his sleep.

CHAPTER NINETEEN

39 Days After the Incident

The next day is quiet, but I know what I am going to do. When the lunch bell rings, I hurry to the usual table, where I find Brandon sitting alone. He flicks absentmindedly at his key chain.

"Come with me," I say now.

Brandon turns to me and his brows furrow. "Come with you where?"

"Can you just come?" I walk out of the lunchroom and do not look behind me, hoping my brother just trusts me. Then I remember that Brandon is so used to being in the lead that he must suck at following, so I check once to make sure. I make my way to Ms. Findley's room, praying she does not have a class. And if she does not, hoping that she is there. I watch my feet swing as I walk and ignore the silent questions emanating from Brandon. When we get to her room, I peer through the window in the door and see her sitting at her desk, eating a salad.

"Your Life Skills room?" Brandon asks.

"Listen," I say. "Life Skills is not just for people with disabilities—"

"I know, but—"

I hold a hand up. "And it is not just for troubled kids, either. It is for life skills. It is for helping you deal with all the crap that life throws at you. It is for navigating the hard parts of life and knowing how to deal with it. It is for all the things. And it has helped me. And you have helped me. So, let me help you. Okay?"

Brandon eyes me with what I think is hesitation but nods.

I nod back and pull the door open.

Ms. Findley looks up and smiles when she sees me. "Aiden," she says now. "And Brandon Wright. To what do I owe the pleasure?" She pushes away the salad and rests her chin on her hands.

"I'm actually not sure," Brandon says.

"I brought him," I say now. "Because everything is awful and falling apart with football and he does not have a clue what to do. And you always know what to do."

"Thank you, Aiden." Ms. Findley smiles. "Is there anything you want to talk about, Brandon?"

Brandon shakes his head.

I push him forward.

After three seconds, Brandon clears his throat. "I'm just

having some trouble thinking about what to do outside of football."

"Aren't you attending college?"

"But where am I gon go without my scholarship?"

"Sorry, I don't mean to presume, but you don't particularly need a scholarship to attend school, right? Your family does pretty well?" Ms. Findley asks.

Brandon frowns. "That's not what I mean, though."

I take a seat in my normal spot and watch the conversation unfold.

"So what do you mean, then?"

"I mean, yeah, we could pay for me to go wherever, but then I wouldn't be on a team. I wouldn't be a part of anything. I wouldn't be who I am," Brandon says now. "I can't go if I can't be—" His voice breaks.

Ms. Findley eyes Brandon as she walks from behind her desk and leans on its front. She always does this when she is getting serious. "Football is a huge part of your identity, isn't it?"

He nods.

"Brandon, do you know that over forty-five percent of student athletes suffer from depression and anxiety after transitioning out of their sport?"

Brandon does not answer. He looks down at the floor.

I try to make out his expression, but I think he is still trying to figure out what to feel himself. His face seems to dither between so many emotions.

"Those numbers increase when the athlete is thrust out of

the sport unexpectedly, whether due to an injury or—"

"An arrest?" Brandon asks.

"Yes, or an arrest," Ms. Findley says now. "What you're feeling is not out of the ordinary, but it would be wrong to call it commonplace. This feeling you're having, it's reasonable. You have never been normal. You've been in the spotlight since middle school, if I remember right, on display since even before then, a subject of public interest since before you could truly comprehend it. I remember when you started here, and everyone already knew who you were. By your sophomore year, college scouts were already looking at you. You have known nothing but the spotlight. You have experienced nothing but excellence. You have exhibited nothing less than perfection."

Brandon avoids Ms. Findley's eyes. He seems almost embarrassed by her observations, but not really. Honestly, he looks a bit sad.

"Have you ever considered what it might be like to be imperfect for even just a few minutes?"

Brandon bites his bottom lip and looks at me.

"Pretend he's not here," Ms. Findley says now. Brandon turns to her. "If you weren't perfect for a day, what would happen?"

The room is silent for thirty-six seconds. "My brother would suffer," Brandon replies. "My family would suffer. I would suffer. I have to be perfect. I have to help everyone. Keep them laughing, keep them going, make them happy. I can't be mad. I can't be upset. I can't be less. I have to be more. I have to stand out. Because then I can take up space."

"What do you mean, 'take up space'?" Ms. Findley asks now.

Brandon looks at me again. This time, there is something else in his eyes.

NOTE: *Is this guilt?*

My brother looks at me for seven seconds before I realize that he is seeking something from me. I search his eyes—looking at him for longer than I ever have—before I recognize what he needs. Permission. I nod, encouraging him to speak.

"I mean, I would get to take up *my own* space."

"Space that Aiden doesn't occupy?" Ms. Findley asks.

I cannot pretend the question does not sting, but I lean forward in my seat. I want to hear the answer.

"But don't you want him there with you?" Ms. Findley adds.

"Yes," Brandon says with a sigh. He seems exhausted by the conversation and a bit frustrated with himself. He paces back and forth now. "Yes, I do, but when it's football, Aiden is coming into my space. It's the place where I take up space. It's the place I dominate. It's the place where I'm the most important. Where everyone looks at me. Where everyone pays attention to me. I want him there, of course, but the space still belongs to me. Now I don't have it. I don't have anything."

So, it is not just about football. It is, but also, it is not. Football is the one place where it does not have to be about me. Because all the rest of the time, it is: Am I okay, am I overwhelmed, am I upset, am I comfortable? Everything has been about me, and Brandon has been taking care of me for so long that I got used to it being that way. He loves that I am playing football, but it was *his* thing. Now, without it, I am taking his place everywhere. I suddenly feel very sad for my brother.

"After all this, I can't just be a student somewhere," Brandon says now. "I'll disappear."

Ms. Findley steps forward and places a hand on his shoulder. "I promise that isn't true. You being a star doesn't dim without football. You will not just disappear, no matter what you do. You aren't who you are because you can throw a ball. You're more than that. You're who you are because of your personality, and you stand out because of that. You still have that. You still have so much. I know it's hard, but the best thing you can do is focus on what you do have. Can you try that?"

Brandon is quiet. I know that one conversation will not fix everything, but I hope it is a step in the right direction.

"I can try," he says.

When we walk out of Ms. Findley's classroom, my brother turns to me.

"Aiden, I—"

"Stop apologizing," I say now.

"But—"

"Stop," I say again. "It is okay. I am okay."

Brandon puts a hand on my shoulder, then hugs me. "I

might take a minute after school before I go home, okay?"

I nod. "Take your time. I have work today after practice anyway."

After practice, I head straight to the library, with Brandon on my mind. I think about what it means to be perfect. How my brother has always kept me in the loop, and whether that was a good or bad thing. Brandon has done so much for me, so much that without him I would have felt lost, but I do not think that is a good thing. I think that maybe my taking up space for him has made him hold me back. I have never had to find friends on my own, I have never had to find activities that were my own—I have never had to take up a space that was not his.

When I reach the library, Isabella is waiting outside, smiling as always.

"Hi, hi!" She waves with obvious enthusiasm.

I grin in greeting.

"Ah, my man of few words."

Something about her tone makes me linger on her words. I cannot fight the warring feelings in my head. I fluctuate constantly between seeing Isabella as a friend growing closer, and another second thing. A second thing that I have not thought about with anyone before.

"Ready to get to work?" I ask now.

"Always!"

We walk inside and head straight to our stations, busying ourselves with returning books to their shelves. I pay attention to the books people check out and whether they have been here before. I notice the woman who comes in every few days with a little boy who might be her son. She always gets romances, and he always gets graphic novels. Today, I suggest a new series to him, and he checks out every book we have. There are two women who come in every day to check out horror and thrillers. I tell them about a visiting horror writer coming next month, and they sign up to be in the audience. There is a man who comes every day in threadbare clothes with a pocket of coins to use the library computers. Today I give him my own change to use after he runs out. He is looking at job applications.

After our shift ends, Isabella and I sit on a bench outside the library. It is twilight, my favorite time of evening. I appreciate the marbled colors painted across the sky, and even more so, I appreciate how the scattered light morphs the color of Isabella's eyes. I watch as they fluctuate between varying shades of gold and brown.

"How are you doing, all things considered?" Isabella's voice snaps me out of my reverie.

I think about my answer. I think about Brandon. I think about all that he has lost so far.

"I do not think I am okay, but I think I am trying to be," I say now. It is the most honest answer I can give.

"That's fair," Isabella says. "Is there anything I can do?"

"I do not think so, not right now." I say now. "But I will let you know if something comes up."

Isabella nods. "You want a hug or a squeeze or anything?"

I reach my hand out to hers and she takes it, squeezing tight. And for right now, this is enough.

When I walk through the front door of the house, I smell nothing. Nothing cooking, no real noise, no lights on. All I see is a dim glow from the kitchen, and I hear the beep of the refrigerator when it has been left open for too long. I walk past the circular table in the foyer, ignoring a few more casseroles and cakes left by neighbors, and walk through the arches to the great room. I see no one. The fridge is open, so I walk around the island to close it and find my mom, sitting on the floor, eating a pineapple upside-down cake, whole, with a spoon.

I stop and stare at her for a bit, surprised by what is unfolding in front of me. I have never seen my mother not composed. Not put together. I take her in now: her hair slightly wild, her shirt unbuttoned halfway, her eyes misty, crumbs on her chin.

She looks up at me when I approach but says nothing. We stay like that for forty-two seconds.

"Mom," I say now. "You okay?"

Mom takes another bite of the cake, a piece of pineapple hanging halfway off the spoon. "We got an all-white jury."

She continues to eat the cake without explaining what that means for the case, but I know it is bad. I can tell it is bad because she looks bad. She never looks bad.

I want to ask questions, but she does not seem to be in the mood to answer.

After a few more spoonfuls, she places the cake on the

floor, gets up on her knees, reaches forward into the dishwasher, and pulls out a fork.

"You can stand there, or you can help me eat this cake," Mom says now.

I want to ask why. I want to ask what eating the cake will do when we have an all-white jury. I want to ask what I can do about this revelation. Instead, I drop my backpack, get down on the floor next to the fridge, cold air blasting at my back, take the fork, and dig into the cake.

We eat like this for ten minutes. Quiet. We work our way through maraschino cherries, caramelized pineapples, and the sweet pineapple-flavored cake. We ignore the crumbs that fall to the clean tile floor and do not stop until the cake is gone.

Once the tin clatters to the floor, I look over at Mom, waiting for her to say something.

"Mom?" I finally ask.

She looks at me. I do not want to break whatever spell is holding us. I reach out and she takes my hand. I see tears gather in her eyes. She is not okay. She is never not okay. I cannot fix it, so I do the only thing I can do. I tell her what she needs to hear.

"There is a casserole on the front table that smelled pretty good when I walked in."

Mom gives me a small smile. "You should grab it for us."

I get up, grab the casserole, and we sit, eating it cold, never complaining.

After a few minutes, Mom finally speaks. "Thank you, Aiden."

I am unsure of what I have done, but I nod in response.

She reaches forward, over the casserole, and grabs me up into a hug. I ignore the tears I feel fall from her face onto mine. Ignore the sniffles that emanate from her every few seconds. Ignore the way she grips me like she is drowning and clinging to a life raft. I ignore it all, and I squeeze.

When I go upstairs, I am full from casserole and cake, and I know what I need to do.

I whip out my phone to text Isabella.

I think I need your help.

I wait for the reply.

Anything.

CHAPTER TWENTY

40 Days After the Incident

O kay," Isabella says now. "So, this is the plan. We ask Tucker. Straight out. We ask Tucker, and he tells us, and then problem solved. Who needs Marcia and Georgia? We don't! We ask Tucker today! And he tells us, and then we know what they're hiding, and we have something to help your brother." Isabella chews on her lip in between sentences.

She is preparing our plan to help Brandon. We know we heard a conversation between Tucker, Georgia, and Marcia. We know they are hiding something. We know it has to do with Brandon. We know it has to do with a video. Marcia wouldn't help us, but we are going to find out what it is.

"If Marcia would not tell us anything, why would Georgia's brother tell us?" I ask.

"Because he is an honest, good person!" Isabella says.

"That is optimistic," I say.

Isabella wiggles her brows at me. "Optimistic is my middle name!"

We walk slowly toward Life Skills, the hallways emptying of students before last bell. Only the squeak of Isabella's sneakers and the slam of a few lockers keep us company.

"I feel like this is our last shot before we just go back to Marcia and force her to tell us!"

That would be a bad idea. I sigh. "Okay, so what do we do?"

Isabella shrugs. "I don't know. Just ask? That's what you did with everyone else, right?"

"And that got us far," I say now.

"Oh, look who's suddenly a master of sarcasm," Isabella says now with a grin.

"Sorry," I say. "Too much time with Reg."

"No, no," Isabella says now. "Sarcasm suits you. Wear it." She laughs. "Okay, but seriously, just try to find a way to ease into it. I know you don't talk to him much, but you guys know each other. This shouldn't be hard, right?"

I shrug. In theory, it should not be hard, but lately, nothing has been easy.

We walk into class, and Isabella sits in her usual seat behind Tucker. I avoid my typical spot and slide into the empty seat next to him.

Tucker eyes me and grabs his camera, flipping through the pictures on the screen. I try to take a glance and notice that they are mostly nature shots—many of them super zoomed in—and they are really good.

I watch Tucker from the corner of my eye. He never looks up from his camera. I look at Isabella, and she motions her head toward him.

NOTE: *I think that means that she wants me to talk to him.*

I clear my throat. "So, Tuck—"

Suddenly, Ms. Findley explains what she needs us to do for the next activity.

"We're focusing on positive self-image development today, so I want everyone to write at least three things that they feel they'd want to change about themselves, and then pair up with a partner. With that partner, I want you to find ways to turn those negatives into something positive and find ways that those traits benefit your life rather than hinder it. Okay?"

A few students nod and she takes it as confirmation from the class.

"Okay, great! Go!" She goes to sit at her desk and lets us choose our own partners.

I glance at Isabella, but she raises an eyebrow at me and gestures toward Tucker.

I nod and move to stand in front of Tucker's desk. His camera rests on the edge of the desk, and I wonder if it can record videos. Does he have video of what happened so that I can finally get an answer, one way or another?

"Hey, Buc—" I clear my throat. "Uh, Tucker. You wanna pair with me?"

"Wouldn't you rather pair with Isabella? She's your girl-friend," Tucker says now. His tone is matter-of-fact.

My face feels hot. I do not look at Isabella, firmly planted in her seat behind Tucker and listening.

"Uh, no." What exactly am I saying no to?

Tucker shrugs.

I grab a desk and pull it close to his, so we are side by side. Isabella gets up and pairs with Dalton. She recently took out her faux locs, and her curls bounce as she walks.

"I'm not done writing my three yet," Tucker says now.

"I actually need to ask you something."

Tucker does not look up from his paper.

"Did you see what happened the night my brother got arrested at Randy's?"

"Yes," Tucker says flatly. He is always so straight to the point.

My eyebrows rise. "Why did you not tell me?" I ask.

"I didn't know you needed to know. You were there," he says now.

Fair.

"I was preoccupied. Can you tell me what you saw?"

Tucker shakes his head.

"Why not?"

Tucker motions toward his camera. "I have footage."

A rush comes up from my stomach. I feel sick and happy at the same time. I do not hug people other than my family, but I throw my arms around Tucker. His body stiffens as I squeeze.

"Consent," Tucker says now.

I let go. "Sorry."

Tucker relaxes but does not look at me. He scribbles at his paper a little longer.

"Can I have the footage?"

Tucker shakes his head.

"Why not?" I ask now. My elation turns to immediate annoyance and confusion. If the video is there, I do not understand what the issue is.

"I don't have it anymore."

"Well, who has it?"

"Georgia."

Shit. Back to square one.

"My three traits are that I'm too brusque, I spend most of my time taking pictures, and I still struggle with eye contact. What are yours?"

I forgot about the activity. I did not write anything yet.

"I still struggle with eye contact, I shut down when I am overwhelmed, and I do not like being touched without warning," I say now. I think the list could be longer.

"You just touched me without warning," Tucker says.

Fair. I nod.

"Do you think Georgia would give me the footage?" I ask now.

Tucker shakes his head, then looks up from his paper and toward the corner of the room. "Eye contact doesn't mean you aren't looking at someone. Shutting down is better than freaking out. People should ask to touch you anyway. Consent."

Tucker looks back down and scribbles at his paper. "And no. She wouldn't."

I consider Tucker's list. "I agree with you. Eye contact does not mean you are not looking, that is a good solution. Taking pictures is not a bad thing, it is a safe way to see the world. And the brusque thing, you know, being straight to the point can be useful in some situations," I say now. "So, how can I get it? The footage, I mean?"

"She gave it to Marcia," Tucker says. "Said it was important." He doodles a rabbit on his paper.

"Why?" I ask now.

Tucker shrugs. "Don't know. Didn't get to watch it." He sighs and picks up his camera. "I think we're done," he says now.

The bell rings and Tucker slings his camera around his neck.

Isabella approaches as I pack my things. "So?"

"We have to go back to Marcia."

The locker room is packed before practice. I make my way to my space—mercifully located at the end of an almost empty block of lockers—and start changing. Coach Davis walks through the room, talking to a few guys before practice. His voice travels, and he slaps the side of my locker when he gets to me, struggling to get my practice jersey over my head.

"This locker location still good? We tried to place you away from all the traffic and noise, but I noticed you've been bonding with some of the other guys. We can always move you if you want to be closer to other people," Coach Davis says. Though he was loud when talking to other players, his voice is low now, so only I can hear him.

I clear my throat. "Yeah, okay. Thanks, Coach."

Coach Davis nods and claps a hand on my shoulder, then goes to help Bernard get his shoulder pads on correctly.

I sit on the bench behind me so I can lace my cleats.

"All right! Just a few more minutes, then I want everybody fully padded up and on the field! We're starting with striders today, y'all, so be ready to sweat!" Coach Davis calls out before leaving the locker room.

Reg comes up and leans by my locker.

"Ready for these striders?"

I shake my head. "I think we would have less if there had not been so many dropped passes at the last game."

Another voice carries over the lockers. Loud and sneering. "Don't understand why we still have someone that causes this much trouble on the team."

Carter.

I focus on pulling my laces tight, working the ends through each hole and securing my ankles in my high-top cleats.

"It's like he just exists to get shit handed to him. I didn't think the football team worked on affirmative action, or is it ADA?" Carter says now, and laughs.

A slamming sound makes me jump. I get up to see what is happening. I walk down two rows and see Carter sitting on the wooden bench between the locker rows. Greg stands over Carter, his hand on the locker where he just slammed it, leering down at him.

"You love to talk, don't you?" Greg says now. "That's your issue—your mouth always writing checks your hands can't ever cash."

"The hell is that supposed to mean?" Carter asks. He stands up, but Greg is taller than him, so it does not have the effect he expects.

"I mean, you talking crap about Aiden when you really still mad that you got your ass beat twice," Greg says now.

A few guys in the locker room whoop and laugh. Carter looks around, embarrassed, and catches my eye.

"What's your real problem with him, man? We all on the same team now. We been on the same team for a while now. It's been almost two months. You're gonna have to get over it," Greg says.

"He just always has something to say." Carter gestures toward me.

I want to respond but I hold back. He is not going to get to me this time, and I do not need another run-in to make the coaches doubt me.

Greg looks back at me with raised eyebrows, then turns back to Carter. "You saying the dude that barely talks to anybody always has something to say? Or is the problem that when he does have something to say, he says stuff you don't wanna hear? Which is it?"

"What can he say that matters that much to me?" Carter asks now.

Greg shrugs. "I don't know, but clearly, whatever he's saying is messing with you. Maybe those dropped passes aching at your soul? I don't get it, bruh. You been gettin' off easy. With everything that's going on, especially. Especially everything with Brandon."

As soon as he mentions Brandon's name, the mood shifts. A few guys look down, avert their eyes from the scene. A few shift back and forth on their feet, fiddle with their fingers, scrunch their mouths. Everyone gets a little less comfortable.

"You think we didn't see how the only injuries you were healing from back when everything happened were the ones Aiden gave you?" Greg asks. "Brandon's paying the price for a fight you started—"

"He started it!" Carter says, and points at me.

"A fight you started," Greg repeats, getting louder.

"Brandon didn't even have to get involved," Carter says now in a pleading tone.

"A fight you started!" Greg's voice rises over Carter's. "With his brother."

Greg and Carter stare at each other for a long time without blinking.

"Don't think a lot of us don't see how your pretty blond privilege helped you out of that tight spot. It won't help you on the field, though," Greg says now.

"Dude, whatever," Carter says. He grabs his helmet off the bench, pushes past Greg, and breezes past me through the doors to the field.

A few guys talk in low voices about what happened, and everyone takes their time filing out the door and onto the field in small groups.

I approach Greg. He is adjusting the visor on his helmet.

"Hey," I say.

Greg looks up and gives me a small smile. "What's up, Aiden?"

"Thanks for that." I rock side to side as I speak.

Greg shrugs his shoulders. "Right thing to do," he mutters.

I nod and look down at the floor.

Greg starts to walk out, then stops at the door and turns back to me. "You coming, A?"

I look up at him. I smile.

"Yeah!" I follow Greg onto the field.

After practice, the mugginess of the air clings to my skin as I walk across the field with Greg, Reg, and Bernard, headed home.

"You trying to chill today, A?" Greg asks me.

I shake my head. "No," I say now. "Trial starts tomorrow, and I have something to do. Things are starting to get really busy. I need to head home."

Greg nods. "I talked to him already, but tell Big-Time good luck from us, all right?"

I bump fists with Greg. "Okay."

Reg and Bernard wave bye, and a surge of happiness swells in my chest when I realize that these boys who were once just somewhere in my orbit are now really my friends. It makes me smile. I pick up the pace as their backs disappear to catch up with Isabella at the gate to the field. It is time for the Plan.

"Hey," I say to Isabella.

"Hey!" Her voice is as bright as ever. "Ready to—"

"Hey, Aiden!"

Everything in my stomach curdles. I know that voice.

I turn to see Carter running up toward me. I freeze. I want to turn around and walk away, but Carter gets close enough for me to see that his face is puffy and the veins in his eyes are prominent, as though he has been crying.

"What do you want?" I ask.

Carter runs both hands through his hair and glances at Isabella. "I came to talk to you, I guess."

I lean against the gate and wait. I focus on the queen palm tree fronds swaying in the light breeze behind Carter. They dance in harmony, cohesive parts of one whole. There is no rain today—only soft breezes.

"Can we?" Carter gestures to the side away from Isabella. Isabella gives me an imploring look, but I shrug and give her a thumbs-up that it is okay.

I take three steps to the left.

Carter sighs. "Okay, fair," he says now. "Look, I was think-ing about what Greg said, and I wanted to apologize."

"For what, exactly?" I ask. My mom used to ask me this when I apologized as a kid. She said that people will say they are sorry without knowing what they are supposed to be sorry for. She told me to never take empty apologies or to give them.

"I'm sorry about the fight at practice," Carter says now. "And I'm—" His voice breaks. "I'm really sorry about Brandon, dude. I was just mad, and I didn't think the cops were going to get involved or anything. Everything got so out of control, and it all happened so fast." He does not cry, but his voice is hoarse like he might. "In the moment, I was just angry, and feeling insecure, and I was really bad to you, and I shouldn't have done that, and now Brandon . . ." Carter's voice wavers. "I just feel like it's all my fault." He puts his face in his hands.

I try to swallow, but my throat feels blocked. My eyes sting. I close my eyes and breathe to gather my composure. Fault. Everyone is carrying it.

"Did the cops interview you?" I ask now.

"Yeah," Carter says. "That's why my mom said she didn't want to press charges, because I asked her not to. I felt bad even then, because I didn't mean for everything to get so out of hand."

That is hard to believe. It could have just been his mom wanting to be nice. I cannot be sure.

"I just never thought anything would happen to Brandon. The night it happened, I blamed myself and I wanted to help by at least making sure you didn't get in trouble, but then afterward I just felt so bad that I started to blame you instead, and then after that I just kept blaming you. I kept telling myself it was all your fault and you started everything. Then at that practice, I just lost it," Carter says now. His speech is hurried, and his words come out somewhat jumbled. I figure he might be anxious.

I study all of his face. His blotchy cheeks. His watery eyes. He has been feeling the way I have felt.

"Why have you had a problem with me all this time?" I ask now.

Carter shrugs. "I don't know. When we were kids, I used to just hate all the stuff we had to replan or readjust for you. Then, as we got older, I think it just turned into hating you because you were you. I never really tried to get to know you. I just put up with you because you were Brandon's brother. I always felt like the adults pushed the rest of us to the side when you were around, you know?"

I consider what Carter is saying. I never thought about how my presence made everyone else feel sometimes—not until Brandon said what he did the other day. It was never on purpose. I know I was a lot of work at times, but at the same time, I should not have to apologize for it. The same way that nobody else should have to apologize for feeling the way they do about me. A few weeks ago, I would have apologized. I would have apologized just to tell Carter what he wanted to hear. Not now. I understand his position, but I have feelings of my own, and my feelings are valid too.

"No, Carter. I don't know," I say now. "Autism is not a privilege. Autism is not something that just gives me extra attention and care. It is work. It is work for me to deal with this conversation right now. It was work for my mom when I had sensory overload. It was work at birthday parties to explain that I was not upset because people were screaming; I was upset because people were screaming, and I could feel the sound of kids rubbing their hands against the rubber balloons under my skin, and the air conditioner whirred too loud. It was always work. I am not going to apologize and understand when all I was doing was working to try to be like you all, when really, you all were never anything to aspire to."

Carter does not look at me and I do not look at him.

"Still," I say now, "autism does not absolve me of guilt. That is a disservice to me." I think of Isabella and her father. "I have been blaming myself. Been blaming you. At the end of the day, we did what we did, but none of us got Brandon arrested. None of us did that. You did not do that."

Carter looks up, and tears finally fall. "Sometimes I feel like I did."

I nod. "Me too."

Carter apologizes a few more times before he leaves. I feel both heavier and lighter after our talk.

I look over at Isabella and she gives me an encouraging smile. "Mind if I rub your back?" she asks now.

I shake my head.

As her hand makes light passes over my back, I think about everything Carter said.

"You okay?" Isabella asks.

"I am not sure," I say.

"You ready?"

"No," I say now. "But we have to go anyway."

We head in the same direction as before and reach Marcia's house in ten minutes. I ring her doorbell again, but this time, her mom comes to the door in a pressed navy oxford shirt so crisp that it looks like it might crack if she moves.

"Did you need something?" Marcia's mom sneers.

"Uh, yes," I say. "Is Marcia home?"

Marcia's mom narrows her eyes. "Is she expecting you?"

"Um . . ." I look at Isabella, whose eyes are wide. "No?"

"Then I suggest you leave right now." Abruptly, Marcia's mom starts to close the door.

"Please, she knows something that might help my brother. I just need to—" I reach my hand out to stop the door.

"Remove your hand before I call the police," Marcia's mom says through clenched teeth.

I lift my hand off the door and she slams it in my face.

I watch as she walks away and ascends the stairs.

That's it. My only chance to help my brother before his trial starts tomorrow, gone.

"I'm so sorry, Aiden," Isabella says now. I look over and she is crestfallen. She reaches for me, and I flinch at her touch, sensitive in a way I have not been in a while. Here we are, standing in front of what looks like the gate to paradise, and we are denied entry. Every hope I have is behind this door and I have no way to reach it. My lip trembles and I feel myself threatening to fall apart.

Isabella squeezes my bicep and I come back to my body. Aware. I close my eyes. I told myself that this was everything. That is the problem. I told myself that this was it. I believed that this was my only solution, but it is not. I can trust in the lawyers to do their jobs. I can trust in my mom. I can trust in the jury to see sense. I have to trust something, because right now, if I don't, everything will seem too bleak.

I pull myself together.

I shake my head. "It is going to be okay," I say now. "We did not need this anyway. It is all going to be okay."

Isabella and I split up and I head home, which is only a few minutes away. I count the sidewalk squares and my steps as I go to calm myself. One, two. New sidewalk square. One, two. New sidewalk square. Then I hear clicks. By the time I look up and catch the flashes, it is too late.

"Aiden!" someone shouts.

"Aiden, here!" another voice shouts.

"Aiden, how do you feel about you brother's trial starting tomorrow?"

My driveway is right there. I am almost home. A huge crowd of journalists pile in front of our—now closed—gate, taking pictures and wagging their microphones in my face. The flashing bulbs blind me momentarily each time they go off. The itch in my skin builds quickly and my throat fills with bile.

"Aiden!"

I try to push past the reporters, praying they will part the way for me, but they barely budge. Now I am lost in the sea of skin, fabric, and questions.

"Aiden!"

Please. I cannot speak.

"Aiden, here! Your brother, is he guilty or innocent?"

Please. Stop.

I fall to the concrete, scraping my exposed knees on the ground, curling up into a ball.

"Aiden!"

The last thing I hear is my name before the ringing. Then

after the ringing, there is screaming. Why is someone always screaming? Why does my throat hurt? Is it me?

Then I am cocooned. Swathed. Cinnamon. Vanilla. Pine trees. Tabasco sauce. Brandon.

"Back up off him!" my brother snaps. "Back up! Now!"

Brandon lifts me and walks with me to the gate. I lean into him, grateful for his presence and calmer in his arms. My erratic breathing slows and I focus on my footsteps.

"Brandon, is this how you saved your brother the night you got arrested?" someone shouts now.

Brandon swings an arm out to clear the way for us.

"Brandon, are you your brother's hero? Are you going to jail for him?"

"No!" Brandon shouts. "No, I'm not. I've never been a hero, and my brother doesn't need one. He's autistic; he's not a victim." He looks at me. "He never needed saving."

Inside, Brandon sits with me and rocks for a while until my body stops vibrating and I feel calm inside my flesh. Mom and Dad call security and get the reporters cleared out. Within the hour, everyone is gone.

After the ordeal, I lie in bed, my body heavy like a rubber weight, aching from practice and a long day. I spend time in my room, resting my eyes, until I hear the doorbell. I wait, but when it seems like nobody answers, I leave my room.

"Mom, Dad?" I call out. "Brandon?"

No answer. Great, now I have to get it.

I head downstairs and open the front door to see Marcia sitting on the stone stairs leading up to our home. Marcia's head is down, and her long black hair falls like a curtain and shines in the dim light of the entryway.

I stand, silent, body close to shut down. Considering her mother's earlier reaction, I am nothing less than shocked to see her.

Marcia turns and stands. Her face is pleading before she even speaks. "You're just going to let me sit here? Not going to invite me in?" Her voice wavers.

I close my eyes, hand still on the door, and tilt my head back.

Marcia clears her throat. "Look, Aiden," she starts.

I lower my head to look at her.

"Why are you here?" My voice comes out low. It is as tired of this day as I am. "You cannot help me, right? You do not have anything else to offer." I do not try for sarcasm. I am not good at it. I just repeat what she said, exactly how she said it.

Marcia looks at me with round hazel eyes and blinks faster.

"You do not have anything else to offer. I came to you for information; you do not have it. I do not have the time, the patience, the aptitude, or the composure—none of it. I am tired. It has been a weird day. I just want to go back inside and go to sleep." My voice comes out louder than intended.

Marcia continues to blink fast, but no tears fall.

My heart begins to race. I let out a slow breath. My heart beats loud in my ears. I try to slow the rhythm.

Marcia twists her fingers up together and bounces on her toes. She looks everywhere but at me.

I slide down the doorframe and settle on the stone porch. I let my arms fall beside me, lean my head back against the frame, and close my eyes.

"I am sorry. It has been a long day for me."

I wait for Marcia's response. I do not want to look at her, blinking and sad, judging me for my feelings. Not now.

"Is everything okay?" Marcia asks.

"No," I say now. I lift my head to look at her. "The trial starts tomorrow."

Marcia looks down at her feet. "Oh."

I tilt my head to the side. "So, why are you here?"

"Do you remember first grade?" Marcia asks.

Oh god, not the kiss. I do not answer. I just look and wait.

"I got glasses, and everyone was making fun of me. I got called 'four-eyes' and 'bat brain.' I remember you came right up to me on the playground, looked at me, and just said, 'Stein.'" Marcia smiled. "You didn't really say full sentences then, just a few words here and there, but I remember I started to cry after you said that, because I thought you were making fun of me too. I thought you were calling me Einstein."

"I was." I do remember. Her hair was loose that day too and got a bit wild after rolling around on the train carpet in our classroom.

"But then you said, 'Smart.' I gave you a kiss for saying that, because it made me feel better and more confident about my glasses. Even though I don't wear them anymore, I still think about that," Marcia says now.

I focus on Marcia's shoes. Slip-ons, no laces. White, like her button-down shirt.

"Aiden, I don't want you to think differently of me. I want you to still look at me and think of the girl with the glasses that you called smart." Marcia rubs at her arms and shivers.

Sweat beads along my arms, a combination of the heat and moisture still hanging in the air from the wet day. She should not be cold.

"I saw what happened to Brandon, but I can't tell you. I can't tell anyone."

I close my eyes and rest my head on the door. A waste of time.

"I swear I have a good reason, Aiden," Marcia says. "You're protecting your brother, but I'm protecting someone too."

Probably Georgia. "Whoever it is cannot be as important," I say now.

"They are," Marcia says. "I swear they are."

"Is there a video?" I ask.

Marcia presses her lips together.

"Can you give it to me?"

Marcia stays silent.

"Why are you here?" I whisper. Tears drip down my cheeks. "Why? You are not helping. You are doing nothing. Why did you come?"

"I just—" Marcia says now. Her voice cracks. "I just need you to understand. I need you to see my side. I don't want anyone to get hurt, but I need you to understand, Aiden."

I stand and do not bother wiping my face.

"Well, I don't," I say.

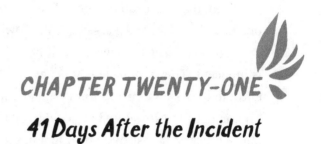

CHAPTER TWENTY-ONE

41 Days After the Incident

Courtrooms are not supposed to make me nervous, but this trial is really ruining them for me. The benches are packed with journalists and a few classmates brave enough to skip school. I scan the room and take in the familiar faces, ignoring the anxious gurgle in my stomach. We are here. I focus now on the back of Brandon's head, sending him all the good vibes that I can muster. He fidgets in his seat, likely nervous for everything to begin. I wish I could comfort him in this moment.

I pull at my fingertips and try to concentrate during the opening statements. Brandon's lawyer talks, and so much of what she says goes in one ear and tumbles out the other in pieces. It is everything I have already heard and everything we have already said. Brandon was perfect. Brandon is innocent. Brandon deserves freedom and a future.

Then the prosecution goes. The lawyer, a man with a pinched, lined face and glasses, speaks slowly and deliberately.

"Brandon Wright's lawyers will have you believe that he is innocent. They will have you believe that this lawsuit is an effort to frame a promising young star and rob him of a future. That is not the case. Brandon Wright is guilty of assaulting a police officer and resisting arrest in a misguided effort to help that boy." The lawyer points at me. "Is it admirable? Perhaps, to some. But does admirability equal innocence? No. This case will prove that emotion clouded Brandon Wright's judgment so much that he felt that attacking a peace official was the only way to assist his autistic brother. A brother who, as you will hear later, was clearly described in a 911 call as a viable and dangerous threat to others—a deadly threat, at that."

Me? Deadly? I look to my dad, who reaches out and gives my leg a squeeze. I want to ask what the lawyer means, but I know this is not a good time. I take a breath and lean back into the pew. This is going to be a long—and personal—day.

"Though Brandon Wright saw it in his heart to do what he felt was right, in the process, he committed a lot of wrong. And for that, we require justice. Thank you." The lawyer finishes and takes his seat.

I look to Mom, and she is stoic and unsurprised. Dad—who still keeps one hand on me—looks slightly sick. Brandon's body is tensed like he would rather run to anywhere but here. The courtroom is not his domain. I know that however nervous I must be, he must feel it ten times over.

The judge declares a break shortly after the opening statements and I rush from the courtroom, suddenly sick to my stomach. I run to the bathroom and heave spit, froth, and the nothing that I ate for breakfast this morning. I am suddenly grateful for that decision. The trial is enough to riddle my body with anxiety, but to hear that I am considered deadly? To have everyone in the room stare and process me as a threat? I am so overwhelmed with emotions that I cannot even put a name to them.

I rinse my mouth out and splash my face with water, not bothering to look in the mirror before drying myself off and leaving the bathroom.

On my way out, I see a flash of long black hair and follow it around the corner. There, I see Marcia, bent over, breathing fast.

I approach, and she appears to be crying. What right does she have to cry when it is my brother on the chopping block? I start to walk away, then double back. Despite the anger surging through my body when I see her, I cannot leave her like this.

"I am going to touch you, if that is okay," I say now.

I see a slight nod from Marcia, so I place my hand on her back. We stay like this for three minutes and twenty-three seconds. Three deep breaths later, and Marcia rises.

"Thank you, Aiden."

"Black men are more likely to be incarcerated for the same crimes as white men," I say. I know she is upset, but I cannot be silent when she knows something that could help my brother.

"Aiden, please—"

"Black men are also more likely to get more time for the same crimes as white men," I add.

"Please, Aiden, don't you see I'm already upset!"

"Why?" I ask now. I barely restrain myself from shouting. "Why are you upset? It is not your brother going to jail!"

"Because it was me!" Marcia shouts. Her voice carries across the lobby, and I freeze. The words tumble from her as though she can no longer hold them in. "The call they're talking about in there. The call that made you sound deadly. The call that made them see all of you as a threat. The call that got your brother arrested. The reason the cops came. Aiden"— Marcia's voice is strained now, and she blinks away tears—"it was me. I called them."

"What?" I ask. That does not make sense. I do not understand. "No, you—"

"I called them," Marcia says now. "You're going to find out anyway when they play the call in the courtroom, so I might as well admit it now. I called. I said that you looked like you were going to kill Carter, and—"

"And what?" I barely get the question out. My throat is tight from shock.

"Georgia said something awful about you looking like a gorilla," Marcia whispers. "It's our fault. That's what we were hiding."

I do not know what to say. Still, not everything is adding up.

"But what about Tucker? You and Georgia were threatening him, and he said something to me about footage," I say now.

Marcia nods. "Tucker had his camera out during the call. He was filming everything. He got the call and the arrest on tape."

My mouth falls open. They have footage of the arrest. They have had it this entire time. If it shows anything we could use in his defense, Brandon could walk away from this. "Could the footage help my brother?" I ask.

Marcia nods. A tear rolls down her cheek. She averts her gaze, and I can tell she is ashamed of herself.

"Do you still have it?"

Marcia nods again.

Anger and relief ripple through me like disturbed water. I want to scream. My body feels as though it is fighting to jerk in every direction at once. My fingers twitch in response to the rush of emotions warring within me. "How could you not say something? How could you let it go on this long? Do you just not care?" I ask.

The tears come faster now, and Marcia's face is soaked.

"No, that's not it!"

"So what is it, then?"

"It's my dad!" Marcia cries. Her face is anguished.

What?

Marcia sobs. "Remember I said my dad is a cop? It's him, Aiden. My dad was the arresting officer. My dad is the one who accused Brandon of assault. I didn't say anything because it's my dad."

I close my eyes and take a few breaths. I stay this way for fourteen seconds. I understand. I get it now. The same guilt I have been carrying, Marcia has carried as well. Her blaming herself for getting her father and Brandon into this by calling the police. Me blaming myself for getting into the fight in the first place.

I pace for a while, then sit on a wooden bench near us. I pat the seat next to me so that Marcia knows to sit. She hesitates for eight seconds, then joins me. She casts furtive glances in my direction as I process.

"Marcia," I say now. "Did my brother do what he is being accused of?"

"From what I saw, no," Marcia replies.

"Then you have to help him."

"I can't," she says now. Her voice breaks.

"So why did you tell me?" I ask.

"Because being here . . . ," Marcia says now. "It makes it real. It's too real."

I pause. I look all over her face. I know she means it, but she still does not get it.

"Marcia, it is real for you today, but for my brother, for all of us, it is reality. It is our reality every single day. If you do something to help my brother, your dad still walks away from this. If you do not do anything, then my brother does not. He does not walk away from this. This is real for you today, but Blackness is not your reality. And look, I am not judging. I have been Black all my life, but until recently, autism has been my whole reality. I never paid attention to how my Blackness made autism much more dangerous until now. And now I see it. I see it, and Marcia, I cannot unsee it. You see something.

Do not close your eyes. Do not try to unsee it. It might not be your reality, but like you said, it is real. Do not make jail Brandon's reality," I say now. "Help him."

We sit in silence for two minutes and forty-two seconds.

"I can't," Marcia whispers.

I close my eyes. Tears gathers in my chest, a sob crawling up my throat. I cough it back down. "Okay," I say.

"I'm sorry," Marcia says.

"Yes," I say now. "You are."

I trudge away from her back into the courtroom. I need to be with my family.

CHAPTER TWENTY-TWO

42 Days After the Incident

The next day in school, I avoid Marcia. I avoid everyone. I know something that could help my brother, but I cannot do anything about it. I cannot tell my mom because then she will pressure Marcia, and I do not think I want that either. What if Mom goes to Marcia's parents and they delete the video? Right now, all I have is Marcia's word and no actual video in my possession, which means that anything can happen if I push too hard.

Yesterday was all opening statements and introductory evidence, so we are not in the weeds yet. I worry about how things will go today. Stress lingers in the pit of my stomach. I am doing okay until gym—the class that I have with Georgia and Marcia. When I exit the locker room onto the track for ten minutes of walking before activities, I see them together, walking and whispering. Probably talking about how they do not plan to help my brother.

I focus on my steps. Moving forward with only the force of my own will. Trying with everything in me not to run ahead, pull Marcia aside, and explain to her again all the reasons why she should do something. I will not beg. I cannot. I have facts. I have statistics. I have truth. So does she. But she will not use it.

I tap along my thigh as I walk. One, two. Stop. One, two. Stop. One step after the next. I watch my feet swing and fall into a mindless pattern, chasing all anxious thoughts from my brain. I lose myself in the motions until they become nothing but swaths of color against the canvas of the ground. I allow the chatter around me to dissolve into whispers that trickle across my skin like wind. I zone out completely until a whistle blows. When our gym teacher calls for us to go back inside, I lag behind everyone else, my head more muddled than it was at the beginning of the day.

I look at my feet and make my way through the doors into the gym until I collide with something solid. I blink away confusion and take my eyes off the floor to see Marcia standing in front of me, eyes wide with an expression that I cannot immediately place.

NOTE: *This might be expectation?*

I am not a mean person. I am never mean to anyone. Mean is not something I do. But I see Marcia looking at me, and I do not know what she wants from me, and suddenly, I feel mean. I feel angry. I do not want her to make me into something else that I am not. First, a killer. Now what?

I sidestep Marcia and keep walking. I ignore the footfalls behind me, louder even than the frantic bouncing of basketballs filling the gym, and try to move faster, my long strides doubling hers.

"Aiden, you can't leave the gym," Marcia says now.

I round on her. "What do you want?" I know my tone is harsh, but I cannot control it.

Marcia steps back, rebuffed by my response. "I . . . I don't know."

I roll my eyes, turn on my heel, and walk away again. Once again, footsteps follow, and I find myself growing more irritated with each step.

"Aiden, please."

I turn again and look at Marcia. "There is no 'please.' There is nothing. There is nothing you can say to me. There is nothing you should say to me. The only thing that I want to hear from you is that you changed your mind and you plan to help my brother. Do you plan to help my brother?"

Marcia opens her mouth twice, but no sound comes out.

"Exactly."

"Aiden, I don't know how. I don't know what to do." Her face is a war of emotions.

"The right thing," I say now. I turn away from her and start toward the bleachers, dodging an errant basketball that flies in my direction.

"Aiden, right and wrong are subjective."

I stop. Isabella said that to me once. But I keep my back turned.

"What's right to you will break me, Aiden. It will break me. It might ruin my relationship with my dad forever. With my mom. With my whole family. My sister might never talk to me again. I have a lot to lose here and not a lot to gain."

"What about a conscience?" I ask now.

Marcia does not answer, so I turn to her.

"What about getting rid of guilt? What about what my brother has to lose? What about that? Is his freedom worth less than your comfort?"

Marcia stammers. "N-no, I didn't mean—"

"You do not have to mean that for it to be true based on your actions. What you say and what you do are two different things, Marcia. And, right now, what you are doing is saying that my brother's life is worth less than yours. You are saying that he is worth less than you."

Marcia looks at the lacquered wooden floor of the basketball court. Around us, people yell and whoop, some playing basketball, some off to the side finding other activities to avoid the raucous undertakings happening in the middle of the gym. Around us, life goes on. Here, two lives are stopped.

"Aiden, I need time to think."

"Everybody to the locker room! It's time to get changed," the gym teacher shouts. He pierces the moment between us like a bubble that has burst.

I close my eyes. I am tired. I have done all that I can. "I do not have any more time." I turn to trudge back to the locker room, exhausted to my bones.

"Wait," Marcia says now.

I turn.

Marcia chews on her bottom lip. "You just need the video?" she asks.

A brief rush of excitement courses through me, but I consider her question. My hopes are almost immediately dampened by reality. Marcia might not agree to help if she has to do more than just give me the video. "I cannot promise you will not be asked to testify. To do this, you will have to be all the way on our side."

Marcia tugs at the ends of her hair. "Can I talk to your mom about it? After school, maybe?"

I stow my shock, reserving relief for when she turns the video over. I nod.

After school, I meet up with Marcia by the gate to the football field. My mood is buoyed when I see her—I figured she would have changed her mind about showing up. I have felt so many things since everything has happened—anger, sadness, joy, guilt—but the one thing I have not felt until today was hope. I have it now, and I do not want to be disappointed.

"Before I call my mom, are you sure you want to do this?" I ask again.

Marcia nods. "Like you said two weeks ago, I know Brandon. I know you both. I don't know if it's the right or wrong thing to do, but I know I have nightmares. I know I can't sleep. This has been eating away at me, and I don't want to feel like this anymore."

"Okay," I say now. My hands shake as with anticipation as I dial my mom's number.

She picks up on the first ring. "Hey, sweetie. You're going to have to talk fast. I'm leaving the office to meet Brandon's lawyers."

"That is actually perfect," I say. "I have someone who wants to talk to you."

Marcia takes the phone and explains, through many tears, everything that happened. She details the assault, the call, the video, and the aftermath. I wait for my mom's response to come through the speaker.

Mom is quiet for only seven seconds. "Where is the video now?" She is in lawyer mode.

"I have it on a memory card at home from Tucker's camera."

"Marcia, I have to be honest with you. We can take the footage and try to get it submitted to discovery, but the law requires that we prove legitimacy of the video," my mom says now. "We can't use it without your testimony. If you agree to testify, then we may be able to do something with the footage, and it may help clear Brandon's name."

Marcia hesitates. "So, I have to go on the stand and testify against my dad?"

"Yes." Mom's answer is immediate.

Marcia looks at me. This is the moment of truth—the only moment that matters. A few tears travel down her face, hanging on her chin before dripping to the ground below, dotting the concrete like raindrops. I hold my breath, waiting for her response.

"Okay," she whispers. "I'll do it."

I hear an audible sigh from my mom. "Perfect. Can you bring the footage to our house?"

"I'm headed home," Marcia replies. "I can drop it off if you're there."

"I'll swing by the house immediately to grab it from you," Mom says now. "And Marcia?"

"Yes?"

"Thank you."

Mom hangs up, and Marcia hands me my phone.

We stand in silence for ninety-two seconds before Marcia sniffles. I finally look up from my shoes and see her rubbing the tears away.

"Are you really ready to do this?" I ask now.

Marcia shakes her head.

"Are you going to do it anyway?"

Marcia nods. "I'm going to go grab the card for your mom. If I don't give it to her now, I might lose my nerve."

I nod.

Marcia walks a few feet away, stops, and turns back. She comes up to me. Her tear-streaked face seems more at peace now.

"Aiden?"

"Yeah?"

"Thank you," Marcia says. She stands on her toes and gives me a peck on the cheek. Then I watch her as she makes her way down the sidewalk, headed to the community.

I rub at my face, ignoring the building itch climbing up my back. I close my eyes. This could be it. This might all finally be over. I check my watch. I need to go.

I have twenty-three minutes before I have to go the locker room for meetings and team meal before the game tonight. This game determines whether we make it to the playoffs, or if our season is over. Our first real way to see if we are a winning team without Brandon.

I wait for nerves to hit me, but there are too many other worries bouncing around in my head. Georgia, Brandon, the trial, and Marcia taking the stand next week with the video that will reveal everything. Too much is happening. My skin starts to tingle and itch, so I wrap my arms around myself and pull in tight. I cannot fall apart now. I need to hold it together and focus.

"Hey, A! I knew you'd be at the field already." Brandon's voice breaks through my thoughts.

I look up as my brother makes his way up the bleachers to sit next to me. When he reaches me, he grabs me and gives me a big hug. "I'm hugging you—accept the hug," he says now. His voice is filled with joy.

I chuckle. "Why?"

"Mom called me. I heard about the video and Marcia and Georgia," Brandon says now, and lets me go. "Mom says this can really be the thing that helps the case for real this time."

I smile. We do not have the video yet, so I do not want to

be prematurely happy, but I will not kill Brandon's light. I let him hope.

"Is that what you were trying to tell me before about Georgia?" Brandon asks now.

"Yeah," I reply. "But I understand why you were preoccupied."

"Nah," he says. "I should have listened. Maybe we would have had this sooner. Maybe I could have been less stressed. I'm sorry I didn't listen."

"You never listen," I say now. "What's new?"

Brandon tousles my locs. "Shut up." He laughs louder than he has since all this began. "So, what are you doing now?"

"Thinking," I say.

"About?"

I shrug. "Everything."

"Like about how male seahorses get pregnant, or how female spiders eat the males after they mate?" Brandon asks.

I smile. "No, I was thinking about how shrimp have their hearts in their heads and how slugs have four noses."

"You mean you ain't thinking about how koalas leave fingerprints at crime scenes and snails can sleep for three years?"

I laugh, finally relaxing into our familiar routine. "No, I was really thinking about laying a frog on its back and stroking its stomach to hypnotize it."

Brandon snorts through a laugh. "I thought you were gonna go for penguin urine in glaciers. I had a good follow-up for that."

NOTE: *Random, weird facts is still our favorite game to play. That, at least, has not changed.*

Brandon's smile makes me feel happier than I have all week. I realize so many of the conversations that we have had lately have been difficult. This is the first time that it feels like we are a step closer to being us again. I lean back in the bleachers and Brandon follows suit. We both gaze ahead at the marigold sky.

"All right, now that you're not feeling so serious, what you thinking about?" Brandon asks.

"The trial," I say now.

"What about it?"

"What if Marcia changes her mind? What if the video does not help? What if they do not care about her testimony? What if—"

"The world blows up right now and we all turn into dust that looks like snowflakes?" Brandon jumps in. "You can 'what if' this to death, but the outcome is gon be what it is."

"This all feels, I don't know, out of control."

"Yeah," Brandon says now. "Because it's out of *our* control. But I'm gon be real with you. I don't think it's totally out of control anymore."

I nod. Finally, nothing is in my hands. I have given it all away, handed it off to someone else, and maybe now I can breathe without the guilt crushing my lungs. Maybe now I can sleep without the stain of red and blue lights behind my eyelids. Maybe now things can really look up.

Brandon looks down at his phone. "Sorry, getting a call."

"You wanna answer it?"

"Nah, it's from Georgia."

I hesitate, rubbing my tongue against the roof of my mouth.

"You should answer it," I say now.

"Why should I?" Brandon asks. He sounds surprised and irritated at the same time. "I know everything now. I know what her and Marcia said."

"We do not know how she meant what she said," I say now. "And she was talking about me, anyway, not you."

"You're missing the point," Brandon says. He shoves his phone back in his pocket, call rejected.

"So, show it to me."

Brandon sighs and rolls his eyes. "It wouldn't matter if she was talking about a random Black person on the street, A. It could just as easily apply to me. And what if those same words landed you in jail instead of me? I mean, honestly, those words could have gotten you killed. So, yeah, I'm mad."

"Maybe she had different intentions. We do not know that she meant it that way," I say now. I want to believe that Georgia did not mean harm. She is friends with Marcia, and Marcia turned out to be good, so Georgia cannot be all bad.

"So how else did she mean it? Even if you take the wild shit she said out of the picture, she knew that her brother had something that could help me but she didn't say anything, A," Brandon says now. "She knew he had this video; she knew that he had video proof that a cop attacked me unprovoked and then accused me wrongfully. She knew that what Marcia said on the phone probably caused the cops to come in how they did. She knew that the cop was Marcia's dad. She knew all that the whole time, and she just been texting me and trying to check on me like shit was all good. Knowing what she knew, she ain't just offer it herself. You had to squeeze it out of Marcia." Brandon shakes his head. "Georgia don't have a damn thing to say to me that could make me feel like she gives a crap about me, A. 'Cause if she cared, she would have told me from the get-go."

I stay quiet for a minute, trying to find the right thing to say to Brandon.

"This is a tough situation," I say now. "Maybe cut her some slack."

"Why?"

"She was not the one who made the call. Marcia is the one who called the cops," I say. "Now she is testifying."

Brandon squeezes his eyes shut. "Then kudos to her. She helped get me arrested, now she's helping fix it."

I tap at my leg. One, two. Stop. One, two. Stop. "I do not want you to be angry and bitter forever."

Brandon smiles at me. "You got a good heart, A. At the end of the day, though, it goes beyond cutting people slack and just handing out forgiveness. It's about privilege, abuse of it, and ignorance of it. It's conversations I don't feel like having and work I don't feel like doing, you know? It ain't my work to do. When Georgia does the work, then we can talk." He chews on his top lip. "And I won't be bitter or angry forever, bro. But I feel like I earned the right to be bitter and angry right now."

I nod. He has.

"Greg said that Louis is reposting a lot of stuff about you. Good stuff. Articles that support you," I say now. Hopefully my brother will be more open to teammate reconciliations.

Brandon shrugs. "I haven't talked to Louis. I don't got an issue with him, really, but I can't help but feel like he took a side, and I gotta wonder why."

"What do you mean?" I ask.

"A, come on, man." Brandon sounds a bit exasperated with me. "I feel like we keep revolving around the same topic and you're not seeing it."

I blink.

"Aiden, Georgia didn't tell me about there even potentially being a video because protecting her white friend—who was using her white girl privilege to get the cops called on us, one of whom was her white dad—was more important than telling me, the Black guy she claims she likes, something that could be of help. Louis took Carter's side even though Carter is, and was, dead wrong, because they're both white. It's really simple."

I shake my head. "I am not saying those things are not factors, but I do not think it is that simple. I do not think that it is the whole picture."

"Well, I gotta sit in a courtroom and I'm Black, so the picture's looking real simple from where I'm at." Brandon snorts out a laugh, but I know he does not think that anything is funny.

"You know, Carter apologized," I say now.

"Good for him," Brandon replies. His tone is flat.

I will have to give that subject more time.

"Georgia and Marcia have known each other since kinder-garten, just like most of your friends. Marcia is Georgia's best friend. What if it was you and Greg?"

Brandon shifts his mouth to the side. The stadium lights come on as the sky darkens above us. They cast a harsh light across Brandon's face, which makes him look more severe than I think he intends.

"You would not turn on Greg for Georgia, and I do not think it is just because Greg is Black. And Carter and Louis have always been closer to each other than everyone else. I mean . . ." I trail off. Brandon has a point. I cannot pre-tend he does not. I do not know if Louis told Carter that he was wrong. I doubt Carter or Louis considered why they got treated better by the cops than we did. I doubt Marcia consid-ered how dangerous her words were on the phone. Brandon has a point. But I have a point too.

"I don't think that's the full story, A," Brandon says.

"It never is," I say now. I am learning that.

Brandon is quiet for a minute. I focus on a dragonfly— the last of the dying day—flitting in between the bleachers. It darts back and forth, and I wonder if it is seeking mosqui-toes to eat. I admire its shadows, which dance in the artifi-cial light.

"If Greg was wrong—if Greg did what Marcia did—I would have said something," Brandon finally says. "But we ain't having that conversation, because at the end of the day, Greg doesn't have the power to cause what Marcia caused. That's the difference."

I rub my tongue against the roof of my mouth again, feeling the textured ridges. I trace my cuticles with my fingertips, scratching at snags and pulling skin free. I ignore the aches as I peel nervously.

"Don't stress about that stuff now, though. You need to focus more on the game and less about all this. You did what you could do for me. Now we gotta focus on you," Brandon says. I glance at him, and he has a smile plastered to his face that was not there a few seconds ago. I can tell that he wants to move on.

"You got people, A?" he asks now.

"What do you mean?"

Brandon shrugs. "On a team, you got the team, yeah, but everybody on the team ain't gon be your people. I'm not out there with you . . ." He closes his eyes and clears his throat. "I'm not out there, so I just wanna make sure you got people. I don't want you to be on the field, on the team, but alone."

"I have Greg and Reg and Bernard and Dustin," I say now. I feel a swell in my chest as I say it. I have thought about it, of course, but to realize and say out loud to Brandon that I have people—my own people—means something to me.

Brandon raises a brow at me. "Oh, now my best friend and brother wanna get along? I just had to get arrested and replaced for it to happen?"

I chuckle. "We never hated each other."

"Yeah. But y'all ain't necessarily like each other, either," Brandon says. "Well, at least you got him."

"Reg, too. And Bernard. And Dustin."

Brandon clicks his throat a few times. "Reg is starting tonight?"

I look down.

NOTE: *I forgot that Reg is our current quarterback.*
  • *Me liking Reg could be seen as a betrayal.*

"Yeah," I say now. I am careful not to seem too excited.

Brandon nods but does not smile. "I taught him all he knows. He'll get y'all there."

I nod with him.

"Well, gon ahead! Go, focus on tonight. Get your head in the game and all that," Brandon says now. He bumps me with his shoulder.

"Put the pedal to the metal, or whatever they say," I respond.

"Nobody says that!" Brandon laughs and tousles my locs before he heads down the bleachers. I watch him descend and consider how my brother has unfailingly showed up for me. All things considered, he never missed a game, even if it made him sad to sit and watch. Though I am sure now that he did not do it all just to be the perfect big brother. Or, if he did, that is not why he is here tonight. He is more than that now—more honest, truer to himself—and I am prouder of him now than I have ever been.

My thoughts shift to everyone else that I want by my side, and I text Isabella.

Game starts at 6. Coming?

Wouldn't miss it for anything in the world.

I smile. This might be our last game. Our last chance to make it to States. I check the clock. It is almost time for the team meeting. Time to get ready.

CHAPTER TWENTY-THREE

42 Days After the Incident

I am standing outside the locker room entrance, huddled up with my teammates, all ready to run out and break the banner the cheerleaders hold open for us. My breath is hot and it echoes in my helmet. I am about to run out onto the field for my first game where I will actually play and not watch from the sideline. I wait for the nervous energy to flood my body. I wait for the urge to tap, or rock, or the need for deep pressure. Nothing comes. I am hyper-focused. I feel and see everything. My team crowding around me, packed in the evening warmth. The rustling of the cheerleaders' pom-poms. The sound of the DJ playing rap music to get the crowd hyped before the game.

"Y'all ready to bust some heads?!" Greg shouts next to me.

Some of the guys yell in response. We are packed tight—not quite in a line, but bunched together, ready to run out.

"Nah, I ain't hear y'all. Y'all ready to bust some heads?!" Greg yells again.

More guys yell back. The noise builds, and I breathe harder. Adrenaline courses through my veins, and everything feels like it is sped up. I let the noise ripple under my skin, becoming a part of me and driving my energy. Hyping me so that I am one with the team.

"I said," Greg yells one last time, "are y'all gon go out there and bust some damn heads?!"

My throat opens up with the team. We all roar in response.

"Let's go!"

We rush forward. The cheerleaders hold a large banner in front of the entrance to the field, and we run through and break it. The lights of the stadium are bright. The field is different when you are on it instead of looking down from the bleachers. I suddenly feel the nerves start to creep up my back.

Someone grabs my shoulders and jostles me. I look to my right, where Bernard yells with excitement. It is loud, but it is almost like I cannot process all the noise at once. This is the same dull roar I have always been used to. I shake it off. Nod my head. Get your head in the game—that is what Brandon said.

We run to the sideline, and the announcer starts acknowledging sponsors before the game. I look out into the stands. I recognize a lot of the faces from sitting with them over the years. I wonder if they know it is me down here. I scan the crowd and see Isabella waving wildly right next to my dad and his unmistakable long locs. Tears sting at my eyes and I blink them away. Next to Dad, still in a suit from work, is my mom. Then, next to her, Brandon. Everyone is here. I cannot stop the tears from falling. For the first time all season, they are all here. All of them.

I wave back to them and then turn toward the turf. I have to show out for them. I have to show Brandon that I am ready for him when he can get back on the field.

Coach Davis walks out to the center line with a microphone and waves for the crowd to settle. It gets quiet on the field and in the bleachers.

"Hi, everyone, and thanks for coming to this game. Thank you to Jupiter Coast High School for coming out and playing us—we always appreciate the challenge." Coach Davis gestures to the other team, gathered in their sky-blue uniforms, and there are scattered claps in the crowd. "Let's get started!"

The first quarter of the game goes by quickly with an early touchdown and field goal from Jupiter Coast. I only get in for one play and then watch from the sideline, judging performances and thinking about what I would have done differently. We are at the top of the second quarter when Coach Nielson calls me over. I push off the bench, put my helmet back on, and run to the sideline.

"Okay, Wright," Coach Nielson yells into my helmet. "Shotgun formation, inside zone run, got it?"

I nod. An easy play. A play I know I can execute. Nothing is going to stop me. Coach Nielson slaps the top of my helmet and I run out onto the field. A few guys stretch their arms out, and I slap them with high fives as I line up for the formation. I glance back up at my family one last time, and Brandon gives me a thumbs-up before I drown out the roar of noise around me and focus on the play. I get to the line and study the numbers on the backs of my teammates' jerseys. Seven, fourteen, seventy-one, eighty-six. I count to four before the play begins.

In my head, it is quiet when the center snaps the ball to Reg and I run up to grab it, pushing forward through an easy hole opened by the offensive line. I break free and a single safety awaits me in the backfield. The last line of defense. He runs to try to meet me, but I am quick. When he dives to tackle me and misses, I run forward, unchallenged, to the goal line. When I cross it, I cannot think of a celebration—I never actually practiced one and I am a little surprised by the touchdown—so I just drop the ball on the grass. Four guys on the team—a wave of red and black—come rushing at me, pushing me and throwing their bodies into mine. I ignore the building itch from all the contact and press my fingers into my palm for feedback. I know they mean well.

"That's what I'm talking about!" I hear them yelling around me. The noise is not enough to overwhelm me. When everything is so heightened, the sound is less of a piercing and more of a blanket of noise. Something so large that it becomes soft.

My first touchdown. I feel a sense of joy that it happened with everyone here. I look up to the stands and my parents are cheering, their arms in the air. Brandon has his hands cupped around his mouth, likely whooping louder than everyone else.

I hold my arm up to wave and he returns the gesture. I smile and run off the field for our team to punt the ball.

The rest of the game flies by. We hold Jupiter Coast back for the rest for the quarter. In the third quarter, Dustin runs the ball in for a touchdown. Then Jupiter Coast gets a defensive touchdown in the fourth quarter, when their linebacker intercepts the ball Reg meant for Louis and runs it all the way back to our team's goal line—a pick six.

NOTE: *Pick six. Pick the ball off (intercept), get six points (touchdown).*

Now there are seven seconds left and we have possession of the ball. We are down three points. We need a touchdown to win.

"Huddle!" Coach Nielsen calls out to us.

We gather around him. There is tension in the huddle, everyone wanting to make the big play and get the win. We listen with an intensity so taut it could snap.

"We aren't tying this game. No field goals. We're thirty yards from the goal line—we can make it!"

We all nod. Thirty yards is a lot, but it is not impossible. The right play could do it.

"Wright, I want you in. They'll be expecting us to throw a Hail Mary to get the touchdown. I want you all in pistol formation for the draw play. I want the defenders focused on Reg. I want them to think he's about to throw. Wright, I need somebody with power, somebody who can knock people over.

I want you to take the ball all the way in. Can you do it?"

I nod.

"We need a clean play! No penalties! No holding! No nothing! Clean play! Y'all get out there and get this win. Do it for Brandon!" Coach Davis yells to us as we head onto the field.

Do it for Brandon. He is here watching, and I have to show him that everything we have worked on means something. I have to do this right.

We line up for the play.

I position myself behind Reg, the ball snaps, and I cut right. He pretends to look for a wide receiver and scrambles in the pocket. The defenders rush him, Reg fakes a throw to Carter, then tosses the ball to me.

It is in my hand and the way is clear. I push forward. Perez blocks for me and stops an incoming tackle. Wind whips in my helmet and my eyes water as I run. Thirty yards. That is nothing. I glance up at the clock. Three seconds left. My breath rushes out in huffs. Helmets clack around me. Bodies hit the grass. I have to trust my team to handle everyone else. I can get to the goal line. I am almost there when I feel hands grabbing at my jersey. I pull free. I can get there.

Then, impact at the back of my legs. My back arches, body falling forward, and I am going down. I am so close. The goal is in my direct sight as I fall. Close enough to reach out and touch. I take the ball out from under my arm, hold it out in both hands, and stretch forward. The ball just needs to be over the line. That is it. I just need to get the ball over the line. I grip the ball tight so that it does not knock loose once I hit the ground. My body bounces once when I am down. The pressure is gone from my legs. I glance at the clock. Time is up. I glance to the sideline. Coach Davis throws a clipboard and Greg cries on a bench. I look at my hands, at the ball. Inches. I am inches from the goal line. I almost got there.

Jupiter Coast huddles together and jumps in celebration. Carter runs up and reaches a hand out to me. I look up at him and take it. He hoists me up and we jog back to the sideline.

"You can't miss tackles like that! You gotta clear the way!" Coach McDonald yells at no one in particular.

I look around at everyone. They are in varying states of devastation. Some openly cry, others just sit on the ground looking dejected. This is not a team accustomed to loss, and as a team, they have already lost so much. *We* have already lost so much. And now our season is over.

Coach Davis claps his hands twice to get everyone's attention, while Coach McDonald keeps yelling.

"Coach!" Coach Davis snaps.

Coach McDonald quiets, though his nostrils still flare with angry breath.

"We're lining up, y'all. It's time to shake hands. Y'all know what I say—we take the loss with grace, and if we don't want to do so, then we have to win. We didn't win today. That's all right. We learn and push forward."

I look around at the guys gathered in a semicircle around Coach Davis. Some nod, others stare at the ground, some still cry. I feel empty. I am angry with myself. It was on me, and I failed. It was on me, and I could not carry the team the way

Brandon would have. If Brandon were here, he could have finished this the right way.

"We wouldn't have lost if we had Brandon," Greg says from the bench, echoing my thoughts.

"What's that supposed to mean?" Bernard asks. This could start a fight. Emotions are high and things are tense. A vote for Brandon is inherently a vote against Reg, and Bernard is not wrong for wanting to defend his boyfriend. "Reg did all he could on the field," Bernard snaps.

Reg reaches out for Bernard, but Bernard pulls from his grip. Reg does not fight to get Bernard back. He seems as disappointed in himself as I feel with myself.

"He couldn't even throw for one touchdown all game," Greg says, standing up.

Reg tugs at his gloves, upset but not arguing back. I feel bad that he is taking the heat.

"They were ready for the pass play, Greg," Coach Nielsen says now, attempting to de-escalate the situation.

"No. Reg wasn't ready to pass!" Greg yells. Though he is normally a bit hotheaded, this is out of character for him. He is more upset than normal.

"I passed!" Reg shouts. "I passed when I could, but they were on me in the pocket! You saw that!" He finally stands up for himself.

"Hey! We will not attack each other on this field! That's not what we do!" Coach Davis yells. He steps up to Greg and grabs him by the face mask. "Greg, line up! All of you, line up! We are shaking hands with the other team, now!"

"No, fuck that! We wouldn't have lost if Brandon was here!" Greg screams. His voice is like a pumice stone. Abrasive. He rips off his helmet and his face is tearstained. "Reg wasn't ready! We aren't ready! We can't do this shit without Brandon!"

"Greg!" Coach Davis reaches for Greg's arm, but Greg pulls away.

"Stop talking about Reg!" Bernard rushes forward and gets in Greg's face. Bernard is taller, so he looks down, right in Greg's eyes.

I want to interject. I want to say that we are all friends and we should not fight. They do not fight. It is not like them. My throat is constricted, though, and I feel sick.

Greg's nostrils flare and his chest heaves as he stares back. "The fuck you gonna do, Bernard?" he asks.

"You're talking about my boyfriend," Bernard says now.

"You're boyfriend's a shit quarterback," Greg sneers.

Bernard cocks a fist back, but Coach Davis catches his hand midair. The other coaches rush forward to pull Bernard back. Reg steps up and starts screaming in Greg's face. Everyone is moving. Everyone is picking a side. The coaches struggle with Bernard, and I cannot hear anything. I am under pillows. Quiet. Everyone is moving at once. I know where they will all go. Carter will swing at Reg. Reg will duck. Greg will step left and dodge a swing from Dustin.

Stop.

Bernard bumps into the Gatorade container and it topples. The orange container hits the turf, the top pops off, and blue liquid gushes from the barrel like an open dam. The coaches wrestle with Bernard in the juice, splashing everywhere as he roars and fights to get to Greg. Greg stands arguing with Reg and Perez, screaming at each other at the top of their lungs so loud that everything is incoherent.

My fingers dance on my leg. One, two. Stop. One, two. Stop.

Everybody, calm down.

"I don't give a shit! This is your fault anyway! You got Brandon arrested!" Perez screams at Carter.

Carter punches Perez and stumbles back, shaking his hand in the air.

Perez holds his jaw and rushes forward at Carter. Carter braces himself.

"Stop." My voice is not loud enough for them to hear.

Everyone is breaking down. Falling apart. Breaking away like fronds on palm trees. We are not dancing together in the wind. We are falling to the floor, detached, dried out, and done.

Perez knocks over the bin with extra footballs. Another container of Gatorade hits the floor. One of the benches flips. The stadium audience reacts with oohs and aahs as every punch lands. The coaches yell to be heard over the screams of our team.

Everyone just needs to calm down. My skin tingles. The tension lives under the surface, in my blood, making the vein in my neck stutter. This is like before, but also it is not. I remember the fights with Carter. I remember the fight with those boys in front of that cop's house. I remember the chaos, the feeling of being out of control, of careening with no anchor toward guaranteed uncertainty. This is not that. I look at everyone losing themselves to emotion around me and realize that I am the only one still in control. Emotion took them where negative touch once took me, and they need to come back down.

I step forward and grab the closest person to me—Carter. He struggles in my grip, but I pull him close and hold him tight. The muscles in his arms tense and harden against mine, taut from effort. His breath comes fast; I hear it through the muffled void in my ears.

"Let me go! I'll kill him, I swear! Let me go!" Carter yells. He struggles against my grip.

I do not let go. I hold Carter—his back to my chest—until he stops struggling. His muscles soften. He goes from ice to water. Then he spills from my hands onto the ground, onto his knees, crying.

Bernard stops fighting. Coach Davis and Coach Nielson have their arms wrapped around him, holding close. The veins in their arms strain against their skin. They are squeezing him.

I look around at the rest of the team. Dustin holds Perez. Reg holds Greg. They are squeezing each other. They are calming down.

Carter looks up at me, snot dripping from his nose like syrup.

"Thank you," he whispers.

I pat Carter on the back.

Everyone slowly gets themselves together. A few wrap their arms around their bodies, even after they separate, trying to squeeze themselves. The other team watches us with interest, and the crowd calms as the tension on the sideline dissipates. I take the scene in, ready to help again at a moment's notice.

Then everything shakes. My teeth chatter. Arms wrap around me. Layers upon layers of arms. Linebacker, quarterback, offensive lineman, wide receiver—a team's worth of arms. All wrapped around me.

I am still.

"We got you, A." Carter's voice in my ear.

"We're right here." Greg's voice in my other ear.

I nod. They squeeze me and I am okay. My team understands me. They understand what I need. They got me.

Sadness spreads out like fog, filling all the spaces between us, connecting us in collected dejection. Still, I feel closer to everyone now. Closer than ever before. Brothers.

"All right." Coach Davis's voice is low as we begin to detach from each other. "We didn't look like ourselves just now. We didn't look like the team I know we are, but we still can be. What do y'all boys want to do?"

Greg and Carter unwrap their arms from me, and a few of the guys look around at each other. Dustin, Reg, and Bernard all look at me. Nobody speaks.

"Brandon would want us to shake. Take the loss. Watch the film. Learn from it. Do better." My voice is small but unwavering. I know my brother. He would be disappointed by the loss, but he would be even more disappointed to see his teammates act this way. "He would tell us that we are better than just one L."

Greg nods and claps a hand down on my shoulder.

"Let's go. We're not bad sports. We can't be that. Let's go, guys," he says now.

We spread out, assembling ourselves into a line. Greg gives Reg a soft bump on the shoulder as he walks past. I think that means they are okay now. Dustin and Carter pat Bernard on the back as he gets into line.

NOTE: *It is like Coach said—we fight, but we come back together.*

For the first time since the game ended, I look up toward the crowd. Mom is watching me. As soon as I look over at her, she waves. The first game where I actually played for a significant time, and it is a loss. I blink back the stinging in my eyes. Dad, Isabella, and Brandon give me encouraging waves, and Brandon even lets out a whoop for me as we move across the turf.

We follow Coach Davis to the middle of the field, where the Jupiter Coast players are lined up. We jog past them, slapping hands as we go. A gesture of good faith and good sportsmanship.

The locker room is quiet, but the guys bump shoulders, rub heads, and give each other small smiles. I wonder what things were like last year, with Brandon at the helm, buoyant after the win, hopeful for playoffs and the end of the season. I do not know if I will ever get to play a real game with my brother where I get real time with him. I cannot stop the tears tipping over my lashes now like rocks over a cliff. I wanted to be Brandon tonight. I wanted to give the team the win. Carry us into victory like my brother. I could not do it.

When I walk out of the locker room, my family and Isabella are waiting with smiles on their faces. Mom hugs me as soon as she sees me.

"Why are you squeezing me?" I mutter from her shoulder.

She holds me out at arm's length, looking me over. "I'm just really proud of you, honey."

"I did not win," I say now.

Mom shakes her head and pulls me in for another hug. "No, baby. You didn't win. You fought hard, though, and that's all that matters."

Brandon steps up, giving my locs a rub and hitting me with a megawatt smile. "Proud of you, loser," he jokes.

"I think losers are pretty cool," Isabella says with a smile. She steps up and reaches her arms out for a hug. I freeze for a second, then Brandon nudges me forward. "I think you did good! Just like Jerry Rice," she adds.

I let her hug me and close my eyes until she lets go.

Brandon laughs. "I get the feeling you did not explain who Jerry Rice was."

I rub the back of my head. "She is working on it. Positions are tough."

"Gotta know football to hang with us," Dad says now, and gives Isabella a smile.

"How hard can it be with twenty-two people on the field and a huge roster, right?" Isabella says. Her sarcastic humor gets the best of Dad.

"Fair." Dad laughs.

Isabella nudges me. "I have to head home, but I really wanted to let you know that you're a winner to me," she says now. Her eyes linger on mine for two seconds, but it feels longer.

"Thank you," I say now. I thought it would feel like an empty platitude. Something people are supposed to say to cheer you up, but I find that her words genuinely make me feel better. I feel warm and almost happy.

"Another hug?" Isabella asks.

I nod. I lean in, taking in her scent this time. Something warm. Pumpkin? And bright. Like cranberries.

This time, when she lets go, I hold her gaze for a second. "Thank you for coming."

"Every single time." Isabella smiles at me.

I watch, maybe for longer than I should, as she bounces away on her toes. I turn, and Brandon looks at me with his brows raised, face full of expectation.

I open my mouth to protest, and he holds up a hand. "I said nothing!" he says, then laughs. I give him a playful push.

Mom claps once. "Let's go home," she says.

We walk across the field, stepping on candy wrappers, hot dog buns, and plastic cup lids littered across the sideline near the stands along the way.

"I swear y'all almost made me die, stressing me out all game," Brandon says as we reach the car. I open the door and slide into the back seat.

I stare down at my lap. "I disappointed you."

Brandon slides in next to me and bumps me on the shoulder. "No, dummy. I was sad for you. The loss is already hard, but the big losses are worse. I know that. I've had 'em. But it's your first year. It's gon happen. I'm still proud of you, A."

I smile and blink away the stinging. Brandon is proud. Still, I cannot fight the sick feeling that has been twisting in my stomach since the football didn't cross that line.

"We would have won if you were there," I say to my brother.

"Maybe," Brandon says. "Maybe not."

"You would have been there if it wasn't for me," I say now.

"You didn't cause this, Aiden." Mom turns in her seat to look at me. "You didn't cause any of this. This isn't your fault. Don't feel guilty."

I stare out the window, watching swaying palm trees as we sit still in the parking lot. "Guilty," I say. "How can I not feel guilty?"

Dad looks at me in the rearview mirror.

"What does guilty mean, Aiden?"

I glance at my dad. We have not done this since I was twelve. Definitions always made it easier for me to remember words. When I could remember them, it was easier to use them.

"Guilty, by definition, means culpable or responsible for a specified wrongdoing," I say now.

"Are you culpable for Brandon being arrested?" Dad asks.

I do not answer.

"No," Brandon says now.

I glance at my brother, who is, for the first time, confirming that he does not blame me for what happened. I fight the gathering tears.

"Did you tell the cops to come that night?" Dad asks.

I shake my head.

"Exactly," Brandon says.

"Were you the only person on the field tonight?" Mom asks now. She settles back into her seat.

I shake my head.

"Are you specifically responsible for any of this?" Dad asks.

I count the queen palm trees as we drive by. One, two. Stop. I consider everything that has been plaguing me. I go back and forth about my responsibility and the part I play in the larger picture. I think about dominoes, about ripples in the water. I understand more now about where I stand in the situation than I did when it began.

"I did not get Brandon arrested," I say now. "I did not call the police, but I was in a fight. I was in a fight and the police showed up and I followed instructions and bad things happened anyway."

"That's true," Mom says.

"But I did not have to fight," I add. "I played a part in all this. We can acknowledge that." I tap on the window. One, two. Stop. "All my life, you guys have not held me fully accountable for anything because I am autistic. You use it as an excuse, but being autistic does not absolve me of guilt. I might not have done every bad thing, but I contributed. I can live with that."

I stare out the window. Once again, the weather fails me. My life really is not a movie. It never rains during my emotional scenes. I look up instead at the clear night sky, and look for the North Star. I follow it to the Little Dipper and think about my place in the world.

"We just don't want you to feel like you need to be different for good things to happen to you, honey," Mom says as she twists around to face me.

Is that what she has been worried about?

"Carter started the fight with me at the diner. I know that. Marcia and Georgia called the cops. I know that. A cop attacked and falsely accused Brandon. I know that. Nobody needed to be autistic for bad things to happen."

Mom's eyes shine with each streetlight we drive past.

"I calmed down Carter after the game tonight. I squeezed him and the other guys saw it work and tried it. I kept my cool when everyone else was falling apart. I am used to everything rushing and crashing around me like oceans tumbling over and over each other. I knew what to do," I say now. "I do not think being autistic causes bad things, Mom. I do not think that I need to not be autistic. I know what I struggle with and I know how to get through it. I don't want to be different. So, do not treat me different."

I stop tapping the window. "I joined the football team because it made me feel good even if it triggered some of my sensory issues. I hesitated because I blamed everyone else for keeping me from it, but I played a part in it too. I had to decide to stick it out, not quit, and be a part of the team. I pushed Marcia for the video of Brandon because I wanted an answer. I needed to know if it was my fault that he got hurt and arrested. I got the answer. It was, but it also wasn't," I say now. "I can deal with guilt, Mom. I can take responsibility. I can handle disappointment. I do not need to always look at the good in things. I can look at the bad and be okay with it. I can do that."

Mom presses her lips together and nods at me.

"And, besides, 'guilty,' by definition, also means 'conscious of or affected by a feeling of guilt,'" I add. "It fits."

Brandon eyes me. "Well, try not to make it fit forever."

"I won't," I say now. I won't.

CHAPTER TWENTY-FOUR

48 Days After the Incident

I take a few deep breaths outside the courtroom. I tap at my leg. One, two. Stop. One, two. Stop.

Today is the day that Marcia testifies. Today we will see the video for the first time. Today we will have all the answers we need.

Dad walks up to me and places a hand on my shoulder and squeezes. "You ready?"

I shrug. I am not the one who has to do the hard part. "Is Mom already with Brandon?" I ask.

Dad nods. I look around until I spot Marcia standing with one of Brandon's lawyers. She wears black—fitting, since it is not the most upbeat of days. She contrasts drastically with the white marble lobby.

"I am going to go say hi," I say now.

Dad nods.

Marcia's back is turned to me. She shifts from foot to foot and rubs at her arm. She looks nervous.

"Hey," I say to her.

Marcia turns. "Hey," she says now. She lets out a big breath.

"Nervous?" I ask.

Marcia nods. "I've never had to testify for anything before. And now, against my dad . . ."

I frown. "It cannot be easy."

"I feel like I'm going to throw up. He didn't even talk to me last night or this morning," Marcia says now. Her voice shakes as she speaks.

"Has he said anything to you about it?" I ask now.

Marcia shakes her head. "No, but my mom said that it's my responsibility to do what I think is right."

I raise my eyebrows.

"She's not a bad person, Aiden. She's just protective."

I nod. I get that.

"But I know that what I'm doing today is the right thing, even if it took me a while to get there," Marcia says now. Her voice strengthens a bit.

I shrug. "My mom used to say that the journey doesn't matter if the destination is the same. You still got there."

Marcia gives me a small smile. "I still got here."

In the courtroom, the defense briefly questions Marcia before playing the video. I steel myself, ready to finally see what I did not see that night, ready to get the answers we have needed all this time. I stare at the back of Brandon's head, where he sits with the lawyers, and hope this will not be too difficult for him.

The lens is zoomed in on one of the coco plum bushes in the stone planters that frame the walkway leading up to Randy's. Tucker zooms in, focusing on individual leaves, then pans back out. In the background, Georgia chatters along.

"He's just in there talking to other girls," she complains.

"Don't stress it. Don't stress," Marcia comforts her. Her voice is low. "He's the quarterback, girls are going to fawn all over him or whatever, but you both know what you have."

The camera zooms in on a group of kids hanging out in the walkway before panning out again. Then the focus is on me, walking down the walkway until I disappear behind another bush.

Tucker pans back out and zooms in on a bunch of yellow jelly palm fruit hanging from a palm tree.

In the background, Georgia changes the conversation. "Wait, are they arguing?" she asks.

"That's Aiden, Brandon's brother," Marcia says now.

Tucker zooms in on the fronds of the tree.

"Oh no, oh no, they're fighting. Shit!" Georgia squeals.

"That looks bad, what should we do?" Marcia asks.

"I don't know," Georgia replies. "I don't know."

The camera pans to the two girls. Georgia holds herself and bounces on her toes, her eyes cast toward the walkway, presumably watching the fight. Tucker zooms in until the lens is so focused, I can count her eyelashes, then zooms out.

"I'm calling the cops," Marcia says now.

A pause as Tucker studies blades of grass in the diner's lawn.

"Tucker, put the camera away, please. Mom's gonna kill me if you break it," Georgia complains. A hand swipes across the camera.

"Stop!" Tucker yells.

The camera is focused on Georgia. She rests her hands on her hips and shakes her head at Tucker. In the background, Marcia's voice is chirpy and hurried.

"Oh my gosh, Marcia!" Georgia screams. "Aiden's so much bigger than him, right?"

Marcia lets out a frightened squeak. "Yes, a Black male. He's attacking another boy. He's much, much larger than him. He looks like he might kill him. Please come quick. We don't know what to do. Yes, at Randy's on Fourth and Sunset." Marcia waits for a response that I can't hear.

The camera pans to us now. Greg and Louis wrestle with Carter to keep him away from me. Sirens grow loud in the background.

"Oh, thank god!" Georgia says now. "That was so brutal. I can't believe Aiden would freak out like that. I've only ever seen him just scream, not fight. He's like a gorilla!"

"I know. That was so scary," Marcia replies.

This is it. I sit up at attention. The camera zooms in on the cop cars filing into the lot. Tucker zooms and pans, so I am not always getting the whole picture. I am hoping I will get it all at the right time.

Cops start to rush the sidewalk. Then, everything happens almost simultaneously.

The camera focuses on a cop car with the number 84477 on its side, then it pans out.

Greg is pinned to the ground and taking hits from an officer. The camera zooms in on me, lying halfway on the grass, waiting to be dealt with. When it pans back out, the scene is organized chaos. Cops divide and conquer. Carter is being redirected despite his best efforts to continue fighting. He pushes against the officer dealing with him but gets little more than a push back. Louis is already sitting and talking to an officer.

The camera focuses on the officers approaching me on the ground. Once they start hitting me, it pans out.

"Oh my god! I can't watch, there's so many of them on him," Marcia says now. Her voice is shaky, like she's crying.

"I mean, he's like a freaking silverback, Marcia. They have to do this. It's like you said, he was going to kill Carter," Georgia soothes her. The camera turns and follows Marcia as she steps away, wiping tears from her face. Georgia follows.

"That's my brother! Aye! That's my brother!"

Brandon's voice echoes in the speaker.

"Oh my god," Marcia says now. "Georgia, it's my dad!"

The camera turns and Brandon cuts to the side, avoiding the walkway and instead jogging down the lawn toward where the cops have me pinned and are hitting me between two planters.

"Hey! He's autistic! Stop! He's not trying to fight. He's—"

Brandon is a few feet from the officers who are hitting

me. One of the officers turns toward Brandon and holds up a hand, and another officer runs up and punches Brandon in the side of the head. From this angle, my brother falls right next to a stone planter and curls up into a ball. The cop descends on Brandon, punching and screaming. "Don't resist! Put your hands behind your back."

"Please stop!" Brandon screams now. "My brother!"

Another cop comes and tries to force Brandon's hands behind his back, but my brother tries to cover his head from the punches.

"Oh my god. Oh my god," Marcia says now. "I've never seen my dad like that, oh my god."

"Stop resisting!" one of the cops yells.

"Please!" Brandon yells. He lowers his hands from his head, exposing his face, and the cop slams his head to the ground, knocking him out.

Brandon stops screaming. The camera zooms in on Brandon on the grass.

"Oh my god! Brandon!" Georgia screams.

"Oh my god, Georgia," Marcia says now. "I'm so sorry. I'm so sorry. My dad. Brandon. I'm so sorry."

The camera pans to Georgia. Tears drip from her lashes and she holds a hand over her mouth.

"Tucker, get that out of my face!" she snaps.

A hand swipes the camera again and the video cuts off.

The air in the courtroom is thick and unmoving. Reporters hold recorders and scribble furiously, but there is no noise.

Not even a cough. Brandon's lawyer takes twenty-seven seconds of silence before speaking.

"Why didn't you report this as soon as you knew about this video, Miss Lewins?" the lawyer asks.

"Because I didn't want to get my dad in trouble," Marcia replies.

"And what made you change your mind?" the lawyer asks now.

"I saw how much trouble Brandon might truly get in and realized that I had to help," Marcia says.

"And what about your father?" the lawyer asks now.

"Objection, Your Honor," the prosecution lawyer interjects. "Relevance."

"Sustained," the judge says.

"Sorry, I'll rephrase," Brandon's lawyer says now. He turns to Marcia. "Are you worried about what comes next?"

"Yes," Marcia responds. "But I figure whatever comes next for me is nothing compared to what would have been coming for Brandon."

Brandon's lawyer nods. "No further questions, Your Honor."

The prosecution questions Marcia a little before finally concluding. Marcia takes two deep breaths before stepping off the stand, and we share a small smile.

She looked at me the entire time. I never once looked away.

This was it. The last of the witness testimony. After a short break, we come back for closing statements.

Brandon's lawyer stands in front of the jury with a picture of Brandon's injuries and a still shot of him being punched by Marcia's dad. "This case is open and shut. You have seen evidence and heard testimony that proves that my client Brandon Wright is not only innocent of the crimes that he is being accused of, but he is also the victim of a different crime. Brandon Wright has suffered exponentially from this case, losing his spot on the football team and his scholarship to the university of his choice, and enduring almost nonstop harassment. These are losses that he cannot get back. Because he is a senior, we cannot give him back his last year of football. We cannot give him back his scholarship. We cannot give him back the peace he lost. But what you can give him today is his freedom. Please, give him what you can. Give him his freedom."

After the closing statements, we finally pack up to leave. Jury deliberations start the next day. Mom, Dad, and I step up to where the defense is packing up and take turns giving Brandon hugs. He looks relieved and happier than I expected. He thanks his lawyers, and Mom has a short conversation with them off to the side before we break away.

On our way out, Marcia stops me. "Hey," she says now. "Thanks for grounding me while I was up there. Being able to look to you for support really gave me the strength I needed to stick to my guns."

"Stick to your guns?" I ask.

"Not chicken out?" Marcia tries.

"Not get scared?"

Marcia laughs. "Exactly. Thank you."

"I would say anytime, but I never want to do this again," I say now.

Marcia laughs, though there is something bittersweet in

her tone. "Yeah, me neither." She bites at her bottom lip and rocks back on her heels. "I'm a little scared to go over to my family," she admits.

I look toward where her parents and sister are gathered with the prosecution. They are subdued—no one is relaxed or joyful. I can understand why.

"They are still your family," I say after three seconds. "Your mom encouraged you, and I am sure that will not be the only encouragement you get."

I have no idea if I am right. I glance over at Marcia's father and consider all that he has caused. In my mind, he cannot be anything more than a cruel man, but I know that he is more to her. And if not, I hope he will be. He has to be more for her.

Marcia gives me a weak smile. "I hope you're right." She glances over at them. "Okay. See you later, Aiden."

I join my family and watch as Marcia walks back to her parents. Her mom puts her arm around Marcia's shoulders. Her dad stands apart from them, and Marcia looks at him. He returns her gaze for twelve seconds, then walks away. Marcia looks down at the floor and then back at me with tears in her eyes before following him.

The interaction makes me sad, but I hope that eventually, they will be okay. None of this is easy, even for her. But what is easy is not always what is right. We all had to learn that the hard way.

CHAPTER TWENTY-FIVE

61 Days After the Incident

My room, a football field, and hell are three places I would rather be than this packed hallway at school the day after the end of the trial. It is chaos. Between the reporters swarming outside the building and the students flocking to Brandon to congratulate him on the "not guilty" verdict, I do not know what is more overwhelming. To think I thought that the normal bustle of the hallways was too much before.

I make my way through the crowds with Brandon at my side, taking in the rush of noise—a mix of classmates excited about the verdict and others happy about having the rest of the week off for Thanksgiving, which is tomorrow. People reach out to us as we maneuver through them, eager to make up for their perceived missteps. Those that are not right on top of us stare from a distance as we walk, the main attraction of the day.

"Brandon, I'm so sorry," someone yells.

"Brandon, we're rooting for you!"

A little late for that, no?

The itch underneath my skin is crawling toward the surface, and not even my noise-canceling headphones are enough to block out everything.

"All right, all right!" Brandon yells. "Thank you, everyone, but y'all gotta back up, please. Me and my bro just tryna get to class."

The crowd parts and Brandon throws an arm around me, guiding me to a quieter corner near my locker. He swipes the headphones from my ears, and my head suddenly feels very cold.

"You good, A?" he asks.

I nod.

"Good."

"This is kind of wild," I say now.

"Yeah," Brandon says. "I expected a turnaround, but not all this."

I expected it. It makes sense for people to flock once they realize they were wrong, once they realize that they wronged someone else. Brandon was not quite treated like a pariah, but everything did fall apart around him. Now everything is coming back to him, as it should.

"You know something really wild?" Brandon says. "I don't know how my number got out, but I been getting all kinds of calls from reporters and people who printed mean stuff about me. The same people who called me a monster now want a statement about my innocence. It's funny how people switch up, ain't it?"

It is funny. Not 'haha' funny, but . . .

"I guess life can kinda start getting back to normal now, right? I can finish out senior year, and you can . . ." Brandon trails off. "What are you gonna do?"

My brows furrow. "What do you mean?"

Brandon leans against my locker. "I mean I'm graduating, little brother. What you gon do without me?"

I never thought about that before. At the start of the year, all I had was Brandon. All I had were Brandon's friends, a spot in Brandon's life, a position on Brandon's team. Next year, he will be gone. I want to feel sad about that. I think maybe, if he had asked me earlier, I would have felt panicked. But now, I think of Isabella, Reg, Bernard, Dustin. I even think of Marcia. I think of all I gained in this chaos of a semester, and I know that without Brandon next year, I will be okay. I have my own friends, my own life, and with football, I think of how my teammates held me, how we took our loss together. I have my own team. I have something now. Something I gained completely on my own.

"I think I will figure it out," I say now. "I think I will be fine."

Brandon smiles and tousles my locs. "Good, A. That's good to hear."

I hear a shuffle, look up, and see Georgia walking by. She curves her neck and I think she is fighting not to look our way. Brandon sees her too. His eyes glaze over.

"You should talk to her, you know?"

"No," Brandon spits out. "Sorry, but no."

I bite my lip. "Now that word got around about the call, I heard she's getting threats."

"I got threats too, on the videos where people thought I attacked the cop. Just because I didn't cry about it means only her emotions matter? Nah, I'm done being less than someone else. Don't get me wrong—I'm not saying that what's happening to her is okay, but I am saying that I don't need to comfort her for pain she dealt to me. I'm tired of wrapping up someone else's injuries while I burn."

I nod. That is fair.

I notice that Georgia and Marcia are not together and am wondering where Marcia is, when she comes stumbling out of the main hallway through a crowd of people. She heads straight for us.

"All right, it's a reunion of the people I don't feel like talking to, so I'm gonna go. Later, A!" Brandon leaves before Marcia gets to us, and her face falls.

"One more person not talking to me, I guess," Marcia says now. She seems a bit crestfallen.

"What do you mean?"

"Georgia blocked me on everything, and more than a few people in school hate me."

"I'm sorry," I say now.

Marcia holds a hand up. "No, don't apologize. Seriously, that would just make me feel worse. I did this. I've been thinking more and more about it, and I lost a lot, but I did it to myself. I've accepted that. My dad will talk to me again one day. My mom and sister, at least, haven't decided to hate me. And I have other friends besides Georgia, but maybe she'll grow and understand her part in this and not see me testifying as a betrayal. Maybe she'll even come back around."

I stay quiet. Maybe.

"Either way, I feel better after doing what I did. Even if Brandon isn't talking to me yet, I'm glad he is here and not in jail. I had to right what I did wrong."

I reach out and give her shoulder a squeeze. "Thank you," I say now.

"Don't thank me, and don't apologize. I'm not some savior, Aiden. I'm not that."

I nod.

"Well, I'll see you later."

I watch as Marcia heads down the hall. Then I grab some books from my locker and head to class, thinking about what she said. She is not a savior, she is right. In the beginning, she only saved herself, but in the end, at the very least, she redeemed herself. That is better than nothing.

In Life Skills, Ms. Findley reminds us that we have to keep up with our reports for our part-time job project.

"Remember to keep your logs and weekly reflections on what you've learned from working in the real world. Now, I want to give you all some time to meet with your partners and discuss what you'll talk about in the upcoming presentation for this project."

I smile across the room at Isabella, and she heads over to me. As she sits, Ms. Findley makes her way to us.

"I heard about the trial," Ms. Findley says to me. "Brandon even stopped by this morning to tell me how you contributed to the outcome. You've done so much already this year. You should be very proud of yourself."

"Thank you, Ms. Findley," I say now.

"Of course. Now, I'll let you both work."

Ms. Findley walks away, and Isabella reaches across the desk, grabs both of my hands, and gives me a squeeze. My hands feel warm in hers and I squeeze back. She looks at me and smiles, but this smile feels different—it feels warmer, like it is just for me.

"I'm proud of you too, you know?" Isabella says, letting me go.

My hands are cool and empty in her absence. I do not like it. I want her to hold them again.

Isabella flips her hair and her scent—cranberries and lemons—wafts over to me. I want to lean in closer.

"I could not have done it without you," I say now.

"Of course you could have," Isabella says. "You don't give yourself enough credit. I was just a tagalong. This was all you. Take the credit. Take the praise." She smiles big.

I bite at my lip and tap at the desk. One, two. Stop. One, two. Stop. I am suddenly so nervous around her, and I realize it is because I feel a little more confident about what I want. A little less unsure.

"Thank you," I say now.

"Of course, Aiden." Isabella gives me that smile again. The one just for me.

And before I can stop myself, words are spilling from my lips. "Do you like me?"

I am too hot around my ears and feel embarrassed, and I stare at the desk instead of her, but I do not regret asking the question. I need to know.

"Of course I like you, Aiden. I wouldn't spend all this time around you if I didn't like you."

I look up at her. I do not think she understands the question.

"No, Isabella," I say now. "I mean do you *like* me?"

Isabella's mouth falls open into a small *O*. I wait a painful eleven seconds for a rejection.

"Well . . ." She tucks a loose curl behind her ear and looks down at her lap. She plays with her fingers on her legs. "Do you like me?"

I did not expect that. I only expected a confirmation or denial, not reverse questioning. How do I explain that I think of her scent sometimes, even when she is not around? How do I tell her that her touch does not make me itch, her squeeze calms me in a way that almost intoxicates me, her smile makes me smile—every time? How do I explain that she is on my mind even when I am not thinking about her and that seeing her is the best part of my day? How do I explain all of that and then explain that I have never felt like this before?

I consider my words carefully, because for once, I have a lot that I want to say, but instead all that comes out is "Yes."

Isabella smiles into her lap. "Well, okay, then."

I am surprised. What does that mean? "Okay, then?" I ask.

She reaches her hand back across the table and I meet her halfway. She grabs my hand, lightly this time, and strokes the back of it, sending tingles up my arm and to my spine. She looks back up at me and gives me the smile again. The one that I know now is just for me. I understand.

"Okay, then," I say now.

After school, I am called to Coach Davis's office, and I head straight there. There is no practice today, so I am confused. When I reach the locker room hallway, I spot Brandon. The confusion grows.

"You get called here too?" Brandon asks now.

I nod.

"Well, let's go see what it's about."

I follow Brandon into the office, where Coach Davis sits, tapping away at his keyboard. He does not look up when we come in.

"Close the door behind you," he says.

I shut the door, then sit.

"I just wanted to call you both in here to acknowledge that we heard about the trial," Coach starts. "Brandon, I know it was a hard semester for you not being able to be on the team given the circumstances, but I'm sure you understand the position we were in. I just wanted to share how happy I am that everything worked out for you."

Brandon nods.

"I also wanted to let you know that some recruiters have

reached back out, so you might be able to keep your options open. No promises, but things might work out in your favor after all."

Brandon is quiet for six seconds. He seems stunned. "Thanks, Coach."

"And Aiden." Coach directs his attention toward me. "I figured both you and your brother would want to know that you're going to be our starting running back next year. No sitting out games, no starting behind anyone—the spot is more than yours."

Now it is my turn to be stunned. I start to trip over my words but then clear my throat. "Thank you, Coach," I finally choke out.

"Well, all right, that was all. We're all really happy for you, Brandon." Coach Davis turns and goes back to typing. Brandon sits still for five more seconds, then stands and leaves the room without a word. I follow.

Out by the field, Brandon is quiet as we walk toward the school exit.

"Ready to head home?" I ask.

He nods.

"Want to talk about it?" I ask now.

"Nothing to talk about," Brandon says. I cannot make out his expression yet. It seems to shift with every passing second. He almost sounds angry, though. "Literally nothing. That was nothing. That was—"

I wait.

"I thought I was gonna finally get an apology. I did so

much for this team, and they just dropped me. I thought, at the very least, I would get an apology."

I consider what Brandon said as we walk. It would have been nice to get an apology. But then again, it would have been nice if he never got arrested. It would have been nice if the cops never got called. It would have been nice if everyone apologized— if everyone regretted everything they did. It would be nice for Georgia and Marcia to be friends, for Louis and Carter to still be Brandon's friends, for everyone to be the way they were before all this. All of that would be nice.

"Sometimes, you do not get the apology," I say now. "Even if you deserve it, sometimes we do not get what we deserve. And sometimes we just have to be okay with that."

Brandon glances at me, then up at the sky, as he walks. "Yeah," he says now.

Yeah.

CHAPTER TWENTY-SIX

77 Days After the Incident

Even though it is almost winter, Brandon still says it is hotter than the devil's ass crack outside.

NOTE: *I have yet to ascertain the temperature of the devil's ass crack.*

The field is quiet, now that the season is over. Brandon and I meander across it together, much like we did before I was on the team. Before everything changed.

"You ever think this is how we was gon end up on the field together this year?" Brandon asks as we walk across the turf. The midday sun beams down, hot on our necks, and I am partially blinded by the light. The empty field stretches out before us, welcoming our presence. I want to sprint across it just to feel something.

"Definitely not," I say now. "This would not be my first choice."

Brandon chuckles. "Mine either, but I feel like I learned something."

"You?" I ask. "Learn something?"

Brandon catches my sarcasm and laughs, pushing my arm.

The breeze blows a light wind on us, and I catch Brandon's scent. The scent that has always brought me so much calm. Cinnamon. Vanilla. Pine trees. Tabasco sauce. A comfort that will never change.

"I saw that you finally talked to Marcia today," I say now.

Brandon shrugs. "Mom said forgiveness isn't for the other person. She said it's for you. So I did it for me," he says now. "Besides, somebody smart told me I shouldn't be bitter and angry forever." He looks at me and smiles.

I walk and bump against Brandon's side on purpose. "Wonder who that was?"

Brandon takes his bag off his back and pulls a football out. "One time for the one time?"

I laugh. "You want to run drills now?"

"I always wanna run drills! That's why they call me Big-Time!" Brandon laughs. "Come on, go long!"

My brother drops back and preps the ball to throw. Even without a season to keep him in shape, he is immediately at home.

"I'm not a receiver!" I yell as I run to catch the perfectly spiraled football. Even though I am totally inept with longer catches, Brandon knows how to throw, and it sails right into my outstretched hands. I rub my palm along the bumpy ball, relishing the familiar texture.

"Perfect as always!" I call from across the field as I make my way back.

When I am halfway to him, Brandon holds up a hand and answers his phone. I pick up the pace now, jogging back to meet him. What could it be now? I fight down the anxiety that begins to creep in. Even with the trial behind us, it is difficult not to worry.

As I get closer, I can hear him talking.

"Yes, no, of course," Brandon says now. "Okay, okay. Yeah, I can definitely talk to my parents about it."

Who is it? I mouth.

Brandon does not see me. He is too busy pacing as he speaks.

I tap at my thigh. One, two. Stop. One, two. Stop. Curiosity is eating me alive. What is this about? Is it bad if Mom and Dad need to be looped in?

"Yes, okay, thank you!" Brandon says now. He sounds excited. Why excited? "Of course. Yes, I look forward to it."

He hangs up. His face is incredulous. As though something amazing happened and he cannot believe it.

"Who was that?" I ask now, practically shouting.

Brandon takes a breath before he answers. His brows are raised. His mouth is open.

NOTE: *I believe this expression is shock.*

"That was University of Alabama," he says. His face begins to morph into a smile.

"Seriously?" I ask. "For what?"

"They said they heard about what happened and had been following my case. They said they also heard about things falling through with UF. They know that UF was my first choice, but they extended an offer anyway. They want me on their team, A! I got another chance!" Brandon whoops into the empty air. It echoes across the turf.

I smile. I want to celebrate with him, but I do not feel the excitement.

"What's wrong, A?" Brandon asks now. "This is good! I got another chance at football! I can play next year! I can play!"

"I know," I say. "I am happy for you." I smile weakly.

Brandon bumps my shoulder. "So, what's up?"

"I just never expected you to go so far. A whole other state," I say now. I want my brother to have football and a team. He deserves that. I just figured it would be somewhere where he was just a short drive away. Somewhere I could visit him all the time, even on weekends.

Brandon smiles. "Yeah, you right. It's farther. I thought about that when they offered."

"And that did not matter?" I ask now.

"Nah, not anymore," Brandon replies.

I frown and sit on the grass. The blades are short and itchy because they've been freshly cut. I reach down and pull at a few, freeing them from the dirt underneath. "Why not?"

Brandon lowers himself next to me. "Because you got people now," he says. "Like you said before, you'll figure it out. I know you gon be just fine."

Tears fill my eyes. He is right. I do. I am in a different place now than I was when the year started and I am proud of that, but I also still need my brother. I think I do, at least. "I am still scared sometimes," I say now. "To do this without you."

Brandon tousles my locs. "Look at what you did without me already! It's pretty amazing, if you ask me."

"What about the future, though?" I ask.

"Aiden, I wouldn't have a future without you, li'l bro. You did this. You can do a hell of a lot more without me in the way."

I smile through my tears. "You've never been in the way."

"Oh yeah?" Brandon pushes me. "How about now?" He grabs the ball and stands. "If you want this ball, then I'm definitely in your way!"

I smile, then pop up and give chase. Brandon dodges me for a bit, then finally, I tackle him and take him down to the turf. We tumble over each other, laughing and breathless.

"There goes that 4.2 again!" Brandon says in between breaths.

"I got the power and the speed," I say now.

"Don't I know it." Brandon tousles my locs again.

"Locs!" I shout.

"They literally don't tangle!"

I get up to run and Brandon immediately starts to chase.

With my brother's laughter behind me and the field in front of me, everything finally starts to look just as beautiful as it did before.

ACKNOWLEDGMENTS

There's something freeing in writing a book, especially one filled with so much of yourself, like this book is for me. So much of it is a marathon and not a sprint, and it takes those people with water bottles and towels at important junctures to keep you going along the way. I have so, so many people to thank, and I know I won't be able to remember everyone, but here's my best try:

To Kat Kerr. You saw something in this book, and then we tore it apart and put it back together. We performed actual story surgery, and look what we made. I may have lost twenty thousand words in the process, but I gained so much more. I'll never forget the work we did to get here, and I'll never forget you for being my partner through it all. Thank you so much for being Aiden and Brandon's biggest fan.

To my editor, Julia McCarthy. You loved this book from

the outset, and you never once let me forget that. I could feel your passion from the minute you offered to the second we finished working on this book, and you always made me feel certain that this book was cared for, needed, and necessary. Nobody made this book feel more important than you did, and I appreciate that more than anything. I couldn't imagine a better partner on this publishing ride than you. Thanks for fighting for our boys.

To my publicist, Alex Kelleher, the speediest replier of emails: thank you for helping me bring this book to light! Your work does not go unnoticed.

To Anum Shafqat, you cared about this book just as much as anyone, and I appreciate you and all the work you've done behind the scenes.

And also to the entire team at Atheneum for making this book happen! The work is never done but it can't happen without all of you.

To my cover artist, Baraka Carberry aka Bokiba. I hope your sister loves the book.

To my husband, James, for taking the kids so that I could write. For being there anytime I needed a sounding board. For giving me every fact I needed about football. For believing in me.

To my mother, for taking me to the bookstore anytime I wanted as a kid. For instilling in me a love of libraries. For nurturing my mind when I wanted to read eight-hundred-page books. For making me a reader.

To Deon. For being you.

To Jaden, Bryson, James, and Naila. For being my constant inspiration.

To Lynne Barrett. This book could not have existed in the form it is without you. You have been there from the beginning and seen this book in its baby stages and pushed me to make it the story it became. You believed it could be something great and kicked my butt when I lagged behind. This is a cheer to every map I drew! I still know exactly where the cop was standing.

To my mentor, Dr. Donna Weir-Soley. You are everything, Mummy. Thank you for always hyping me up and for knowing I could do this from the beginning.

To everyone at FIU's MFA program. Every class I took got me here.

To my friends, who are magic and got me through it. There are too many of you to name, but I couldn't have survived sub without you all. When I needed someplace to scream, I screamed with you all, and that means everything.

To Jordan and Audrey especially. For being everything to me as my friends. For supporting me always. And for being there for me. Every. Single. Time.

To my very secret society of wordy crones. The snark is all I need to get by.

To every person who ever boosted a post, added me on Goodreads, preordered my book, and just in general supported this book just because you saw this idea and loved it before you read the words. Thank you! My books can't exist without you all.

And lastly, to little me. We did it, babe. We did it.

Love always,
DeAndra